THE
ATLAS
MANEUVER

THE ATLAS MANEUVER

STEVE BERRY

GRAND
CENTRAL

NEW YORK   BOSTON

Copyright © 2024 by Steve Berry

Cover design by Eric Fuentecilla
Cover images by Shutterstock and Getty Images
Author photo © Carey Sheffield
Cover © 2024 Hachette Book Group, Inc.

Grand Central Publishing
Hachette Book Group
1290 Avenue of the Americas, New York, NY 10104
grandcentralpublishing.com
twitter.com/grandcentralpub

First Edition: February 2024

Grand Central Publishing is a division of Hachette Book Group, Inc. The Grand Central Publishing name and logo is a trademark of Hachette Book Group, Inc.

The publisher is not responsible for websites (or their content) that are not owned by the publisher.

The Hachette Speakers Bureau provides a wide range of authors for speaking events. To find out more, go to hachettespeakersbureau.com or email HachetteSpeakers@hbgusa.com.

Grand Central Publishing books may be purchased in bulk for business, educational, or promotional use. For information, please contact your local bookseller or the Hachette Book Group Special Markets Department at special.markets@hbgusa.com.

Library of Congress Cataloging-in-Publication Data

Names: Berry, Steve, 1955- author.
Title: The Atlas Maneuver / Steve Berry.
Description: First edition. | New York, NY : Grand Central Publishing,
    Hachette Book Group, 2024. | Series: Cotton Malone
Identifiers: LCCN 2023040927 | ISBN 9781538721032 (hardcover) |
    ISBN 9781538766491 | ISBN 9781538721025 (e-book)
Subjects: LCGFT: Spy fiction. | Novels.
Classification: LCC PS3602.E764 A94 2024 | DDC 813/.6—dc23/eng/20230905
LC record available at https://lccn.loc.gov/2023040927

ISBNs: 978-1-5387-2103-2 (hardcover); 978-1-5387-6649-1 (large print);
    978-1-5387-6870-9 (Canadian trade paperback); 978-1-5387-2102-5 (ebook)

Printed in the United States of America

LSC-C

Printing 1, 2023

ACKNOWLEDGMENTS

My sincere thanks to Ben Sevier, senior vice president and publisher of Grand Central. To Lyssa Keusch, my new editor, whom I've greatly enjoyed getting to know and working with. Then to Tiffany Porcelli for her marketing expertise, Staci Burt and Ivy Cheng, who handled publicity, and all those in Sales and Production who made sure both that there was a book to read and that it was available. Thank you, one and all.

A continuous deep bow goes to Simon Lipskar, my agent and friend, who makes everything possible.

A few extra mentions: Jessica Johns and Esther Garver, who continue to keep Steve Berry Enterprises running smoothly; Jon Baldwin, who taught me all about tents (and demonstrated a diabolicalness I was not aware of); our drivers and guides in Morocco, who first showed us the Atlas Mountains; Ray Simmons, who told me about navy showers and other interesting things; and Ami Richter, who made sure my Japanese was correct.

As always, to my wife, Elizabeth, who remains the most special, and most intuitive, of all.

When I moved to Grand Central Publishing in 2020, that came with a new editor, Wes Miller. Wes was a seasoned pro, an executive editor, managing bestselling authors who are among GCP's most valued and reliable producers. People like Douglas Preston, Lincoln Child, Harlan Coben, Joe Ide, Kanae Minato, Robin

Peguero, Stephen Chbosky, Chuck Palahniuk, Jason Schreier, and many others.

I was fortunate to be assigned to him, even more so when I learned that Wes had been a fan of my work prior to me coming to Grand Central. It's always good when your editor likes the work. Recently, Wes left Grand Central for a new career outside of publishing. He and I worked together on only four manuscripts, but I came to greatly respect his opinions and insights. He was a man of few words but, when uttered, you listened.

Here's a perfect example.

In the finished draft of *The Omega Factor* there was a problem. A detail that I could not adequately explain or tie together with the main plot. Nor could Elizabeth when she performed her edit. We were both stumped.

But not Wes.

When he reviewed the manuscript he not only found the problem, but offered the perfect solution.

That's what great editors do.

I wish him nothing but the best.

I'll miss him.

This book is for you, Wes.

For Wes Miller,
editor extraordinaire,
and an even finer person.

A faithful man will abound with blessings, but he who makes haste to be rich will not go unpunished.

Proverbs 28:20

THE
ATLAS
MANEUVER

PROLOGUE

Luzon Island, Philippines
Monday, June 4, 1945
11:54 p.m.

General Tomoyuki Yamashita toasted the group for the final time. A hundred and seventy-five men stood before him in the dimly lit underground chamber. All engineers. Specially selected. Each having accomplished his task to perfection. They'd performed so well and so fast that he'd ordered a celebration. Fried brown rice, boiled eggs, grilled sweet potatoes, and dried cow's meat. All washed down with copious amounts of sake. For the past two hours they'd sung patriotic songs and shouted *banzai*, long life, until they were hoarse. All the harshness of war had been set aside for a few precious hours.

He'd been reassigned to the islands last October, charged with stopping the rapidly advancing American forces. Prior to that he'd led the Imperial Army during the invasion of Malaya and the Battle of Singapore. Both resounding victories. He took pride in how Churchill had described the fall of Singapore. *The worst disaster and largest capitulation in British military history.*

But everything here had gone wrong.

Now he was doing nothing more than delaying the inevitable. The war was lost. MacArthur had returned. Japan was isolated. And he was trapped in the mountains north of Manila, low on supplies, with the Americans rapidly closing in. For the past few

1

months he'd been less a military commander and more a miner. And banker. Taking deposits. Building vaults. Securing their presence for future withdrawals.

"For you," he said to the engineers, his metal cup held high. "And a job well done. *Banzai*."

They echoed his good wishes.

The underground chamber around him was the largest they'd constructed, perhaps as much as twenty meters square, illuminated by battery-powered bulbs. Rectangular bronze boxes, filled with gold bars, were stacked eight-high against the walls, each bar around seventy-five kilograms and individually marked by weight and purity. A little under thirty-seven million total kilograms.

An enormous amount of wealth.

And there were 174 other buried vaults, each containing a similar hoard of treasure. All plundered from Asian countries, starting with China in 1937. More came from Korea, Thailand, Burma, French Indochina, Cambodia, Malaysia, Hong Kong, Timor, Indonesia, and New Guinea. National treasuries, banks, religious shrines, private estates, museums, factories, homes, galleries. Anything and everything had been looted. A grand larceny of wealth that had been accumulated by its owners for thousands of years. A lot of it had already made it to Japan. The rest was to go by sea. But the Americans had stopped that redistribution with a submarine blockade. No way now to ship anything, much less something as heavy and bulky as gold.

So another way had been conceived.

Hide it all in the mountains of Luzon and come back for it after the war.

The plan had been formulated at the highest level, all the way to Emperor Hirohito himself. Several of the lesser royal princes had headed teams of thieves that had fanned out across the conquered territories, but the emperor's charming and cultivated brother, Prince Chichibu, had supervised the overall plunder, along with its secreting away, naming the entire scheme *kin no yuri*, Golden Lily, after a poem the emperor had written.

"To each of you," Prince Chichibu said, his metal cup raised. "The emperor extends his thanks for your dedicated work. He wishes great blessings to you all."

The engineers returned the toast and offered long life and blessings to the emperor. Many of their eyes were watering with emotion. None of them had ever been this close to someone of the royal house. Nearly all Japanese, Yamashita included, spent their life in awe of the imperial family. The emperor controlled the entire sovereign state, commanded the armed forces, headed the national religion, and was believed to be a living god.

Chichibu stepped close to Yamashita and whispered, "Is all ready?" He nodded.

Months ago, Prince Chichibu had moved his headquarters from Singapore to Manila and ordered all plunder still on the Asian mainland to be brought to the islands. Thousands of slave laborers and prisoners of war had spent the past few months digging tunnels and fortifying caves with concrete. Each site had to withstand earthquakes, aerial bombing, flooding, and, most of all, time. So the vaults had been constructed like military bunkers. As each was completed the prince had come to personally inspect, like tonight, so there was nothing unusual about his presence.

The men continued to enjoy the revelry, their job completed. The last of the 175 vaults—this one—had been finished three days ago. All of the architectural drawings, inventories, instruments, and tools had been crated and removed. With each vault's completion the prisoner-of-war laborers had been shot, their bodies sealed inside. Also, some Japanese soldiers had been included with the doomed so that their spirits would help guard the treasure in the years ahead. Which sounded good, but it only masked the real purpose, which was to limit the number of eyewitnesses.

"Is the map secure?" the prince asked him.

"In your car, awaiting your departure."

Everything had been sped up after MacArthur landed at Leyte. Two hundred thousand enemy troops were gaining ground every day, the Japanese forces slowly retreating ever higher into the mountains. A submarine awaited Prince Chichibu to take him back to Japan, along with the map that led to each of the vaults. Natural markers that worked as pointers had been left across the lush landscape. Subtle. Hard to decipher. Part of the jungle. All of it in an ancient code called Chako. The map would be returned to the emperor, who would hold it until the time for retrieval arrived. They might lose the war militarily, but Japan had no intention of losing financially. The idea was to hold the Philippines through a negotiated peace so they could return and retrieve the gold. How much wealth had they hidden? More than anyone could have ever imagined. Somewhere around fifty million kilograms of precious metals.

For the glory of the emperor.

"Time for us to leave," he whispered to the prince. Then he turned his attention back to the engineers. "Enjoy the food and the drink. You have earned it. It is private, quiet, and safe here. We shall see you in the morning when we evacuate."

The group offered him a collective *banzai*, which he returned, noticing the smiles all around from the men. Then he and the prince left the chamber and made their way to a crude elevator that led back up seventy meters to ground level. Along the way he noticed the dynamite that had been set in the shaft while the celebration had been ongoing. A separate access tunnel had also been rigged to explode, the charges spaced far enough apart to seal the passage, but not close enough to totally destroy the path.

He and the prince left the elevator and emerged out into the steamy tropical night. Three demolition experts waited for them. Once the shaft and tunnel were blown the last remnants of human consciousness, the 175 engineers who knew the precise location of the caches, would be dead. Most would suffocate, but some would surely commit ritual suicide in service to their emperor.

He turned to one of the soldiers and nodded.

The charges were ignited.

Explosions rumbled and the ground shook, the charges detonating in a predetermined sequence, each one bringing down a portion of the excavation. The final charge obliterated the main entrance in a cascade of dirt and rock. Before dawn it would be smoothed and dressed and, within a few weeks, the jungle would replace the lost foliage completing the camouflage.

They walked toward a waiting vehicle.

"What of these soldiers?" Chichibu asked of the demolition team.

"They will be dead by morning."

Which should end the killing. And with 7,107 islands in the Philippines, even if the enemy knew what had been done, searching for those 175 caches would take decades.

But he had to wonder.

"What of me?" he asked the prince. "Am I to die as well?"

"You are a high-ranking general in the Imperial Army," the prince said. "Sworn by oath to allegiance with the emperor."

They reached the car.

"So were all the soldiers and engineers who died," he said.

The prince opened the rear door and retrieved a leather satchel. From inside he withdrew a Japanese battle flag. A red disk atop a white background, with sixteen rays emanating from it, symbolizing the rising sun.

Chichibu laid it out flat across the hood. "I thought you might be apprehensive. Let us be frank. The war is over. All is lost. It is time now to prepare for the future. I have to return to Japan and work with my brother to secure that future. You have to stay here and hold the Americans at bay for as long as possible."

Which made sense.

The younger man withdrew a small ceremonial blade from the satchel and pricked the tip of his little finger. Yamashita knew what was expected. He took the knife and punctured his own little finger. Together, they dripped blood onto the flag in a ritual that dated back centuries, one that supposedly bound the participants together in a blood oath.

"We are one," Chichibu said.

He suddenly felt the same pride that those engineers had experienced. "I will do honor to the trust you have shown in me."

"You will be needed," the prince said, "once this war ends and we return to retrieve what is ours. And we will, Tomoyuki. We will be back. Japan will survive. The emperor will survive. In the meantime stay safe, and I will see you then."

Chichibu climbed into the vehicle. The driver was already behind the wheel. The engine coughed to life and the transport drove off down the narrow, rutted road. One of the demolition experts approached, stood at attention, and saluted. He knew what the man wanted to hear. "Set the traps. Secure the site."

Every one of the caches had been rigged with explosives and a variety of other lethal, defensive measures. If anyone dared to breach the vaults they would pay a heavy price.

In the distance he heard gunfire and mortars.

It would not be long before the enemy controlled the islands.

Thankfully, though, Golden Lily was finished.

PRESENT DAY

CHAPTER 1

COTTON MALONE COULD NOT DECIDE IF THE THREAT WAS REAL OR imaginary. He'd been sent to assess the situation, keep an eye on the target, and intervene. But only if necessary.

Did this qualify?

The streets of Basel were busy. Not surprising given this city of two hundred thousand had been a commercial hub and cultural center since the Renaissance. Six hundred years ago it was one of Europe's great cities. Location helped. Strategically placed where Switzerland, France, and Germany converged, downtown was divided by the Rhine River into two distinct sections. One from the past, the other rooted in today. Its old town filled two hills that rose against the river's southern bank. A place full of ivy-clad, half-timber houses reminiscent of a long-ago medieval town, the cobbled paths a mix of pedestrian-only and light-traffic streets.

He stood, bathed in sunshine, beside one of the more congested traffic routes and enjoyed a bag of roasted chestnuts purchased from a nearby vendor. His target was inside a small boutique, on the other side of the street, about two hundred feet away, where she'd been for the past thirty minutes. Windows of fashionable stores drew a continuous stream of patrons. Lots of cafés, shops, jewelers, designer clothing, and, his personal favorite, antique-book stores.

Plenty of them too. Each reminiscent of his own bookshop back in Copenhagen. He'd owned it now for several years, the store modest in size, tastefully appointed, and well stocked. He catered not only to bibliophiles, but also to the countless tourists who visited Copenhagen. He'd netted a profit every year, though he spent more time away from the shop than he liked. He was also the current secretary of the Danish Antiquarian Booksellers Association, a first for him as he was not much of a joiner.

But what the hell?

He loved books. They loved books.

People moved steadily in every direction, his brain attentive to the slightest detail that had signaled trouble in his former profession. No one stared or lingered too long. Nothing at all out of sync, except for one car. A dark-colored Saab. Parked thirty yards away among other vehicles nestled to the curb. All of the others were empty. But not the Saab. It contained two people, whose forms he could make out through the lightly tinted windshield. The driver and another in the back seat. None of which, in and of itself, should spark any suspicion in most people.

But he wasn't most people.

He was a trained intelligence officer who'd worked a dozen years for the Magellan Billet, a covert investigative unit of the United States Justice Department. He'd been one of the first people recruited by his old friend Stephanie Nelle, who both created and continued to run the unit. She'd recently found some trouble with the new American president, Warner Fox, but all that had been resolved and now she was back in command. And though he'd been retired from the Billet for a while now, he continued to work freelance for Stephanie whenever she managed to entice him away from his bookshop. He liked that he was still needed, so he rarely refused her. Sure, there'd come a day when she would ask less frequently and he would become only a bookseller. But thankfully, for now, he still had his uses, though he wasn't here for Stephanie. This favor was for another friend whom he'd encountered a few months back in Germany.

Derrick Koger.

Recently promoted European station chief for the Central Intelligence Agency. Who'd piqued his curiosity with an amazing tale of lost treasure.

Billions in plundered gold.

General Tomoyuki Yamashita, who'd commanded the final defense of the Philippine Islands, along with supervising the secretion of that loot, surrendered to the Allies in September 1945, then was quickly tried and convicted of war crimes in December 1945. Two months later Yamashita was hanged.

Why so fast?

Simple.

The Office of Strategic Services, precursor to the CIA, had learned about 175 buried vaults. Yamashita flatly refused to cooperate with locating them and the last thing the Americans wanted was him still alive, able to tell the world about the gold.

So they hung him.

Once that loose end had been eliminated, and the island of Luzon militarily secured, the OSS moved in and managed to retrieve several of the larger caches, tons of unaccounted-for precious metals, all shipped off to repositories in forty-two countries across the world. All done with the full knowledge and blessing of both General Douglas MacArthur and President Harry Truman.

Why was it taken?

Three reasons.

First, if the recovery of such a huge mass of stolen gold had become known, thousands of people would have come forward to claim it, many of them fraudulently, and governments would have been bogged down for decades resolving ownership.

Second, the sheer volume of the gold, if dumped back on the open market, would have devalued the price. At the time most countries linked their currencies to the U.S. dollar, and the dollar was tied to gold, so an unexpected plummet in value would have caused a worldwide financial disaster.

And finally, once Hitler and Japan had been defeated, the greatest threat to world security now came from the Soviet Union. Communism had to be stopped. At all costs. And hundreds of millions of dollars in secret wealth could certainly be channeled into that purpose.

So, slowly, over time, the retrieved gold and silver were consolidated to one location under the control of what came to be known as the Black Eagle Trust. Where was it centralized? The Bank of St. George in Luxembourg. And there that wealth had sat since 1949, safe behind a wall of secrecy that had only, according to Koger, fallen in the past few months.

Fascinating stuff.

The car with the two occupants cranked to life.

Cotton's attention shifted from the vehicle to the boutique.

His target had appeared, stepping from the front doorway and turning onto the busy sidewalk. Had the car cranking been just coincidence?

Doubtful.

He'd only seen one photo of Kelly Austin, who was employed by the Bank of St. George. Her job? He had no idea. All he'd been told was to look after her and intervene only if absolutely required. Koger had been emphatic on that last detail. Which was why he'd positioned himself across the street, among people walking here and there, oblivious to anything around them outside of their own concerns.

Kelly Austin walked away from the Saab, which swung from its parking place and crept forward in the street. No cars were behind it, but one was ahead. The one in front accelerated and headed off past Cotton. The Saab, though, never changed speed.

No question. This was a threat.

Austin kept walking his way, on the other side of the street. No head turns. No looking around. No hesitation. Just one step after another with a shopping bag dangling from one hand, a purse slung over her other shoulder.

Oblivious.

He tossed the chestnuts into the waste can beside him and stepped from the curb, zigzagging against the lanes of traffic to the pedestrian bay at the center. There, at the first break in the cars, he crossed, fifty feet ahead of Austin. People passed by, heading in the opposite direction. The Saab kept coming, moving a little faster, now nearly parallel with Austin.

The rear window descended.

A gun barrel came into view.

No time existed to get closer to Austin. Too far away. So he reached back beneath his jacket and found the Beretta. Magellan Billet issue. Which he'd been allowed to retain after retiring out early. The appearance of the weapon sent a panic through some of the pedestrians. No way to keep the gun out of view.

He told himself to focus.

In his mind the all-pervasive background noise common to cities around the world ground to a halt. Silence dominated his thoughts and his eyes assumed command of the rest of his senses. He leveled the gun and fired two shots into the open rear window. The Saab immediately accelerated, tires grabbing the pavement as the car squealed past. The danger from return fire seemed great. So he sent another bullet into the open window.

People scattered. Many hit the ground.

The Saab raced away.

He focused on the license plate and etched the letters and numbers into his eidetic memory. The car came to the next intersection, then disappeared around the corner. He quickly stuffed the gun back under his jacket and looked around.

His lungs inflated in short, quick breaths.

Kelly Austin was nowhere to be seen.

CHAPTER 2

Kyra Lhota pressed the throttle forward and powered the boat across the water. The lake's statistics were mind boggling. Formed from an ancient rift valley thirty million years ago. The world's oldest reservoir. Containing one-fifth of the planet's fresh water. Three hundred rivers fed into it, but only one drained out. Seven hundred kilometers long and up to eighty wide, its deepest point dropping fifteen hundred meters down.

On maps it was a crescent-shaped arc in southern Siberia, part of Russia's great empty quarter near the Mongolian border. Two thousand kilometers of shoreline stretched in every direction and thirty islands dotted the crystalline surface, all of it a haven for the rich and poor. The latter huddled in villages and towns that hugged the pebbly-beached shores. The former occupied the forested high ground inside expensive dachas, the real estate remote and desired, commanding the highest price per square meter in Russia.

Summer was fading, autumn always short-lived, a long winter not that far away. This was also the stormy season and soon the freezes would come, transforming the lake into one continuous block of thick blue ice solid enough for trucks, cars, and railroads to move across.

But not today.

The surface remained wet and frothy.

Kyra marveled at the overwhelming sight of water and sky, both deep and saturated, each slightly different in hue, the blue colors blanketing everything with a mystical sense of calm and order. A stiff north breeze chopped the surface, which had little effect on the thrust from the triple outboards against the fiberglass hull. She'd rented the speedboat at a marina on the southern shore, one that catered to high rollers who loved to use Lake Baikal as their personal playground. Hers was a little over ten meters long and came with enough power to send the boat streaking across the surface at nearly fifty knots.

She stood at the center console, the wheel tight in her hands, and spotted another long narrow muscle boat about half a kilometer away. She yanked back on the throttle and brought her engines to neutral, then switched them off. Their roar faded until the only sound was the distant hum of the other boat. She grabbed her backpack, found the smoke grenades, and pulled two pins. They ignited, sending a dark plume up into the late-afternoon sky. From everything she'd read about the occupant of the other boat he should react to the sign of a fire. Part of his egotistical gallantry.

But the other vessel kept going.

She added a third grenade that generated more smoke.

The other boat turned and sped her way.

Finally. As predicted.

She prepared herself, unzipping her leather jacket and allowing it to hang open, revealing her tight toned body. More of her intel pegged the target as a rich narcissistic playboy who'd managed to make billions off copper mining with dabbles into agriculture, construction, and telecommunications. In Russia that success meant this oligarch had political connections, ones that surely reached deep into the Kremlin.

Which advised her to proceed with caution and make no mistakes.

The other boat approached and slowed, pressing against its wake and easing up alongside. The lone occupant matched the photograph she'd been sent of Samvel Yerevan. Medium height. Coils of coal-black hair atop a muscular frame. An Armenian who'd relocated to Russia after the fall of the Soviet Union. There, he'd become enormously rich then reconnected with his Armenian homeland, buying a seat in the national parliament for his brother, eventually elevating him to prime minister. Net worth? In the five-to-eight-billion-euro range. A few international magazines labeled him the richest ethnic Armenian in the world. A title he reportedly cherished. He lived outside of Moscow in a palatial estate. Married, with five children. But that did not stop him from enjoying a variety of mistresses.

Women were his weakness.

And she'd dressed for the part.

A black neoprene bodysuit showed off her petite body's every curve, her blond hair tied back into a cute ponytail.

"Are you having trouble?" Yerevan called out in Russian.

She raised her arms in confusion and kept to his language. "The motors started to smoke, then died. Can you take look?"

He nodded and began to ease the powerboat closer, tossing over mooring lines, which she attached to hull cleats. She made sure to position herself between him and the grenades, which were still spewing out smoke, obscuring the engines from view. Yerevan was an avowed thrill seeker. He owned fast boats, cars, and planes, along with a huge dacha not far away that overlooked the lake. No doubt he was heading there before she'd interrupted the journey. The intel she possessed had informed her that he spent a lot of time in Siberia, as some of his mines were located nearby.

She'd learned that the easiest way to entice someone was to keep things normal. Nothing odd or questionable. Just the expected, which provided her with the advantage of being one step ahead. She was good at her job, which was why her services commanded such a high price. The client that had contracted for these possessed some of the deepest pockets imaginable, so she'd seized the opportunity and altered her fee from a flat rate to a commission.

And not in dollars or euros.

Bitcoin would be her payment.

One percent of the amount she recovered.

And if the intel was right, that would mean around seventeen million euros for this day's work. There'd been some pushback on her terms, which she'd expected, but she reminded the client that the victim possessed connections not only to the Kremlin but also to the Russian mob. There could well be retaliation, so part of her task was to make sure she left nothing that could lead anyone anywhere. And that added protection the client had been willing to pay for.

Yerevan finished securing his boat and powering down his outboards. He then hopped up on the gunwales and was about to step over onto her boat when she leaped up and joined him. She noticed his nose, broken long ago and never set properly, which added a touch of hardness to his face that some women might find attractive.

She used her index finger to signal for him to come closer.

Which he did.

She wrapped her arms around his neck and kissed him hard. He did not seem the least bit surprised or intimidated, and pressed his lips into hers, willing to accept whatever this stranger might offer.

She pivoted and swung them both around, then pushed off with her legs and propelled them over the side and into the freezing water. She was ready, having worn neoprene to insulate her pale skin.

He was not.

Her arms were already wrapped around his neck and, during the plunge over, she swung herself around so that her spine hit the water first, her hands and arms changing to a vise grip on his throat. They submerged and she kicked, keeping them under. He struggled, trying to free himself, but weightlessness evened the score and gave him no leverage.

She tightened her hold.

His hands tried to break her grip, but she clamped even harder.

17

The water temperature was well under twenty degrees Celsius, which would quickly affect Yerevan, who wore only a bathing suit and light jacket over a bare chest. She kicked and popped her head up above the surface and grabbed another breath, not allowing Yerevan the same luxury. Back down they went and she could feel his grip on her arms lessen, his body going limp, and finally no movement at all. To be sure she kept the hold in place a few more seconds, then released and kicked to the surface.

Yerevan was not moving.

She checked for a pulse.

Nothing.

Good. One more thing.

She found the gold chain that she'd seen before the attack, the one Yerevan wore night and day, and yanked it free of his neck, her grip tight on the small steel cylinder that dangled from the loop.

She then swam away from the body, which floated facedown. Back at the two boats she climbed aboard hers. The smoke grenades had played themselves out. A quick glance around in every direction revealed no one else in sight. They were toward the lake's center, kilometers from the nearest shore, with dusk rapidly approaching.

She'd timed her move well.

She untied Yerevan's boat and allowed it to drift away. The assumption would be he went for a swim and drowned, the cold water erasing any evidence of strangulation. A tragic accident. For which no one was to blame.

She took a moment and gathered herself.

Only the gurgling of the water beneath the hulls disturbed the silence.

Part one done.

She powered up her engines.

Now for part two.

CHAPTER 3

Luxembourg City
Grand Duchy OF Luxembourg
10:00 a.m.

Catherine Gledhill enjoyed the first Thursday of each month. She was in her twenty-sixth year of employment with the Bank of St. George, one of the oldest financial institutions in the world. It had started in Italy and first received deposits and made loans nearly a hundred years before Columbus crossed the Atlantic. By the 17th century it was heavily involved in the maritime trade, financing kings, queens, and emperors along with such concerns as the Dutch East India Company. Unlike most of its competitors it withstood the centuries, possessing a sense of greatness and destiny, weathering financial panics, wars, and revolutions. After Napoleon invaded Italy he suppressed independent banks, which led to its closure in 1805. But not its eradication. The bank moved west from Genoa to Luxembourg and, after Waterloo, restarted its business, becoming one of many private financial institutions the duchy harbored.

There were no shareholders or regulators. A special Luxembourg law allowed the bank to freely communicate internationally, like an embassy, and it was exempt from local taxation. The institution was capitalized, in perpetuity, with private equity. Its customers were few and special, all by invitation only. Some individuals. Most corporations and institutional investors. A smattering of governments. Royalty. Even other banks. Nothing retail, though, like checking or savings accounts. Everything was done at the wholesale level, providing services such as asset management, the buying and selling of foreign exchanges or precious metals, and selective loans and credit extensions, most to finance ultra-high-risk projects, which all accrued an above-market return on investment. Its business model was a delicate balance of risk and reward for clients who could afford to play, and pay, for those high-stakes games. They had one long-standing customer, though, which they'd spent the past seventy-five years quietly satisfying.

The Central Intelligence Agency.

But all that was about to end.

"Are we prepared to begin?" she asked the six others, each settled comfortably in a black leather chair around the long oval of a glass-topped conference table.

They each bore the title of consul. One for every continent, with the South American desk also handling Antarctica but, as of yet, no investment opportunities had materialized there. Each was highly successful with varying degrees of international finance experience. Two counts, one French, the other Spanish, heavy with inherited fortunes. Three others were former heads of competing financial institutions who retired early to take the positions. Another the retired creator of a European hedge fund known for high risk and equally high returns. She was the seventh member, the first consul, chosen by the others, not representing any particular territory but instead acting as board chairman and chief operating officer. They all resided in Luxembourg, a requirement for membership, but most retained dual citizenship.

Nothing about the bank's operations was ever publicly discussed. It worked in total secrecy behind closed doors. She was the third generation of her family to serve. Her grandfather had been first consul too. But her father made it only to North American chair, understandable given his propensity for alcohol, which eventually killed him.

"I call the September meeting to order."

20

She sat upright in the leather chair, her graying blond hair coiled tightly in a bun to the back of her head. She wore a gray silk blouse and charcoal skirt that clung to her thin frame. Both Chanel. No jewelry, save for a small pendant. A gift from her grandfather. St. George atop a horse. Fitting.

And symbolic.

The room around her reflected the solemnity of the gathering. Mahogany paneling with the matted patina that wood acquired after decades of polishing. Thick ornate draperies. Tasteful antiques. The only touches of modernity came from the glass conference table and a monitor that constantly scanned for electronic devices. She'd always liked the feeling of accomplishment the room oozed, the walls decorated with framed photographs. No captions or titles. Only successes that they all knew. The current batch included an offshore North Sea oil platform. A natural gas facility in Ghana. Italian textile mills. A British motion picture studio. And a German automobile plant. Three times a year the photographs were changed to display the most current of their investments.

They moved through the eight-point agenda, dealing with various scenarios from around the globe, some showing promise, a few not so much. Rarely did the bank become entangled in a failure, given its rigorous underwriting requirements. Sure, they took risks. But never foolishly. The main check and balance on recklessness was the fact that the seven around the table were compensated solely on the bank's overall performance. So any losses would, quite literally, come out of their own pockets. It took a little less than an hour to deal with the agenda. The monthly meetings never lasted long. She closed the leather portfolio in front of her, the Cross of St. George embossed into its cover, foiled in red.

"I now need to update everyone on what's currently happening," she said. "Everything internally is secure."

And it was.

The bank controlled, at last count, 4,556,298.67523984 bitcoin, procured over the past decade by a variety of means. Some legal, most not so much. Unknown to the world the bank was by far the largest possessor of bitcoin on the planet, now owning about twenty-three percent of the entire total. Those coins existed anonymously within the cyberworld inside 4,312 separate electronic wallets, each protected by a twenty-four-digit access code.

A private key.

The keys were encrypted and changed every few days on a random schedule to ensure the highest level of security. No paper record of the 4,312 keys existed. All of them dwelled inside a special server, not connected to the internet, that stored them behind a complex computer code designed to thwart any intrusion. Hence the label *air gap*. Only five people could access the server. She was one of those. Three more were currently inside the bank, at work. The last was Kelly Austin. But she had left yesterday for a previously scheduled holiday in Switzerland.

"And Samvel Yerevan?" one of them asked.

"That is being handled, too. As we speak."

Another task that also involved private keys.

At its heart bitcoin was nothing more than ones and zeros amid a computer program that generated mathematical challenges, requiring some of the fastest and most powerful computers in the world to solve. But if solved by people who cleverly called themselves miners, that same computer program sent a reward in the form of bitcoin. At present, that success was achieved, and 3.125 bitcoin were issued, every ten minutes. Four hundred and fifty a day. Was the whole thing strange? Odd? Not really. Little different from the other miners who once scoured the earth, or panned a stream, in search of gold. Both actions generated wealth. One traditionally, the other through something new and different.

But nonetheless valuable.

Gold was heavy, bulky, and difficult to transport. Bitcoin dwelled in the cyberworld, easily stored and capable of moving around the globe at the speed of light. At present, twenty million or so coins existed within over three hundred million online wallets, each accessible only through that owner's unique twenty-four-digit alphanumeric private key. Have the private key, and you have that person's bitcoin. The current value of the bank's holdings? A little under 220,000,000,000 euros, all safe and secure.

But Samvel Yerevan's bitcoin?

For him, those were in dire jeopardy.

Over the years the bank had acquired bitcoin through covert mining, front-running purchases, and trading. But stealing had, of late, become the fastest and easiest way. It was actually quite easy, provided the person doing the stealing was bold, competent, and knowledgeable. Which perfectly described Kyra Lhota.

"We should be able to transfer Yerevan's wallets to us by the end of the day," she told the other consuls.

Nods signaled all was good.

And she agreed.

On to other matters.

"The event in Morocco will happen, as planned," she told them. "Everything is being prepared. So we all fly there tomorrow. I look forward to seeing each of you there. I'm also anticipating some good news later this evening from Mexico, and will alert you once that happens."

"And the CIA?" one of the consuls asked.

That was the wild card in all that was about to happen.

"Surely they know that our relationship is at an end. But I have a plan to make that point absolutely clear."

CHAPTER 4

Cassiopeia Vitt walked down the corridor. The walls around her were stainless steel and shiny to the consistency of a mirror, the floor a polished gray terrazzo. Every ten meters windows of double-thick glass provided a view into dimly lit refrigerated rooms. The underground facility had first been built in the 1970s with stone walls a meter thick, surrounded by heavy support pillars to protect against earthquakes. It had served as a repository for Swiss banks, the perfect place to safely store large amounts of gold bullion. But that business ended years back. Now the whole thing had been converted into something unique, one of only a handful of such places in the world.

A wine vault.

Dedicated to aficionados worldwide who wanted a safe and secure place to store their precious bottles. Her research, done before coming, told her that, at present, there were forty-one thousand bottles, with room for fifty thousand more. Wealthy collectors, bankers, diplomats, and corporate executives made up the bulk of the clientele. Some owned as many as two thousand bottles. The fee? A mere quarter of a Swiss franc per bottle, per month. Quite a bargain considering the underground space came with zero temperature variations, controlled lighting, little to no vibration, and a constant humidity.

She kept walking.

She'd never been much of a wine fanatic, despite living in southern France among world-famous vineyards. True, she enjoyed a glass now and then, but never would she sink tens of thousands of euros into something to drink.

Not her idea of an investment.

But to be honest, business was not her forte.

Her parents had left her sole ownership of one of Europe's largest corporations. Terra. Her Spanish grandfather started the business in the 1920s, when he began to import coal, minerals, precious metals, gems, and gold from all over the world. Her father grew the company even more and today that output was used in everything from high-end electronics to parts for planes and missiles. Demand never seemed to cease. He also hired the right people to run things, a practice she'd continued after his death. Which allowed her time to focus on her rebuilding project, which was progressing. The idea was to erect a French castle, from the ground up, using only 13th-century materials, tools, and techniques. Daunting, for sure, especially for a passion project, but she was about a quarter of the way complete, though a few setbacks of late had definitely cost time and money.

She'd been working at the construction site three days ago when the call came from Cotton. He'd been asked to help out an old acquaintance, Derrick Koger, with something in Basel, Switzerland. Simultaneously a repository in Geneva needed to be visited. Time was of the essence. Why? That had not been explained. Which was not unusual when favors like these were requested. Little information seemed the norm. But when Cotton asked if she was in or out her decision was never in doubt.

If you're in, I'm in.

Truth be told, she'd do pretty much whatever he asked.

The intel she'd been provided indicated that the wine was actually a front for another vault, one left over from the facility's former days, one that should contain a staggering amount of bullion. Part of Yamashita's gold, unearthed in the Philippines after World

War II and secretly brought to Europe, eventually consolidated and managed in what came to be known as the Black Eagle Trust. The ownership of the wine vault itself was connected through a series of shell companies to the Bank of St. George in Luxembourg, which had maintained a long-standing covert relationship with the CIA, the organization that had initially created the Black Eagle Trust. Did the gold still exist? That's what Koger wanted to know, so he'd provided her with a confidential password that should gain access to the hidden vault.

Which had worked.

When she'd given the password to the attendant back at ground level she'd been immediately shown to the elevator and told to descend to this level and walk past the cold vaults to a steel door at the end of the hall. There she should enter her personal code, which would release the lock. Only the owner of the vault knew the code.

She turned a corner and spotted the steel door.

Everything about this intrigued her. How could it not?

In 1945, with the emperor's blessing, Japan had hidden tons of looted wealth underground across the Philippines, part of an operation known as Golden Lily. All of that wealth had but one ultimate purpose. To enrich the imperial family. Neither the Japanese government, nor its people, would ever see or learn of any of it.

But none of that happened.

Japan lost the war, along with the Philippines. And in 1946 a portion of the gold was unearthed by American intelligence. The rest? Most likely still in the ground. Though some say Ferdinand Marcos obtained chunks of it during his twenty years in power, and that treasure hunters here and there had found even more. But here? In Switzerland? According to what she'd been told, the vault on the other side of the steel door should contain the bulk of what the Americans had retrieved of both the Nazis' and Yamashita's gold. Which seemed a misnomer. As the Japanese general had never possessed a speck of ownership over any of it.

She stared at the keypad.

The password had worked so maybe the code was spot-on too.

Six letters. Which she'd memorized.

She tapped the screen.

A red light changed to green, accompanied by a click that signaled the electronic lock had released. Apparently, Koger's intel had been correct.

She opened the door.

Fluorescent lights in the windowless room flickered to life. The space was about ten meters square with the same shiny steel walls and polished floor as the corridor.

And empty.

Not a thing there.

An alarm sounded.

Loud. Blaring.

CHAPTER 5

KELLY AUSTIN STOOD INSIDE THE BAKERY. SHE'D RETREATED THERE AS the shooting started, catching only a fleeting glimpse of the car with the window down. Somebody on the street had been firing at the car, but amid the chaos she'd not been able to see who. Nor had she waited around to learn more. Instead, she'd rushed in the opposite direction and darted into the first doorway she'd encountered.

More people followed her inside and she caught the concern on the faces. Which she echoed. Fear had settled in a ball of burning pain right in the pit of her stomach. She'd never contemplated the danger of what she was doing, thinking it all under control. But if the person on the street had not fired, she would have been dead.

She'd left Luxembourg City yesterday on a supposed five-day holiday. Nothing unusual there. She'd taken many over the course of her years with the Bank of St. George. Her title was director of special technology, which meant she'd created and managed some of the most sophisticated computer systems in the world. Though the Bank of St. George prided itself on a deep heritage, the backbone of its modern existence turned on cutting-edge technology.

Most of which she'd created.

She eased her way past the others in the bakery and stepped close to the front windows, keeping to one side. The car was gone.

The person shooting from the sidewalk? Nowhere to be seen. Dozens of sirens converged outside. Who had just tried to kill her? The bank? That made no sense. For a variety of reasons.

So who?

Only one culprit came to mind.

A quick scan beyond the window and she saw no more obvious threats. No one was headed her way. No one searching around. She caught a quick glimpse of her own reflection in the plate-glass window. Her face was rattled. How could it not be? Inside the bakery no one appeared threatening. But how good were her instincts? She'd never seen that car coming.

She tried to breathe slower, but each inhale came like a mouthful of broken glass. The sweet scent of fresh bread and chocolate confectionaries filled her nose. One of the reasons she'd chosen Basel for her holiday was for the sweets. She loved them.

Always had.

She'd come a long way from a small town in southern Illinois. Her dad had been blue collar and worked in a tractor factory. Her mother, a housewife, mainly ignored her and focused on her two brothers. To survive she'd immersed herself in sports and computers, both of which allowed an escape from reality and a chance to compete. She spent her teenage years on the lacrosse field, honing her skills and testing limits—or at a computer, teaching herself how to code in Pascal, COBOL, Fortran, Python, and C++. She developed into an impressive athlete. During her sophomore year in high school Big Ten and Pac-12 schools came calling and she eventually realized her dream of playing college lacrosse.

She obtained a degree in computer science and went to work for the United States government, first with the military, then with the National Security Agency. Her life changed forever at age twenty-eight, one Saturday night, when a deer darted out from nowhere and caused the car she was driving to plunge over an embankment. It took an hour to cut her out with the Jaws of Life. During the ensuing emergency surgery she lost twenty-one pints of blood. Her spinal cord had been severely damaged, and she spent two years in a wheelchair. It had taken an intense amount of physical therapy and multiple plastic surgeries to rebuild her face and get her walking again. At one point she actually died on the operating table and experienced some sort of out-of-body phenomenon, floating overhead, perched on the edge of a wall looking down at the surgeons as they worked to save her. The face staring up, her face, had been like a waxen mask, the skin dull and lifeless, her eyes closed and distended. A bright light warmed her right side, and sitting beside her had been an angel. *Are you ready to go home?* the apparition asked. She'd shaken her head. *There's more I need to do.* The angel smiled and vanished. Then she was resuscitated, her heart shocked back into rhythm.

She took two things away from the experience.

First, angels were badass. And second, from that day forward she sought and understood absolute truth. Her superpower. One that had served her well. One that, weeks ago, told her something had to be done.

So she'd called Langley.

Two police cars arrived out on the street, lights flashing, sirens blaring. Uniformed officers emerged. She thought about enlisting their aid, but the bank's reach was enormous. Catherine Gledhill knew a lot of people who knew even more people. No. Better to stay put. No one on the street, other than her, realized she'd been the target.

Or maybe not?

Who'd been shooting at the car? Was that in her defense? Or just fortuitous. Time to find out.

She stepped over to an empty corner, set her shopping bag down, and rifled through her purse, finding the phone Derrick Koger had supplied to her. She hit #5 and the unit dialed the preset number.

"There's a problem," she told Koger in a whisper, facing the corner. "Talk to me."

She'd only known Koger for a short time, their first encounter coming during the early-morning hours at her house, in Luxembourg, nine weeks ago. Koger was tall, with sparse, ash-blond hair and candid brown eyes topped by bushy eyebrows. He toted a bit of beer gut, though he'd told her he was trying to lose it. He also liked to flash a cheeky smile that seemed designed to disarm. When she'd made contact with the CIA she had no idea who would come. But the European station chief? That was higher than she'd imagined. Still, she was glad he was on board—he seemed a straight shooter.

She told him what had just happened.

"I thought you said the bank was unaware of us?" Koger said. "You were careful, right?"

She knew what he meant. Their contacts had been intentionally minimal and all through burner phones Koger had supplied. Only the one face-to-face. Their first meeting. She'd quietly taken all of the necessary steps at the bank before leaving on holiday, which had been routinely scheduled for over two months. Nothing should have aroused any suspicions.

"I was extremely careful," she whispered into the phone. "I'm not an amateur. And, news flash, the problem here is not the bank. It's on your end."

And she did not like the lingering silence that greeted her suggestion.

"Okay," he said to her. "I'll check."

"You do that. What now?"

"I have a man on the scene."

Who may have just saved her life.

"Tell me where you are and I'll send him your way."

She did.

"Stay put," Koger said.

CHAPTER 6

CASSIOPEIA REALIZED IMMEDIATELY THAT SHE'D WALKED INTO A TRAP.
There really was no other way to view the situation. Koger had
said that this vault should be filled with tons of gold bullion. To
identify it he'd provided her with the lettering and specialized
marks that had been stamped into each bar long ago, denoting its
ownership and purity. The newly formed CIA had supervised all
that in 1949. His intel was good, he'd assured her. But he'd been
wrong. What did Cotton like to say? *It's never fun being the fox
in the hunt.*

No kidding.

The alarm stopped blaring.

She turned from the door and headed back down the corridor
between the wine vaults. There were two ways out. An elevator and the stairwell. She came to the elevator and saw cameras
mounted high in the corners, then her gaze locked on the floor
indicator. The elevator was coming down. Her way. She positioned
herself to the left of the doors and waited for the car to arrive. No
telling how many people were on it or whether any were armed.
This was Switzerland, after all, and guns were rare, even for the
police.

Ding.

The doors opened and two men stepped out.

Uniformed. Guards she'd seen above.

She pounced from their right, clipping the legs out from under the nearest man, then pivoting and kicking the second back into the elevator. The guard slammed into the metal wall hard. She reached in, hit the button for the second floor, then allowed the doors to close and the car to rise. She then turned her attention back to the first uniform who was trying to stand, planting her boot into the side of his face. Breath and spittle spewed out, then the guy slumped to the floor, not moving. She realized the attack had been witnessed by the cameras, so she would not have the element of surprise again. Disturbing was the fact that the guard toted a weapon at his waist, the safety strap unbuttoned. She'd apparently made her move before he could withdraw it. She freed the gun, chambered a round, then fired twice. One bullet into each of the two cameras, obliterating them.

At least they were blind now.

She opened the stairwell door. Risers led up and down. Going up was definitely the way, but there would surely be more guards waiting. And she couldn't shoot them all.

So she opted for down.

She descended, wondering where this was going to lead. At the bottom was another elevator entrance and a metal door, opening into what appeared to be a storage room. Lots of furniture, shelving, and equipment.

But no way out.

Here she was again. Right in the middle of trouble. She and Cotton seemed to stay in the mix. Truth be known they both loved the rush, though neither one of them would ever openly admit it. Their relationship had certainly been a rocky one, plenty of ups and downs, but they'd been in a good place for some time now. She loved him. No question about it. And he loved her. Once they both admitted that fact and realized it was no weakness, things had become much easier. There was no one on the planet she trusted more. Where were they headed? Hard to say. Marriage seemed to scare them both, so it was a subject they shied away from. They enjoyed spending time together, alternating between her château in southern France and Cotton's bookshop in Copenhagen. And there was the occasional joint endeavor—like here. They worked great together. A team. Watching each other's backs. Unfortunately, Cotton was currently 250 kilometers north in Basel. She and Koger were supposed to connect with him later today.

She stood in the storage room and waited for a new wave of guards to find the two from above. It would not be long before they arrived.

Then what?

She still held the gun, but it seemed unlikely she would use it. No sense making matters worse. Besides, she was surely going to be outgunned. True, the vault was empty, but there was an overabundance of security around just for wine. Cameras, high-tech sprinklers, alarms, and armed guards. Sure, there were some pricey bottles, but nothing to warrant this level of protection. Koger was nearby, waiting for her, but of no help at the moment. Whoever sprang this trap had done so with precision. She knew herself to be a woman of instinct, surviving in a world where today's friend became tomorrow's enemy. And she'd always utilized those instincts to overpower the doubt that sometimes crept into her thoughts.

Like now.

She stared at the only way out.

Not a sound from the stairway. Odd. What was taking so long?

She stepped over and opened the door. All quiet.

Okay. Why not.

She climbed the stairs back to the wine vault level and looked inside past the steel door. The guard she'd dropped to the floor was gone.

Strange.

She decided to avoid the elevator and continued up the risers to ground level. There, she carefully eased the exit door open. The small elevator lobby from earlier came into view. No one in sight.

Cameras filled the corners here too. Once she stepped out, she would be under surveillance.

No choice.

She exited the stairwell and gave one of the cameras a quick glance, then walked back to the main foyer.

Waiting for her were five men.

Four had weapons trained on her.

The fifth stood behind them. Slightly plumpish with a round balding head.

"We saw no need to further pursue you, since there is only one way in and out of this facility," the fifth man said. "Please drop the gun."

Like she had a choice.

She slowly bent down and placed it on the marble floor.

"Now," the man said. "Come with me."

CHAPTER 7

Cotton searched the street for Kelly Austin. He'd been supplied a physical description and photo of her, which he'd committed to memory. Curvy, fit, with ginger-colored hair cut short, and perfect teeth. He envied folks with straight white teeth. His own had always been a challenge. She was obviously quick on her feet too, as she'd fled in a rush and disappeared, though she could not have gone far.

Police cars arrived.

Hopefully, no one would point him out as the shooter. But conscious of the urgency to move away from the scene, he headed farther down the sidewalk. He wondered if the rounds he'd sent into the car had done any damage. The idea had been to distract and deter and the Saab had sped away fast so, on that point, mission accomplished. And though he had the car's license plate committed to memory he doubted that was going to lead anywhere.

Still, he should report in.

He drifted toward an alley between two of the shops. There, he took out his cell phone and called Koger. Police had fanned out to both sides of the street, talking to people. Thankfully, no one was pointing them his way.

Koger answered and said, "I know what happened. Austin called me."

"Did she bother to say where she is?"

Koger chuckled. "You lose her?"

He was already irritated, so smart-ass comments just made things worse. "Derrick, what's going on here?"

"We got ourselves a first-class mess. One that could turn into a world-class situation."

He did not like the sound of that. "I thought this was a simple babysit. A quick favor for a friend. That's what you told me. But somebody just went to a lot of trouble to take her out, and if I hadn't been here—"

"I get it, and I appreciate it. But that's what Captain America does, right? Saves the day?"

He heard the sarcasm the praise carried. That was Koger's style. Just enough bullshit to keep everyone off guard. Koger was career CIA. Part of the spies-and-make-believe culture, America's eyes and ears abroad and all that bullshit. But the agency had a long history of incompetence, arrogance, and abuse of power. In the old days, when he'd been active with the Magellan Billet, working with them was out of necessity, not desire. Until a few months ago Koger had been with special operations. Now he was European station chief, thanks to a White House promotion, and all because of what he and Koger had done in Germany a few months back. Every enterprising CIA field officer aspired to a desk at Langley and Koger was no exception. But to obtain that reward you had to match a timeline. Fail to rise fast enough and the train passed you by. Koger was more than twenty years into his career, definitely into overtime on the career clock. But a little luck had finally fallen the big man's way when the president of the United States owed him a favor.

Their paths had crossed several times back when Cotton was active. Some good. Others not so much. A lot of people with Koger's longevity were retired, now writing revelation books or appearing on cable news as talking heads. But Koger was still on the job and, to his credit, had turned down that desk at Langley, which had finally been offered to him, choosing to stay in the field as a station chief. It fit the man's tough, no-nonsense reputation. No one who'd ever worked with him doubted his loyalty or ability. But that didn't mean they'd enjoyed the experience.

Himself included.

"Derrick," he said. "I'm helping you out here. The least you could do is level with me."

"I hear you, and I want to. Believe me, I do. But I'm working with at least one hand tied behind me. Can you cut me some slack a little while longer?"

He got it. How many times had he worked a situation half blind? More than he could count. But that was when he was a full-time agent, on the payroll, with benefits. This was a freebie. One that had just turned violent. So he wanted to know, "How important is this?"

"On a scale from one to ten . . ." Koger paused. "An eleven."

Overstatement was not a Koger trait. Okay. He got it. This was serious. "You have any idea who just made that attempt on her life?"

"I'm afraid I do. Which may elevate this to a twelve or thirteen on that importance scale."

Koger's problem, not his. "Is Cassiopeia in trouble?"

"I hope not. But I've got her back."

Good to hear. "What do you want me to do?"

"Babysitting just turned into chaperoning. Can you handle that?"

"Where do you want her?"

"Bring her to me here, in Geneva. In one piece. That last part is really important."

"Where is she?"

"You see a bakery?"

He stepped back to the end of the alley and looked around, spotting one farther down the street. "I see it."

"She's in there. I'm sure that perfect memory of yours will help you recognize her."

It would. A gift from birth. Not photographic, as television and movies liked to say. Eidetic. An ability to recall an enormous amount of detailed information that never seemed to fade.

"I'm on it," he said.

And he ended the call.

He stepped from the alley back onto the sidewalk and turned left, making a beeline for the bakery. Which reminded him he was hungry. He hadn't eaten since the two breakfast rolls he'd managed to snag a few hours ago. A bag of pastries would be wonderful.

The police continued to canvass the area, talking to people, trying to figure out what had happened. Surely there were cameras somewhere on this street. The damn things were everywhere. That footage would be studied and he could well be identified from those images. Since he was here at the request of the CIA, hopefully, any further action from the locals would be quashed by Koger. That's what European station chiefs did, right?

He made it to the bakery and entered.

Nice place. Sparkling glass cases displayed chocolate croissants, apple turnovers, cakes, pastries, and quiche. About ten people were inside, most of them focused on what was happening out on the street. He spotted Kelly Austin in the far corner, her back to the others, facing the wall, the shopping bag she'd been toting resting on the floor beside her. Koger had said she was shaken up, so he needed to go easy. He stepped over, but stopped short of coming too close, which might frighten her.

"Ms. Austin," he said.

She whirled and faced him and he caught the fear in her eyes.

"Derrick Koger sent me. I was the one shooting at the car out there. I'm glad you're okay. My name is—"

"Harold Earl 'Cotton' Malone," she said.

He was surprised. "Koger told you my full name?"

She shook her head. "No, he didn't."

The eyes had calmed and something else entered them. Curiosity. Then amusement.

"You don't recognize me, do you?" she asked.

He shook his head. "Have we met?"

"It's me, Cotton. Susan Baldwin."

CHAPTER 8

KYRA POWERED ACROSS LAKE BAIKAL, THE COOLNESS OF THE EVENING air biting at her thoughts. She was satisfied with Samvel Yerevan's demise.

Another good kill.

Which was the only way she liked them.

She never considered herself a murderer. More a problem solver. Keeper of the peace. Delivering exactly what the client wanted. She'd worked for the Bank of St. George before on other acquisitions. Apparently, death had worked its way into their business plan. Understandable since, if done right, murder could eliminate a multitude of issues quick and easy. The bank came with the added benefit of paying exceptionally well. The only qualification? It expected nothing less than total perfection.

Fine by her.

She expected the same thing from herself.

The collar of her windbreaker was turned up against the chill that rushed across her body, drying the neoprene and her hair out from the dunk in the lake. Darkness was approaching, which meant it would be tomorrow, at the earliest, before Yerevan's boat and body were discovered. Plenty of time for her to leave the country. The plan was to drive south into Mongolia to its capital,

Ulaanbaatar, a trip of about 450 kilometers. From there she'd catch a private flight west.

To where?

That remained to be seen.

Across the lake she spotted Yerevan's dacha perched high on a forested bluff. Dachas were more than a Russian architectural and cultural phenomenon.

They were a way of life.

Back in the 17th century they started out as small country retreats where a noble could escape palace protocol and engage in simple pleasures like planting a garden or growing a vegetable patch. Today, Russians living in crowded urban apartments all wanted an even smaller dacha out in the countryside where, from May to October, they could enjoy walks, picnics, boating, and bike rides. This one here in central Siberia, a massive, sprawling country estate worth millions of euros, reflected what only a tiny percentage of Russians were able to enjoy.

She slowed to a crawl and brought the boat close to a concrete dock. Engines off, she tied off and hopped out. At the end of the dock, stairs cut into the limestone led up to the house.

She'd been born and raised south of Moscow to parents who lived in a small clapboard farmhouse, which she recalled fondly. They were workers all their lives, never causing any trouble and always focused on each other. Both dead now. The life expectancy of a Russian was nothing like that found in Western countries. A shame, too, as they were good people. And she knew what they would think of her chosen profession. Both had been impeccably honest and deeply religious. Neither would understand why she'd chosen to kill for money. But disappointing them had never factored into her career choices. Survival. Living comfortably. That's what mattered. Along with being dependent on no one, able to buy her own magnificent dacha if she wanted.

She stopped at the top of the stone stairs.

Modern dacha owners were free to build as they desired. More of the reforms that came with the end of the Soviet Union and the rise of the new Russia. Some re-created Chekhov's idyllic getaway, others leaned more toward a Spartan place to write and read, most immersed themselves in nature. Samvel Yerevan chose something else altogether.

Obscene luxury.

A modernistic style dominated the multistory structure with sleek lines, soft colors, and few adornments. Plate-glass windows offered great views of the lake. A large terrace dotted with outdoor furniture faced the water. It looked more like a museum of modern art than a house. Through the windows she saw that the inside, lit by warm incandescent lights, was a collage of marble and stone.

On the terrace she found a glass door that opened.

Unlocked? Why not.

More of a rich man's arrogance. Who in their right mind would break in? The repercussions would be swift, violent, and permanent. Which explained the lack of cameras or guards.

Yerevan was unique among the Russian oligarchs. As a class they all came into existence after the fall of communism when the collective ownership of state assets like oil, gas, minerals, and coal became cloudy. Informal deals were eventually made by well-connected entrepreneurs, with former USSR officials, to acquire or control much of that former state property. The name itself, *oligarch*, came from the Greek *oligarkhia*, meaning "rule of the few."

And rule they did.

Lining the pockets of government officials while acquiring massive amounts of personal wealth. Yerevan made a fortune mining copper. But, of late, he'd amassed even more in bitcoin. In fact he was Russia's self-proclaimed largest miner and investor in cryptocurrency. Which had surely brought him onto the Bank of St. George's radar.

Bitcoin was legal to possess in Russia but it could not be used as payment for goods or services. As in the United States, and most of the world, it was treated as property, not legal tender, unrecognized as a monetary unit. All of the things that made it attractive—decentralization, confidentiality, financial autonomy, non-seizability, and accessibility—also made it suspect. For a while now oligarchs had been stockpiling cryptocurrency as a hedge against American financial sanctions, imposed on them for the Russian government's various maligned activities around the globe. Yerevan had been one of the most prolific acquirors, quietly amassing over two billion euros' worth.

Luckily, for all bitcoin's sophistication, confidentiality, and modernization, stealing it was remarkably easy. Owners guarded their private online wallets in a multitude of ways. Some high-tech. Others not so much. Yerevan chose an old-school approach. He kept the key to his wallet protected behind a two-step process, one part of which he wore around his neck. The other was an outer steel cylinder consisting of twenty-four separate disks, axled together, with etched letters and numbers on each disk in random order. Separately the two parts yielded nothing. But when the smaller cylinder was inserted into the larger, then the disks twisted, notches in the smaller locked the disks in the larger into a preset order, revealing Yerevan's twenty-four-character code—which, if her intel was to be believed, would open his wallet.

A one-of-a-kind device.

No way existed to duplicate the code with any other cylinders.

So she had to find the other half.

Her information said that Yerevan brought both pieces with him wherever he traveled. But this was a big house. She stepped inside and withdrew the small steel cylinder from her jacket pocket, considering where to start looking.

"Who are you?" a female voice asked in Russian.

Which momentarily startled her.

Her gaze shot to the staircase, another eclectic combination of steel and glass that seemed to float in the air. On one of the risers a woman stood. Tall, svelte, with long dark hair and skin to match, dressed in a yellow silk bathrobe that barely made it past her waist. The curve of her breasts against the silk seemed to promise pleasure, but the tight lines at the corner of her lips hinted at a price to be paid.

"A friend of Samvel's," Kyra said, keeping to the same language, her voice low and calm.

"He has no friends. He's a pig. You look like you've been swimming."

Beneath her jacket she still wore the neoprene bodysuit and her hair remained damp. "The water was invigorating."

"Is he dead?" the woman asked.

"Why would you ask that?"

"What you're holding. He never takes it off. Not ever. Nor does he allow anyone to touch it."

The voice was matter-of-fact.

She held up the small cylinder. "Do you know where the other part to this is hidden?"

The woman descended the stairs. At the bottom she said, "I might."

A formality dominated their interaction, and though it seemed congenial both of them were wary.

She told herself to stay friendly.

For now.

CHAPTER 9

Cassiopeia was escorted from the main foyer back into the wine repository's inner workings and a small conference room. Two plate-glass windows opened out, past the curtains and sheers, to the afternoon sun. The four men with guns waited outside, and the fifth—attired in a blazer with shiny brass buttons, a flashy tie, and creased gray trousers—sat across from her at the conference table.

"You are a trespasser at this facility," he said.

"I had the proper password and code for access to the vault. That doesn't make me a trespasser. Who are you?"

"I am Wells Townley, the duly authorized representative of BHTR Limited, the owner of this facility."

"Now, we both know that's a lie. This facility is owned by the Bank of St. George."

Which she knew all about.

Her father had established a relationship there long ago, and the men and women who continued to run her family's multinational corporation had maintained that relationship. A unique institution. Part investment banker, hedge fund, and high-risk venture capitalist. Terra, like many other corporations, had utilized the bank's services several times for an influx of capital. She'd met Catherine Gledhill, its chief operating officer, twice. A true Luxembourger.

Which made her part Celtic, Gallo-Roman, and Germanic. A challenging combination of daring and caution, pleasant in manner and voice, reasonable, easy to deal with.

"I want to speak to Catherine Gledhill," she said.

And she found her cell phone.

"Those do not work inside this building."

Of course they didn't. How silly of her to think otherwise. This whole thing made her feel a bit foolish, which she did not like. She slipped the phone back into her pocket. She decided that to receive she had to give. "I was sent here by the Central Intelligence Agency, which, to my knowledge, was the owner of gold that was supposed to be in that vault. And, by the way, you have a lot of security and guns for wine bottles. Where's the gold?"

"We have none."

"That's not what the CIA says."

She was unarmed and four men with weapons were on the other side of the conference room door. Or at least somewhere in the building. Could she deal with them? Probably. The question was, should she? As Cotton would say, she didn't have a dog in this fight.

Or maybe she did.

Life had dealt her a lot of ups and downs. A happy childhood, pleasant teenage years, then a time after college when she became estranged from her parents. That had been tough. She lost both of them within a year of each other. It had taken her a long time to recover, especially with so much between them left unsaid. Thankfully, they'd settled many of their differences and all was reasonably good before they both died. She missed them. Lately she'd been forced to deal with demons from her past, settling old scores, learning things she never knew about her father, even selling her family's Spanish estate in an attempt to excise all of the bad spirits.

And it worked.

She was in a good place.

So why not spread a little of that goodness around and help out

Cotton, who was helping out Derrick Koger, who was obviously *not* in a good place?

Seemed like the right move.

And still did.

She stood. "I'm walking out of here. Anyone who tries to stop me is going to get hurt. Bad. And that includes you, Wells Townley."

"I have no intention of harming you. Of course, you harmed two of our personnel."

"Like I said, there are a lot of guns around here for wine."

"While you were skulking about in our basement," he said, "I made a call and received explicit orders. You did possess the correct password and code, which once gained the CIA access to this vault. But no more. I have been instructed to inform the CIA to walk away. None of this concerns them any longer. The bank is severing all ties, effective immediately. The Black Eagle Trust is no more. Leave. Us. Alone."

Now her curiosity was piqued. Who was *us*? She decided to try a bluff and see if more could be learned. "They want their gold."

"That bullion was deposited with the bank almost eighty years ago. No documentation exists relative to any of it, a fact that they insisted upon. That includes any and all inventories, which do not exist. The United States wanted that stolen war loot to disappear, and that is what happened. It's gone. They don't get it back. Not now. Not ever. The bank is tolerating this intrusion as an opportunity to send a message."

That was a mouthful. And fascinating. "Okay. I'll pass that along."

"Please do that, and do not return here. As you have discovered, there is nothing here to find."

He stood and opened the door, gesturing for her to leave.

She approached him but hesitated a moment. "You're an odd fellow."

He tossed her a thin smile. "You have no idea."

She walked back toward the front of the building and the main foyer. None of the men with guns were around. She left from the front door and soaked in the midday sun. Historically, Switzerland had been a favorite sparring ring for diplomats, the birthplace of grandiose schemes to achieve world peace and prosperity, a place that had always inspired people to settle their differences with reason instead of blood. But it was also a place of secrets. Many, many secrets. Like a wine vault that wasn't a wine vault?

The repository sat at the end of a busy commercial boulevard at the edge of Geneva's financial district. Koger had dropped her off earlier, and she saw his car parked fifty meters away. He apparently saw her and pulled away from the curb, heading straight for her. When he stopped, she opened the door and climbed inside. She assumed the people inside the repository were watching.

"How'd it go?" he asked.

She slammed the door.

"Drive and I'll explain. But you're not going to like it."

CHAPTER 10

C<small>OTTON STEPPED UP ON THE COVERED PORCH AND ENTERED THE WHITE</small> *clapboard house. He never knocked. No need. Suzy always left the door unlocked. Their affair was in its sixth month. He was a young navy lieutenant, fresh out of law school, beginning what would surely be the next twenty years as a JAG lawyer. He'd wanted to fly fighter jets and had made top marks in flight school, but other people, older and supposedly wiser, friends of his dead father, had different ideas for his life and he ended up at Georgetown law school. Now he was less than a year into his first assignment at the Naval Air Station in Pensacola, Florida. There he'd met another twenty-six-year-old. A petite blonde who worked in the data storage facility. Computers were becoming more and more important and people who understood how to use them were likewise valuable. Suzy Baldwin, "with a 'y'" as she liked to say, was one of those people. Smart, cute, sassy. They'd hit it off immediately. She lived a few miles from the base in a small subdivision typical for the Florida panhandle. He lived on base, behind the fences, which made this the perfect place for their regular trysts.*

She stepped from the bedroom wearing a short sundress stretched tautly over her curves, the legs that emerged beneath beautifully tapered. She had high cheekbones with a sprinkle of freckles over a delicate upturned nose. Her hair cascaded past her shoulders in long, soft curls, just the way he liked it. She was from a small town in southern Illinois, born into a middle-class family, just like himself. Their entire relationship had played itself out here, within these walls. Never had they been out in public.

And for good reason.

He was married.

She wrapped her arms around his neck and kissed him.

Hard.

She never dilly-dallied much when it came to lovemaking. Both of them seemed anxious for the experience, though he'd become less and less enthralled.

Thanks to the guilt.

Which was why he'd come over today.

"We need to end this," he said.

He could still see her puzzled face, baffled by the declaration. Only it was not the same one he was now staring at. "What happened to you?"

She smiled. "You don't like what you see?"

He shook his head. "That's not what I mean. It's just that you look completely different."

"A lot happened to me since Pensacola," she said.

Obviously.

"What do you mean, end this?" she asked him.

"I can't come here anymore. I have a wife."

"Yes, you do. Her name is Pam. Who you've cared little to nothing about these past few months."

That hurt. But it was true.

"You seemed to enjoy climbing into my bed," she said. "I haven't heard a complaint."

"This is not about you."

"Excuse me. Last I looked there were two people in this relationship."

50

That was the problem. There was no relationship. Only sex. And she was the latest in a series of affairs that started in law school. Women here and there who meant little to nothing. Why did he cheat? He had no idea. He'd tried to analyze it. Understand. Stop it. But nothing had worked. True, his relationship with Pam had been strained for some time. Did he still love her? Hard to say. But she did not deserve what he was doing to her.

Did Pam know?

He didn't think so.

And he wanted to keep it that way.

What an idiot he'd been.

A selfish, narcissistic fool.

Twenty years had passed and he still felt the guilt. Even with all that happened between him and Pam since that time, he'd never been able to shake his failings. The hotshot law student, then naval officer, thinking himself the cock of the walk, able to do whatever he wanted. He'd cheated on Pam with four women.

Suzy the longest in duration.

"What's happening, Earl?" she said to him. "You growing a conscience?"

His real name was Harold Earl Malone, but he'd been called Cotton since childhood. There was a story to that. A long one. He'd told it to Suzy, but she'd still insisted on using either Harold or Earl. Terms of endearment? Maybe. More a sign, at the moment, of her growing anger.

"Can we make this easy?" he said.

"What's going on with you? You act like neither of us knew you were married. Why now? What's different?"

He wasn't going to explain himself. Feelings were hard for him. The last thing he wanted was to discuss them with someone else. That was another problem between him and Pam. Neither of them was good at sharing. "I'm really sorry. But I can't do this anymore. I should have never done it in the first place."

"Get out."

Anger had arrived. Bold and clear.

"You're not going to make any trouble, are you?" he asked.

"Is that what you're worried about? That I won't tell anyone? That your wife won't know. Or your commanding officer. You don't give a damn about how I feel, do you?"

"Of course I do. I don't want to hurt you. Not at all. But I also don't want to hurt my wife anymore. Can't you understand that?"

She pointed at the door.

"Get. Out."

They never spoke again.

A few weeks later she was gone from Pensacola. Now here she was, two decades later, in Basel, Switzerland, with a new name, new face, and people trying to kill her.

"You and I were a long time ago," she said to him. "I'm over it. A lot has passed by since then, and I want to tell you all about it, but this is neither the time nor place."

An old reality, from long ago, returned in a steaming wave of uncomfortableness. He hadn't thought about that part of his life in years, and he felt strange as those distant, disturbing memories flooded back. A familiar shallow righteousness ripped through him that left his gut empty and weak. Once a struggle had raged within his brain—one of right or wrong, happiness or misery— but he'd long since acquired a hold on the anchors that now firmly rooted his life. He'd known, even as a young man, that there'd be a moment when he'd be tested, a moment when he would come face-to-face with the truth, when his actions would affirm or deny everything.

Suzy Baldwin had been his moment.

He was no longer the man who'd cheated on his wife, having learned his lessons and never repeated them. He was now an honorable soul. More than that. He was a cautious soul, careful about his mistakes and mindful of others. And here, standing before him, was a vivid reminder of his former shortcomings.

People were again coming and going through the bakery's front door. Beyond the front windows he saw the street returning to normal, the police leaving. She was right. This was not the time for reunions. But—

"What have you gotten yourself into?" he quietly asked her.

He saw the concern on her face.

"More than you can possibly imagine."

CHAPTER 11

KYRA STUDIED THE WOMAN SHE'D FOUND INSIDE YEREVAN'S DACHA. Slender, sophisticated, reserved. And the eyes. Brown dots. Cautious and measuring. But Kyra had not survived in her line of work by being reckless, stupid, or naïve. The house was supposed to be empty. And this woman, naked beneath a silk robe, with the calculated demeanor of a mortician, raised a multitude of alarms. An unexpected new player in the game.

But who was she?

"What is your name?" she asked.

"Roza."

"Do you have a last name?"

"It's unimportant."

Okay. She wanted to remain a bit anonymous. Kyra gestured with the cylinder she'd taken from Yerevan. "What do you know about this?"

"You don't have a name?" Roza asked.

"It truly is unimportant."

Roza shrugged with a coyness she found irritating and pointed at the cylinder. "He liked to show it off, especially in bed. He said it was the key to bitcoin worth billions of euros."

"And what do you know of this bitcoin?" she asked.

They stood inside the dacha's great room, its ceiling held aloft by pillars wrapped in brass bands set into sparkling stone, like bracelets around a pale arm. Beyond the wall of glass, past the terrace and a row of low hedges, darkness was rapidly enveloping the lake.

"He called it his digital children," Roza said. "Odd, considering he has real children whom he never spoke of."

Not really. It seemed perfectly in character.

Roza stepped across the room, closer to the bar that dominated one side, the mirrored wall behind it fronted by glass shelves displaying a variety of expensive amber-colored liquors. Kyra noticed that she walked with a slight limp, a pain in one leg.

"Are you hurt?" she asked.

"The bastard kicked me before he left on the boat. He said I wasn't...enthusiastic enough."

"The hazards of your line of work?"

Roza studied her with a casual intensity. "There are risks associated with what I do." The woman paused. "But there are also rewards."

"Designer clothes? Shoes? Jewelry? Staying in a house like this?"

"All those. And more."

"So you're a whore?"

"Is it necessary to insult me?"

"I meant no harm. But that is what you seem to be."

"And what are you?"

"I like to think of myself as a problem solver."

"Did you kill him?"

No need to lie. "I did."

Roza seemed unfazed by the admission. Which was odd. But since Kyra planned on killing this woman anyway, what did it matter? The more important question, though, was whether this whore could be useful in finding Yerevan's highly specialized device. So she returned to the point. "There's another part to this. A larger cylinder with dials, letters, and numbers on it that this part fits into."

"And if I show you where it is?"

"I won't kill you, and you can take what you like from here."

"What if I report you to the authorities?"

She smiled. "You won't."

Roza considered the proposal in silence, and Kyra took the moment to make the kind of critical assessment that had saved her life on more than one occasion. Nothing she'd just said should be believed by any reasonable person. No way was she going to allow an eyewitness to just walk away. Slowly, but clearly, all of the pieces of the puzzle swirling around inside her head began to fit together into something that made sense.

Bitcoin was born on January 3, 2009, when the program that created it first appeared on the internet. By 2014 seventy percent of all the then-bitcoin transactions were handled from one world exchange. Mt. Gox. Based in Japan. But in February 2014 Mt. Gox suspended all trading and announced that 850,000 of its bitcoin had been stolen by hackers. About $450 million U.S. at the time. Which shocked the bitcoin world. Subsequently 141,000 were reclaimed, but 709,000 coins remained missing. The hacker was eventually identified and hunted down, but before he could be arrested by the FBI he transferred those bitcoin to Russia's Federal Security Service.

Quite a bold move.

Which spoke volumes.

She'd dealt with the FSB before. The successor to the infamous KGB. Its main responsibilities included counter-intelligence, border security, and counter-terrorism. From its headquarters in Moscow's Lubyanka Square, which the KGB once occupied, the FSB worked independent of anyone and everything. The Kremlin had long proclaimed its hatred for bitcoin but, privately, through the FSB, it was one of the world's largest owners of cryptocurrency. So she wondered. Had the FSB set its sights on Samvel Yerevan's stash? Why not? He was an easy mark.

Everything about this woman pointed in that direction.

This was no whore.

"Come with me," Roza said, and she hobbled her way down a short hall and into another spacious room that also faced the lake. Some sort of office or study. More glass, stone, and wood mixed in a contemporary style. But it wasn't the décor that attracted a visitor's gaze. It was the busts. Classical statues on high, verdant-green marble pedestals that gazed out with an ageless silence. She counted eight against the walls, each fashioned of white marble.

"My best guess," Roza said, "is that what you seek is in this room. He called this his fortress."

The desk contained no drawers. Just a stainless-steel frame that held a thick glass slab aloft. Behind it glass shelves were built into the wall with drawers and cabinets beneath. No books. Just porcelain vases, small sculptures, and stone carvings. All impressionistic.

"He had strange tastes in art," Kyra said.

Roza walked behind the desk to the shelves and leaned against the counter. "He was imperious and sanctimonious, thinking himself innately better than all of us. He never liked anyone or anything to have more meaning than himself. The busts? They are his heroes."

She recognized some of the images. Napoleon. Alexander the Great. Charlemagne. Julius Caesar. Stalin. "He seemed to like dictators and conquerors."

A cold tension tightened her body, which brought her alert, sharpened her movements, and heightened her senses. Roza still showed no fear, no impatience. Instead, she remained methodical, calculating, and, above all, capable.

But of what?

Certainly not more than Kyra herself could display.

Her fits of fury had always frightened her parents. As a child she would periodically flail wildly, the anger tough to control. They'd never really known how to deal with her, and psychotherapy in Russia, especially for children, was nearly unheard of. Eventually, on her own, she mastered the process of harnessing rage and using it to wipe away depression, along with an occasional bout of helplessness. Her first kill came at age nineteen. Done on a dare. A way to be accepted. More favors followed until she realized that a market existed for the service. At first she'd been hesitant about the urge, which seemed to come from deep inside her, a place she'd tried to repress and deny. Eventually she came to accept that a terrible violence seethed just beneath her amicable exterior. And instead of frightening her, it provided a sense of strength.

Along with an insight she'd learned to trust.

The obviousness of this situation broke through her clouded thoughts and she could delay no longer. If she'd read this scenario right, reinforcements were surely on the way. More FSB agents, backing up this one here in the dacha.

As a teenager Kyra had first learned that she possessed an acute sense of color. Strong and clear, seeing things—like rainbows inside pieces of ice—that others never saw. Some colors triggered manic and euphoric episodes, others produced giggle fits. Oddly, the malady faded with age, replaced by an exceptional degree of peripheral vision. A German optician explained to her that such acuity was normally not possible because the majority of vision receptors, the cones, were packed in the central part of the eye. Her abnormality? She had an overabundance of cones. Which had temporarily heightened her view of color and permanently increased the range of her peripheral vision beyond normal limits.

A hidden asset she used to maximum advantage.

Which was why she'd shifted her position closer to the Napoleon bust, her eyes clearly angled away from Roza, who still stood behind the desk. But she was able to see out of the corner of her eye as the woman, propped against the counter, eased open the drawer behind her in the wall unit and slid one hand inside, out of view.

Kyra reacted, grabbing the marble bust, spinning around, and launching it across the room. The heavy mass crashed into Roza just as the woman's right hand came into view, from the drawer, with a gun in her grip. Roza raised her left arm to shield herself from the impact but the heavy bust pounded into her hard and she collapsed to the floor, dazed and in pain. Kyra darted across the room and relieved Roza of the gun.

A cold rage devoid of all feeling engulfed her.

She stared at the gun. Clean. Well oiled. Loaded with fresh rounds.

Ordinarily she avoided factory ammunition, preferring custom loads that she made herself with less powder, which provided lower velocity and less noise. But this would have to do. The gun seemed alive, power surging into her hand, up her arm, and into her entire being.

Which brought her life.

Like always.

She fired twice into the woman's head.

CHAPTER 12

CASSIOPEIA WAS TRYING HARD NOT TO BE IRRITATED. BUT SHE'D LEFT her castle rebuilding project in the hands of her employees and traveled to Switzerland, at her own expense, only to be set up? She told Koger what happened and passed along the message. They were motoring north, out of Geneva, at a fast pace.

"It was fifty-fifty if the gold was there," he told her.

"Which you failed to mention, before I went inside."

"There's a lot more I didn't tell you too," he said.

"Like the Black Eagle Trust?"

Koger nodded. "Yeah. Like that."

They rode a few minutes in silence. The day was turning cloudy and overcast. Something was happening here, something that the big man sitting across from her was definitely bothered about. Something Cotton had thought important enough to involve himself in.

Koger slowed the car and turned into a small parking lot that accommodated an office building. Trees encircled the asphalt and only about half the spaces were occupied. He parked in one and switched off the engine. He then reached back to the rear seat and grabbed a leather satchel. From inside he removed a few pages stapled together.

"I need you to read this," he said. "Then I'll answer your questions.

INTERNAL MEMORANDUM
CLASSIFIED—TOP SECRET
FOR DCI EYES ONLY

<u>Text:</u> Until September 1945, Edward Lansdale was an immaterial advertising copywriter, who spent the war writing propaganda for the Office of Strategic Services (OSS). With the disbanding of the OSS, Lansdale was offered an opportunity to transfer to the Army's G2 operation in the Philippines. There, he was placed in charge of supervising a Filipino American intelligence officer named Severio Garcia Diaz Sanata. By then Japanese General Tomoyuki Yamashita had surrendered, been tried for war crimes, found guilty, and executed. Yamashita was questioned extensively about gold and other assets he hid across the Philippines, but refused to say anything. Once dead, attention turned to Major Kojima Kashii, who had driven Yamashita all over the islands.

Sanata tortured Kashii and learned about 175 hidden caches of Japanese treasure. Edward Lansdale joined in those sessions. Kashii eventually led Sanata and Lansdale to the location of a dozen sites in the mountains north of Manila. Two of those were opened and revealed huge amounts of gold, precious metals, and gems. Sanata then recruited a team and started to open more sites. Lansdale flew to Japan to brief General MacArthur and then on to Washington to speak with President Harry Truman, who decided to proceed with the gold recovery, which would be kept secret and classified. Roosevelt's Secretary of War, Henry Stimson, was the first to propose using gold recovered from the Nazis as a secret, post-war slush fund. The Nazis had already re-smelted their looted gold, making it nearly impossible to trace its origin. Further, many owners had perished in the war and most of the pre-war governments had ceased to exist. With many of the eastern European countries falling under the influence of the Soviet Union, returning any gold to those countries was out of the question. So the Allies decided to retain whatever Nazi wealth was possible. In 1946 the decision was made to consolidate that gold with what was being recovered from the Philippines into what became known as the Black Eagle Trust.

After briefing Truman, Edward Lansdale returned to Tokyo in November 1945. From there General MacArthur accompanied Lansdale on a secret flight to Manila where MacArthur personally inspected box after box of gold bullion stacked yards tall in underground chambers. That gold was then covertly moved by ship to banks in 42 different countries. Classified documents (viewed by several retired assets in the 1980s but no longer existing) confirmed large deposits of gold, silver, and platinum were made to those institutions. These same assets confirmed that the Black Eagle Trust was formally created in 1948.

Total secrecy was vital to success. The United States had openly declared that Japan was broke from the war, with no money to rebuild itself. Communism had become the common enemy of America and Europe. The United States wanted Japan to become a staunch anti-communist state. But a problem arose when the most ardent of the anti-communists in Japan were indicted as war criminals. These individuals were needed post-war. So few were ever punished, due in large part to MacArthur absolving both them and the Japanese emperor of all war crimes. The end result was that those most responsible for the war (and its atrocities) were left in power. A formal peace treaty with Japan was not executed until September 8, 1951. To shield Japan from war reparations, John Foster Dulles, the American envoy, secretly negotiated specialized terms with Japanese officials. Article 14 of the ratified treaty states:

> It is recognized that Japan should pay reparations to the Allied Powers for the damage and suffering caused by it during the war. Nevertheless it is also recognized that the resources of Japan are not presently sufficient to make such payments. Therefore the Allied Powers waive all reparations claims for themselves, and their nationals, arising out of any actions taken by Japan.

By this article, any claims, including those by Allied nations, citizens, and servicemen forced into slave labor by Japanese warlords were waived. This also essentially placed anything looted by Japan off limits to legal action thereby ensuring that no one could lay claim to any of the recovered gold. Classified records that have survived indicate that the value of the gold recovered exceeded $200 billion 1947 dollars (which would exceed $2 trillion dollars in today's value). More caches were eventually unearthed and added to the total. But not all of the 175 underground vaults were found and a map, created by Yamashita to be used for their eventual re-location, disappeared after the war.

By 1950, all of the gold acquired was physically consolidated at a single institution, the Bank of St. George in Luxembourg, under the guise of the Black Eagle Trust. Any and all records associated with that trust are currently the property of the bank and in its sole possession. This was part of the initial agreement between the agency and the bank, a safeguard to insulate the United States government from any official involvement, which created full deniability. Until recently, the CIA enjoyed a congenial relationship with the bank, but that is no longer the case.

Background: The Central Intelligence Agency was formed on September 18, 1947. But its overall purpose was unclear from the start. Truman simply wanted a centralized group to organize the information that reached him each day. The Department of Defense wanted high-level military intelligence and covert action if needed. The State Department wanted to use it to create global political change favorable to the United States. A confusion of purpose contributed to the CIA's early lack of success. It failed to provide sufficient intelligence about the Soviet takeovers of Romania and Czechoslovakia, the Soviet blockade of Berlin, and the Soviet atomic bomb project. It was caught off guard by the Chinese entry into the Korean War. The famed double agent Kim Philby was the British liaison to the CIA and worked for years undetected. Arlington Hall, the nerve center of the then-CIA cryptanalysis, was compromised by a Soviet spy.

The 1948 Italian elections were the first known uses of the Black Eagle Trust. The idea had been to prevent the communists from taking over Italy, so money was funneled to opposition candidates and the election outcome bought. Next, communist uprisings in Greece and Turkey were defeated through covert funding of counter-insurgents. In Japan the Black Eagle Trust propped up the government and funded the royal family, along with the fight of communism in Asia. When the socialists won big in the 1946 Japanese national elections, trust money was used to discredit the newly formed coalition. More was used to eventually elect and replace key members of the Japanese government.

The Black Eagle Trust has been utilized for over seventy years to fund covert operations around the world. And while these operations were certainly odoriferous and most likely criminal, the real danger came in keeping trillions in unaccounted-for gold out of the hands of private individuals.

But on that goal we failed.

CHAPTER 13

Cotton led Kelly Austin from the bakery back onto the streets of Basel. He could see that Kelly remained apprehensive. Understandable, given that someone had just tried to gun her down. Even if you did this for a living, which he had for a dozen years at the Magellan Billet, nerves still got rattled. Guns and bullets had a way of doing that.

Even to him.

The afternoon had turned cloudy and cool, but Basel remained bustling with cars and people. Koger had said to bring Kelly Austin to him. But they needed a few minutes to regroup. Her hotel was out of the question. If the people in the car knew where she was on the streets, they definitely knew where she was staying. His hotel was off limits for a variety of reasons. So he decided a café would be best. Public. Lots of people. A good place to have a chat.

And they needed to talk.

They made their way across the Rhine and through old town. Many of its former residences had been turned into businesses. Bright brass plaques adorned the buildings. The streets were spotless, the windows clean and bright. Flowers sprouted from sill boxes in a profusion of late-summer color. They entered the Marktplatz, the cobbled square dominated by the vivid red façade of the old rathaus. The crowds pressed together, constantly moving. Winding alleys led off to a maze of more shopping and eateries. He headed down one of the narrow, cobbled paths and found an eclectic café with lots of windows, vaulted ceilings, and what he liked best, plenty of open space. On entering he caught the pungent scent of curry in the warm air. Not his favorite. He led the way through a series of booths spaced against winding walls, surely calculated to provide diners with privacy. Atop each table sat a small shaded lamp that illuminated white linen tablecloths. They claimed a booth toward the rear. A woman in a long tan dress took their request for two bottled waters. He told her they might order some food, but to give them a few minutes.

Once she was gone, he asked, "What happened after you left Pensacola?"

"How is Pam?"

"We've been divorced a long time."

"Your fault or hers?"

"Long hours and travel played hell with both the nerves and home life."

"As did adultery."

Blunt, as always. "We both did our share of bad things."

"Both? Was she a bad girl too?"

He wasn't in the mood to relive ancient history. "It doesn't matter."

"Did she ever know about us?"

"I think she knew everything about all the women I cheated with. But she was good at keeping things to herself."

It really hurt to talk about the past. He'd spent years making amends for the pain his recklessness caused. It had only been in the last few years that he'd come to fully understand all that happened. He had affairs. Pam had an affair. But from hers came a child, Gary, who he'd thought was his until learning, years after the birth, that he was not the boy's biological father. Gary was seventeen now and they'd both dealt with the lies. All was finally good among him, Pam, and Gary.

"I thought I loved you," Kelly said.

That was new.

"It was stupid, I know, considering the situation. You were married. But when we're young we do stupid things."

That we do.

"It hurt when you ended it that day," she said. "I didn't handle it well. I was mad. My instincts were to run, so I got a transfer to another base."

He was hoping that talking would calm her down, take her mind off the attack. It also bought him some time until Koger provided further instructions.

"A few years after I left," she said, "I was in a bad car accident. A deer jumped out in front of me and I went over an embankment. I was paralyzed and disfigured. It took three years before I walked again. I also got a new face from too many plastic surgeries to count. My life changed totally. So I decided to get a new name to go along with all that. Suzy Baldwin became Kelly Austin. I went back to school and earned some advanced degrees, then landed a job with the National Security Agency. They always need computer people. From there I moved to the CIA, then to the Bank of St. George."

The woman returned with their waters. Kelly indicated she wasn't hungry. He had been half an hour ago, but not anymore.

"That's quite a career move," he said to her.

She drank from the bottle. "Not really. They're all related."

He waited for her to explain.

"What about you, Harold Earl? What happened with you?"

"My name is Cotton."

"Not to me."

All of the physical changes had not altered her sharp personality, which had been one of the things that had attracted him to her in the first place. God help him, but he liked strong women. "I left the navy and went to work at the Justice Department. A special covert unit."

"The Magellan Billet?"

"You've heard of it?"

She nodded. "It came to my attention a few times. But never your name."

"I was there a dozen years before retiring out early, divorcing, and moving to Denmark. I own a bookshop in Copenhagen."

"And yet the CIA calls on you to look after me."

"A favor for a friend."

"Koger?"

He nodded.

"Still the master of opaqueness, I see."

"As are you," he said. "I noticed you changed the subject instead of explaining the connection among all your career moves."

"I like to keep you guessing."

"Considering your life is, literally, in my hands, that's a stupid move."

"Yeah, I get that," she smirked.

He came to the point. "What did you do at the Bank of St. George?"

"I created something utterly unique. Something wonderful. Something the world desperately needed."

"You going to tell me what that is?"

"Ever heard of blockchain?"

His eidetic brain recalled what he knew on the subject.

An expandable list of data linked together. Each block contained a cryptographic hash of the previous block with a timestamp, along with data. The timestamp proved that the data existed when the block was created. Together the blocks formed a chain, with each additional block reinforcing the ones before it. Blockchains were impervious to modification because, once recorded, the data in any given block could not be altered retroactively without altering all of the subsequent blocks. Which was impossible. Ingenious and quite clever. *Immutable* was the term those in the know liked to use.

From what he knew blockchain was invented in 2008 by a person, or group of people, using the pseudonym Satoshi Nakamoto, as part of the creation of the cryptocurrency called bitcoin. But no one knew the identity of Nakamoto. Never been seen or heard by anyone. The name more a legend than a fact. People had speculated as to the identity for over a decade to no avail. Secrets were hard to keep in the cyberworld, but this one had endured.

He told her what he knew.

She smiled. "That memory brain of yours?"

He nodded.

"That's one trait I wish I'd acquired along the way."

Her eyes, always a pale shade of violet, had remained unchanged. He recalled them with fondness. He'd hated hurting her, but he hadn't been able to keep hurting his wife. His actions became a wedge, sharp and clear, a thing of substance, slicing between him and Pam, forcing them apart. And it would be years before the piper of that parade was fully paid.

But paid he was.

With a lot of pain.

Not the least of which had been Suzy Baldwin's feelings. But he'd just saved her life. Which counted for something.

Right?

"Cotton," she said to him. "I am Satoshi Nakamoto."

CHAPTER 14

KYRA STARED DOWN AT THE DEAD WOMAN.

Definitely not a whore.

This one was a trained operative sent to get her hands on the same thing Kyra was after. She'd caught the look in Roza's eye when she'd first displayed the cylinder. That momentary flash of desire. How many times had she seen that look before?

Especially in her own eyes.

She'd encountered FSB agents before. But never had she killed one. No choice had existed here. She had no time to try to squeeze the information out, and there was no way anything of substance would have been voluntarily revealed. If she was right, people were on the way and there'd be consequences for what she'd just done. Time to figure this out.

And leave.

Roza had brought her to this room for a reason. True, there was a gun that she knew existed. But what if there was something else?

She stared around.

Clearly this had been Yerevan's personal haven. Everything about it screamed *male arrogance*. The house itself seemed like a middle finger to the Russian government, which could do little to stop the oligarchs short of jailing them. But that also came with repercussions since the rich definitely looked after the rich.

She'd been advised that Yerevan was in deep financial trouble. Lenders were openly pressuring him for repayment on several balloon loans. The Bank of St. George was one of those, as it had invested in Siberian copper mining. Yerevan, like other oligarchs, borrowed heavily from Russian banks, invested that capital in the stock of his own companies, then took out more loans from Western banks against the value of those shares. Everybody knew the scheme. But the interest rates charged were too good to resist. A collapse in share price was about to force Yerevan to sell some of his holdings to satisfy the margin calls. To both hide and shield his assets, Yerevan, like other Russian billionaires, had bought a lot of bitcoin.

Easy to acquire and hide, even easier to retain.

Provided you controlled the private key.

Online exchanges offered custodial services to the smaller owners. But the high rollers, like Yerevan, eliminated the middleman and held their coins in one of two ways. A hot wallet connected to the internet allowed an owner immediate access for buying and selling. The trade-off for that convenience was an exposure to hackers. So most opted for cold storage, where the private keys were held directly and not left on any internet-connected computers. No one, other than the owner, knew where the keys existed, which included governments, lenders, creditors, law enforcement, and thieves.

Like burying a gold bar in your backyard.

Past experience had taught her a lot about cold storage.

An Irish drug dealer she'd killed wrote the key to his digital wallet, containing six thousand bitcoin, on a piece of paper and hid it inside a fishing rod case. Another buried hers in a half-full detergent box, which sat innocently in her laundry room. Another slid a handwritten key into the hollow of her master closet rod. A particularly innovative German had his etched into the bottom of a colorful ornament that sat inside an aquarium in his Bavarian estate.

To work, a private key had to remain secret at all times. Revealing it was the equivalent to ceding control over the bitcoin. Many owners backed up their primary hiding place, and protected from accidental loss, by storing the code in a safe or a bank deposit box. Surely Yerevan had done that. But that was of little help to her current dilemma.

She had to find the second cylinder.

Think.

Her background work on Yerevan indicated a love of history. Though Armenian, he was fascinated with Russia's past. His boat, the one she'd left drifting across Lake Baikal, was named *Rus*. Russia started with Viking adventurer-traders who opened trade routes back to Scandinavia. They settled on rivers all the way south to the Caspian Sea, ruling for over two hundred years. Eventually they were assimilated by indigenous tribes, who called them Rus. Okay, so he named his boat after them.

Her eyes scanned the room, focusing on the busts.

Napoleon. Alexander the Great. Charlemagne. Julius Caesar. Genghis Khan. Tamerlane. Francisco Pizarro. But she did not recognize the eighth image. Intrigued, she stepped closer. She found her phone and snapped an image, then entered it into her search engine for more information.

Which appeared.

Rurik. From the 9th century. A Viking warrior who ruled northern Russia. He conquered Novgorod and, through his heirs, established a dynasty that lasted seven hundred years. Certainly the type of personality Yerevan would have admired.

She examined the bust. White marble. Matte finish. The face of a bearded man with a thick mustache and heavy eyebrows. He wore a pointed helmet from which long strands of hair fell. She tapped on the helmet with her knuckles. Solid. Dense. She lifted the heavy bust from the pedestal and felt beneath. Something there. She laid it down on the floor and saw two strips of black tape affixed to the bottom. She peeled them away and exposed a circular opening bored into the marble.

And saw the second cylinder.

She smiled. Not bad.

She freed the cylinder. About twenty centimeters long with twenty-four separate rings affixed with letters and numbers to their exterior. One end was solid, the other had a hole into which she slid the smaller cylinder taken from Yerevan. She knew what to do next and rotated the rings until each locked into place.

She stared at the now-revealed access code.

And wasted no time.

On her phone she opened to the web address the bank had provided for the transfer of Yerevan's bitcoin. They'd already learned where Yerevan's online wallet was located, which was no small feat, but the bank had sources no one else possessed. Of course, the account information was useless without the private key. Which she now entered with a few taps. The screen acknowledged that she controlled the wallet, which contained 41,867.45 bitcoin. She'd also been provided account information and another key into a wallet the bank owned. She tapped TRANSFER, then copied and pasted the information onto the screen from her NOTES app. For security her smartphone did not sync the NOTES app to any cloud server. Whatever she typed stayed only in her phone. Per her arrangement with the bank, one percent of what she'd acquired belonged to her. So she entered 41,448.78 to be transferred. In the blink of an eye, bitcoin worth billions moved from one wallet to another.

Confirmation appeared on the screen.

She then deleted the information from NOTES and accessed her own wallet, transferring the remaining 418.67 bitcoin to herself. Right at seventeen million euros with current values.

She tapped in a text message confirming her success.

DEPOSIT MADE.

And sent it to Luxembourg.

She heard the growl of car engines outside. She fled the study and headed back to the great room. Three vehicles had stopped and doors, front and back, opened. Men emerged, each shouldering automatic rifles. FSB. No question. Roza had definitely called for backup.

She smiled.

Too late.

She hustled out the back door into the dim twilight of day.

And headed for the dock.

CHAPTER 15

1:30 P.M.

CATHERINE ENJOYED ANOTHER PIECE OF CORDON BLEU. SHE WAS ordinarily a light eater at lunch, but on meeting days she splurged. After completing their monthly business the consuls always retired to the third-floor dining room to enjoy a light buffet. The others were now gone. The meal had ended a short time ago. She'd lingered. Cordon bleu was a personal favorite. Chicken, Danish ham, and Swiss cheese, breaded and sautéed. This particular version added paprika and a creamy white wine sauce that she'd always thought superb.

Her phone lay on the table.

Which had yet to signal a new incoming call or message.

The last call, though, had been instructive.

From the wine repository in Geneva.

An unexpected breach. But not unwelcomed. The CIA had come for a look. She'd expected that at some point. So she made good use of the opportunity and instructed her representative there to deliver a clear unequivocal message backed up by an empty gold vault. Hopefully, that would be the end of the bank's association with the CIA. Decades of doing their bidding was now at an end. Other first consuls had tried to terminate the relationship.

They all failed.

But she succeeded.

She was enjoying the quiet, studying a square shaft of white sunlight that angled through the windows to the floor, waiting on confirmation from Russia. Kyra Lhota was an extraordinary woman who seemed to function on two totally different levels at the same time. One civilized and refined, the other utterly barbaric. Kyra was engaged in another private acquisition, one of many the bank had financed over the past few years. The consuls were aware of each one, but never apprised of the details. Better that way. Those she and Kyra handled alone.

It helped that their targets were scattered around the world, usually in lawless places and relatively reckless with their own personal security, thinking themselves invincible. Murder was not always involved. In fact, most of the acquisitions had been through thefts cleverly carried out by Kyra, leaving not a trace of a trail back to the bank. Yerevan had been different. A Russian oligarch was a special breed. Better to end that life than allow any opportunity at retribution. The bank needed to acquire as much bitcoin as possible. Every one of them strengthened their upcoming position.

Incredible, really.

History seemed to be repeating itself.

In the 1800s gold rushes started all across the world, which led to extensive mining that lasted for generations. Most of those entrepreneurs immediately spent their newly acquired wealth on tools, food, horses, gambling, liquor, and women. Just like today, gold then was not a currency in and of itself. The real value was in the IOUs, the paper certificates that banks handed out to individuals in exchange for keeping their gold safe—certificates that could be returned later and traded back for gold. Over time, as more and more gold came from the ground, and more and more governments stockpiled it as their reserve to back up their national currencies, less and less gold was available on the open market.

So the price rose.

As more time went by, new gold veins became harder and harder to find. Today, the amounts of gold being mined were trivial compared with two hundred years ago and the price remained sky-high.

Bitcoin worked in a strikingly similar way.

Mining gold from the ground, or filtering it out of a river, was mimicked by solving a complex mathematical challenge fed to computers through a specialized program. Like a lottery number that the computers must decipher, scrolling through the billions of possible combinations, searching for the right sequence. If found, a block on the chain was sealed and the miner earned a coin. Proof of work, it was called. The rewards themselves known as a subsidy. The challenge came from landing on the right answer before anyone else. In the beginning miners used ordinary computers, but then, smartly, they moved to ultra-high-speed machines. In the beginning, back in 2009, 50 bitcoin were generated with each block solved. After 210,000 blocks, the subsidy was cut to 25. At 420,000, to 12.5. Then 630,000 down to 6.25. The latest halving at 840,000 blocks dropped the subsidy to 3.125. On average, halvings occurred roughly every four years. Thirty-two in all. No more. And, like gold, there was a finite amount of bitcoin. The program would only create 21,000,000. That number had been set when blockchain was first made public on the internet.

The idea?

A limited amount would lead to greater demand, which would lead to higher value. Just like gold. Reflexive. A bitcoin today was worth a little less than forty thousand euros.

Things had come a long way.

For the first year and a half of its existence only seven people mined for coins. But word of mouth spread, aided by the bank's covert publicity campaign about open-source software, available to all, where wealth could be found, and more joined in.

The first bitcoin transaction happened on May 22, 2010, inside an online chat forum when a man in Jacksonville, Florida, offered to pay ten thousand bitcoin for two large, delivered Papa John's pizzas. Someone on another continent accepted the offer, called the local Papa John's, bought the two pizzas, had them delivered. In exchange, that person received ten thousand bitcoin. At the time the pizzas cost $25, while ten thousand bitcoin were worth around $41. That day had evolved into crypto folklore as Pizza Day, not because of the transaction itself, but more the price. Today, those same ten thousand bitcoin would be worth around four hundred million euros.

And it all started right here.

In this room.

"Katie, it can be done," Kelly Austin said to her.

They were enjoying lunch. Just the two of them. When alone they were Katie and Kelly. Friends. Colleagues. A lot had happened over the past few weeks. Revolutionary things. And thanks to them the world was about to change.

"I've worked it all through," Kelly said. "It's ready to go. We can do this."

Four months ago they'd been secretly briefed by the CIA. America was in the midst of the worst economic disaster since the Great Depression of 1929. A perfect storm had formed from risky investments by banks into questionable home mortgages, fueled by an overall drop in real estate prices, compounded by an inability of large lending institutions to cover the losses. It started in 2007 and now, by August 2008, had spread across the globe like a fire burning out of control. A worldwide recession loomed, threatening nearly every economy with a full-scale depression. She agreed, something had to be done.

But she wanted to know, "Are you sure this is the solution?"

"It's what they asked for."

The CIA had been specific in their wants and desires. An alternative financial system needed to be created. One independent of government control. Private. Easy to operate. Widely accessible. Peer-to-peer. But under CIA control.

"Blockchain is revolutionary," Kelly said. "This is the answer. It builds onto itself, keeps itself honest, and just grows, one block at a time. It's a central source of truth. Unflinching. Incorruptible. And the best part is no one else has it. We'll be the first.

I've tested it over and over. It's totally hackproof and can become exactly what the CIA wants."

"If they are to be believed," she said. "It had better work or the world may be without any viable financial systems."

"It will work."

"I want to hear every detail before I give the okay," she said to Kelly. "It's important I understand what you created. But I'm curious. Have you thought of a name?"

"Bitcoin."

Short, clever, and self-explanatory.

The perfect label.

And it caught on. In a big way.

On January 3, 2009, they anonymously released the source code. In the Genesis block Kelly embedded the text from that day's *London Times* cover story titled CHANCELLOR ON THE BRINK OF SECOND BAILOUT FOR BANKS. First, they wanted the world to know that the program was new and real, then second they wanted to highlight the instability caused by the world's fractional-reserve banking system, alerting everyone that bitcoin was free from any central bank manipulation. Since everything needed a creator they invented the name Satoshi Nakamoto. No credit would ever be given to Kelly Austin. That wasn't possible. Nothing could be traced back to the bank or the CIA. Then they watched as financial freedom spread around the world one block at a time.

Kelly had been so dedicated. Loyal.

And smart.

Brilliant, actually.

With degrees in applied mathematics and computer science. One of those rare intellects that came along only so often. And she'd been right. Blockchain was a central truth. It changed the world. As had bitcoin. But things were about to change again. And this time Kelly Austin was the enemy.

Her phone dinged.

She checked the text message.

DEPOSIT MADE.

Perfect. Samvel Yerevan's stash was now within the bank's control. Kyra had come through again.

More good news.

She left the cordon bleu on her plate and fled the dining room, taking the private elevator down to the basement. All of the bank's computer servers were housed two floors belowground.

Once the realm of Kelly Austin, but not anymore.

Through a series of doors where both retina verification and digital codes were needed to release the locks, she entered a small windowless room with a single server and two desktop terminals. The air-gap server kept a record of all of the bank's bitcoin accounts, constantly updating the private keys. Its isolation, with no internet access, assured that no one could breach the server without being physically inside this room. One of the desktops was linked to it by cable. The other desktop was connected to the bank's mainframe and all of its assorted systems, open to the world through the internet. Usually others would do what she was about to do, but Catherine thought it better, under the circumstances, to handle this transfer herself.

She sat down in front of the terminal for the air-gap server and gained access to the bank's bitcoin accounts. Only herself and three others had such privileges, the room monitored 24/7 by closed-circuit cameras. She located the wallet that she'd directed Kyra to use and saw that 41,448.78 bitcoin had been deposited. Their intel on Yerevan placed his ownership at that amount. But that was the thing about bitcoin. You never knew exactly what the other person owned until you were able to identify their wallet.

Thankfully the bank possessed that capability.

She also confirmed that Kyra had withheld the agreed-upon one percent for her fee.

She needed the most current keys for the six wallets where she planned to store the new acquisitions. That was another thing about bitcoin. The original source software encrypted each transaction with a string of characters. A ledger of every coin's movement was published across the entire network, which meant that every wallet in the world, and there were over three hundred million, was listed on the internet. No owners were named, no buyers and sellers identified, but every buy/sell to and from each wallet was there for all to see. That meant, unlike other forms of wealth or currency, the world knew exactly how and where every bitcoin existed, just not with whom. This transparency was another popular trait bitcoin owners cherished. But it also allowed the bank to keep a close eye on everything.

She slid the chair over on its casters and tapped the keyboard for the air-gap server, securing the latest six private keys for the designated wallets. She then entered those into the other desktop and, through the internet, set up a transfer of the 41,448.78 bitcoin to the six wallets in equal installments of 6,908.13 each.

She tapped ENTER.

The move happened in an instant and the screen for the desktop verified the deposits into the six wallets.

Perfect.

She was about to leave when the screen for the air-gap desktop suddenly changed. On its own. Odd.

A message appeared.

IF YOU'RE READING THIS THEN YOU'VE REQUESTED A NEW KEY OR KEYS. IT OR THEY ARE YOUR LAST. BEFORE I LEFT I MADE SOME CHANGES. YOUR ACTION HAS ENCRYPTED THE AIR-GAP SERVER, OVER WHICH I NOW HAVE TOTAL CONTROL. I ASSURE YOU, THERE IS NO WAY TO OVERRIDE OR DISCONNECT FROM WHAT I'VE DONE. ANY ATTEMPT WILL ERASE THE KEYS TO ALL OF THE WALLETS, ALONG WITH THE INTERNAL HARD DRIVE BACKUPS. YOUR ONLY WAY TO ACCESS THOSE WALLETS NOW IS THROUGH ME. AND, BY THE WAY, I QUIT.

She struggled to breathe.
Oh, no.

CHAPTER 16

Cotton heard what Suzy had said.

I am Satoshi Nakamoto.

A friend of his back in Copenhagen was big into bitcoin. They'd talked about it several times and he'd learned all about Nakamoto. Or at least what was supposedly known, which was not much.

The general consensus?

A pseudonym for the person or persons who created blockchain. One of the few contacts Nakamoto made with the world came in an internet paper published on October 21, 2008, that first explained blockchain. Every year that day was celebrated worldwide by cryptocurrency enthusiasts, and some say that document was one of the most innovative ever written. But who was Nakamoto? Some postulated that it might be a team of people. The use of words like *we* and *our* in the paper gave credence to that conclusion. But, in reality, Satoshi Nakamoto was a total and complete mystery.

Which, to Cotton, also described bitcoin.

Truth be told, it seemed more like high-stakes gambling based on blind faith that, one day, somebody would come along and pay you more for the coin than it had cost. But as his friend back in Denmark would say, that also explained nearly every government-issued currency in the world, which were also unsupported by anything tangible. For that fiat money to work the holder had to believe in the government issuing it. For bitcoin to work the holder had to believe in Satoshi Nakamoto.

So he said, "You're going to have to explain yourself."

"I can do that, but I hope you're not the same naïve young lawyer who liked to cheat on his wife and hop into my bed."

"I assure you," he said. "I'm anything but naïve. You just told me that you're the one who started bitcoin. That's a little much."

"It may be. But it's true. I created the name myself. *Satoshi* in Japanese means 'quick-witted.' It seemed appropriate."

He smiled.

"Some people thought the name came from a merger of Samsung, Toshiba, and Nakamichi, all major Japanese concerns," she said. "That was a stretch. One theory says Nakamoto remained anonymous to avoid being prosecuted in the U.S., and other countries, for creating a new currency system. That actually made sense, but no cigar."

He smiled.

"I made sure the name bore no relation to anyone or anything, living or dead. It's wholly fictitious. Totally made up. Fleeting as a fairy tale."

"You must have laughed at all the speculation."

She nodded. "It's amazing how so many people read so much into absolutely nothing."

He checked his watch: 2:40 P.M. Still nothing from Koger.

"Suzy. No. Sorry. Kelly—"

"I like it when you call me Suzy. Brings back memories."

She gently laid her hand on his forearm, which lingered a little too long. He kept still until she withdrew her grip.

She seemed to sense his hesitancy. "You said you were divorced."

"I am. But that doesn't mean I'm unattached."

"Now, that raises some interesting questions."

"Which we don't have time to explore."

She grinned. "Mr. Down-to-Business. Okay. We'll put a pin in that subject for later. You have more questions for me?"

More than he thought possible.

"Look," she said, her voice low. "I know it might be hard to believe. But I created bitcoin for the CIA in 2008. There was a real fear that the world's economic systems might all fail from the worldwide financial crisis. They wanted something in place in case that happened, where financial transactions could safely be made peer-to-peer without any financial institutions involved. I'd been toying with the concept of blockchain. So I finished my research and made it happen."

He was still not convinced.

"Maybe this will help," she said. "There are only twenty-one million bitcoin. After my wreck, during surgery, they gave me twenty-one units of blood. There are only thirty-two halvings. My lacrosse number through college was thirty-two. These facts are easily verifiable. So you tell me. That can't be a coincidence."

He was a realist by nature, so normally he would laugh all of this off, but he was actually starting to believe her.

"I know all this is complicated and hard to believe. But it happened. Now something else is happening. Something that threatens all the good that was done. I left the bank yesterday knowing I would never return. I walked away from my life's work."

He wanted to know, "Why?"

"It was the right thing to do. The bank has embarked on a course that will lead to disaster for a lot of people. I decided to stop all that."

"You contacted the CIA?"

She nodded. "I thought they were on my side. I assure you the bank does not want me dead. So that leaves only one candidate who just tried to kill me." She stood from the table. "Hold that disturbing thought for a moment. I'll be right back. My bladder is screaming for relief. I'm lucky I didn't wet my pants out there on the street."

He shook his head. "I see you didn't develop any filters for that mouth over the past twenty years?"

She grinned. "I wouldn't be me if I had."

True.

He watched as she headed off toward the restrooms. Yes, he'd ended things with her because he came to detest the lying and cheating. But another reason had been that he'd begun to like her far more than he should have. She was so different from Pam. And, back then, he'd been on a serious search for different.

Not anymore, though.

He checked his phone on the off chance he'd missed a call or text. But nothing was there. Koger was with Cassiopeia and he hoped everything was all right.

She *was* the love of his life.

No question.

And his best friend.

He'd long given up on the breathtaking, pulse-quickening, love-at-first-sight encounters, thinking no one would come along and be that. Then Cassiopeia appeared in a French village, shooting at him before speeding away on a motorcycle. Ever since, there'd been bells, incredible highs, unbearable lows, calls, texts, dinners, weekends, soul searching, pleas, jokes, arguments. Good and bad. A lot of time had passed since Pensacola. He was older and a whole lot wiser. Long ago he'd analyzed his mistakes and learned from them. He'd also been tried, convicted, and sentenced by his ex-wife for all of his failures. He served his time and had moved on, forging a new life.

All was good.

"Cotton."

Suzy's voice. Loud. Sharp. Troubling.

And no Harold or Earl.

Not good.

He bolted from the chair and headed toward a small alcove that led to the restrooms. He banged on the door for the ladies' room. No answer. He pushed it open. Empty. His gaze darted to the left and another door marked EMPLOYEES ONLY. He pushed through and entered a short corridor that led to another door marked EXIT in three languages. He turned the knob and opened the metal panel, exposing a small parking lot at the rear of the building and a car, a light-colored BMW, speeding away.

He caught a quick glimpse of Suzy in the back seat, struggling with two men. He reached for his gun to take out the tires, but the car made a sharp right turn and disappeared. But not before he locked the license plate into his brain.

CD BS
375 • 48

Working twelve years at the Magellan Billet had taught him a lot about license plates. They could be really informative.

Especially in Switzerland.

He knew that BS at the top right stood for the canton of Basel-Stadt, one of twenty-six political subdivisions that existed across the country. The CD confirmed that the car was a diplomatic vehicle, and 48 was the code for the particular country that plate was assigned to. The 375 denoted who was utilizing the vehicle. An embassy? Consulate? Special envoy?

Hard to say.

He found his phone and typed an inquiry into the search engine. A moment later the screen flashed with information. The number 48 within the Swiss diplomatic plate scheme was assigned to Japan. He then inquired about the 375 code and received another answer.

One that told him precisely who was operating the BMW within Basel.

The Japanese consulate.

CHAPTER 17

Cassiopeia absorbed what she'd just read about the CIA. Lost gold? The Black Eagle Trust? The U.S. government keeping war loot? Using it to finance covert operations?

Wow. That was a lot.

They were back on the road, a four-laned autoroute, heading north, paralleling Lake Geneva.

"That classified summary report you just read was prepared a few weeks ago for the director of Central Intelligence," Koger said.

"Should I be reading it?"

"Probably not. But you need to know what we're dealing with. A lot of people at the agency have no idea what happened back in the 1940s and '50s when the CIA was first formed. It was a different place then. The bottom line is we kept all that war loot and did a lot of bad things with it. Now we've lost every ounce of that gold. Trillions of dollars' worth. Gone. I had no idea if that vault would be empty, but I had to find out."

All of which would have been nice to know beforehand. "Cotton said you were a pain in the ass, and he was right."

"I pride myself on directness. Captain America prides himself on—" Koger paused. "I have no idea what he prides himself on. But I'm sure it's something heroic. He's always heroic."

She grinned. "Cotton only prides himself on getting the job done. Have you heard from him?"

"He has the situation in Basel under control."

Good to know. "So what are *we* doing?"

Koger did not immediately answer and she allowed him the luxury of his thoughts. She could use a little quiet herself, so she stared out the window at the blue water of Lake Geneva. A cloudy overcast day made it impossible to see the Alps far to the south. She'd visited the town of Montreux, which lay ahead nestled to the lake, several times. A few four-star hotels and a variety of fashionable boutiques and pricey restaurants dotted its shoreline. She wished she was there, enjoying a delicious glass of wine and some sharp cheese. Instead, as Cotton would say, she was doing *God-knows-what* for no discernible reason other than she'd been asked to help.

"I have a big problem," Koger finally said.

Okay. Maybe this was truth time.

"In 1950 the CIA entrusted the Bank of St. George with the gold recovered in Europe from the Nazis and all of the gold found in the Philippines. An incredible amount. Why do something so stupid? Chalk it up to eighty years ago. Everybody was terrified of communism. So anything and everything was okay in order to fight it. Including totally entrusting billions of dollars in stolen wealth to a tiny, unregulated bunch of civilians in freakin' Luxembourg. Amazingly, all was okay with that arrangement until about three years ago. Then things began to drastically change."

"Why then?" she asked.

"We discovered the bank was dipping into the gold and using it to buy bitcoin."

"You know why it was doing that?"

"I know some, and it's not good. But Cotton has the person who knows it all."

Fair enough. "So what just happened here?"

"We pushed. They pushed back. So we're going to push again."

She was concerned about the *we* part. "I thought I was only in for the one trip to the wine vault."

"Somebody tried to kill the woman I sent Cotton to watch over. He handled it, like always, and he's fine. He's damn good, but if you tell him I ever said that I'll call you a liar."

She smiled, but didn't like hearing that Cotton was in danger. He was a big boy, though, and could handle himself.

"You don't know me," Koger said. "And I shudder to think what Malone had to say about me. But I'm a career agent. Twenty-four years on the job, all in the field. Along the way I've managed to piss off just about every boss I've ever had. It's an art form to me. I'm really good at it. But recently I managed to do something different. For once I made a friend in high places and was finally offered a desk at Langley, but I turned it down. Instead, they made me head of European operations. Which I like. I can work a few more years in the field and retire out. Then this cluster of a mess dropped into my lap out of nowhere. It has CAREER-ENDING stamped all over it. But I don't care. I have a problem. A big one. And I'm not too proud to say I need your help."

She heard the hint of desperation in his voice. A guy like Koger would never let anyone see him sweat, so she appreciated his honesty. Okay. "What can I do?"

Koger did not immediately answer and the car kept speeding down the autoroute. The sound of the tires humming on the pavement lulled her. She grabbed her bearings, staring out at the countryside, seeing fields of hay and villages dominated by sharply pitched church steeples in dark red and green. They were now headed more eastward, around the northern shore of the boomerang-shaped lake toward Lausanne.

Away from Geneva and Basel.

"I thought we were going to meet Cotton," she said.

"Not anymore."

Koger's phone buzzed. He found the unit in his pocket, tossed it over, and asked her to answer it on speaker.

She did.

"We have a big problem."

Cotton.

They both listened to what had just happened in Basel with Kelly Austin.

"She's gone," Cotton said.

"Damn. Damn. Damn," Koger muttered, shaking his head and pounding the steering wheel. "You sure it was the Japanese?"

"I'm only sure that car was assigned to the local consulate."

"I'm here, Cotton," she finally said.

"Everything okay?"

"Not really. Your friend Koger is a bit high-strung."

"To say the least, but he's no fool. Something is definitely happening here."

"Did Austin say anything?" Koger asked.

"She told me she created bitcoin."

What?

"She actually did," Koger said.

Even more surprising.

"I have to have her back, alive, intact," Koger said. "That woman has information no one else on this planet has. I need it. More than you can imagine."

There was that desperation again.

She had to say, "Then aren't you glad Captain America is on the job."

"Okay, I deserve that one," Koger said.

"Cotton, is this our problem?" she asked.

They'd made a pact that when one wanted to involve them in something, the other would keep a clear head. Since this was Cotton's party that she'd been invited to, that duty fell to her. So she added, "Koger has a lot more resources at his disposal to solve this than we do."

"Ordinarily," Cotton said, "I'd agree with you. But this is not ordinary."

She was puzzled. "Care to explain that?"

"I will. Just not now."

She heard what had not been said.

Cut me some slack. Okay?

"Help me out there," Koger said. "I need her found and fast. I'm countin' on you. We'll handle things here. And I don't care what rules you break, I got your back. Understand?"

"I got it."

"Be careful," she had to add.

"Always. Same to you."

The call ended.

She glanced over at Koger and asked, "Where are *we* going?"

"To see a man who knows an awful lot about stolen gold."

CHAPTER 18

Catherine stabbed the button for the third floor and stood alone in the elevator car. Her analytical mind raced. She detested chaos. Her world was one of order. Facts. Figures. Balance sheets. A precise sequence of things. One thing after the other leading to a reasonably predicted result. But what had just happened was the precise definition of a disaster.

The elevator arrived and she stepped from the car, telling herself to slow down. Be calm. Show nothing. On the way across the floor she passed a couple of subordinates, one she stopped and chatted with for a moment. When finished, she walked into the office for the bank's director of information and technology and greeted the administrative assistant, saying that she was expected.

She entered the main office and closed the door.

Lana Greenwell worked at the bank as a senior vice president. She was a tall, elegant woman, her hair, sliding to gray, cut in a fashionable tight coiffure. An American, lured away twenty years ago from a Fortune 500 company, she knew every aspect of their computer systems, which represented an investment of many millions of euros for some of the most sophisticated data processors in the world. Kelly had not worked under her, only with her, as the two women had never cared for each other. There'd been continual interdepartmental feuds that Catherine had refereed on more than one occasion. They were each top-notch and the bank needed their respective expertise, so a truce had always been found, one fueled by their individual ambitions and, to a large extent, greed. Both women had been paid generously, though Kelly had garnered more in the way of rewards. Catherine had already spoken to Lana on the phone before heading up from the basement.

"Explain to me what happened?" she asked.

Lana turned from the terminal on her desk. "We've only had a few minutes to take a look, but it appears Kelly directly infected the air-gap server with some ultra-sophisticated malware that was programmed to activate the first time new wallet keys were requested. I just had someone run a diagnostic. The server is frozen with a kill switch. If we try to bypass or affect it in any way, everything gets erased. All of the keys and the internal hard drive backups will be gone. It's clever and sophisticated. But I would have expected no less from her."

Kelly had been brilliant. No doubt. She'd created something utterly unique. Blockchain. Which led to something equally novel. Bitcoin. Both crazy ideas, for sure, but ones that had become revolutionary.

"*Governments can adopt bitcoin as their formal currency,*" Kelly told her. "*A means of exchange for goods and services within their nation. They could even use bitcoin value as their reserve currency, backing up whatever currency they currently use. No more dollars or euros. Right now gold is the most valuable asset on earth. But by the time the fourth halving occurs, bitcoin will be the rarest asset on earth. Twice as scarce as gold. Bitcoin could, quite literally, replace gold in value.*"

And here they were, at the fourth halving. She'd never considered such a broad-reaching possibility. But Kelly was right. People thought gold infinite. Nothing could be farther from the truth. There were maybe 171,000 metric tons of it aboveground in the world, at the most. Compressed, that would be a cube measuring around twenty-one meters square. Not a lot.

Just like bitcoin. Finite.

Valuable.

"Can't we just unhook the hard drives from the air-gap server and access them externally?" she asked. "Securing the keys."

"That was my first thought. But a preliminary analysis shows that if the power supply stops, the program triggers and erases the drives as a fail-safe. She thought of that possibility."

Of course Kelly would. She thought of everything.

Like always.

"Katie, think about it. If nations adopt bitcoin as their currency, or simply back up their existing currency with its value, we would then be in a new era. The world would fundamentally shift away from tangible metals, away from fiat currency that is worthless, to ones and zeros in a computer program. The value of which the users themselves will determine. There was a time when salt was the currency of the world. Or cattle. Or animal skins. Each replaced by something else, which was replaced by something else. Change always happens. We may be at one of those crossroads when it will happen again."

So brilliant.

"Why would she do this?" she asked, more to herself.

"That was the thing about Kelly. She was really good at showing you only what she wanted you to know."

Yes, she was. Fooled her completely.

"It could take months—years—to undo the damage," Lana said. "And we could activate that kill switch at any point in the process. Which would be catastrophic. My recommendation is to leave it alone, until we know more."

The bank had long ago stopped keeping hard copies of the bitcoin wallet keys. Too risky and nearly impossible to secure. Instead, they'd opted for the air-gap server, with three electronic hard drive backups that were generated each time the server changed the keys. So clever they'd thought themselves. But how foolish that false sense of security had turned out to be. The bitcoin world was replete with stories of how investors lost the private keys to wallets. Once gone, the bitcoin was gone too. At present it was estimated that around fifteen percent of the twenty million or so existing coins were forever lost, inaccessible in the cyberworld.

Now the bank's were at risk.

"Everything is happening over the next two days," she said to Lana.

"I haven't forgotten."

"We must have access to that bitcoin."

"I realize that, and we'll be working on it. But Kelly timed her actions carefully."

The second call Catherine had made before coming up from the basement was to Kelly's office, verifying where she was staying in Basel. That information was passed on in her third call, made to Kyra in Siberia, ordering her to find Kelly, in Switzerland, and fast.

"*This is ordinarily not what I do,*" *Kyra had said.*

"*We'll double the bitcoin you received if you find her, unharmed, and return her to me.*"

She knew that would work.

Kyra, though born Russian, was a capitalist at heart.

She shook her head, frustrated.

The greatest struggles through human history had all been fought over wealth. Sometimes those wars happened on battle-fields with armies. Other times they occurred in private, behind closed doors, in courtrooms, legislative chambers, boardrooms, or on the floors of mercantile exchanges. Control the distribution of money and you controlled the world. That singular act conferred immense power and influence.

Which she intended to acquire.

Everything was truly about to change.

"We keep going," she told Lana. "As planned. But we can't allow anyone to know we've been breached. Make sure your people keep silent. In the meantime, we have to get inside that air-gap server."

"Have you tried to call her?"

She shook her head. "Her message on the server made things perfectly clear. But I will have her located."

"That would be wise, as the fastest way, at the moment, to those keys is through Kelly."

CHAPTER 19

KELLY WORKED HARD TO CONTROL HER PANIC. SHE'D LEFT COTTON TO go to the restroom. While washing her hands she'd been accosted by a woman who had a narrow, low forehead, thin mouth, and shoulder-length straight dark hair. At first she'd thought her another patron, but the woman produced a weapon and two men, both Japanese, like her, burst in, one clamping a hand over Kelly's mouth, the other securing her arms behind her back. She'd resisted, but they forced her from the restroom, the other woman leading the way. She'd managed to bite the hand over her mouth and yell out Cotton's name right before the door leading out had closed behind them. They'd stuffed her into a car and driven off, but she'd stolen a glance out the back windshield and caught a glimpse of Cotton with a gun.

"What do you want?" she asked in English.

"I have what I want," the woman said from the front seat.

She did not like the sound of that.

"Did you try to kill me earlier today?"

"You have no value to us dead."

Encouraging. But of little consolation.

Silence settled inside the car.

No way to escape, nor resist.

So she did the smart thing and sat tight with her mouth shut.

Twenty minutes later the vehicle angled off into a quiet neighborhood, turning eventually into a driveway, the mansion beyond barely visible past a curtain of trees and high shrubs. A painted crest held a commanding position between two enormous pillars that supported an electronic gate. A bronze plaque affixed to one of the stone pillars read JAPANESE CONSULATE.

Which meant she was no longer on Swiss soil.

The car parked and the woman led the way from the BMW inside the building, the two minders in tow. Kelly ended up standing in what was once, surely, a bedchamber, now an office, on the second floor, decorated with glass-fronted cabinets filled with curio objects of fine workmanship, including some impressive jade. On a polished teak table against one wall rested a carved Buddha that sat beneath a colorful Japanese wall hanging. Afternoon sun flooded in through the windows, past the sheers. The two armed men watched over her until, ten minutes later, the woman returned.

"My name is Aiko Ejima," the woman said, stepping behind a desk clear of clutter.

She ran through her brain the sound of the name. *Eye-ko. Eh-jee-mah.* She took a stab at connecting the dots. "What are you? PSIA?"

The Public Security Investigation Agency served as an appendage within Japan's Ministry of Justice and handled national security matters both inside and outside the country. She knew all about it. Created in 1952 to deal with communism within Japan, it currently was staffed by a legion of investigators. Its main focus? Watching the far left and right, as well as the Japanese Communist Party. It also kept a close watch over Koreans. Its Second Department of Investigation was in charge of foreign intelligence and she knew that PSIA investigators were routinely sent abroad, just like the CIA and FSB. Every employee at the Bank of St. George had been repeatedly briefed and warned about them. Any contact had to be immediately reported on threat of instant termination.

"How did you know where to find me?" Kelly asked.

"I know a great deal about you."

She smirked. "Nice to be appreciated."

"You're being quite modest, Ms. Austin...for the creator of bitcoin."

That statement shocked her. Only a handful of people in the world knew that fact. And none of them would ever utter it publicly.

"You are Satoshi Nakamoto. Millions of people have speculated about your existence, yet here you are in the living flesh."

This woman was remarkably well informed. Or was she? "You listened in on my conversation at the café."

Ejima shook her head. "There was no need."

"Forgive me if I'm skeptical. But for the past fifteen years I've lived within a bubble of maximum security. Few on this earth know much about me or of what you just spoke."

"*Atorasu sosa.*"

"You're going to have translate that one."

"There's not an exact meaning. But it is the closest description in Japanese to something you know a great deal about."

She waited.

"The Atlas Maneuver."

Cotton had taken a taxi from downtown to the Japanese consulate, thinking that was the first place he would look. He had no idea if Suzy was inside or not, but Koger had said to get her back in one piece and he didn't care what rules had to be broken. He'd left Suzy's shoulder bag at the café, no need to haul it around, but retrieved her passport, wallet, and phone.

Those could be needed.

The building before him was an art deco mansion among other equally impressive structures in the city's diplomatic district. Three stories, its stone in varying hues of white and gray, and all surrounded by foliage and an iron fence. One gate led in, flanked on each side by stone pillars. No one guarded the portal, but he spotted cameras. Three he could see. Surely there were more he could not. But he was, as yet, not in their field of view. The answer as to whether this was the right place came when he managed to work his way closer. Parked behind the gate was the same light-colored BMW with the same license plate he'd committed to memory.

Okay.

Time to go to work.

KELLY WAS SHOCKED BY WHAT SHE'D JUST HEARD—*THE ATLAS Maneuver*—three words grouped together that only a few on earth knew existed. Yet this stranger did. Which meant, "You have eyes and ears inside the Bank of St. George."

Her captor nodded. "We've been watching for a long time."

All bad. But maybe it could work to her advantage. "Then you know I don't give a damn what happens to that place."

"I fully understand that, which is why we are talking."

"The bank needs me alive," she felt compelled to say.

Ejima nodded. "On the trip here, in the car, I was informed, by text, of your seizure of the bank's bitcoin keys. You have them at quite the disadvantage."

This woman *was* remarkably well informed. The bank prided itself on its security. It spent millions every year ensuring it. Yet this foreign agent was privy to things that had only happened in the past few hours.

"Catherine Gledhill now knows just how important you are," Ejima said. "My congratulations on besting her. She's a smart, capable, dangerous woman."

And her friend. But that was now over too.

That part she regretted.

"What do you want?" she asked.

Ejima smiled. "I must confess, the answer to that inquiry has now become fluid."

"You want to trade me for the Golden Lily wealth?"

"Hardly. We both know that is impossible."

She wanted to know, "Is the air-gap server frozen?"

"It appears so. And you are the only one who can reverse that."

Good to know. But that did not mean she liked being a prisoner. The entrance of the Japanese changed everything. She'd never figured them into the equation.

"We are a culture thousands of years old," the woman said. "One of long-standing traditions. Finding that lost gold was once a matter of imperial honor. That wealth belonged to our emperor. It was acquired in his name, for his benefit, as part of a war we fought for him."

She laughed. "You can't be serious? Japan looted that gold from across Southeast Asia. It's contraband."

"Which the United States stole from us."

"And which has been hidden under a blanket of secrecy for eighty years. Officially, that gold doesn't exist. And since you know of the Atlas Maneuver, you know the bank can't do what it wants to do without that gold."

"We are hoping you might cooperate with us," her captor said.

"In what way?" she asked.

Ejima stood impassionate, not a hint of anything on her face. In that way she was a lot like Katie Gledhill. Listening. Missing nothing. Plotting. Planning. You either were important to her endeavors or you were not. Nothing in between. This entire mission had been about stopping the bank from doing something catastrophic. But becoming a pawn? A token? A unit of exchange? Something negotiable?

That was never part of the plan.

"Katie will never bargain with you," she said again.

"On that I am afraid you are correct."

Ejima motioned to the men standing behind Kelly.

Suddenly, something swept across her face from behind.

A cord.

That tightened around her neck.

She tried to swing her body around and lessen the pressure, but to no avail. Her throat constricted, cutting off air. She kept trying to free herself. Which only made things worse. Her eyes went wide, mouth frothing, hands still clawing at the cord, slashing, trying to break free.

The air in her lungs exhausted.

But no new breaths were possible.

Her hands fluttered at her sides.

Shrill, whining sounds seeped from her contracted throat as she tried to stay conscious—*have to stay awake*—but to no avail.

The world went black.

And silent.

CHAPTER 20

Aiko Ejima watched as Kelly Austin's limp body was carried away. Regrettable that violence was needed, but sometimes there was simply no alternative. It was important that Austin be incapacitated. The American had already shown, back at the café, a willingness to fight.

Usually, the room around her was occupied by an official of the Japanese foreign ministry. But that man was in Bern for the day at the main embassy, and the rest of the consulate's staff all worked for the PSIA. Japan had long maintained a robust intelligence presence within Switzerland, especially in Basel, thinking that what remained of Yamashita's gold was stored somewhere nearby. Which made sense. Switzerland was a haven for bullion.

The PSIA had quietly sought the Golden Lily wealth for decades but had found nothing. Only a year ago, after they'd finally cultivated a source inside the Bank of St. George, had they begun to make significant progress. Especially so in the last few hours when things had unexpectedly begun to move at light speed. Before heading out to secure Austin, Aiko had made an initial report to Tokyo, and she had been ordered to make an additional report once Austin was questioned. So she sat before the desktop LED screen and connected to Tokyo by a secure channel.

The political situation within Japan was unusual, to say the least. The current holder of the Chrysanthemum throne, the 127th to carry the title emperor, was a healthy fifty-six-year-old, married, with two children. But he'd not ascended to the throne by the death of his predecessor. Instead, his father, eighty-nine years old, had abdicated, saying that it had become more and more difficult, because of his health, for him to carry out his duties.

Or at least that's what the nation had been told.

Instead, the emperor emeritus, who was old but relatively healthy, had spent the past six years quietly focused on something that his father, Emperor Hirohito, had started during World War II.

Kin no yuri.

Golden Lily.

An unfulfilled promise.

But where his father had been in search of ill-gotten wealth, the son wanted something altogether different.

Or at least that was what she'd been told.

Her contact was the emperor emeritus' chief of staff. A dour, middle-aged man with little personality. But when the screen lit up the face was different. This one was wizened by age, the hair a thick patch of silver, the eyes dark and piercing. Never had she expected this man to be on the other end of the call and immediately, out of respect, she diverted her eyes from the screen.

"*Daijō Tennō,*" she said, bowing her head.

She'd utilized the proper means of address. Emperor emeritus. His son, the reigning emperor, was known as *Kinjō Heika,* current majesty.

"Raise your head, please," the old man said in Japanese. "Tell us, Ejima-san, what have you learned from your captive?"

"We have Satoshi Nakamoto," she told him.

"An elegant way to describe the situation," he said. "So the legend has finally been revealed, in all her glory."

The emperor of Japan was the head of the imperial family, the Symbol of the State and the Unity of the People. Few laws applied and no court possessed judicial power over him. He was also the head of the Shinto religion, regarded as a direct descendant of the solar goddess Amaterasu. He was the only remaining head of state in the world with the monarchical title of emperor, the Japanese imperial house among the oldest, dating back to the 6th century B.C. Once regarded as God-like, a heavenly sovereign, but everything was rewritten after World War II. On New Year's Day 1946, Hirohito, at the prompting of General MacArthur and with little choice, renounced his heavenly status, declaring that relations between the ruler and his people could not be based on the false conception that the emperor was divine or that the Japanese people were superior to other races.

A shocking declaration.

But necessary.

Since then, the emperor had possessed little to no political power. Instead, the country was run by an elected prime minister, the emperor's powers limited to ceremonial functions. But that did not mean the position was without influence. The emperor remained a symbol, a uniter, with nearly ninety percent of the Japanese people harboring great affection for the entire imperial family. The man she was speaking with had been especially popular. An innovator. The first to marry a commoner. The first to raise his children at home. The first to have been stripped of all political power under Japan's American-inspired postwar constitution. And the first to renounce his throne in favor of his son.

"What did your captive have to say?" he asked.

"She agrees with us. The gold is lost."

"But we may have come across something far more valuable. Patience is indeed rewarded."

They'd known of the Atlas Maneuver for many months, first reported from their spy within the bank. It had then seemed a bit inconceivable but, to its credit, the Bank of St. George had managed to transform an abstract idea into a functional reality. Kelly Austin's betrayal had altered that course in a totally different direction. Making things much easier. With Austin, now *they* controlled everything.

"From this point forward you will communicate only with us," the emperor emeritus said. "This situation will require immediate decision making, so we will personally oversee everything."

"Of course, *Daijō Tennō*. As you command."

"We are assuming that your prisoner harbors no affection, or loyalty, toward her former employer."

"That is correct. But getting her to work with us might prove difficult."

"You gathered that from speaking to her."

"I did. She is strong-willed."

"You performed well in securing her quickly. Your assessment from earlier is correct. The Americans wanted her dead. Understandable, considering it would solve a multitude of problems for them simultaneously. But they tried and failed. Does she comprehend that?"

"We did not discuss it, but she is smart and has surely already come to the same conclusion. The CIA is the only logical culprit. She's been incapacitated and will shortly be transported from here to a secure location. There, I will endeavor to convince her that we are on the same side."

He seemed pleased. "You are the daughter of a warrior who served us faithfully, with great honor and dignity. We met your father once and told him how proud we were for what he'd done."

She had no idea. That had never been mentioned within her family.

"We tell you this, Ejima-san, so that you will know that we place a great deal of trust in you. We have been offered a great opportunity here, one that we hope you will help us fulfill."

She felt a swell of pride. "I will not fail you, *Daijō Tennō*."

"When will the bank know that we are involved?" he asked.

"Quite soon."

"Excellent. *I no naka no kawazu taikai wo shirazu*."

She'd not heard that saying in a long time.

A frog in a well knows nothing of the sea.

"We have for so long viewed the world through a limited

perspective," the old man said. "It is hard not to. We are quick to judge and think big of ourselves. Such arrogance comes from living an exalted life. But like that frog in the well, there are things bigger than us in the world. Things we never saw before. But we have stumbled upon a sea, Ejima-san. A massive, sprawling, limitless sea that almost no one knows exists."

She knew what he meant.

The Atlas Maneuver.

"Obtain it," he said. "For us. For Japan. And we will set things right."

She bowed her head in respect. "I shall do that."

The screen went blank as the video call ended.

A swell of elation swept through her.

What a feeling.

CHAPTER 21

CASSIOPEIA WATCHED AS KOGER KEPT THE CAR IN LOW GEAR ALONG a twisting roadway, the grade steep up into the Alpine foothills through dense Swiss woods. They passed more farms and *gasthauses*, then began climbing with increasing steepness to where the road became more a shelf, a bank on one side, a sharp drop on the other. Eventually, they motored out onto a level plain with a magnificent view reaching kilometers to the south and highlighting the dull grays and muted greens of trees and shrubs, with an occasional eruption of flowers. The road continued until Koger turned into a narrow entrance set between brick columns supporting statues of a man atop a horse sporting a lance.

"St. George?" she asked Koger.

"The one and only."

"As in the Bank of St. George?"

Koger nodded.

They drove toward a rambling stone mansion, three stories tall, topped by a steeply pitched slate roof studded with dormers. Interesting were the satellite antennas that dotted the roof, the kind that facilitated contacting anyone around the globe.

Koger stopped the car and they both stepped out.

A chilly light fog had settled, with a wind blowing in off the faraway Alps that stung as it swirled around her. She closed her eyes and braced herself against the biting wetness. In the distance she heard the steady, strong, somehow reassuring boom of a bell.

"Somethin's wrong," Koger said. "I've been here several times before. Always the curtains were closed. Even in the middle of the day."

She focused on the many windows. Ivy had invaded the stone exterior, framing each one in thick leafy vines. And yes, past the paneled panes, nothing obstructed the glass.

"The person who lives here is not one for open windows," he said. "Just the opposite, in fact."

Koger stepped back to the car and opened the rear door. He fished through a leather attaché case and removed an automatic pistol. He slammed the car door and handed her the gun.

"Do I need this?" she asked.

He reached beneath his jacket and unholstered his own weapon. "I don't know. But I want to be ready."

She did not like the sound of that.

He marched toward the front door and she followed.

It was impressive, with herringbone panels inlaid between strapping timbers studded with wrought-iron bolts. As they drew closer she saw that the heavy slab hung open a few centimeters.

"The guy who lives here also never leaves a door open," Koger said.

"Sounds like he's paranoid."

"When people are actually out to get you, it's not paranoia."

Good point.

He motioned and they fanned out, each to either side of the door, Koger nearer to the iron latch. He risked a peek into the open crack then gestured her way. She knew what to do and, with her left hand, pushed open the door.

Which eased inward on its leaf-shaped hinges—

Emitting a grinding sigh.

COTTON STOOD ABOUT THIRTY YARDS AWAY FROM THE ENTRANCE to the Japanese consulate. He realized that consulates were not embassies, which usually displayed a far higher level of security. But they were still secure locales. An electric iron gate barred entrance, obviously controlled from within the building. There was a call box that a visitor was required to use from the driver's-side window.

He stood amid a clump of beech trees that occupied a patch of green among the other buildings lining the street. The direct approach seemed best but he'd lose the element of surprise, which could be helpful. If he didn't handle this right he'd end up without Suzy and probably in a Swiss jail.

But Koger had his back.

Right?

A white van motored down the quiet street and approached the consulate gate. On its side was stenciled EDELWEISS CATERING with a local telephone number and a website address. The van came to a stop and he watched as the driver punched the call button and communicated with someone inside the consulate.

Now or never.

The gate camera angled to focus on the open driver's-side window. Cotton used the moment to flee his hiding place, positioning himself with the van between him and the camera. He made it to the rear of the vehicle as the gate began to slide open.

The van's engine revved.

He stepped up on the rear bumper and grabbed hold of the handles for the two doors, careful not to reveal himself in the rearview mirrors. Thankfully, the rear doors were windowless. The camera could be a problem but he noticed as they entered the compound that it had turned to where its point of view was back on the street leading up to the gate.

The van motored around to the side of the building and came to a stop. He released his grip and dropped to the pavement, hustling toward the parked BMW a few feet away where he crouched down on the far side and watched. A man emerged from the van and headed off toward a short flight of wrought-iron-bordered stone stairs that led up to an entrance alcove, the door held open by a young Japanese male.

The two disappeared inside.

He decided *Why not.*

He hustled to the door and tried the latch.

Which turned.

He eased the door open and stepped inside, walking down a short corridor that ended at a kitchen.

Lying on the tile floor was the young Japanese male he'd just seen letting the van driver inside.

With a bullet hole in his forehead.

CASSIOPEIA STARED PAST THE OPEN DOOR INTO THE FOYER. THE FLOOR was an expensive inlaid ceramic tile over which were strewn rugs in brilliant designs. The massive furnishings were of wood. Large armoires, carved in bas-relief, added an Old World presence. Art dotted the walls. Past that space she spotted a parlor of some sort where the furniture was upended, the drawers and cabinets open, their contents strewn about. Even the heavy draperies had been ripped from the wall and lay piled on the floor like dark wet stains.

"Somebody was looking for something," she whispered.

"You got that right," Koger muttered.

They entered the parlor.

She took her cue from him and kept her weapon level and ready. They both heard it at the same time. A dull thump, then a scraping from somewhere far off in the house.

Their expressions said the same thing.

We're not alone.

CHAPTER 22

CATHERINE GRABBED HOLD OF HERSELF.

The day had started off just as any other. A consul meeting. Lunch. A new stash of bitcoin secured. All was good. Even the incident at the Geneva wine vault, though unexpected, had played out well. Message delivered. Sure, the CIA was going to be a problem. The agency would not easily walk away from billions of dollars in bullion that it regarded as its own.

But what could they do?

The bank had exclusively controlled that wealth for a long time with no outside paper trail. Seventy-five years ago, when priorities were different and the world a much larger place, that secrecy had been workable. The Black Eagle Trust had done its job, funneling countless millions of dollars to an assortment of clandestine activities across the globe. Her father and grandfather had been involved with administering the trust and facilitating those expenditures, creating plausible deniability for Washington. And she'd heard the stories. Both the successes and failures. But she'd managed to finally acquire total control and ownership of the gold.

And she'd put it to good use.

Kelly's betrayal still vexed her. Nothing had been said or occurred between them to indicate that Kelly would take such a drastic step. She was a friend. About as close a friend as Catherine possessed. So what was happening? What had made Kelly do a total about-face? They needed to talk, but she wasn't ready.

Not yet. But soon.

Lana's people needed more time with the server. They had to know and understand what they were facing.

She sat comfortably in a bank-owned car, being driven home a little earlier in the day than normal. A guest was expected for dinner, one she hoped would bring good news after the day's disaster. Another major gathering, long scheduled for tomorrow evening, could not be delayed, no matter what was going wrong. The last thing she needed was to send panic through those they'd worked tirelessly to convince that the new way was the right way. Representatives from Panama, Paraguay, Venezuela, Nicaragua, Brazil, Argentina, and Malta would be in attendance, each of them on the verge of adopting bitcoin as legal tender, following the lead of half a dozen other countries that had already done the same, making it the primary monetary instrument within their respective nations for the settlement of debts and the meeting of fiscal responsibilities.

Just like fiat money now.

Some were also pondering going all the way and adopting bitcoin as their reserve currency, backing their own against it, as had been done with gold or U.S. dollars in the past. Revolutionary things, which the United States opposed.

And for good reason.

People and governments around the world had painfully learned that settling any international transaction in U.S. dollars gave America legal jurisdiction over them. And Washington was not shy about interjecting itself, imposing its mores and laws on people across the globe. She'd heard the same complaint over and over. So if something other than American dollars could be used, something safe and effective, something outside the reach of American regulators, the United States would lose that power.

Like bitcoin.

Which was stateless, apolitical, totally inclusive, non-inflationary, and not subject to any governmental censor. All attractive qualities for an eager entrepreneur or emerging political state. And now, after fifteen years of near-constant development, bitcoin was ready to disrupt the international power structure and hammer the final nail in the coffin of American imperialism. Or at least that was the spin they'd pitched to the 128 undeveloped nations around the world looking for a way to be less dependent.

She was comfortably ensconced in the rear seat, the car equipped with high-speed internet so she could stay in constant communication. She'd sent a text to Kyra Lhota just as she'd entered the vehicle, wanting to know the status of Kelly Austin. An answer appeared on her laptop's screen.

TOLD THE PACKAGE HAS YET TO BE LOCATED. NOT AT THE HOTEL. I HAVE PEOPLE ACTIVELY WORKING. WILL REPORT WHEN SUCCESS IS ACHIEVED.

Dammit. Nothing seemed to be going right.
Including the weather.
A thunderstorm raged outside and rain poured down as the Mercedes sped out of Luxembourg City. She hoped the storm would not delay her dinner guest.
A car passed them on the left.
Accelerating.
Odd, considering the wet road and limited visibility.
Then it abruptly pulled back into their lane, causing her driver to pump the brakes and slow their speed.
"What's happening?" she asked.
"I don't know, but that car should not have done that."
She saw more brake lights from the vehicle ahead.
"There's another one right behind us," the driver said.
She turned. Through the rain-smeared rear window she saw a second vehicle keeping pace with them, way too close considering the conditions.
The car in the rear tapped their bumper.

113

Which startled her.

Her driver's foot smashed the brake and the Mercedes swerved, skidding and swaying on the soaked surface. The rear wheels shrieked, trying to grab the pavement, and the entire car veered right onto the shoulder, dangerously near the guardrail at the road's edge. At the last moment her driver succeeded in regaining control and bringing the tires back into the lane.

The car ahead sped away.

The one behind passed, then accelerated away too. She could see nothing but blurs out the rain-soaked windows.

What was that?

Her nerves were rattled.

But she quickly grabbed hold of herself and said, "You did good."

One of the prerequisites for all the bank's drivers was attending a special course on executive protection, which included defensive driving lessons. She'd once thought the precaution overkill, but that schooling had just paid off.

She took a moment and gathered herself.

Her reputation was one of calm and cool. Rarely did she raise her voice and never had she lost her temper while at work. Not even today. If she was bothered, or angered, she dealt with those emotions in private. Which did not mean she was weak. No. Only careful.

Always.

She was about to close her laptop when a soft ding signaled that a new email had arrived. Nothing unusual. She received a hundred or more each day. But the subject line was not usual.

DID YOU RECEIVE OUR MESSAGE?

She tapped the keyboard and called up the information.

No message or name anywhere.

Only a symbol.

One she knew.

Used in Chinese, Korean, and, most relevant, Japanese.

For gold.

She shook her head.

A bad day just got worse.

CHAPTER 23

COTTON CAME ALERT AT THE SIGHT OF THE DOWNED MAN, REACHING beneath his jacket and finding his Beretta. Magellan Billet issue. From his old boss, Stephanie Nelle. Who made sure he always had one on hand.

Okay. Be ready.

He stepped from the kitchen.

The consulate filled what had surely once been an opulent Swiss villa. The numerous rooms on the ground floor had been converted to staff offices with desks, computers, and filing cabinets. Everything neat and orderly, the décor decisively Japanese. Consulates were like branches of a bank, stationed throughout a country to offer services to their respective nationals and monitor things at a local level, each reporting back to the main embassy. He was seasoned enough to know that their staff usually included people from the intelligence branches of their respective governments. For Japan that meant the PSIA, which he'd dealt with before in his other life as an active Magellan Billet agent. What concerned him here was the lack of people. Consulates never closed. Yet this place seemed deserted.

The kitchen corridor ended at a double-leafed door, the right half open. To the left was a dining room.

He heard pops. From past the double doors.

Sound-suppressed shots.
Then, others.
Unmuffled.
Return fire?

AIKO HEARD THE SHOTS AND STOOD FROM THE CHAIR.
What was happening?
She headed for the office door.
More shots rang out from the other side.
She eased the wooden panel open and peered out, seeing two of her men pinned down at the top of the stairway.
"There is a man with a gun, below," one of her men reported.
Who? How had he made it inside?
She'd been waiting for a transport to arrive. Kelly Austin had to be secured away from Basel, in a safe place. Keeping her at the consulate, or the embassy in Bern, was not an option. No one outside of the highest levels in the imperial household knew anything about this operation, and she'd been ordered to keep it that way. The PSIA was administered by the Ministry of Justice, tasked with internal security and dealing with espionage. To prevent abuse and provide some oversight, any investigation conducted by the agency had to be first approved by a special commission. But this operation had remained secret with no approvals. She'd been specially assigned and provided with a support team, and she reported straight to the imperial palace.
Now someone had breached the consulate?
She fled the doorway and darted across to the window. Below, parked, sat a van, just as she'd ordered, complete with business credentials that were surely fake. The van was here.
Yet a man was shooting?
What was going on?

Cotton snuck a few quick peeks around the corner and spotted one shooter on the ground floor firing a sound-suppressed pistol upward toward the second floor. The intruder was pinned down as shots were returned from the unsuppressed weapons that had caused the shooter to take cover.

Hard to know the players here without a program.

But the guy shooting up surely killed the man in the kitchen.

And that was enough for him.

"Hey," Cotton yelled.

The guy with the sound-suppressed pistol whirled.

Clearly surprised.

Cotton shot him in the chest.

Aiko heard somebody call out, then a gun banged from below. Unmuffled. No more pops came up their way.

Somebody else was here?

She gestured for her men to retreat and get Austin while she assessed the situation. They both slipped into a room to her immediate right, which placed them, and her, away from the second-floor railing.

"Excuse me. People up there," a male voice said from below. "I took the shooter out. He killed one of yours in the kitchen."

She stayed silent.

"My name is Cotton Malone. You have Kelly Austin. I want her."

They'd known Malone was in Basel since yesterday, as he'd followed Kelly Austin around town. They'd maintained loose surveillance, more just a look-and-see, until today and the shooting.

Which Malone had thwarted.

Allowing her to take more drastic action.

The advanced billing on Malone seemed correct. He was indeed most resourceful.

She made two decisions.

The first was transmitted by hand gestures to one of the men in the other room watching her from the doorway. He understood and moved toward Austin. The second was a gesture to the remaining man, who returned to a position at the second-floor railing.

And fired below.

COTTON SPOTTED THE SHOOTER IN THE INSTANT BEFORE THE TRIGGER was pulled. Which allowed him to drop back, away from the corner, right before three rounds thudded into the woodwork, generating a blast of splinters. Apparently, no one was grateful for what he'd done.

Okay. He'd shoot his way in.

He snuck a couple of quick peeks around the corner and saw no one above.

He waited a few moments.

Checked again.

Then climbed the risers to the second floor, gun extended and ready. At the top a corridor stretched about thirty feet to his left, doors on either side. A couple were open, most closed. He checked each as he went and found more empty offices. Toward the end of the corridor was another stairway that led down, this one smaller than the main risers. Most likely at one time for the hired help. Now a convenient escape route. The last door opened to a corner space, larger than the others, lined with glass-fronted display cases and an impressive carved Buddha.

A man stood inside, near the windows.

Japanese. Young. Thin. Fit. Unarmed. Shirtsleeves rolled up. Bare feet at the end of his dark trousers.

The guy moved with blinding speed, advancing and throwing a vicious kick that caught Cotton square in the chest, sending him staggering backward, the gun dropping from his grasp.

A shower of colors burst before his eyes.

Air fled his lungs in harsh gasps.

He caught himself at the doorway with an outstretched arm and steadied his balance. Okay. He'd give him that one.

Martial arts.

Never something he'd mastered, though several had tried to teach him.

Over the years he'd learned that most people trained in such had never really used the skills. They mainly exhibited them in controlled situations or competitions. Movies and TV loved to choreograph two opponents showing off their abilities with unnatural chops and nearly impossible kicks. All in slow motion for added effect. But a real fight was something altogether different. No rules. No style. Winning was all that mattered.

And he knew how to win a fight.

He advanced toward the guy, cutting off room to maneuver. The man waited, planting one foot on the carpet and pivoting to uncork a spinning kick, trying to catch Cotton on the jaw.

But he was ready.

His left hand clamped onto the man's swinging foot. He wrenched the leg up, then down, sharp and hard, at an odd angle, sending a wave of pain through his smaller adversary. The man tried to break free but Cotton only tightened his grip. He then released his hold and planted his right fist straight into the face. He had a few inches in height and fifty pounds on this guy, and that advantage paid off.

The body spun like a puppet, then flailed backward.

He delivered another blow to the face.

The younger man shrank to the carpet, spread-eagled, out cold.

He heard an engine crank outside, rushed to the windows, and saw a woman and another man at the BMW consulate car. The man was dropping Kelly's limp body into the trunk, slamming it shut, then they both climbed into the car, which sped toward the gate.

Now he knew.

The other fella had been left here to buy time.

He fled the room and descended the stairs. Once outside he saw the BMW clearing the gate, speeding away.

He darted to the van, spotted the keys in the ignition—thank God—then climbed inside and roared the engine to life.

CHAPTER 24

CASSIOPEIA WAS IMPRESSED WITH HOW KOGER HANDLED HIMSELF, moving toward trouble, never hesitating. Say what you want about him, the man was no coward. The stairway was a beautiful curve of polished wood that rose to a landing where it turned and ascended to the next floor. She followed him up, keeping a close watch behind. He seemed to know his way around the house. Good thing. As she was at a loss. Her senses, though, were at full alert as they steadily advanced toward the source of the sound.

They passed bedrooms that had each been tossed like the parlor downstairs. Somebody had definitely been looking for something. What? She had no idea, but Koger surely knew. A set of double doors were partially open at the end of the corridor. Solid wood panels carved in bas-relief. Koger flanked to one side, she to the other. Their gazes met and she understood that, like downstairs, he was going in first and she was to watch his back. Ordinarily she liked to lead the parade, but this was Koger's show so she deferred to the big man. He pushed the door open and stepped into the room.

Movement caught her attention.

She angled the gun toward it.

A large tan-and-white cat raced past them, out into the corridor.

A vase lay shattered into pieces on the hardwood floor. Apparently the source of the noise.

"I hate that damn cat," Koger muttered, lowering the weapon. She did the same.

They stood in a large bedchamber that had also been thoroughly searched.

"What's going on here?" she asked Koger.

"The man who owns this house, Robert Citrone, knows more about World War II gold than anyone on the planet. He was the CIA's resident expert and managed the Black Eagle Trust. Of course, that was back when the agency, the bank, and Citrone were all on the same page."

"I didn't realize CIA officers made the kind of money needed to afford an estate like this?"

Koger was pacing. "They don't. But like I said, Citrone knew where the gold was buried. I assume he dug some of it up for himself."

"And that was okay?"

"When it came to Yamashita's gold there were no rules. In return for deniability Langley granted its people a wide latitude. Too damn wide, though. Which is why this whole thing is a cluster—"

"I get the point," she said. "Who did this?"

"I have an idea."

But he did not offer anything more. So she asked, "What were they looking for?"

"Let's find out."

He left the room and she followed him back down the corridor to the staircase.

"When Yamashita created the 175 underground vaults, each one was added to a map," he said. "One map. No copies. Trillions in wealth hidden in booby-trapped underground vaults, and the only way to find them was with that sole map. It was taken back to Japan from the Philippines, by Prince Chichibu, in June 1945 when he fled the islands. Chichibu was the emperor's brother, a general in the Imperial Army who headed up Golden Lily, though the official version was that he spent the war convalescing from tuberculosis and had nothin' to do with anything. Along with every other high Japanese official, the prince was pardoned by MacArthur for war crimes and lived until 1953. After the war he became Mr. Wonderful. He headed up a lot of athletic organizations, promoting skiing, rugby, and other sports in Japan. He was a big supporter of the Boy Scouts in Japan. There's even a stadium named after him and statues of him everywhere. A regular 'prince' of a man."

"I assume he was a cold-blooded killer too?"

"In every sense of the word. He ordered hundreds of workers and engineers murdered. Chichibu cared about one thing and one thing only. Securing all the gold, silver, gems, and platinum for the imperial family. He spent every day from 1945 to 1953 trying to get it all back. But failed."

"And the map he had?"

"It passed through a lot of hands and eventually ended up at the CIA. That's where Rob Citrone got his hands on it."

Koger crouched down in front of the thick railing. It was supported by heavy stone spindles shaped like pears, fatter at the bottom than the top. He grabbed hold of one, toward the center of the span, and twisted counterclockwise. The spindle turned, then released from beneath the railing. Koger carefully sat it upright on the floor.

"Best place to hide something is right in front of people," he said.

She agreed. "I've never seen a hiding place like that before."

"Citrone loves secrets. It's his life."

She saw that the spindle had been hollowed out in a perfect circle, a few centimeters in diameter. Inside the cavity rested a metal tube. Koger uprighted the heavy spindle and allowed the half-meter-long tube to slide out. She reached down and grabbed it as he laid the spindle back on the floor. She handed him the cylinder and he twisted off the cap.

"Hold your palm out," he said.

She did and he shook the tube.

A rolled-up sheet of white paper slid free into her hand. She unrolled it to reveal a map drawn in washed-out sepia, the contrast clear between the many scribblings and symbols.

"It's a photograph of the original," he said. "Nobody knows where the original is now, or at least that's what Citrone says."

"This leads to all those hidden caches across the Philippines?" she asked.

"That's the legend, provided you can figure out the codes and understand the symbols. Unfortunately, everyone who could have done that is now dead."

"That gold is still there, after all these decades?"

He nodded. "The majority was never found."

"How did you know about this hiding place?"

"Citrone and I have always gotten along. I used to help him out some. Recently, he let me in on a few of the secrets. He and I shared a dislike for authority."

"Is he the one who pointed you to the wine vault?"

He nodded. "The one and only."

She heard a noise from outside.

Distant. An engine roaring to life.

Koger heard it too and they rushed back into the bedroom, to a set of half-open French doors that led out to an upper terrace with a magnificent view of Lake Geneva. Citrone's house sat about a hundred meters from the shoreline, a lawn of thick grass and trees in between. A dock jutted out into the blue water where a boat was tied and another was pulling away, revealing the source of the noise. Cassiopeia spotted a pair of binoculars lying amid the rubble of the tossed bedroom and quickly retrieved them, handing them to Koger. His eyes were better than hers on this one since she had no idea who or what she was looking at. Koger handed over the map and focused on the lake.

"Citrone is on the boat with two men. Damn."

She caught the frustration.

"May I?" she asked, gesturing for the binoculars.

She traded him for the map and gazed out on the lake. The boat moving away was maybe six meters long, with a single outboard engine containing two Japanese men and another heavyset man. She then adjusted the angle and found another boat tied to the dock. A sport cruiser. At least ten meters, V-hulled, with a teak deck, brass fittings, a flying bridge, and inboard engines. Probably at least two. More power. Definitely.

She lowered the binoculars and asked, "You want him back?"

"We need him back."

"Are the Japanese the people you thought responsible for tossing this place?" she asked.

He nodded.

"I assume those men were after that map?"

"That's a good assumption. Citrone told me the PSIA has been looking for it a long time."

"I can get Citrone back."

And she told him what she had in mind.

He smiled. "I like the way you think. The key to the boat is down in the kitchen. I've been on it before."

She pointed at the map. "We'll use that as bait."

CHAPTER 25

KELLY BLINKED HER EYES.

Her face was on fire and she was shaking. Badly. She hadn't felt such fear in a long time. Not since that night when her car crashed.

That awful, awful night.

Consciousness came in slow gentle waves as she rebounded from the turmoil that had assaulted her stunned mind.

Had she bitten off way more than she could chew?

Maybe.

She was enclosed in a tight, dark space with little room to move. More reminiscent of the car crash where she'd been trapped.

Except this time she was moving.

A wave of cold apprehension passed through her.

Was she inside a car trunk?

Her throat hurt from the choking and she struggled to calm her burning lungs. The chain of events she'd initiated had definitely spiraled out of control. Take a moment. Grab hold.

Think.

What started out as trying to do the right thing had gestated into a free-for-all that now involved a hostile foreign government. One that had just tried to kill her. Or had they? She'd never, ever considered that possibility. Nor had she expected Cotton Malone.

Seeing him again, after so long, had been amazing. Incredible, actually. Yes, he'd hurt her. More than he ever realized. But she hadn't been innocent in the situation either. Having affairs with married men came with consequences. And she should know. Cotton had not been the first, but he had been the last.

Her problems went way back. She'd never really been close to anyone. In every relationship that had ever hinted at a possible commitment, she was the one who ended things. If not her, when nothing they gave was returned, they always went elsewhere. A vicious destructive cycle, one she'd never been able to break. Cotton's reemergence here, after so many years, had released a flux of ugly, long-suppressed recollections. Apparently, she'd been living in the illusion that her emotional wounds had scarred with time, but seeing him had revived the pain and humiliation she'd felt long ago.

And it wasn't anger.

No.

Regret.

Unfortunately, she could not have children. Another side effect of the wreck, which had necessitated a full hysterectomy. She was alone. On her own. Dependent on no one.

She rid the last wisps of fog from her brain and began to assess her situation. The good thing was that the PSIA and the bank needed her alive, only for different reasons. That choking? Surely designed to send a message that they were not playing around.

Okay. Message received.

She was unbound and felt around in the dark, finding the latch that held the truck lid closed. Thankfully, she'd never been claustrophobic. Sight was impossible in the dark, but touch worked and she examined the spring-loaded catch with her fingers, finally managing to release it. But she held the lid closed with a tight grip on the catch.

Careful.

If she allowed it to open too far, the car would surely alert the driver. All cars did that now. Instead, she eased the lid open just enough to peer out and see a car following on the road.

COTTON STAYED WITH THE CONSULATE CAR, ALLOWING ANOTHER vehicle to move between him and the BMW. The time was approaching 4:00 P.M. and they were headed out of Basel, south, toward Geneva, which lay about 150 miles away. The consulate car was maintaining a steady pace with no evasive maneuvers, indicating that his target was unaware of any tail. He had to stay with them and retrieve Kelly.

Then he noticed something.

The trunk of the consulate car opened. Not far.

But enough.

Oh, crap.

Kelly was making a move.

He pressed the accelerator and spun the steering wheel, powering around the car in front in the opposite lane. Thankfully, no vehicles were coming his way. But the van had little get-up-and-go, the engine dragging. The gap between the car in front of him and the BMW was not much. He'd need more room to get over and he'd surely announced his presence now to the BMW's driver.

He edged the van back into the right lane, forcing the car behind the BMW to brake. Its driver laid on the horn, which he ignored. He was now right behind the BMW with a clear view of the trunk. More important, Kelly would have a clear view of him. The trunk was still partially open and he caught a glimpse of her concerned face. Their gazes met and he shook his head, gesturing with one hand for her to keep the lid down.

She nodded her understanding.

His front bumper was only a yard or so from the BMW and they were moving at a steady clip down the rural road. Nothing defensive, as yet, from the other driver, so he decided to go on the offensive. He yanked the wheel again hard left and floored the accelerator, speeding past the BMW, then easing his way back over in front of the consulate car. Ahead he spotted an intersection with a traffic signal.

Opportunity?

Maybe.

The light was green, so he slowed to allow time for the signal to change to yellow.

The cars ahead of him reacted.

Two rushed through the intersection, then the rest congealed, stopping in a line.

He brought the van to a halt and watched in the rearview mirror as the BMW did the same. He slammed the transmission into reverse and sent his rear bumper into the BMW behind him, which lurched from the impact, surely startling everyone inside. Then he stuck his head out the open window and yelled.

"Now, Kelly. Fast."

CASSIOPEIA CROUCHED DOWN, OUT OF SIGHT, BELOW THE MAIN DECK where Koger stood at the helm of Citrone's boat. She'd been right. It came with twin diesel inboards, plenty of power to overcome the other boat, which had a solid five-minute lead. Her idea had been for them to use the horsepower advantage, and the expanse of Lake Geneva, to their benefit.

They'd found the key in the kitchen, exactly where Koger had said it would be hanging. He explained that he'd been out on the lake a few times with Citrone. They both loved to fish, and who didn't enjoy a thirty-foot cabin cruiser with all the amenities? Citrone employed a staff of five, including a boat operator, who'd been nowhere to be seen in the house.

"He liked to show that map off," Koger said from where he stood behind the helm. "Like I was harmless or somethin'. It really irritated me."

"Or maybe the map is useless."

"Yeah, I considered that too. But it has to be deciphered, and he always said only the Japanese had a way to do that."

Koger swung to port and she felt the bow press into the swells.

"Tokyo has been obsessed with Yamashita's gold since the 1950s. They tried repeatedly with the Eisenhower administration to learn more about what we'd done after the war. But Allen Dulles stonewalled them."

Koger shoved the throttle forward. Propellers bit the water and the stern dug in, spray flying up. The air was chilly and she assumed the water would be even colder.

"Dulles was an asshole," Koger said. "His philosophy with running the CIA was to make it a private army. Political meddling, coups, wars, even assassinations. Everything and anything was in his playbook, and he financed most of it through the Black Eagle Trust."

She'd read some on the Cold War and knew that, in its early days, the CIA struggled for an identity.

"If Dulles had been good at any of that, things might have been different," Koger said. "But he was terrible at the job. He overthrew the duly elected prime minister of Iran and replaced him with the shah. Twenty-five years later that came back to bite us. He led a coup in Guatemala and that country has never been a friend of ours since. Then there was the Bay of Pigs. A total fiasco. Everything about that was wrong from the start, but Dulles plowed ahead. Kennedy fired him shortly after."

"And the Black Eagle Trust?"

"It just kept chuggin' along. All under the supervision of the Bank of St. George. Eventually, Rob Citrone became the agency's rep to the bank. He served in that capacity for nearly twenty-five years."

Which now explained Koger's initial description of Citrone. *A man who knows an awful lot about stolen gold.* Bet he does.

"You don't find it strange he showed you the map *and* its hiding place?" she asked.

"At the time? No. Now? Damn right. Somethin's off here."

She agreed. As if Citrone wanted him to know.

"How far away are we?" she asked from below.

"Maybe a quarter mile and closing," he said.

The chaos in the house certainly indicated something had happened. Citrone being taken to a boat, then out on the lake, was clearly a cause for concern. His abductors being Japanese? Another red flag. But what did it all mean?

Too soon to tell.

She was three steps down in the forward cabin, below the main deck. The metal tube lay on the pilot's chair. Koger had placed the map back inside the spindle, minus its container, and returned it to the stair railing. They'd brought along the empty metal tube, planning to use it to attract the men in the other boat's attention, hoping the map had been what they were after and they'd simply failed to locate it.

The boat pitched and poked its way ahead.

"I can see how you and Captain America get along," he said to her. "You're a lot like him."

"I'll take that as a compliment," she said.

Koger pulled back on the throttle, slowing gradually, the bow wave diminishing as they came to a slow swinging stop and settled on the water.

"Get ready. We're here."

Aiko had watched the van from the consulate speed past, then weave back in front of them.

And the driver?

Cotton Malone.

Who apparently had avoided the obstacle she'd left for him with her man. The idea had been to delay Malone enough so they could leave the consulate. He was a known commodity within the intelligence community, though one from the past. Smart. Competent. Proof positive of which had just been shown as he'd backed the van into their car. The jolt had jostled them all around but the shoulder harness had done its job and kept her in the seat.

"The trunk has opened," her driver said.

Kelly Austin rushed by outside.

"Stop her," she ordered.

Her driver opened his door.

COTTON HOPED KELLY HAD SEEN HIM PASS THE BMW.

And she had.

He saw her spring from the trunk and run his way. He decided to provide cover and slipped out the driver's-side door, sending one round from his gun ricocheting off the BMW's hood. Kelly reacted to the shot with a momentary hesitation, but he urged her forward with a wave of the weapon.

The BMW's driver emerged, surely reaching for a gun beneath his jacket. Kelly kept coming from the passenger side and he sent the driver to the ground with another round to the car's hood. Taking out a tire would be good, but the angle was wrong. So, for good measure, he blew out the driver's-side door window. He was trying not to kill anyone unless absolutely necessary.

Kelly hopped into the front passenger seat.

He climbed back inside and rammed the accelerator to the floor, spinning the steering wheel. The rear tires broke loose on the asphalt, then bit. He whipped the steering wheel hard left and swung around into the opposite lane, speeding ahead.

"What now?" she asked.

Good question.

AIKO STARED AT HER DRIVER, WHO STOOD AFTER TAKING COVER FROM Malone's bullets, slipping back behind the wheel and slamming his door shut.

"Pursue them," she said.

CHAPTER 26

Cassiopeia had removed her jacket along with her shoes, leaving on her shirt and jeans, ready for a swim. Some neoprene would be great but, unfortunately, none was available.

Step one, overtake the boat. Step two, show them the metal tube. Step three, hope this grabbed their attention so Koger could occupy them long enough for her to swim over. Step four, neutralize the threat and take control of the other boat with Citrone on board. The whole thing sounded good back in the warmth of the house, but out here, in chilly air and about to go into even colder water, the whole thing sounded a little crazy.

The boat bobbed in the water, its engine in neutral. Koger was standing at the helm, holding up the metal tube.

"They see it," he muttered, not moving his lips. "And, lo and behold, they want it. I'm going to swing around to the far side of 'em. When I tap my right foot, over the side you go."

She climbed up the three risers on her hands and knees, keeping low and out of sight. Koger had laid down the tube and was now working the throttle and wheel. She felt the boat turn in a wide swing, slowly fighting its way across the lake. She readied herself, her brain at full clarity. Nothing but clear, calm, quick thinking, without the impingement of any distractions, would be needed in the minutes ahead.

Koger's right foot tapped the deck.

She finished the climb up to the deck and stayed below the gunwales, moving to Koger's right. A careful glance back over her shoulder and she saw the boat they'd been pursuing bobbing in the water about fifty meters away. The view from its occupants was momentarily blocked by the angle Koger had achieved. She slid over the gunwale headfirst and entered the water with barely a splash.

The cold was swift and immediate, radiating through her body. Maybe twelve to fifteen degrees Celsius. She shivered for a moment, then settled down and focused, powering herself downward. Above her, Koger kept going and she used him as a bearing, bisecting his path and swimming directly toward the other boat. Koger would shortly be turning, completing his circle, drawing the occupants' attention in the direction opposite her approach.

She prided herself on staying slim and lean with hardly a gram of unnecessary body fat. But at the moment that lack of insulation was adding to her discomfort. So she kept swimming.

Hard.

A look upward and she saw the keel of the first boat and heard the churn from Koger's idling engines.

Her lungs started to burn.

Time to head up.

COTTON ASSESSED THE SITUATION WITH GOOD NEWS / BAD NEWS. The good part was that he had Kelly back. The bad news was that the BMW from the consulate was in pursuit.

"I'm glad to see you," Kelly said.

"I knew it was serious when you called out 'Cotton.' "

"Don't get used to it."

"Any idea what they wanted?"

She shook her head. "We didn't get that far before they choked me unconscious."

"You okay?"

She rubbed her throat. "I'll live. Right now we have to lose that car behind us."

He agreed.

The intersection was just ahead. He decided that he had to take the chance and sped around the three cars stopped at the light into the opposite lane. He approached, braking, looking for an opening between the cars moving perpendicular to his path. Horns blared. In the rearview mirror he saw the BMW trying to keep pace. This was going to be close. He slowed and timed his approach, waiting for an opening.

Which came.

And he sped through, barely avoiding two other cars.

Kelly was watching through the outside rearview mirror.

He heard the squeal of brakes, horns, then a crash. A quick glance in his own mirror and he saw that the BMW had not been as lucky, colliding with another car and spinning around.

"That should stop them," Kelly said.

He added speed and kept going.

"I never counted on the Japanese showing up," she said. "Neither did Koger, I bet."

"Why are they involved?"

"The answer to that will have to come from Koger. Sorry, Harold. But this is his show."

"Which you invited him to. So you're the host of this party."

He'd read once that smart people exhibited ten qualities. Highly adaptable. Understood what they didn't know. Possessed an insatiable curiosity. Read a lot. Open-minded. Liked their own company. Had a high sense of self-control. Were funny. Sensitive to other people's experiences. And always, always, thought creatively.

He liked to think himself smart.

So to get to the truth, he was going to have to apply all ten.

The problem?

Suzy Baldwin was smart too.

AIKO STOOD OUTSIDE THE WRECKED CONSULATE CAR AND WATCHED AS a police cruiser appeared and two officers worked the wreck. Witnesses confirmed the presence of the van that had run the intersection first, along with its markings. Her car being registered to the consulate meant diplomatic immunity was in place, which the Swiss protected with a religious fervor.

So no explanations would be required.

The consulate breach was serious. Her transport van driver had disappeared, replaced by another man who'd entered the building shooting, then had been shot dead. Killed by Cotton Malone. Another of her contingent had also been killed. An awful lot of bloodshed.

The culprits?

Had to be CIA.

Who else?

CHAPTER 27

CASSIOPEIA EASED HER HEAD OUT OF THE WATER JUST ENOUGH TO SUCK a few breaths through her nose. She treaded water and saw that she was about five meters from the boat, its three occupants facing away. Her body had adjusted to the cold, but she wasn't looking forward to climbing out. She heard voices and assumed Koger was engaging them, as planned, dangling the metal tube, supposedly negotiating a trade for Citrone. She kept down, swept her arms out and in, and eased closer. Luckily, it was a small craft, low in the water. Which should make what she was about to do a touch easier.

The boat's engine was off. Thank goodness.

That prop could pose a real danger.

More voices back and forth.

English.

She timed her approach with the bobbing and waited for a down swell. When it happened she planted the palms of her hands on the gunwale and kicked as the boat rose back up. There'd be noise that would alert the two men standing only a couple of meters in front of her, facing away.

So she had to be quick.

Citrone, a rotund man with legs out of proportion to his bulging torso, stood off to one side.

Up and over and she was on the deck.

Water dripped from her soaked shirt and pants.

She met Citrone's gaze. For an instant.

Then the two Japanese turned, but she gave neither time to react, calling on her experience-trained reflexes. She kicked the one on the right hard at the shoulders, sending him over the side and into the water. As he fell she saw he was holding a gun. She spun on her heel and prepared to deal with the second man.

Citrone moved out of the way.

The man leaped and struck at her exposed neck with the edge of his hand.

Which hurt.

She buckled but did not go down.

Instead, she lunged, grabbing hold of an arm, throwing her weight forward, then bringing the arm up and into her right armpit. With her left elbow she struck backward, the point burying deep in his ribs. She twisted again and, locking onto the man's wrists, used her leverage to spin and press backward against his arm.

Which broke with a snap.

The man cried out and tried to break free, but the pain and confusion caused him to flail and miss.

She released her grip and shoved him over the side.

The boat's motor roared to life.

Citrone stood at the wheel, working the throttle.

Koger was watching from his own boat and tossed a thumbs-up.

She returned the gesture.

"I know the scoundrel on my boat over there," Citrone said. "But who might you be?"

"Cassiopeia Vitt."

"You seem to be quite brave and nimble."

She smiled. "I try."

They powered ahead for a short way, then Citrone shifted to neutral and shut the engine off, fifty meters from the two swimming men. Koger's boat motored around, crossed in front of their bow, then eased close, touching, and she helped Citrone to make his way to it. She then hopped over, taking the keys in the ignition, leaving the motor off. With a little luck the two men in the water could make their way to it but would have nowhere to go.

Cassiopeia stood with a towel wrapped around her wet clothes, back inside Citrone's messy bedchamber. The big man appeared unfazed by the ordeal. She estimated him to be in his sixties, with a large, pockmarked nose, skin pale as ivory, a thatch of thin hair atop a partially bald head, and the watery eyes of someone who liked alcohol. A smile seemed to always fill his lips, which cast an odd warm glow of pleasure she thought not real. His fingernails were immaculately manicured. Still, the most poignant first impression came from his voice—smooth and mellow, the English spoken with a clipped, upper-class accent, like some audiobook narrator.

"Cassiopeia," Koger said. "Meet Robert Kenneth Citrone, or as he likes to be called, Sir Rob, formerly of the Central Intelligence Agency, assigned to the Bank of St. George, now retired. As you already know, this is his home."

Citrone offered her a slight bow of welcome.

"Are you an actual knight?" she asked.

"Of the Order of the Gold Lion," Citrone said, adding another bow. "At your service."

"Don't get him started," Koger said. "The royal house of Luxembourg granted it to him a long time ago. For what? I don't want to know."

"I'm familiar with the order," she said. "That honor is meant only for royal families. I've never heard of it being bestowed on an outsider."

"It was given to me in secret. For meritorious service to the royal family," Citrone said.

"Yet he tells everyone," Koger added.

Citrone waved the criticism off. "He's just jealous."

"Yeah," Koger said. "Let's go with that."

The boat ride to the house had been uneventful and Citrone had said little. Koger had apparently decided not to press until they were back inside and alone.

She stepped over to an open panel in the wall that Citrone had revealed. When closed, it appeared to be a set of inlaid shelves. Citrone had accessed it when they arrived. On the other side was a small, windowless room that housed six LED screens. One showed the front of the house where their car awaited. Others showed various rooms and hallways. Another replayed a loop from earlier with the two men entering the house.

"The PSIA paid me a visit," Citrone said. "Unannounced."

"And you didn't see them coming?" Koger asked.

The big man grinned. "They caught me napping."

"A lot of good all these cameras do you asleep," she had to say.

"Where's the house staff?" Koger asked.

"Most are on their day off. The others were out on errands."

"What did the PSIA want?" Koger asked, his tone suggesting he needed an answer.

"They demanded the map. I told them no. They searched, found nothing, then took me prisoner."

"And where were they taking you?"

"That wasn't mentioned."

"Why did they think you had the map?" Koger asked.

"I suppose my inquiries to certain Japanese sources seeking help with its deciphering did not go unnoticed."

Koger shook his head. "Does Langley know you have the map?"

"Not that I'm aware. But I doubt they care. Having the map is one thing. Digging any gold from the ground in the Philippines is another matter entirely, bordering on the impossible."

That she could believe. Once, the country was an American ally, with Marcos heavily under Washington's thumb. But in recent years the politics there had veered to the far right and were openly anti-American. The last thing anyone would want was to reveal the locations of huge amounts of buried gold for that regime to enjoy.

"The vault in Basel was empty," Koger said. "Not a speck of gold. And they knew we were coming."

"Not surprising. But you had to take a look. Catherine Gledhill is a careful, careful woman." Their host waddled across the room, his gate oddly undulating, stopping at the windows. "This situation is escalating, Derrick. Operation Neverlight in full swing. Everybody is expendable. No untidy ends will be left."

"I need you to explain things to Cassiopeia," Koger said.

"Really?" Citrone said, beaming.

"Yeah. No more secrets."

"It's classified."

"Yet you, retired, know all about it," Koger said.

Citrone smiled. "I still have friends. And I told you this wasn't going to be easy."

"Yeah, you did."

"My dear," Citrone said to her. "How are you with stories?"

She knew the right answer. "I love them."

CHAPTER 28

6:00 P.M.

CATHERINE HAD SHOWERED AND CHANGED, NOW SPORTING A strapless, pale-blue evening gown, her trademarked hair bun replaced by free-flowing, stylish curls. She'd never considered herself attractive. Her features lacked the symmetry of perfect beauty, her mouth too wide and full-lipped, the nose a fraction strong. But when she smiled all of the pieces fit. That smile had always served her well.

This evening was important, but it also demanded a certain informality. Pressure, but not too much. Enthusiasm, yet tempered with caution. The consuls had been working toward this day for several years. Tonight would be the culmination of some intense lobbying and liberal bribing. The trick came in balancing the right measure of each ingredient. Too much of one, too little of another, and nothing would materialize. Thankfully, she was an expert in the art of political persuasion.

She lived an hour north from Luxembourg City, near the village of Esch-sur-Sûre, one the most picturesque spots in all of Europe. The estate sat on a rocky loop in the Sûre River Valley, surrounded by distant hills that dropped from steep cliffs down to the river. Not far away stood the crumbly ruins of a 10th-century castle, a place that conjured up images of knights, horses, and invading armies. Belgium bordered on one side, Germany the other, a mere twenty kilometers of dense Luxembourg forest in between.

Her château was no antique. She'd built it a decade and a half ago, among twenty acres of trees, with the first millions made from her employment with the bank. Then she was a senior administrator, before graduating to the board as European consul. From there she was elevated to first chair, now serving at the pleasure of the other consuls. Her reputation was one of a consummate professional. Financial leaders across the globe called on her for advice. She'd served on the board for the World Bank, and the duchy of Luxembourg depended on her, and the bank, to manage its long-held wealth.

But no one really knew her.

How could they?

She never revealed much about herself to anyone.

Before all this started the complex question of who she was contained too many variables to answer. Now, at least, she'd identified, solidified, and quantified most of those. She knew exactly who and what she was.

With no apologies.

She decided that pearls would be the proper accent for the evening and found the strand of Majorcas she'd bought in Spain a few years ago. Kyra Lhota was on her way back from Siberia via private jet. At least they now knew where Kelly was located. In Japanese custody. So she'd reported all that to Kyra, who assured her that she had eyes and ears on the ground in Switzerland, waiting for her to arrive. Good. They would be needed as the Japanese would be making contact again. They wanted something and, to get it, they'd use Kelly to make a deal. Of course Catherine had no intention of surrendering a thing to them. Instead, Kyra would strike, with the when and where of that all being part of the bargaining process.

She clipped the pearls around her neck, smoothed the wrinkles from her dress, and left the bedroom, descending to the ground floor. She passed through a large archway that separated the entrance foyer from the main parlor. The intricate parquet floor beneath her Christian Louboutins was dotted with expensive Turkish rugs she'd bought herself in Istanbul. The room beyond was filled with light. A crystal chandelier hung over Louis XIV furnishings. Pale blues and eggshell white predominated. The furniture was all custom-designed, another luxury that obscene amounts of money afforded. High ceilings with hewn exposed beams added spaciousness, all done on the advice of her Parisian interior designer. A fire crackled inside one of the many stone hearths.

Her guest waited inside her study.

Medium height. Swarthy skin. Mid- to late forties. Dressed in a well-cut suit of European design. The flared waist of the jacket accentuated his trim build, and his stylishly groomed short brown hair and pencil-thin mustache spoke of a man in charge.

Which he was.

"Minister, it is good to see you," she said, adding one of her smiles and accepting a hug.

Benito Gómez Farías headed the Secretariat of the Treasury and Public Credit, Mexico's equivalent of the United States Treasury. He was a member of the federal executive cabinet, appointed by the president of the republic, with the approval of the Chamber of Deputies. Farías directed all of Mexico's economic policies, including taxes, spending, and public debt.

"I have been looking forward to this day," he said. "Much work is about to bear fruit."

She exhibited the composure that was needed and stepped over to the serving cart, lifting a gold-sealed bottle chilling in an ice bucket. She deftly worked the top and the mushroom-shaped cork made a popping exit. She then poured the bubbling froth into two stemmed glasses and brought one over to Farías.

Her pulse began to quicken.

Anticipation always caused her to be anxious. Occupational hazard. But she was good at appearing indifferent. Tonight it was important that she control the dialogue, spot any inconsistencies, alleviate fears, and, most important, bring the result home. But she'd mastered the jargon of power that converted polite conversation into political capital.

She sat opposite her guest, hoping her smile, pleasant personality, and cultivated manner had a salutary effect.

"You sound encouraging," she said to him. "Are we celebrating?"

They both sipped their champagne.

Through the bank's private lobbying, which had included massive amounts of bribery, nine nations in Central and South America had already adopted bitcoin as their legal currency, placing it on the same international status as the dollar or euro. There, citizens now had the legal option to use bitcoin, instead of other currencies. And they were doing just that. Every day. Millions of transactions. Six of those nations had gone one step further and certified bitcoin as their reserve currency.

Which was revolutionary.

A reserve was a large quantity of wealth maintained by a nation's central bank for investments, spending, international debt obligations, and meeting exchange rates. Since 1944 the U.S. dollar had been the primary reserve currency for most countries.

And for good reason.

At one time the American gross domestic product, a measure of the total national economic activity, represented fifty percent of the world's entire economic output. Following the famed Bretton Woods Agreement in 1944, delegates from forty-four nations formally adopted the U.S. dollar as their official reserve currency. After that, other countries also pegged their exchange rates to the dollar. Which, at the time, was a good move. Dollars were backed by gold, which meant their own reserves were backed by gold.

But in the 1960s America needed money for Lyndon Johnson's Great Society and to fight the Vietnam War. So it started printing dollars by the billions. With all that new money in circulation the amount of gold backing those dollars diminished, which reduced the value of the dollars held in reserve by foreign countries. As the United States flooded markets with new paper dollars, understandably the world grew cautious and began to convert their dollar reserves back into gold. The run on gold was so extensive that in 1971 Richard Nixon decoupled the dollar from the gold standard, which gave way to the floating exchange rates still around to this day. It also led to a huge escalation in the price of gold and a steady decline in the value of a dollar. Decades later, the almighty dollar remained the world's primary currency reserve, but only because countries simply could not get rid of it. The euro was a distant second. Now the Bank of St. George was introducing a third option.

Bitcoin.

If someone had told her in 2009 that fifteen years later nations would fully recognize ones and zeros from a computer program as legal currency, she would have laughed. No way. Impossible. But the concept had developed far quicker than anyone had ever thought. Like a religious movement in many ways, as Kelly had told her on more than one occasion. Now Mexico was poised to be the next to do just that.

Farías smiled. "A vote will be taken in the Congreso de la Unión early next week. We have polled the 628 members, and nearly three-fourths support the measure. Which was no small feat. Currently, the government is composed of eight varying political parties, along with the independents. Consensus is—challenging, if nothing else."

"They'll be pleased with that decision," she said. "Nothing else allows so much value to be transferred with no interference from the United States."

"We did have an incident," he said. "One of the representatives stripped to his underwear on the floor of the Congreso. He took the podium and yelled, 'You are ashamed to see me naked, but not ashamed to see your people moving on the streets naked, barefoot, and hungry after you have stolen all their money and wealth.' A bit melodramatic, but it made headlines."

She sipped more of the champagne. "Did it sway any votes?"

"Not a one. He's from one of the smaller parties, an extremist, who opposes everything."

Good to hear.

The bank had been heavily involved in the drafting of the new Mexican legislation, which stipulated that all businesses must accept bitcoin as payment. To promote bitcoin's use the government would also launch a nationwide educational campaign designed to encourage citizens to make the switch. All financed, of course, by the bank.

"My chef has prepared a lovely dinner," she said, "in honor of this occasion. Chile ancho en nogado. I'm told it is one of your favorites."

Farías nodded. "I adore it."

"We even wood-roasted the chicken," she said.

"You spoil me."

"This is a momentous day. Mexico can finally come out from under the United States' thumb. Freedom. At last."

Farías tipped his glass to her. "Screw Washington."

She returned the toast. "I agree."

CHAPTER 29

INITIALLY, THE BLACK EAGLE TRUST WAS USED TO CULTIVATE POSTWAR Japan into an anti-communist bastion. Part of that involved financing a death squad, headed by a U.S. Army colonel, which targeted student leaders, liberals, leftists, union organizers, journalists: anyone and everyone who got in the way of the revival of capitalism in Japan.

Joseph Keenan, the chief prosecutor in the Tokyo war crimes trials, drew on the funds to bribe witnesses to falsify their testimony so that the reputations of the emperor, right-wing politicians, and other war criminals could be rehabilitated, those men eventually used to solidify Western influence in postwar Japan. A succession of Japanese governments were bought and paid for. The fund also bribed witnesses of Japan's chemical and biological warfare program to commit perjury so that the deadly knowledge they held could be kept secret and passed on to the U.S. military. And there were violent deaths and suspicious suicides among people who resisted those efforts.

By 1950 a branch of the Black Eagle Trust, called the M-Fund, had been created especially for Japan. Its value amounted to almost ten percent of Japan's entire gross national product at the time. The dividend from this fund financed Japan's self-defense army *and the formation of its right-wing Liberal Democratic Party. Huge inducements were paid to support Nobosuke Kishi, who had been actively involved in the use of slave labor as a wartime minister, as the Liberal Democratic Party leader, against a less pro-American rival. During his three-year reign as prime minister, from 1957 to 1960, the Liberal Democratic Party received millions each year from the CIA, all drawn from the M-Fund.*

In the decades after the war both government and private treasure hunters flocked to the Philippine burial sites, but little gold was discovered. Yamashita had done his job well, and the sole map that detailed the location of all 175 caches had disappeared. Philippine president Ferdinand Marcos entered the fray in 1965 and found a few of the caches. At the time he was courted by the United States as an Asian-Pacific friend. He even used CIA aircraft, U.S. Air Force planes, and U.S. Navy ships to transport bullion out of the country. That Philippine gold rush continued for decades, quietly, in the background.

Initially, banks across Europe were the major repositories of stolen war loot and billions were deposited in vaults. But the Bank of St. George eventually became the record owner of it all, secretly administering the fund in conjunction with the real owner, the CIA. From the 1950s through the 1990s the Black Eagle Trust was used to interfere with sovereign nations, buy elections, undercut the rule of law, control the media, and carry out assassinations. Additionally, monies were channeled to fund the dictator in South Vietnam, spread anti-communist propaganda during the Cold War, and reinforce the treasuries of anti-communist allies. Both the Black Eagle Trust and Golden Lily war loot became a highly guarded state secret. So much so that, in the late 1990s, President Bill Clinton allowed the CIA to remove all references to both from about-to-be-declassified U.S. records on the war in Asia.

Cassiopeia listened in amazement.

She'd had no idea about any of what Citrone had just told her.

"Needless to say," Koger said, "none of that is the agency's finest hour."

"You think?" she asked. But she wanted to know, "Is that gold still around? After eighty years?"

"Oh, yes," Citrone said. "I have seen it with my own eyes. It's quite an amazing sight."

"And where was that?" Koger asked.

"Actually, it was in that wine vault. But that was years ago. That's why I suggested that a look was warranted."

Maybe so. But she had a lot of questions, and started with "What is Operation Neverlight?"

She listened as Koger explained that the expansion of terrorism had created unique pressures on intelligence work. A new strategy evolved, one that stressed speed, secrecy, and certainty. But the CIA, unwieldly by nature, was ill equipped to deal with those changes.

So a special unit was created.

Neverlight.

"It cleans up the messes," Koger said. "But the potential for abuse is obvious. No oversight means no rules. No accountability. Anything goes. Here, the covert relationship between the agency and the Bank of St. George is gone. The bank is now the enemy. Langley wants no evidence of anything to do with the Black Eagle Trust to exist. Nothing at all. Wipe it clean. That includes records, gold, and people. Which brings us to here and now. Somebody tried to kill Kelly Austin earlier."

She saw that Citrone was intrigued by that news.

"Part of Neverlight?" she asked.

"Absolutely," Koger said. "There is no other explanation. A few months ago Kelly Austin made contact and I reported what she told me. Then, strangely, I heard nothing. Not a word from anyone. And considering what she told me, that was unusual. So I talked with Rob, who found out that Neverlight had been activated."

"You knew that before you asked Cotton to go to Basel?"

"I had no idea they were targeting her there. But yes, I knew there might be trouble."

Now she was angry. "And the Japanese?"

"That was unexpected," Citrone said. "But they have their own nationalistic interests at stake, which have always been directly contrary to the CIA. The Japanese are conflicted. They want that gold back. They've been searching for a long time. But even they realize that it will be impossible. Of late, the thinking has been that they want to expose the Black Eagle Trust and show the world that America is a lying hypocrite."

She felt like she was at a party and everyone else knew something she didn't. A party she didn't even really want to attend but had only gone to because a friend asked. "You both realize that, as I've heard said on more than one occasion, Cotton and I don't have a dog in this fight. This is your battle."

"I get it," Koger said. "But I need your help. Confiscating Japanese and German gold, then using it to fund covert activities, broke myriad laws. Not to mention it was beyond unethical. The agency does not want any of that to become public. The political embarrassment would be enormous. And now with the Japanese this close, things are going to be dicey."

She pointed at Citrone. "You never explained what you were doing on that boat."

"I had little choice but to go. They tossed my house, then led me away at gunpoint."

"Where were you going?" she tried again.

"That was unclear. They were not the most talkative of people. I suspect I was being taken to someone higher on the authority pole within the PSIA."

Citrone was hedging, so she pivoted. "I know you have some sort of map out there in one of the spindles, a photograph of the map for where Yamashita buried the 175 vaults. Do you have the original?"

"Is she cleared to breathe this rarefied air?" Citrone asked.

Koger spread his arms out wide. "Fill her lungs."

"I have the original." Pride entered his voice. "The opportunity presented itself, so I bought it."

"Like Rob told you, Golden Lily was headed up by the emperor's brother," Koger said. "A piece of garbage named Prince Chichibu. He died in the early 1950s and left behind the map, which he'd brought to the Philippines in 1945."

"Then denied that fact to his brother, the emperor," Citrone added. "It was a source of tension between them. I never understood what he planned to do with the map. Perhaps he intended to reclaim the gold for himself? How? I have no idea. No member of the imperial family would have been allowed anywhere near the Philippines. So the map stayed in the prince's family, hidden away. Being the good loyal Japanese they were, they told no one until one of the grandchildren needed money in the 1990s. He was quite negotiable. Of course, by then, fifty years had elapsed and few knew anything about that gold. Even fewer knew about the Black Eagle Trust, and most of them worked for the CIA."

"Seems the Japanese know something," she said to Citrone. "Otherwise, what was their redecorating about today? Which, by the way, you've still not fully explained."

"I must say, I don't appreciate your brisk tone."

"Forgive me. I get this way when I'm being played."

"Really, now?" Citrone asked.

An accusatory pause filled the room, which she and Koger allowed to fester.

Finally, Citrone said, "I must admit, I thought Tokyo's memory had faded on this subject. I thought they had given up. But I was dreadfully wrong. To answer your question more fully, after searching here, and finding nothing, they made a call. Then I was led at gunpoint from the house. I decided not to resist, hoping to learn more."

Smart move, considering Citrone was at least a hundred pounds overweight and in terrible shape. But he did not appear to be a fool.

Quite the contrary, in fact.

"You managed the Black Eagle Trust for the CIA?" she asked, shifting gears again.

"For twenty-three years, I was the agency's sole representative, granted a wide element of autonomy."

He seemed amused by the thought of his own importance.

"Which means," Koger added, "that he pretty much did whatever he wanted."

"Apparently, the job paid well," she said, motioning around her.

"Indeed, it did. One of the perks of managing a covert, illegal cache of stolen wealth with a bank that operates by its own rules."

She noticed that Koger was staying close to the open terrace doors, keeping a watchful eye out toward the rear yard and lake.

"I have a proposition," Citrone finally said.

Koger turned back. "I'm listening."

"Let us find that gold. Together."

CHAPTER 30

AIKO HAD COOPERATED WITH THE LOCAL POLICE AND PROVIDED A statement, corroborated by her driver, as to how the wreck occurred. Operators from other vehicles had backed up their version of the collision—that it had all been caused by a white van marked EDEL-WEISS CATERING. She'd offered the officers the explanation that the van had trespassed at the consulate, and they were in pursuit when the wreck occurred. The police assured her that the van would be located and released her to return to the consulate. Things had definitely become convoluted. Certainly not according to plan. But that was nothing unusual.

Her line of work was full of surprises.

Years ago she'd been involved with investigating Aum Shinri-kyo, the murderous cult that committed many heinous crimes, including sarin nerve gas attacks that had murdered hundreds. The group disseminated a unique doctrine, one proclaiming that it was okay to kill another human being, so long as that person was committing "evil deeds." Of course, the definition of *evil deeds* was one the cult set for itself. Its leader prophesied the coming of Armageddon and, after failing to win any meaningful support in a national election, transformed a political party into a ter-rorist group that used violence to make its points. It even went international, establishing branches in the United States, Germany, Russia, and Sri Lanka.

She'd been assigned to the task force that kept Aum Shinrikyo under nearly constant surveillance. She'd also been the investigator who first detected the profit-making businesses used by the cult to finance its operations, even locating where their account books were secretly stored and their monies deposited. It took a little over two decades but finally the cult's leader, a psychopath named Shoko Asahara, was caught, tried, and executed. She'd been there, watching, as Asahara was hanged. His final words assigned his remains to his wife and third daughter. But fearing that the ashes would be enshrined where followers might honor them, she defied her superiors and poured them into one of the prison toilets, flushing them to the sewer.

That had earned her a reprimand.

But nothing more.

She spent fourteen years tracking Aum Shinrikyo, and that dogged determination had brought her to the attention of superiors. She steadily rose to her current rank of chief investigator. From there the imperial family had chosen her for this specialized task. Why? That had never been explained. But emperors were not noted for explanations. Not even retired ones. She learned a lot from pursuing Aum Shinrikyo. That group institutionalized paranoia so, to get inside, you had to be clever.

The same was true here.

They'd tailed Kelly Austin from Luxembourg to Switzerland, expanding their already tight net on the bank. But when they noticed that Cotton Malone was also on Austin's trail, that had elevated their interest. Aiko and her men had watched the attack on Austin and Malone's spirited defense, then bided their time and taken advantage of Austin's trip to the bathroom in the café to make a move. Taking Austin seemed the prudent course considering that somebody, most likely elements in the CIA, wanted her dead.

Austin didn't help by biting the hand that had shielded her

mouth and calling out. True to form, Malone had traced the car to the consulate. What she'd not counted on was an outside attack and bloodshed. Malone had even managed to follow in the van and succeed with a rescue. She'd underestimated Austin, who freed herself from the trunk, and the collision at the intersection had allowed them both to escape. Would the bank become aware that Austin was free? Would Austin reveal that there was a spy within the bank? She doubted either would occur since Austin had no reason to make contact and could not care less if the Japanese had infiltrated.

The man whose job it had been to deliver the van to the consulate was still missing. Most likely dead. The intruder at the consulate dead too, thanks to Malone. They'd run an identification on him, but she already knew that trail would lead nowhere. Most disturbingly, thinking she had the matter under control, Aiko had alerted Catherine Gledhill to the PSIA's presence.

Taunting her.

Which was fine when she had control of Kelly Austin.

But not now.

COTTON SWITCHED OFF THE VAN IN THE PARKING LOT OF A BUSY rural shopping center, parking near a grocery store, nestled safe among other cars. They were maybe a dozen miles south of Basel, beyond the metro sprawl, in the Swiss countryside. The van had surely been reported stolen, and fleeing the wreck at that intersection had not helped, so further driving around seemed foolish. Shoppers were coming and going from the stores. His eyes scanned the building's exterior and saw no cameras. Thankfully, they were not as prevalent in Europe as they were in the United States.

They climbed out and he noticed that the EDELWEISS CATERING on each side was an attached stencil, which was easily ripped off. Apparently, this had been a hastily prepared transport. He

155

removed both signs and tossed them into a garbage can near the grocery store's entrance, which should help keep their location secret. They then walked inside among the other shoppers.

"You okay?" he asked her.

She nodded and rubbed her neck. "I'll survive."

"Tell me what happened."

He listened as she recounted what occurred after the café.

"What are the Japanese after? And please don't bullshit me."

"Stolen gold they consider theirs."

He'd figured as much. "Why take you?"

"I can't tell you that. Koger has to be the one."

That's not what he wanted to hear. So he asked, "How did they know you were here, in Switzerland?"

"They have eyes and ears inside the bank. The PSIA woman, Aiko Ejima, admitted that. They know a lot about a lot."

"Like what?"

She hesitated. "I want to tell you, but I need to speak with Koger first."

Okay. Fine.

So did he.

CASSIOPEIA CHANGED CLOTHES, REPLACING HER DAMP ONES WITH A fresh shirt and pants from the travel bag she'd brought with her from France, which had been sitting in Koger's car. They should have been on their way north toward Basel and Cotton, this favor over and done with, but that plan had changed. Koger and Rob Citrone were still talking. Koger had asked for some privacy and she'd obliged them by walking downstairs.

The house was a wreck.

It would take time to put the place back in order.

She wandered through the rooms and admired some of the paintings, statues, vases, and figurines. Beautiful objets d'art, all surely acquired over the years by a devoted collector, an eclectic mixture of old and new.

A lot like Citrone himself.

She was trying to assess the man, but she'd noticed that Citrone liked to divert a listener's attention with false modesty and unrequested courtesies. She'd also noticed that Koger was not all that enamored either, asking questions, pressing for answers, more humoring Citrone than believing him.

Which made her wonder.

Was Koger thinking the same thing?

She entered one of the trashed rooms. A small salon. A case clock caught her eye. Cobalt blue. With an elaborate pastiche of gilt and bronze topped by two smiling and garlanded gold cherubs. Not working. Still impressive. And oddly still standing. Unaffected. Unlike the framed paintings that lay scattered across the parquet floor. One grabbed her attention. An oil portrait of Martin Luther, the patina cracked and muted from age. In the lower right corner she saw the image of a small winged snake supporting a ruby ring.

And instantly knew the artist.

Lucas Cranach the Elder.

From the German Renaissance of the 16th century. He specialized in portraits of kings, emperors, and prelates. This one was typical for a Cranach. Loaded with exceptional detail. She knew most of Cranach's work hung in museums. His paintings were expensive and not all that much in demand. A pall had settled over his work in the mid-20th century when Hitler took a liking to him. The Nazis looted many a Cranach. Lawsuit after lawsuit had been fought in courts all across Europe by owners trying to get their originals back.

Yet here was one.

Owned by Sir Robert Citrone.

Then she noticed another painting hanging askew on the far wall. A watercolor framed behind glass. Of Neuschwanstein in Bavaria, one of King Ludwig II's fairy-tale castles. She'd visited the site a couple of times. There was nothing special about the work, a reasonable interpretation with muted colors and simple lines. But it was the signature at the lower right corner that made it noteworthy.

A. Hitler

Adolf Hitler.

She knew Hitler painted. About three hundred of his works had survived. From time to time they came up for sale at auction houses. Most people considered it immoral to buy one. Apparently not Rob Citrone.

She heard her name called out by Koger.

"In here," she said back.

Koger stomped down the hall and stopped at the parlor's open doorway. "Citrone is gathering some information for us."

"Anything useful?"

"I doubt it."

"He's a liar."

"Tell me something I don't know."

"What's his bio?"

Koger shrugged. "He has a doctorate in political science and Pacific studies. He was a college professor before the agency brought him on board. It's rare we go to academia for people anymore. Langley generally stays with the military or other intelligence community veterans. Easier to train and far less trouble. But for some reason, Rob made the cut and was hired about forty years ago. He worked clandestine operations and was the one who persuaded Muammar al-Gaddafi to abandon Libya's nuclear weapons program. That put him on everyone's radar, which led to him being named special envoy to Luxembourg. He had the gift of gab, if you know what I mean."

She did.

"He was in charge of the trust," Koger said, "for a long time, reporting directly to the director of Central Intelligence. Why the third degree on him?"

She pointed at Hitler's painting. "He has interesting tastes in art."

Koger stepped close and admired the castle. She explained its provenance, along with the Cranach.

"Doesn't surprise me. Rob has a lot of eccentric tastes. You should see what he eats."

"Yet he was placed in charge of a covert fund worth billions, reporting only to a single political appointee. And he apparently helped himself to some of the proceeds."

"I agree. It stinks. But go figure."

"How well do you know him?"

"We've never been in a foxhole together, if that's what you mean."

"Yet he took you into his confidence about the map."

"I know. That stinks real bad."

"You don't know me," she said. "So take this with whatever you think it warrants. But something's definitely not right here."

CHAPTER 31

Cotton said to Kelly, "I've been doing this a long time, and I've managed to stay alive by being careful, smart, and observant."

"And your point?"

"First somebody tries to kill you. Then you're kidnapped by agents of the Japanese government. You seem overly popular today. And not for a good reason."

"What can I say? I always was the life of the party."

"This is not a joking matter. Far from it, in fact."

"Why'd you quit the government? You're a little young to be retired."

She was pivoting. Okay. He'd bite. "I was shot in Mexico City. Not the first time. But I wanted it to be the last. So I got out."

"Is that when you divorced?"

He nodded. "Quit my job, ended my marriage, moved to Denmark, and became a bookseller."

"Damn, Harold, you burned all the bridges."

"Not irrevocably. You see, while I was screwing around with you and all those other women, being a first-class fool, my wife had an affair of her own that resulted in a child being born. A boy, that she led me to believe for years was *my* son. He's seventeen now. Both he and I learned the truth not all that long ago."

"That had to have been tough," she said.

"More than you can imagine. So payback is hell."

"I know that, too, from firsthand experience."

"Thankfully," he said, "my family worked our differences out."

"And the boy?"

"He's *my* son. In all the ways that matter."

And he meant every word.

"Sounds like that selfish, cocky navy lieutenant grew up and became a man."

"He did. And now here I am, standing in a Swiss grocery store, looking at a part of my past that doesn't look anything like what I remember, who's gotten herself into a world of serious trouble."

"Comes from being the smartest person in the room."

"That arrogance will get you killed."

"Is the new and improved Harold Malone always so blunt?"

"It's the truth."

They had not, as yet, called Koger. He was waiting until he had a better handle on what was going on. There was definitely more to this than anyone wanted to say. How to find out more? That could prove difficult. He was no longer an active field officer with a high-level clearance. He was merely a guy doing another guy a favor. Throughout his career at the Magellan Billet he'd never been one to overburden Stephanie Nelle with minutiae. Some agents loved to constantly report anything and everything. Not him. He was a big-picture guy and worked best when he worked without inter-ference. Stephanie ran the Billet with an iron fist, but she also was smart enough to allow her people the freedom to do their jobs. Never a micromanager. More an I've-got-your-back-when-things-go-to-hell-so-get-it-done style.

Which he liked.

Koger?

He was a help-me-out-while-I-keep-you-in-the-dark kind of guy.

He glanced at his watch. It was getting late in the day. "We need to lay low. And food would be good. Then we both will speak with Koger."

"You're irritated with me."

"More irritated at myself for getting in the middle of this circus in the first place."

"I changed the world, Harold. I invented something that has altered the way people use money. It's turned into something magnificent. Beautiful. But it's about to be misused by a woman who wants to control the economies of countries around the world. She's going to mangle and manipulate what should be sacrosanct. People will be affected. Nations will be affected. And all so she can have power and profit. She was my friend, but I don't think I ever really knew her. She can't be allowed to succeed. I thought I was doing the right thing by going to the CIA. Koger said he would help. But now I'm not so sure."

Finally, a little truth. And some new information.

Mangle and manipulate?

"It looks like all I've got is you," she said.

"That isn't much."

"Don't sell yourself short, sailor."

He smiled. Her confidence had always been infectious.

"I'll do what I can," he told her.

"That's good enough for me."

CASSIOPEIA FOLLOWED KOGER OUTSIDE AND THEY WALKED TOWARD the lake, away from the house. Nighttime had arrived. Citrone was somewhere inside. They needed privacy.

"Tell me what you're thinking," he said to her, his voice low as they walked.

"We saw Citrone on the boat with two men, one armed. But were they there to take him? Or protect him? Or were they all working together? I just met the man, but he strikes me as a true opportunist. His house is like a museum. He likes rare, expensive things, some of which are really odd. Perhaps he saw an opportunity with the Japanese? They want the map. He certainly knows a lot about that gold. Information they need. He has the map secreted away. Sounds like the perfect scenario for a deal."

"And what does Citrone get out of it?"

"Money. Probably a lot of it. With his lifestyle, I assume he needs it."

"And the house being trashed was for my benefit?" Koger asked. "Did he know we were coming?"

He nodded. "I spoke with him earlier, while you were inside the wine vault. I told him that if there was no gold, we were coming to see him." Koger paused a moment. "So he prepared a little show for us?"

"I noticed that nothing was broken, or ripped, or destroyed," she said. "As if it had all been carefully laid down to look like a search."

She saw that Koger was connecting the dots too.

"You don't think the PSIA is involved?" he asked.

"I think the whole thing was designed to make us think they are involved."

"The two on the boat did respond quickly when I showed the tube," he said. "Damn. He knew exactly what I would do."

"When I climbed onto that boat, in the instant before I took those guys out, I locked eyes with Citrone. There wasn't a shred of fear or gratitude."

Koger ran a hand through his hair and sharply exhaled. "You a hunter?"

She shook her head. "Never."

"Me neither. Not now anyway. Years ago? Different story. I was huntin' once in Appalachia and watched as two bucks got into it over a doe. A chocolate-horn lowered his head and crashed into the antlers of a rival so hard it sounded like a board cracked in half. The white-racked buck was thrown back, his hooves scrabbling over snow-covered oak leaves. But, being a buck, he dug his hind feet in and pushed back. For nearly ten minutes those two bucks mashed antlers. Twice they stood in a stalemate, their flanks exposed, heaving. That's when it occurred to me that I could send some hot lead into one of 'em. Or both. Easy kills. But it didn't seem right. So I stood there and watched."

It seemed to her the memory was a good one.

"The white-racked was definitely stronger, but each time he'd shove, the chocolate-horn would slide his back legs into the ground and hold. Finally, he drove hard, twisted his head, and flipped the white-racked on its side. Then he plunged his tines into the exposed ribs. Amazingly, the white-racked popped to his feet and fled. The chocolate-horn then chased him out of sight."

She wondered about the point of the story.

"Here's the thing about that fight. The doe, the whole reason for the encounter, just stood off to the side and watched. Then she slipped into the brush. A smaller buck, who'd watched the whole thing too, followed her. Chocolate-horn got nothin' for his trouble."

Now she got the point.

"Am I being played too?" he asked her.

"There's one way to find out."

CHAPTER 32

CATHERINE UNDRESSED AND SLIPPED ON HER NIGHTCLOTHES. THE evening had been a resounding success. Mexico seemed slated to become the next government to fully adopt bitcoin as both their reserve and the national currency. One by one they were bringing country after country into the fold. All the planning and hard work was paying off. It helped that the nations that had already made the move universally applauded their choice. The media coverage had been exemplary. All of the respective economies were prospering, no longer tied to the dollar or the euro or dependent on others for the value of their own money. Instead, they now determined their own destinies.

Or so they thought.

The Mexican finance minister was back in Luxembourg City, safely ensconced in a five-star hotel suite paid for by the bank. Normally he would have stayed at the Mexican consulate. But this trip was off the books, unofficial, part of a previously scheduled European vacation. As was the fifty bitcoin that had been quietly transferred to an e-wallet under the minister's control. All part of the miscellaneous "expenses" incurred by the bank to ensure that the Mexican congress made the right decision. For that to happen it was imperative that the finance minister be on board.

Sadly, few people in this world acted without either provocation or consideration. Either one worked for her. Some violence had been necessary within Mexico to persuade a few of the more stubborn representatives, but bribery had proven far more effective. Well-placed payments had added grease to the rails and guaranteed no sudden curiosities. Thankfully, that had only been required with a handful of key delegates since, as she'd come to learn, the more joints a pipe contained the greater the chance of a leak.

She found her silk bathrobe and slipped it on, tying the sash around her waist. The clock beside her bed read 10:20 P.M. Though late she was still alert, her mind stirring with scene after scene from the past few hours.

The house was quiet, only a handful of overnight staff on duty, cleaning up from dinner and closing things down for the day. She opened the bedroom door and walked down the wide hall to a staircase that led up to a private wing on the third floor. At the top she navigated another short hall and lightly rapped on a plain wooden door. She did not wait to be invited inside and turned the knob. The bedroom beyond had been specially created for its occupant. Soft colors. Hardwood floors. A low-sitting poster bed, dresser, and armoire, along with two rocking chairs. All of it crafted by a Dutch carpenter to the delight of the room's occupant.

Madeleine Gledhill sat in one of the rocking chairs, a blanket draped across her lap, before a stone hearth with a crackling fire. Her mother slept little. Maybe three or four hours a night, a trait she'd passed down to her only child. They both agreed with Margaret Thatcher. *Sleep is for wimps.*

"Is it over?" her mother asked in Luxembourgish.

She sat in the other rocker atop a crocheted cushion depicting the Cross of St. George. "We have Mexico."

The old woman rocked, the chair squeaking from each pitch like a clock in perfect rhythm. They'd just celebrated her ninety-fourth birthday with a Belgian chocolate cake, the layers thin, like she liked it, sweet crystallized icing in between, a single candle on top. Her mother had lived a long life, surviving her father by over thirty years. And though by the time of his death alcohol had dulled his senses to the point of uselessness, her mother's had always remained laser-focused. The old saying *Behind every great man is a woman* seemed the precise definition of cliché, but in this case the idiom was correct. Her father had a laughing, unfocused, doubting approach to life. Her mother had been the mirror opposite. An intelligent listener who absorbed details, cataloged them in proper order of importance, then made swift, smart decisions unaffected by emotion. Thankfully, though blessed with a noble and prepossessing countenance, her father had allowed her mother to develop most of the ideas he ultimately proposed.

"But, Maddy," she said, "there is a problem."

Though in her mind she thought of her as Mother, she rarely called her anything other than Maddy. She'd started the moniker as a child, maintained it all her life, and never once had her mother asked her to stop.

The older woman continued to rock as Catherine explained all that had happened during the day, leaving out no detail. Never had she misled, held back from, or lied to her mother. All three would be counter-productive. Good decisions were always made with good information. Her mother sat in the chair with perfect posture, taught to her long ago at a British finishing school. Catherine mimicked the same pose, learned at the same school decades later.

For the first time her mother's head turned from the fire and stared at her. The once striking face had aged and the features now held a vague hint of melancholy. But the eyes remained undimmed, hard points of crystal buried in sockets sunken and masked in shadow.

"This cannot be allowed to fester," the older woman said.

"I have Kyra on the way to Switzerland, as we speak. She has people there looking for Kelly."

"And the Japanese? Any previous indication they were nearby and attentive to the bank?"

She shook her head. "Nothing."

The rocking stopped.

The room went silent, except for the crackling embers.

She knew better than to interrupt those thoughts.

Her mother's maiden name was Flanagan, born in County Clare on Ireland's west coast. She obtained a degree from Trinity College in Dublin, then another from the London School of Economics, on her way to a career in high finance until she met a young apprentice at the Bank of St. George, Rowan Gledhill. They married and birthed a daughter. Then her mother did what many women of that time chose, devoting herself to her family, abandoning her personal ambitions.

But that did not mean she went silent.

Instead, she worked through her husband, providing him with courage and self-respect, both of which he lacked. It helped that he desperately wanted to prove himself to his own father, who'd risen to be first consul. Eventually, longevity and nepotism earned him a seat at the consul table, but it had been her mother who'd helped her father keep it. She possessed a brilliant mind and was well read. Together, they'd been quite formidable. Behind his cultivated wit and charm had been an insecure and weak-willed man, seemingly content in living secretly within his wife's shadow. And when her father's liver finally succumbed, it was the only time Catherine ever saw her mother cry.

But she'd often wondered.

Were the tears for him, or for Maddy herself?

Catherine's rise within the bank had been thanks to a combination of her own innate abilities, along with her mother's natural cunning. Maddy was a devoted Presbyterian, and religion had always been important. But economics was her passion. Catherine had sat here many a night listening and learning. Her mother had played a major role in formulating the Atlas Maneuver, her genius all over it. She'd always seemed larger than life, carved rather than molded, her face that of a woman who'd suffered but had not been defeated.

Her real gift?

An ability to place things in their proper perspective.

As she'd done, right here, one late night many years ago.

Money was invented twenty-five hundred years ago.

All sorts of things, at one time or another, acted as legal tender in a variety of cultures. Salt, tobacco, dried fish, rice, cloth, almonds, corn, barley, coconuts, tea, butter, reindeer, sheep, oxen, cacao seeds, animal skins, even whale's teeth. Eventually, metals became popular. Copper rings, strips of flattened iron, brass rods. Why? They lasted longer, could be easily divided, and had the enviable trait of retaining their intrinsic value. Perishable goods could be swapped for hard metal, which could then be used to buy other goods.

The Roman Empire brought coins to the forefront. But after the empire split in the 4th century into East and West, Rome's mint closed. When Rome was sacked for the second time in 426 its economy, then a little over a thousand years old, collapsed. From that point, until the Renaissance began in 1350, money played only a minor role in society. People retreated into a rural economy, based on feudalism. Coins existed, but they were of little value. Trade was governed by the barter system.

In the 14th century something new emerged.

Prosperous men would travel to the many markets and fairs where they traded goods, made loans, and accepted payments. They acquired a name from the benches they used. Banco. Which eventually morphed into bank. This practice started in northern Italy and, over the next hundred years, spread rapidly. These men did not deal in coins, though, which were heavy, hard to transport, and easily stolen or counterfeited. Instead, they traded in bills of exchange, a written promise that ordered the payment of a certain amount of designated coin to a certain person at a certain time and location. Similar to a modern-day check. These bills were easily transported and, if stolen, useless, as they could only be redeemed by the individual specified in the bill.

Then something new appeared.

Huge amounts of gold and silver from the New World, thanks to Columbus' discovery, flooded into Europe. The quantity of goods could not keep pace with all the new wealth, so prices rose, which ate away at the value of all that gold and silver. Western civilization for the first time experienced inflation, where the value of wealth depreciated. By then gold and silver coins had totally replaced bills of exchange.

Everything changed again, though, in the 18th century.

The American Revolution was the first war financed by paper money. And as long as that paper was supported by gold or silver it remained desired and people believed in it. By the turn of the 20th century gold was the ultimate value behind nearly all of the world's currencies.

And for good reason.

It was hard to acquire, did not rot, rust, or deteriorate, and was continuously recycled, generation after generation. For a nation to create more money, or borrow money, it had to have more gold. The two were linked together. The gold standard united the world, doing what no conqueror or religion ever could. But all that collapsed during World War I, when nations came off the gold standard so that they could issue more paper money, unbacked by gold, to finance the fight. After the war none of those governments wanted to return to the gold standard. They liked the power they'd acquired over their own economies. New social systems had also emerged. Communism and national socialism particularly, which both echoed absolute control over financial systems. Money was no longer issued in accordance with gold reserves. New money came into being whenever the government wanted. The United States came partially off gold in 1933, then completely in 1971.

Other nations did the same.

And money became merely fiat. Government-issued currency unbacked by any physical commodity like gold or silver, its value derived solely from the relationship between supply and demand and the stability of the issuing government. By the turn of the 21st century over two hundred national currencies existed around the world, each one controlled by their governments and backed by nothing more than faith. A gold-based currency had been limited *by the amount of gold in the world, which constantly fluctuated. But with fiat money governments could print as much money as they liked. Literally generating wealth out of thin air.*

But printing more money came with consequences.

Each time it was done, the value of the money that already existed diminished. Which simply forced the printing of more money, which drove down the value even further.

A vicious cycle that continued to this day.

And would eventually render all money worthless.

Her mother had been right.

Money was merely a tool that could be manipulated.

The trick was in knowing how.

"Katie, an economy is not a single, monolithic creature," her mother said. "Contrary to what governments want you to believe, there is no central decision-making mechanism, no single state of being. Analysts talk about an economy being in good or bad shape. They use terms like bull *and* bear *for stock markets. Academics refer to the desired state of an economy as being in equilibrium. But those are poor ways to think, because, as I said, an economy is not one single thing.*

"Instead, an economy is far more like an ant colony, where thousands of insects act both independently, yet collectively, at the same time. Economic activity involves hundreds of millions of independent actions made each day by businesses, governments, people. It's an aggregate. And the amazing thing is that it's never the same from one minute to the next. Constant change. Constant evolution. Constant problems. Understanding this is key to understanding everything."

She recalled every word her mother had said next, as it had been vital to what they had in mind for the world.

"There are three critical, decision-making principles you must never forget. The first is that no economic decision is made in

a vacuum. What happens in the world will, without question, shape and influence every economic decision. The second is that the past informs the present. History matters. Every human choice is influenced by the past, and those choices directly influence economies. And finally, never forget that fear and uncertainty always, and I mean always, hinder good decision making. Especially when that fear morphs into anger."

"You're angry," her mother said. "I can see it."

"I'm furious. Kelly was my friend. It was her idea that governments could use bitcoin as their reserve currency. She planted that thought in my head. We did all this together, then she betrayed me."

"You should be angry. But not at her. At yourself. *Betrayal oozes out at every pore.* Freud was right, and you missed the signs."

The words stabbed her, like a knife.

She had missed the signs.

Totally.

"Do you think the Japanese know anything about Atlas?" her mother asked.

"I have no idea. You would think, if they did, it would have been mentioned."

But not a word.

"You must assume that they do," her mother said. "And the CIA breaching the Geneva vault today? That cannot be coincidence. Something is happening, and it's coming toward you from different directions."

She agreed and smothered the countless questions forming in her mind, wanting to shift ground and find a safer level of conversation, but her mother's calculating emotions, though old, were not deadened.

She knew what was coming.

"Correct your error," her mother said, the eyes staring at her icy blue, cold, and confident. "Freud was right about something else too. *The goal of all life is death.*"

Her mother had been the one who encouraged the hiring of

Kyra Lhota. But that had been about acquiring bitcoin. This was now a matter of survival.

For them all.

"I have to get back those private keys," she said.

"Why would she return them to you? If she planned to do that she would have never secured them."

She disagreed. "You taught me long ago. *Find what your adversary wants most of all, acquire it, then bargain it away.*"

Her mother started rocking again, the unfathomable eyes turning away. "You know what Kelly Austin wants most of all?"

"I do."

And she explained it all to her mother.

CHAPTER 33

Aiko sat in the second floor office at the consulate, no lights on, waiting for dawn, her mind draining away yesterday's unsatisfying events.

She'd groped for sleep all night but only found a welter of disturbing thoughts. She'd come a long way from a junior PSIA investigator after a murderous cult. Now she was working directly for the imperial family on a mission that stretched back to the last great war, an opportunity that few, if any, in Japan were ever afforded. Two years ago she knew little to nothing about Golden Lily. But she'd been granted unprecedented access to information and documents that had long been held in secret. Unfortunately, none of the actual participants remained alive. Only their stories had survived. Some true. Others false. The rest a combination of the two extremes. It was important that she deliver on what the emperor emeritus wanted. Not only for the gratitude of the imperial family, but for herself. The rewards would be immeasurable. And not monetary. More abstract.

Giri.

That sense of duty, honor, obligation, justice, courtesy, and gratitude. A concept hard for Westerners to accept. But a person flush with *Giri* could always be relied upon.

Like her father.

He enlisted in the Imperial Japanese Army at age eighteen. In December 1944 he was sent to the Philippines to destroy an enemy airstrip and ordered not to surrender, under any circumstances. Unfortunately, all but her father and three other soldiers died during the operation. The four survivors fled to the hills and kept fighting, even after the war ended in 1945. Leaflets were repeatedly dropped from the sky informing them, and other Japanese holdouts, that the war was over. One, printed with a message from General Tomoyuki Yamashita of the Fourteenth Area Army, ordered them all to surrender. Most did. But her father, and his three compatriots, were not persuaded, thinking it all a trick.

Seven years they kept up a terrorist campaign.

In 1952 letters and family pictures were dropped from planes urging them to surrender, but the four warriors again concluded that was another trick. One of them was killed during a shoot-out with local fishermen in 1953. Another died in 1954 from a shot fired by a search party. A third died in 1972 from two rounds delivered by local police.

Which left her father as the last man standing.

Then fate intervened.

In 1974, her father, by then forty-eight, met a Japanese national who'd come to the Philippines and ventured up into the mountains looking for him. They became friends but her father still refused to surrender, saying that he was waiting for orders from his immediate superior. The man returned to Japan and found her father's former commanding officer, who traveled back to Lubang Island and fulfilled a promise he'd made in 1944 that *whatever happens, we'll come back for you.*

And her father finally surrendered, overflowing with *Giri*.

He returned to Japan and reunited with his wife. Aiko was born a year later. The Japanese government offered him a huge amount in back pay, which he refused.

More of that *Giri*.

He lived forty more years, always unhappy with receiving any

175

attention and troubled by what he saw as the withering of traditional Japanese values.

You are the daughter of a great warrior. Who served faithfully, with honor and dignity. We met your father once and told him how proud we were for what he'd done.

The emperor emeritus' own words. To her. Just yesterday.

That legacy was now hers.

And she'd failed. Losing Kelly Austin.

A fact that she'd not reported, as yet.

A soft rap came to the office door. One of her men entered and stepped to the desk, stopping in front.

"Forgive the interruption, but we have located the cell phone."

They'd already determined that the dead intruder from yesterday was hired help who had worked for the CIA before. Then there was the matter of her missing man, the one who'd been charged with obtaining and delivering the van to the consulate. He had to be located. So they'd searched for his phone.

"Where is it?"

Her subordinate showed her a cell phone screen with a map of northwestern Switzerland, along with a flashing blue dot.

She stood. "Let us go and see where that leads."

Kyra had made excellent time.

A fifteen-hour flight from Mongolia, aided by the seven-hour time difference, had placed her on the ground in Basel by dawn. She'd slept on the plane, eaten two meals, showered, and changed clothes, her toned legs now clad in tight jeans tucked into high leather boots beneath a black sweater. She'd also received three reports from Switzerland and one from Luxembourg on Kelly Austin. So far the elusive computer scientist was still among the missing. She'd not returned to her hotel and one of the people she'd hired to make a search reported a street shooting yesterday.

Was it related to Austin? Hard to say as the details were sketchy. But apparently no one had been hurt, which was encouraging. The entrance of the Japanese had definitely added a new dimension. To what extent? Another unknown. But she'd ordered her people to monitor the consulate in Basel for activity. Nothing had happened there so far.

"It is imperative that Kelly be found," Catherine Gledhill told her during an in-flight call. *"The situation is critical and I need her secured somewhere, isolated, away from anyone and every-one. But under no circumstances harm her. Is that clear?"*

She'd provided the correct response.

A car had been waiting at the Basel airport inside the charter company's hangar. She'd driven herself into town, traffic light in the early-morning hours, deciding to head for the consulate, as it seemed the only tangible lead. No doubt existed that, at some point, Kelly Austin was going to die. Betrayal often commanded that price. For now, though, Austin was to be found and held alive, unharmed.

She operated her business on a select few rules. No emotional involvement. No targets under the age of eighteen. No pregnant women, though once the child was born they were fair game. No remorse. Not ever. It was just a job, like everybody else had. And, above all, always give the client what they want.

So her course was clear.

Especially considering the bonus of another seventeen million euros in bitcoin.

She entered Basel's diplomatic district, the quiet, tree-shaded neighborhood speaking of power and dignity. Her acolyte, some-one she'd used before, was stationed half a kilometer away from the Japanese consulate in an empty parking lot, out of sight and camera range, but with a view of the gated entrance. She eased up alongside the vehicle and lowered her window. The man in the other car did the same.

"A car just left," he said. "Mercedes coupe. One occupant. Female."

"Who?"

"Aiko Ejima. She's known around here as the local head of the PSIA. I sent one of ours to follow."

She needed to keep on the move.

And that PSIA woman intrigued her.

"Find out their location," she ordered. "Send me the information. I want to head that way too."

CHAPTER 34

COTTON HAD TAKEN HIS USUAL NAVY SHOWER, JUST LIKE HE HAD for the past forty years. His father, a full commander and submariner, taught him.

"It's pounded into your head from day one at boot camp. Turn the water on. Wet down. Water off. Soap up. Scrub down. Water back on. Rinse off. Water off. Towel-dry. The whole thing takes about three minutes. No reason to take any more time, since it's really only about getting the stink off."

But it was also about saving resources, since fresh water was one of the most valuable assets on a bluewater vessel. Cotton had been bathing like this since he was seven, a way for a young boy to connect with a father he idolized. After his father disappeared at sea when he was ten he kept up the habit as a tribute. Once he too joined the navy he continued as a matter of practice and procedure. To this day he still felt guilty if he let the water run for more than three minutes.

He was clean, but could not shave. No razor. He stared into the mirror, hair tousled, a day's growth of stubble sprouting from his jaw, more than a few of the whiskers a disturbing gray. He didn't feel nearly fifty, but was starting to look it. Not the body, though—he'd always kept himself in reasonably good shape. Not the hair, either. Still full and tawny, with only an accent of gray at the temples. But the neck. Yes. That was it. The skin there a little loose and thin. And around the eyes. When had the wrinkles invaded? Not a lot of them. But enough.

He and Suzy had left the van, without its markings, parked in the supermarket lot and managed to snag a ride with a local to a small *gasthaus* farther into the Swiss countryside. A first for him, actually. Hitchhiking. But it had been necessary. No Ubers, taxis, or anything traceable could have been used.

He'd let two rooms for the night, Suzy next door in the weathered-wood building. Luckily, he had enough cash on him to cover the costs. The front desk, for a few more euros, had managed to provide some toothpaste and a couple of brushes, which had been welcomed. A change of clothes would be great, but that wasn't possible. It felt like the old days as a field officer, working for days, sometime weeks, the necessities of everyday life taking a back seat. Getting the job done was all that mattered. Results. Wins. That's what made the difference. And he'd been a winner. Sure, he made mistakes. Who hadn't? But he always recovered, and rarely had he outright failed.

He wasn't going to start now.

His cell phone vibrated. The guy at the front desk had also allowed them to use his charger. He answered the call.

"You having fun?" Cassiopeia asked him.

"It's definitely more than I bargained for."

"And that's something new?"

He smiled. "Each time still amazes me, though."

"We've got a mess here too," she said. "You want to tell me why we are still in this? What's really going on here?"

He needed to tell her everything. No. He wanted to tell her everything. There was a time when they jousted, dodging around the truth, holding back far more than they ever revealed. That song and dance eventually led to a breakup, which they'd both taken badly. Luckily, they came to recognize that they needed each other. More than either one of them wanted to admit. So they made a pact. No more secrets.

"You're right," he said. "There's something you need to know."

CASSIOPEIA LISTENED AS COTTON EXPLAINED ABOUT THE WOMAN Koger had sent him to watch.

Kelly Austin aka Suzy Baldwin.

From the past.

She'd not seen that one coming and didn't know how to handle the information. Jealousy was not her thing, and Cotton had never given her any reason to doubt. He'd told her about his youth and the mistakes, and all about an encounter with another woman from his past that happened recently in Poland. Like there, this was not a scenario that warranted irrational emotions. It seemed that Kelly Austin had managed to dig herself a deep hole. Clearly, her life was on the line. And something big was unfolding. Koger needed Austin, and Austin needed Cotton. But she had to say, "I know we never talk about feelings. But you have to be experiencing something."

"I am. Mainly shame and confusion. Neither of which is helpful here. I was young and stupid when I knew Suzy Baldwin. I ended it. And never made that mistake again. I also became someone else. Someone better. Or at least I like to think so."

She heard cracking in his voice. Rare. But she appreciated the fact that he felt close enough to share what was going on in his head.

That was a tough thing for them both.

"I never knew that Cotton Malone," she said. "And I'm glad. I would not have liked him. But I love you. So do your job and take good care of her. Koger says she's important."

"Apparently so. I need to talk to him."

"I'll tell him to call you. But we have our own mess here to deal with."

"I look forward to a report."

"Same with me from you."

"Oh," he said. "I love you too."

KELLY SAT ON THE EDGE OF THE BED. SHE'D MANAGED ONLY A FEW hours of sleep. One thought kept racing through her mind.

Who tried to kill her yesterday?

It definitely wasn't the bank.

No way. And not the Japanese. They'd made their play afterward and wanted her alive. That left the only likely suspect. The CIA. But why? She'd come to them. Told them things they had no idea existed. Offered them everything. So why kill her? Probably because they'd decided to expunge the situation rather than exploit it. The gold was gone. Bitcoin was beyond their reach. So just get rid of it all, along with all the key players. She'd badly miscalculated on the CIA, thinking they were on the same page as her. Clearly, they were not.

And the Japanese?

They just made a bad situation worse.

Time to cut her losses.

Cotton had left, saying he was going back to the van. He'd managed to get her wallet, passport, and cell phone from the café after she was abducted but, in all the confusion yesterday, her passport had slipped from his pocket. It could be in the van so he'd gone to check and get them some breakfast. Fifty euros had obtained him the use of the *gasthaus* maintenance man's car for a couple of hours. Cotton had removed the battery and disabled her cell phone as a precaution. So she gave the same guy fifty more euros from her wallet in return for the use of his cell phone.

And he'd obliged.

She tapped in the number. One she'd called many times. Two rings and it was answered by Catherine Gledhill.

"Katie," she said. "It's Kelly."

"I was told the Japanese had you."

"They did, but I managed to escape."

"Let me come get you."

"That's not possible."

"Why are you doing this?"

"Because I don't agree with what you're doing."

"It was your idea."

"No, that's a lie. I wanted to help countries off the gold and dollar standard. Not provide you with a way to manipulate their economies. You've lost all sense of right and wrong."

"Come back, and we can discuss it. Work something out."

"We're beyond that. Somebody tried to kill me yesterday."

"It wasn't me," Katie said.

And she heard the shock in her voice.

"I know. It was the CIA. They're going to purge us all. You included."

"I can take care of myself. When did this bout of conscience come over you?"

"*From the least to the greatest of them, everyone is greedy for unjust gain, and from prophet to priest everyone deals falsely.* Jeremiah 6:13. Then there is *A faithful man will abound with blessings, but he who makes haste to be rich will not go unpunished.* Proverbs 28:20."

"I never knew you were religious."

"I'm not. But sometimes the Bible can be instructive. What I am is an American. Loyal and true. Years ago, I did everything that was asked of me. We all did. And we created something marvelous. Now you're going to weaponize that into something monstrous."

"Does your newfound conscience also include returning the millions of euros you've been paid?"

"I consider that compensation for my services, and the risks I'm taking right now."

"Amazing how you rationalize your own participation, but condemn the rest of us. Like I said, this whole thing was your idea."

"I never intended anything like you're planning. I believed in the revolution bitcoin could create in the world, taking central banks out of the mix. I wanted people to be independent and free with their money and investments."

"Bitcoin can still do all that. And more."

"It's the *more* I have a problem with. Look, Katie. We were friends. Close ones. I cherished that. I still do. So I called to tell you that you have a spy in the bank. When I was with the Japanese I learned they know all about the Atlas Maneuver."

Catherine was stunned.

Secrecy was vital to success. The full extent of the bank's reach in bitcoin must remain limited to a precious few. All of who stood to greatly profit from the venture.

"You told them?" she asked.

"They already knew. Like I said, they have a spy on the inside."

For some strange reason she believed what she was hearing. "Tell me about the Japanese."

"Her name is Aiko Ejima. She's PSIA at the Basel consulate, and is remarkably well informed about your business."

Which might explain how those two cars located her yesterday on the highway north from Luxembourg City.

"She also knew I'm Nakamoto and that I now control the bank's bitcoin private keys," Kelly said. "How is that possible?"

An excellent question. "Kelly, I need you to listen to me. What you've done is bad. You've hurt me beyond measure. But I'm not your enemy and I certainly brought no harm to you. If your life is in danger, let me help. Come back and we'll work this out. I can offer you full protection."

"Will you stop the Atlas Maneuver?"

"I can't do that."

"Katie, you have more money than you could ever possibly spend. You have power. Prestige. A glowing reputation in the financial community. Leave the world alone."

"It's far too late for any semblance of morality," she made clear. "And I'm doing nothing more than offering nations a choice. A way to free themselves from American and Chinese monetary influence. They don't have to take what I'm offering."

"But they will. It's too enticing. They just don't know that they've traded one problem for another."

A fear pulsated through her. She realized that Kelly could use the private keys as a bargaining chip with the CIA. They'd surely make a deal for that kind of control.

Yet Kelly had called her. Why?

"What do you want?" she asked. "What can I give you?"

"Sadly, Katie, you have nothing that I want."

The world would be a different place if everybody thought alike. If people spontaneously conformed to other people's every wish, every thought, every feeling. But life did not work that way.

Which was why negotiating came to be.

She'd learned five things over the years that made all the difference in deal making. First, establish a relationship, get a feel for the other side. Be open. Sincere. And, most important, believed. Second, focus on the win-win. Never think only of yourself. Know what the other side wants and try to give it to them. Third, embody your inner adult. Never, ever think childishly. Be the stable adult at the table. Don't argue. Instead, understand. Fourth, respect the rhythm of the relationship. Don't force things. Allow them to flow naturally so the other side has time to reflect and consider. And finally, always choose honey over vinegar. But the honey must be genuine. Real. Desired.

Never just create an agreement.

Instead, cultivate a long-term relationship where the other side wants to willingly make a deal.

This was perhaps the most critical negotiation she'd ever faced.

Everything was on the line.

You have nothing I want.

Time for that honey.

"You're wrong, Kelly. I have what you want most in this world."

CHAPTER 35

CASSIOPEIA REPLAYED THE CONVERSATION WITH COTTON IN HER HEAD. She understood his dilemma and reservations. Confronting your past was tough. She herself had come face-to-face with a man from her own a while back in Denmark. That had ended badly and nearly cost her entire relationship with Cotton. So who was she to judge? Cotton was a big boy and he'd deal with the situation, and she had to trust him to handle it. She realized this was not about an old lover resurfacing. That was way too simple. Instead, this was about mistakes and memories.

And Gary Malone.

Cotton's wife had dealt him a blow there. Deep. Hard. Painful. Becoming pregnant by another man, telling no one, and allowing Cotton to raise the boy thinking him his own. That took a huge amount of callous resentment. Pam had only revealed the truth, in anger, as the marriage dissolved, to hurt him, fifteen years after the boy was born. Luckily, Gary had grown into a fine young man, handling all of the revelations in a mature manner. He and Cotton enjoyed a great relationship. They were close. The boy was even talking about following his father and grandfather into the navy. But they were still a year or so away from that decision. How Pam Malone held that truth in for so long was hard to understand.

Anger for Cassiopeia had always been open and immediate, with no hesitation. Long ago she had learned that nothing good ever came from keeping volatile emotions inside. They were like a cancer that affected everything.

Excise and heal. That was what worked.

At least she now knew why they were still in this fight.

She and Koger had stayed at Citrone's house for the night, taking turns keeping watch. Interestingly, their host slept soundly in his room, deep snoring signaling not a care in the world. Which added more suspicion to their already growing list. She'd showered and even washed her hair, now ready for the day. The staff were arriving, shocked by the state of the house. Some had started cleaning up, while the kitchen crew prepared a light breakfast of bread, cheese, juice, and coffee, which she and Koger enjoyed.

"Interesting that none of these people were here yesterday," she said to Koger.

"Especially considering that I doubt Citrone even wipes his own ass."

Their host appeared, dressed in chest-high rubber waders over jeans and a plaid shirt. His head was topped by a black felt hat with a broad flat brim, wrapped by a white headband into which were hooked a few salmon flies.

"Are we goin' fishing?" Koger asked.

"I thought we might," the big man said.

Citrone sat at the dining room table and ate while she and Koger, cups of coffee in hand, retreated outside. Air pressure was dropping, the skies fading to a nasty shade of gray. Wind clubbed at the trees. Rain squalls were coming, promising a stiff blow across the water.

"Fishing?" she asked.

Koger shrugged. "He does like it. But I suspect there's more to it."

"And, by the way, neither one of you fully explained Operation Neverlight," she pointed out.

"It's pretty simple, really. They clean and whitewash. Not a speck of anything to find is to be left behind. It's supposedly why

I was dealing with Kelly Austin. Bringing her in. Securing what she knows."

"Then somebody tried to kill her."

"They used me to set her up. You just can't get all the rot out of a bad tooth. There are people at Langley that still think killing is the way to go. I made some calls last night. They're not backing down from Neverlight."

Which alarmed her. "Does Cotton know?"

Koger nodded. "I called and told him. But he says he has Austin tucked away safe and sound. Here's the rub. The agency doesn't want anything about that gold to ever come to light, but they also wouldn't mind gettin' it back. And apparently, they don't care how. So they sent me to do one thing, then others to do another."

"Why is Kelly Austin so important?"

"She holds the key to everything. I've been instructed to stand down, but I don't follow orders all that good."

"That's what Cotton said too."

"Something is dead up the creek and I intend to find out where the smell is coming from. I'm sure my superiors know me well enough to know that I'm not walkin' away."

"Which now makes you a target."

Koger pointed. "No. It makes *us* a target."

An excellent observation.

"Sir Rob is a resourceful guy," Koger said. "A seasoned professional who is, at the moment, a few steps ahead of us. But he thinks we're idiots. Okay, let's act like idiots and see where he leads."

Cotton had left Suzy at the *gasthaus*, telling her to stay in the room out of sight. No one knew where she was. Her cell phone was disabled and his, a Magellan Billet–issued unit, was untrackable. He'd somehow lost her passport in all the chaos yesterday. It was probably in the van and, since he hadn't checked the vehicle out, a quick look seemed in order.

Finally, last night, before they'd both gone to sleep in their separate rooms, Suzy had opened up.

"The CIA and the bank created bitcoin in 2009 for good reason. It made sense to be ready, just in case the world collapsed. After the crisis passed the CIA lost interest in bitcoin. Typical. They have the attention span of a three-year-old. I don't think they ever saw the potential. But the bank kept going, morphing bitcoin into the phenomenon it is today. One coin is worth, what, fifty grand? Pretty damn good for something that is nothing more than a blip on a computer program. Now the bank is poised to use bitcoin to gain control of a sizable portion of the world's financial systems."

"I want to hear that part."

"More and more countries are adopting bitcoin as their currency and reserve," she said. *"Which was my idea. I thought it a good thing. Why not? The world was ready for a change in value. What the world doesn't know is that the Bank of St. George can control the value of bitcoin. They can make it go up or down, at will. Bitcoiners love to say how they're free of governmental regulation and have total anonymity and independence. They do. But both of those traits also make it easy to manipulate."*

"How is that possible? There are twenty million bitcoin out there."

"It's actually quite simple. About fifteen percent of those twenty million are gone. Meaning their owners lost the digital keys. Once gone, those coins are no longer in play. They can't be retrieved without the key. That leaves about fifteen and a half million active coins. At present, the Bank of St. George owns four and a half million of those. That's nearly a third of the whole pot. Of course, no one knows that since ownership is completely anonymous. Bitcoin pricing is governed by the market. Buying and selling determines the daily value on each exchange. So all the bank has to do is buy and sell its own coins to itself. With every transaction the overall price of bitcoin in the various exchanges is

affected. They can send it up or down, whenever they want. The whole bitcoin market is like penguins on the edge of the ice about to leap into the water. They all bunch up and freeze, waiting for one to take the plunge. Once that happens, they all move until another hesitates, then they stop. There's little to no independent thinking. It's a collective mind that simply reacts."

He recalled reading about countries that had adopted bitcoin. Mainly in Central and South America, though several Eastern European nations were openly flirting with the possibility. According to Suzy the Bank of St. George was actively involved in lobbying those countries to make the change.

"The more nations that switch," she said, "the more influence the bank possesses. Here's an example. Venezuela is now on the bitcoin standard. Let's say one of the bank's clients wants to invest there, or buy something, and the government is not cooperating to make that happen. There are fees, commissions, and interest to be made by the bank if the transaction happens. So the bank starts buying and selling bitcoin to itself. They control thousands of online wallets, so those transactions are spread out across many different trading exchanges and would raise no alarms. Billions in buy/sells happen every day. But enough activity would affect the price, and if those buys and sells are carefully manipulated, the overall bitcoin market would react up or down, depending on the manipulation. Since the bank is buying and selling to itself, with its own money, it's losing nothing. They can buy their own coins at lower than current market, which will simply drive the market price down. Or they could do the opposite and raise it. Venezuela would be affected by any rise or drop in price. Its reserves would be affected. The bank, though, assures the Venezuelan government it can remedy the matter, which it does with more buying and selling, and a grateful government returns the favor and takes care of the bank's client. The bank, in essence, controls the Venezuelan economy, but nobody knows that."

It was clever. Damn clever, in fact.

"It's called the Atlas Maneuver," Kelly said, "because that's where it was first formulated. In the Atlas Mountains of Morocco. Katie Gledhill has an estate there. I was present, along with a handful of others, when the plan was conceived. They have already tested it several times across the globe. And it works. Every time. They're now poised to take it to the next level."

"And the Japanese know about it?"

"That's what the woman, Aiko Ejima, told me. If people know that the bank owns that many coins, Atlas collapses. The manipulation would be out in the open. It only works if no one knows."

"Why not just expose it all? Tell the world."

"That could be a problem, without proof. Remember, bitcoin ownership is anonymous. The bank would have a lot of deniability. It would simply just stop the manipulation. I'm the proof, and they want me dead."

That they did.

"Stupid me thought we are all on the same side. Big mistake. Those bastards have the loyalty of a great white shark."

Which had made him wonder.

He knew what they wanted for Suzy.

But what were they planning for the Bank of St. George and Catherine Gledhill?

CATHERINE TAPPED THE PHONE AND CONNECTED WITH KYRA. "WHERE are you?"

"South of Basel following a lead from the Japanese consulate."

"I just spoke to Kelly Austin. I need you to stand by. There may be some new instructions."

"I'll be here."

She ended the call.

Employees within the bank, when hired, were subjected to rigorous background checks, which were periodically updated. The idea was to ascertain if there was anything that could lead to blackmail or a compromise of their position. Participation was a non-negotiable condition of employment. Kelly's file contained a name change that happened years ago. A terrible car accident. Massive injuries. Multiple surgeries. A prolonged recovery. No surprises there.

But there'd also been something else.

She and Kelly were friends, and she could count on one hand the number of people ranked in that category. They'd spent time together and shared things. Catherine had spoken of her father, a little about her mother, careful with her words but grateful for the ear. Kelly had also spoken about her past and the awful experience she'd bravely rebounded from.

Brilliant and courageous.

That's how she'd many times described Kelly, who seemed invincible. Except for one weak point. Something else they'd also discussed. Along with the anguish. So she'd played that card with Kelly on the phone.

Now she waited to see.

Would it work?

CHAPTER 36

AIKO FOLLOWED THE TRACKER FOR THE VAN DRIVER'S CELL PHONE. She'd never anticipated the CIA making such a bold move with an armed intruder at a foreign consulate, or the death of one of her own, or the appearance at the consulate of Cotton Malone, who managed to retrieve Austin. The old saying she'd heard as a child rang true. *Spilled water never returns to the tray.* Yes. Mistakes had been made.

But she would rebound.

The tracker indicated that the cell phone was ahead, a few kilometers down the road. Interestingly, they were not all that far from the scene of yesterday's intersection collision where Malone absconded. She kept driving, following the signal, spotting a small shopping complex busy with cars. Among them was a white van. The same one from yesterday? Minus its markings?

One way to find out.

She motored up and parked in an empty spot, approaching the van from behind, creeping close to the passenger-side door and glancing inside.

No one there.

The rear compartment did not open into the driver's cab.

So she walked back to the rear and faced the windowless doors.

Kyra followed the car from the Japanese consulate, taking over for her man who'd started the task. She was biding her time, doing as Catherine Gledhill instructed.

Staying ready.

She watched as the car parked, then a woman exited the vehicle. Middle-aged. Dark hair. Japanese. And examined an unmarked white van. The angle gave her a good view of the face, so she snapped several pictures with her cell phone through the front windshield.

Kelly thought she had the upper hand. Control the bitcoin private keys and she controlled the bank. It had all seemed so simple. But a shadow of constraint had now enveloped her.

I have what you want most in this world.

And she'd listened in astonishment to Katie Gledhill.

"You confided in me," Katie said. *"You told me something so personal, so painful, that it affected me."*

She had indeed done just that. A few years ago. Why? At the time it seemed okay. One friend to another.

"You mentioned back then that you'd like to know the truth," Katie said. *"So I hired people to find out. I was going to surprise you, and offer the information, if you wanted it. I could sense that you wanted to know. I thought it would make you happy. Provide some peace. Then all this happened and I discovered you were not the friend I thought you were."*

"So you use it now, as a bribe? A way to get the keys back? Is that what a friend does to another friend?"

"Don't talk to me about abuses. You've put us all in a terrible position."

"Do you truly have no shame?"

"You started this, Kelly. I'm simply doing what I have to do. Now you have to decide how bad you want that information."

"If you found it, so can I."

"Don't be so sure. It wasn't easy. It took three years, and I can erase the trail as fast as it was found."

"I don't want to know."

"If that were the case then you would have already hung up," Katie said. *"After all, you hold the superior hand."*

"Then why do I feel vulnerable?"

"Blame that on the choice you made long ago."

She'd grossly underestimated her opponent. Katie Gledhill had found her soft spot. The one thing she could not ignore.

Not again.

Damn. Damn. Damn.

She redialed the number.

What had before been purely business had just turned deeply personal.

CATHERINE SAT IN HER DINING ROOM, HER HAIR TIED BACK WITH A silver scarf that matched the one at her neck. Her business suit was dove gray, tailored, elegant, from a Parisian couturier. Fine clothes were, to her, tools. The right ensemble, chosen carefully and worn properly, portrayed authority. Confidence. And first impressions counted, since a strong one left a lasting impact. The world was judgmental. People were quick to make assumptions based simply on what they saw, and a proper appearance radiated self-respect and self-worth. It also made her more productive. Feeling good led to working good.

She poured herself another cup of hot water and prepared her tea.

A lot was happening.

Far more than she'd ever imagined would be present at this point in their plan. The visit with her mother last night still rang loud in her mind. New strategies had been discussed. Plans altered. The older woman remained sharp as a piece of broken glass. In the bed later she'd thought back to lessons from the past. So many. But one in particular she'd never forgotten.

An evening when she was younger and just out of university. An impressionable twenty-two-year-old. Her mother took her to see a bull, a huge, sleek, powerful beast confined to a corral. She'd watched as a man with a rifle calmly shot the animal in the head. The bull fell to the ground with a thud, kicked the air, then lay still. More men then tied its legs with ropes and lifted the carcass into the air by a hoist supported on steel bars. A butcher plunged a knife into the chest and dragged the blade down, releasing a cascade of blood and guts that stained the ground. The body of the skinned animal had glistened white in the hard-edged glare from pole lights.

Strangely, she'd not been revolted.

"Look closely," her mother said. "That bull, the embodiment of male vitality one moment, is nothing but beef for the table in the next."

A dichotomy.

Life and death.

Two parts of one existence. Yet separable.

She'd learned that keeping those two extremes apart wasn't callous insensitivity. More mental compartmentalization, a skill she'd mastered, one that had served her well. Along with remembering that bull. Over the past twenty-four hours she herself had gone from beast to beef.

There'd been many other lessons from her mother through the years. Some helpful, others not so much. Sometimes she daydreamed about a fictitious Greek island, sunny, tropical, where a woman with money and charm could open a small, elegant inn, the sort of place where people would come to retreat and relax. Her inn. Where she could live at her leisure and never deal with the decisions she now faced. But that was unrealistic. And boring. She was going to change the world. But was she getting too old to feel the thrill of the dangerous games she'd long played?

Not in the least.

In fact, her nerve was solid, her resolve even more so. She'd meant what she said to Kelly. She was fully prepared to do whatever was necessary. She was a Luxembourger, born and raised, tough and resilient. But not reactionary. Nor was she an anachronism. Her eloquence, confidence, and empathy were widely known and respected. And she'd need all three of those attributes in the days ahead.

Along with courage.

She glanced over at the floor clock her grandfather had bought at the turn of the 20th century: 10:09 A.M.

Her cell phone vibrated.

The same number from a few minutes ago.

She answered.

"All right," Kelly Austin said. "You win. What now?"

She closed her eyes and breathed a silent sigh of relief. Thankfully, she'd already thought about the next steps in the event Kelly took the bait.

They spoke a little more, then she ended the call.

So many parts were moving all at once across the globe. Representatives were working to convince governments on three continents that it was in their best interest to ditch the dollar, avoid gold, and stake their national treasuries on bitcoin. Kyra Lhota was in Switzerland, ready. And now Kelly seemed back under control. She had to trust the people working for her. All were consummate professionals, well paid and motivated.

Only one thing though.

They have a spy in your midst. They know all about the Atlas Maneuver.

One of her people was a traitor.

And that had to be dealt with.

Right now.

By her.

CHAPTER 37

COTTON STOOD INSIDE THE GROCERY STORE AND WATCHED THE WHITE van still parked in the lot. He'd arrived a few minutes ago and come inside. So far it appeared no one was interested in the vehicle. Suzy was safe back at the *gasthaus*. He'd spoken to Koger and reported the situation. The big man told him to hang tight, transportation was on the way. But it would be a few hours. More than enough time for this errand and a little food.

He was a boots-on-the-ground guy. Always had been. The inside scoop, a firsthand look, was preferable to anything else. To really understand you had to be there to hear and see and, if that wasn't possible, then you needed someone who could be there for you. All the intel in the world only provided a partial picture. The whole picture came from knowledge that could only be gained on the ground.

Like here.

He grabbed some cheese, bread, and orange juice and headed for the checkout line. Through the front plate-glass window he saw a car park and a woman emerge.

Japanese.

Which sparked his interest.

He paid for the food and continued to watch as she approached the van, peeked inside, then moved to its rear double doors. He hadn't locked the van yesterday. No need. He still carried the gun from yesterday and readied himself to make a move.

Two new vehicles sped into the parking lot, brakes screeching to a stop. Three men sprang out, each carrying a weapon.

The woman froze.

The men with guns converged.

KYRA'S PHONE BUZZED AND SHE ANSWERED.

"I've made contact with Kelly Austin," Catherine Gledhill said.

She'd been watching as the woman from the consulate car inspected a white van.

"I have eyes on the Japanese right now," she told Gledhill.

More cars appeared. Men with guns stepped out.

She debated what to do, but Gledhill decided the course for her.

"Forget the Japanese. A better avenue has opened."

KELLY SAT STUNNED IN THE QUIET ROOM.

Like Cotton, who'd come face-to-face with his past, hers had found her through Katie Gledhill. How could that be? Was it possible?

She closed her eyes and thought back.

"Sign here," the lawyer said to her.

She lay in the hospital bed. Her abdomen ached. But it was finally over. The pregnancy had been uneventful, routine. The labor anything but. Twenty-nine hours. No epidural. The doctor had said there could be issues. So all natural it had been, one damn contraction after another. Finally, it ended with a last push and the birth of a daughter.

Whom she hadn't been allowed to see.

And for good reason.

She accepted the pen and studied the page.

The top was headlined FULL AND COMPLETE SURRENDER OF PARENTAL RIGHTS. *The body of the document was clear and straightforward. Being solicitous that my newly born female child shall receive the benefits and advantages of a good home, I do hereby surrender the child and promise not to interfere in the management of the child in any respect whatever; and, in consideration of the benefits guaranteed by the adopting parents, I do relinquish all right, title, and claim to the child, it being my wish, intent, and purpose to relinquish absolutely all parental control.*

Further down in the annoyingly long paragraph was a provision that she would have ten days to withdraw the surrender, which had to be done in writing at the address provided.

"This document is the final one necessary for the adoption to be completed," the lawyer said. "I regret this has to be done here, in the hospital, but it's necessary. The adoptive parents need to take the child home. They can't, without this surrender."

She understood. But that did not make it any easier.

She signed her name.

Quick. Decisive. She'd thought about the decision for a long time. There was no other path to follow. None at all. Or at least that's what she kept telling herself. She was not cut out for motherhood.

"Are the adoptive parents here?" she asked.

"You know I can't answer that," the lawyer said. "We talked about this. This is a closed adoption. Everything is sealed. Forever."

Apparently not.

"She has grown into a fine young lady," Katie said over the phone.

Her eyes closed and began to tear.

"I even have a photo of her. Nineteen years old. Short blond hair, cute face, petite. Perhaps she looks a lot like you before the accident?"

Perhaps. She'd fantasized many times about just that.

"Tell me your location and I'll send someone to get you," Katie said. "Then we can make a deal."

AIKO FROZE.

PSIA agents rarely carried weapons. That practice dated back to post–World War II when weapons were outlawed in Japan. She'd authorized her men to be armed yesterday, especially after the attack on Kelly Austin.

But today? She'd seen no need.

The two vehicles had pinned her in, the van blocking the way behind her. Could she turn and run?

Doubtful.

The three men advanced.

Guns aimed.

COTTON LEFT HIS PURCHASES AND FLED THE GROCERY STORE, USING the cars in the parking lot as cover to make his way toward the trouble. He decided to get their attention and fired a shot into the air.

Which worked.

All three of the men with rifles whirled around his way.

The woman dove to the ground behind another parked car. The men kept striding toward her. Cotton, off to one side, aimed his weapon and fired, dropping one of the assailants. He anticipated the other two's movements and leaped behind one of the cars. A barrage of rounds came his way, the bullets ricocheting off the cars. He'd only have a few moments before they turned their attention back to the woman. So he stayed low and advanced to the next car, coming up and sending two more shots at his attackers.

Which were returned fivefold.

This firefight was not good. They had rifles. He had a pistol.

Somebody was going to get hurt. Especially himself. So he hugged the pavement and searched beneath the cars for feet. There. One set. He sent a bullet into them, then retreated behind the rear tire next to him for protection. The guy screeched out in pain and fell. He risked a look and saw that the two men were retreating to the cars that had brought them, the one man helping the injured one, whom he stuffed into the back seat. Two more rounds came Cotton's way, designed to keep him pinned and allow them an escape.

So he let them go.

The car reversed, tires screeching, then it raced away.

He stood.

The woman also came to her feet.

The guy he'd shot remained on the pavement, not moving.

He hustled over. "We need to leave."

People from inside the grocery store were now out, some with cell phones aimed his way. Someone said the police had been called. So they both ran to her car, climbed in, and sped away.

"Thank you," she said.

"And you are?"

"Aiko Ejima."

"PSIA?"

The woman nodded. Interesting admission.

They kept speeding down the road.

"Those guys were CIA?" he asked.

"Like the one yesterday in the consulate. We appreciated that gesture too, Malone-san."

She was there, and knew him?

Okay.

But was this friend or foe?

CHAPTER 38

CASSIOPEIA STOOD AT THE DECK'S STERN. SHE, KOGER, AND CITRONE were back aboard Citrone's V-hull powering across Lake Geneva. The sky had carried through on its earlier threat. A soft morning drizzle had turned into a light gale, the wind moaning across the surface, coiling the fog around like a snake. Definitely not a day to go fishing.

"That vault was empty," Citrone told them. "Which means we have to explore other possibilities. One of those is here, on the lake."

Koger swung the bow around toward the southeast, taking the swells. Water pecked at the windscreen. He kicked up speed, the engines responding with a surge of power hurling the boat ahead with a smooth dull roar. Citrone had explained that the gold belonging to the Black Eagle Trust had been held in various vaults around Switzerland from 1950 until sometime in the late 1990s. That was when the bullion was moved to Geneva and the underground vault. With the location's conversion to a wine repository the gold was supposedly left in place. Or that's what Citrone was led to believe.

"I heard various stories that conflicted," Citrone said. "That's why I suggested a firsthand look inside the wine vault. Now that we know it's empty, there is one other possibility. A story that can no longer be discounted as fiction."

Bank secrecy in the Swiss region can be traced back to 1713 and the Great Council of Geneva, which outlawed the disclosure of any financial information about the European upper class. The Congress of Vienna in 1815 formally established Switzerland's international neutrality. Landlocked, the Swiss saw banking secrecy as a way to build an empire similar to the use of armies and navies by France, Spain, and the United Kingdom.

And it worked.

The mountainous terrain provided the perfect place to excavate secure underground vaults for storage of gold, diamonds, and other valuables. During World War I, when European countries began to increase taxes to finance the war, the wealthy moved their holdings into Swiss accounts to avoid taxation. The French banked in Geneva, the Italians in Lugano, the Germans in Zurich. Banking secrecy was codified in 1934 by the Swiss Federal Assembly, which quelled all controversy over the alleged tax evasion of wealthy French business-men, military generals, and Catholic bishops. That law also protected Jewish assets from the Nazi party and Nazi assets from the world.

After the 2008 financial crisis pressure increased to eliminate Switzerland's long-standing banking secrecy. But the Federal Assembly resisted the lobbying and increased the prison sentence for violations of secrecy from a maximum of six months to five years. Eventually Switzerland signed the U.S. Foreign Account Tax Compliance Act, which required Swiss banks to disclose non-identifying client information annually to the Internal Revenue Service, but only if the client consented.

Which rarely happened.

More laws were passed in 2015 and 2017, which allowed for additional disclosures, but nothing far reaching. Most dealt with ongoing audits and the level of cooperation that a Swiss bank could offer. In the end secrecy remained an integral part of Swiss banking. So much so that the Justice Ministry declared that that disclosure of client information in any pending court case was subject to federal espionage and extortion charges, in addition to charges relating to banking secrecy laws. Employees working in Switzerland and abroad at Swiss banks had long adhered to an unwritten code, similar to that observed by doctors or priests.

Never. Reveal. Anything.

Since 1934 Swiss banking secrecy laws had been violated by only four people. Christoph Meili in 1990, Bradley Birkenfeld in 2007, Rudolf Elmer in 2011, and Hervé Falciani in 2014.

"Those breaches of secrecy sent shock waves through Swiss banking," Citrone said. "They were deemed unthinkable."

Koger stood at the helm and kept them powering ahead through the storm.

"That was particularly true for the Bank of St. George," Citrone said. "They took extreme measures to guard their Swiss assets. I was there and participated in those efforts. Since the gold is no longer in that wine vault, and if the story I was told is to be believed, they moved it south, across the lake, to a new underground vault."

"And why was this not mentioned before?" Koger asked.

"Because it was just a story, until yesterday. Now it may indeed be a fact."

"Where are we going?" she asked.

Citrone shifted his bulky frame over to the GPS navigation unit. The boat was equipped with a variety of electronics that included a satellite radio, high-frequency radar, and a sonar unit. Citrone removed a slip of paper from his shirt pocket and stepped close to the GPS display. He then tapped in a set of numbers and the boat's compass projected a course on the screen before Koger at the helm.

"Follow that route," Citrone said.

Koger tossed her a look that asked what she was thinking. So Cassiopeia said, "Is the story over?"

"Are you enthralled?"

"You do seem to enjoy its telling."

"Mysteries intrigue me. They always have. I simply can't help it."

"Please, then," she said. "Keep talking."

"The gold was shipped by barge south. Supposedly it sank here, in the lake. But no one was told. Nothing reported to the CIA or anywhere." Citrone paused. "They wanted no one to come searching."

She was skeptical. "You're saying that billions in gold is lying at the bottom of this lake?"

"I have no idea. But, like that wine vault, we must take a look."

"How long ago did that happen?" Koger asked.

"If the story is to be believed, twenty years."

"And no one has found the wreck?" she asked, skepticism in her voice. "Diving is a popular pastime here."

"Dear lady, this is one of the largest lakes in Western Europe. Two hundred and twenty-five square miles. Deep too. It has three distinct sections, which worked to the bank's advantage."

She listened as Citrone explained about the *Haut Lac*, the Upper Lake, the eastern part from the River Rhône estuary. The *Grand Lac*, Large Lake, the deepest basin with the largest width. And the *Petit Lac*, Small Lake, the most southwest portion, narrow and shallow.

"That barge is in the *Grand Lac*," Citrone said. "Thirty meters down. The divers prefer the *Petit Lac*, where the water is shallower and clearer. And then there is the pollution. It became catastrophic in the 1960s and, by the 1980s, it nearly wiped out all the fish. Few swam in these waters then. There have been cleanup efforts since and today we can enjoy the lake, but I would not recommend it for long, especially the deeper parts where the pollution remains."

"So you're saying nobody has dived that wreck?" she asked.

"I'm saying nobody knows it even exists, outside of Catherine Gledhill and a few others at the Bank of St. George."

"And you," Koger added.

Citrone cast a grin. "And me."

"And how did you come to know?" she asked.

"I became suspicious during my time as liaison. I made inquiries, which Gledhill denied. Of course, she also would not allow me a look inside the vault. Finally, I decided to look for the barge and discovered it had disappeared."

Now she understood the presence of all the electronics. But she had to say, "And yet you did not report what you knew to the CIA."

"No. I did not."

"And you never came to explore or check it out?" she asked.

"There was never a need. Until now."

She decided to press. "No one at the bank knew about this?"

"They kept that information quite close."

Hard to know what to make of this. So she simply said, "This could be another shot in the dark."

"It could. But we have to rule out all the possibilities."

"What do you mean by *we*?"

"I'm hoping one of you is a diver," Citrone said.

Koger cast her a questionable look that said, *Not me.*

She faced Citrone. "How did you know?"

"I did not survive forty years in the intelligence business without being able to learn things. I'm told you are fully certified and quite experienced."

This guy truly believed himself to be a step ahead.

She had no choice, so she asked, "I assume you have equipment?"

"Of course."

CHAPTER 39

Cotton was unsure of Aiko Ejima, but he'd created this opportunity so now he had to exploit it.

"I need to know what the PSIA is doing here," he said.

"Better question is, what is a retired Magellan Billet officer doing here?"

"I'm doing a favor for a friend."

"That must be a good friend."

He shrugged. "Not really. Call it a weakness. I can't say no."

"Is that friend Derrick Koger?"

He nodded. "You acquainted?"

"Only by reputation. And, I might add, yours preceded you as well."

"Don't believe everything you hear. There's a saying where I come from. Even the blind-eyed biscuit thrower hits the target occasionally."

"Modest, too. The reports on you were definitely correct."

Enough sparring. And when all else fails, play dumb. "Why is Kelly Austin so important?"

She smiled. "Come now, we both know the answer to that."

AIKO COULD NOT BELIEVE HER GOOD FORTUNE. FATE HAD INTER-vened and provided a surprising alternative.

But life was like that.

"This is for you," her father said.

And he handed her a small round object.

Her seven-year-old brain was baffled. "What is it?"

"Something quite special. A daruma."

She'd been intrigued.

Eventually, she learned that a daruma was a traditional Japanese good-luck charm, used for making a wish or setting a goal. Typically round, made with papier-mâché, and painted with blank eyes and the exaggerated face of a bearded man. They were modeled after a sage monk named Bodhidharma, who lived in the 5th and 6th centuries. Supposedly he spent nine years facing a cave wall in deep meditation, his eyes wide open, never blinking. His commitment to enlightenment was so strong that his arms and legs atrophied and fell off. Yet his spirit remained undaunted. The dolls represented that limbless body and spirit.

Have a goal, a wish, or a promise to fulfill?

Paint one eye with a circular dot. Then work toward the goal every day. Once accomplished, paint the other eye. The dolls were everywhere in Japan, on bedroom dressers and tables, or on shelves in businesses, restaurants, and temples, an auspicious charm, a constant reminder of *ganbaru*, the ability to persevere. She'd kept hers from childhood as a reminder that life was full of pitfalls, bumps on the road, false starts, and good fortune. The daruma embodied a wise proverb.

Fall down seven times, stand up eight.

"It's not just a doll," her father would say. "It is a physical manifestation of your goal, a reminder of fate and everything in between. It keeps you accountable."

As a child she'd been intrigued.

"Which eye do I paint first? To set the goal?"

"The left side, from the doll's perspective. Left is always considered higher in rank."

And here she was, sitting in the left seat of the car.

Moving toward her goal.

With Cotton Malone.

COTTON DECIDED TO SHIFT GEARS AND TRY THE HONEST APPROACH. "I know that Kelly Austin created bitcoin and now the Bank of St. George is weaponizing it. Something called the Atlas Maneuver. But I have to say, I have doubts. Bitcoin has been around for a long time. It's a niche product. Something long-term investors and people who think they're going to get rich quick toy with."

"That's where you are wrong," Ejima said. "True, it is an investor tool. Mainly used by people who have no idea what they're doing. But it is also something much more potent. A weapon that, if channeled properly, can be wielded with devastating results."

Okay. This woman knew things. Clearly. And he recalled what Suzy had told him. *They have a spy in the bank.* "You've been watching all of this?"

She nodded. "For some time now."

"To what end?"

"At first? We were after the gold. But that changed once we learned of the Atlas Maneuver."

The PSIA had long been a friend of the United States, working closely with American intelligence. He'd always found them top-notch and trustworthy. And this woman seemed no exception.

"Our intent was to stop the bank," she said. "How? That remained to be seen."

He knew better. "And by stopping you could expose everything the CIA had been doing?"

"I will not deny that we remain irritated by America's hypocrisy. Kelly Austin forced the issue, though, when she unexpectedly involved the CIA. We had no choice but to act. We took her for her own protection."

"Then strangled her."

"It was merely a means to acquire her undivided attention. But she is the one who placed herself right in the middle of a war."

"Between the bank and Japan?"

She shook her head. "Between the bank and the CIA."

He recalled more of what Suzy told him last night.

"There've been countless bitcoin transactions. The whole thing has become everything I imagined it to be. And more. Much more. So much that a few years ago the CIA demanded the Bank of St. George shut the platform down. But the bank refused, saying that it had expanded and grown far beyond what was practical to end. So when the CIA could not get the bank to stop, it began a massive, worldwide disinformation campaign. People were told how bitcoin was being used by terrorists and criminals, with little to no accountability. By money launderers and tax evaders. The whole concept was painted as something sordid and nefarious. If you owned bitcoin you must be trying to hide something. All designed to scare people into staying away from it. Then there were the so-called environmental impacts. Supposedly, all those computers mining for coins consumed a huge amount of electricity, which affected the planet."

"That doesn't make much sense."

"Because it's false. There have been countless studies on this. Bitcoin accounts for about 0.001 percent of the world's electricity consumption. That's a pretty tiny percentage. The energy wasted in the American electrical grid is three times the energy used by bitcoin globally."

"But no one checks the details. Right?"

"Exactly what the CIA was counting on, and the wasted-energy argument gained some traction. But it still couldn't stop the momentum."

"So why did you go to them?"

She shrugged. *"I wanted to stop the bank, so what better place to head for help than its sworn enemy."*

"Is Kelly Austin safe?" Ejima asked.

"She is."

"Then perhaps we might work together, toward a common goal."

"I'm not sure our goals are aligned."

They rode for a few moments in silence.

The enemy of my enemy is my friend.

From the Gospel of John.

Good advice?

Hard to say.

CHAPTER 40

CATHERINE CARRIED HER PRIZED GOSHAWK OUTSIDE INTO THE morning air. The bird sat balanced atop her gauntleted wrist. The sight in her mind always conjured images of medieval nobility exhibiting notions of dignity, wealth, and status. *The sport of kings* was how history described falconry. But it had actually been much more widespread. Its main purpose had been for food. Like fishing today, the birds were a way to obtain fresh game. What differed was the birds used. Where a saker falcon would be owned by a king, the masses might use a kestrel. Back then the birds were all caught in the wild, then trained. Today most were bred from captivity and she employed several falconers who maintained and nurtured hers. The goshawks were her favorite. Humans had never successfully domesticated the species. Too wild. Not to mention they were capable of doing serious harm with their sharp beaks and talons. Only licensed zoos and falconers could legally possess one in Luxembourg.

She owned four.

Opinions varied as to the best ways to train them. Some preferred to take the bird away from its parents as a chick, rearing it so it thought itself human. But she disagreed with that approach since it made a natural predator needy for human company and caused it to screech more than it should. She kept the young with their parents for the first few months. That way they knew they were hawks. Gradually, they were weaned away until fully independent.

She surveyed the impressive bird.

Dark feathers streaked its back and the top side of its wings, with lighter-colored feathers on the bottom of the wings and underbelly. The red eyes, like blood dots, set them apart from other hawks, along with their size, about a full kilogram with a wingspan a meter across. Goshawks were so successful at hunting that falconers called them the cook's hawks, because they provided so much food.

They have a spy in your midst. They know all about the Atlas Maneuver.

Kelly's words. Said to rattle her?

Throw her off guard? Maybe.

But they could also be true. And something told her they were. Which begged a question. If there was a spy, then who?

She'd quickly clicked down the list of likely suspects. Of course the consuls knew all of the details regarding the Atlas Maneuver. But there was little danger of any of them being a traitor. All were compensated based on performance, and what they were about to do would be the first steps in making them the most powerful and richest people on the planet. Outside of the board only she, herself, Kelly, and Lana Greenwood knew the full story. Others within the bank worked blind, thinking they were simply selling the advantages of bitcoin over dollars or euros. Lana had been brought in out of necessity. Somebody had to lead the charge with the various governments as point person, and that person had to know what was at stake. Lana was the natural choice. So she'd been told. And she'd done her job.

Masterfully.

Catherine stood outside before the rookery. The building lay about half a kilometer from the main house, near the northern border of her estate. Stone-built, square, constructed on high ground that looked out over an immense span of firs and conifers broken periodically by small meadows. She'd driven over to prepare herself for what was to come.

She hated these unpleasantries.

So unnecessary.

What happened to friendship, loyalty, and trust?

Those qualities seemed to have vanished, replaced by betrayal, lies, and greed. The old Italian proverb was right. *Big mouthfuls often choke.* Then there was the more simplistic approach. *Many have too much, but none enough.*

Of course, all of those wise words could apply to herself.

She was worth hundreds of millions of euros. More than enough for her to spend over several lifetimes. She'd never had the desire to marry or have children, which she knew disappointed her mother. Instead the bank served as both her spouse and child, and she intended to see it grow into full adulthood. This was not about money.

At least not for her.

This was about changing the world.

About time somebody stepped up and did that.

She removed the hood from the hawk and loosened its jesses. The bird flung its wings wide and rose into the morning air, climbing, becoming black, then ghostly white, finally golden in the sun. Goshawks claimed their prey with short bursts of amazingly fast flight, often twisting among branches and crashing through thickets. They liked grouse, crows, squirrels, rabbits, snakes, even insects. A determined predator.

Like herself.

The goshawk swung around in the bright sky. She whirled the lure, summoning the bird back to her wrist. The hawk dove, coming straight at her in a steep powered descent. At the last moment the bird's wings arched back, slowing its speed, talons extended as it hovered above her wrist, then gently dropped onto her sheathed arm.

She offered the bird a morsel of red meat, which the hawk

devoured in short pecks from its hooked beak. She gently stroked the wings, which the bird accepted with gratitude.

Like the nations they'd already enticed.

Eager, hungry, aggressive, but trainable. Responsive to a lure. Oblivious to their own vulnerabilities. Central and South America, Eastern Europe, and Africa offered the prime initial opportunities. Economies that teetered on the brink, existing from month to month, with little to no cash reserves. In Central America, Guatemala was the largest and most stable economy. Panama and Costa Rica followed behind, with El Salvador, Honduras, and Nicaragua the least stable. South America showed more promise. Brazil, Argentina, Chile, Colombia, Peru, and Paraguay possessed natural resources and cheap labor, but not the skill and expertise to maximize those advantages. They were all like her goshawk, who continued to stand docile, perched on her arm, waiting for another handout.

Which she offered.

Most of Central and South America were now, or about to be, within the fold. The rest would soon follow. Already for those countries that had adopted bitcoin as their reserve currency there'd been economic growth. All were pleased. No complaints. So far, several multibillion-dollar contracts from bank clients had been directed toward Chile, Honduras, and Argentina. More were being negotiated. The bank possessed contacts across the globe, all looking for the best deals at the greatest return, and she intended to deliver. A win for the country, the client, the bank, and the world.

But all that was now threatened by Kelly and a spy.

Overhead, a pair of buzzards quartered the ground, drifting at about thirty meters high, crossing, one below the other as they traced the lines of some invisible grid, treating the sky as their territory. Broad wings grabbed the breeze, and she felt just as light and untrammeled as those birds. She envied the casualness of their hunting. Never in a hurry. Not like the hawk, who wasted no time circling its prey, certain of success.

In the distance across the meadow she spotted a doe. The animal dragged a hoof back and forth, dipping into the grass with gentle plunging strokes of her neck, then raising her head to full height, allowing her ears to flare wide open. Then she spotted a fawn without spots standing tautly among the trees. Coming out into the open could be foolish. But hunting was not permitted on her property, so the animals had developed an aversion to caution.

The fawn followed the doe out into the open field, both feeding on the grass. She angled the hawk so it saw both animals. The red eyes locked like radar. A gesture with her arm and the bird took to the air, soaring up into a sky that gleamed like a bright pearl. She watched as the hawk angled its flight, placing the sun behind it, shielding its presence from anything watching from the ground.

Smart.

The doe and fawn were now in the center of the meadow, still eating, oblivious to any danger that was not at ground level.

Big mistake.

Danger came from all around.

The goshawk tucked its wings and dove in a burst of blinding speed. The doe sensed something, raising her head, then rushing off in a quick run. The fawn hesitated, unsure what was happening, seemingly deciding between the delicious grass and the fast exit of what was surely its mother.

That moment would be fatal.

The hawk swooped down, wings out, talons extended, plunging them into the fawn. The deer tried to break free, but the hawk knew to go for the neck, its beak ripping into the flesh. The fawn dropped to the ground and tried to kick its way free, but the hawk worked its talons deeper, pecking away, squeezing harder, until the fawn stopped moving.

Amazing.

Such a small predator able to subdue such large prey.

Today she would be like that goshawk.

Equally certain of success.

CHAPTER 41

CASSIOPEIA SLIPPED ON THE WET SUIT, WHICH COVERED HER FROM NECK to ankles. The neoprene fit perfectly. Which made her wonder.

How far ahead of them was Rob Citrone?

Everything from Koger signaled that he wanted them to keep going, and she agreed, as she was more than curious about what lay below the surface of Lake Geneva. Was it an old wreck? Or something else entirely? Citrone seemed to think that he had them under control. So whatever he was going to do, there'd be no reason not to do it.

"The wreck is about thirty meters down." Citrone said. "We are floating right above it."

"And what about all that pollution you mentioned," she asked.

"This part of the lake is quite clean. You will be fine."

But she was not comforted by the words of a pathological liar.

She slipped her hands through the straps and lifted the air tank up and over her head, wiggling her outstretched arms and allowing the harness to settle on her shoulders. It had been a while since she'd last dived. She'd learned in her early twenties, experiencing many dives in the chilly Mediterranean off the Spanish coast. Over the past fifteen years she'd periodically enjoyed the Med, but she'd also dived in the warmer waters of the South Pacific, Hawaii, and the Red Sea.

She donned the buoyancy compensator, then slipped a flashlight into its pouch.

Citrone stood toward the stern, holding a fishing rod. He'd already offered another to Koger. "We'll see if we can get a couple of the arctic char or brown trout to bite. They seem to like rough weather. A little cover, as you investigate."

She sat on the gunwale and buckled six pounds of weight around her waist, tightening the belt. Then she stretched a pair of skin-tight rubber boots over her feet and fitted flippers over the boots. She pulled a hood over her head and ears.

"It was a barge and the gold was supposedly crated," Citrone said. "If there's anything to find, it should be lying across the bottom."

Koger cast his line out into the blue water. "Don't be long."

She did not have to be told that twice.

At thirty meters she'd have about twenty minutes of down time without worrying about a decompression stop on the way up. She knew that number from experience. Anything longer would require a stop at about five meters for ten minutes to allow the nitrogen to bleed from her bloodstream. Ignore that and she risked getting the bends.

Citrone cast his line out into the water. "Enjoy the dive."

She adjusted the mask onto her face.

Then moved onto the stern platform.

And stepped off into the water.

COTTON KNEW WHEN TO KEEP HIS MOUTH SHUT. EXPERIENCE HAD taught him that most valuable skill. The hardest thing for most people to do was nothing. This PSIA agent was here and talking. For a reason? Absolutely. So let her. She'd stopped the car at a fueling station, parking off to the side away from the pumps.

"I want to hear your take on the Atlas Maneuver," he said to her.

"That's a complicated subject," she said. "One we have studied for months."

"Then you surely have some insight to share."

"And what would I get in return?"

"I do have the creator of it all."

She smiled. "Yes, you do. All right. In late 2009, after bitcoin went live on the internet, Satoshi Nakamoto supposedly mined more than one million coins by himself. At the time few knew the opportunity for mining existed and bitcoin had practically no value. But from an analysis of the various blocks that were created, we know that a single entity, using a single computer, mined thousands of blocks and racked up around 1.1 million bitcoin in rewards. Folklore attaches the ownership of those coins to Satoshi Nakamoto. We now know that Kelly Austin, through the bank, mined those coins. They are now worth around fifty billion U.S. dollars. But they are the key to everything."

He'd heard that before from his friend back in Denmark. "I don't get it. Why does it matter about those million coins? Who cares? There are millions more in existence."

"You're not that familiar with bitcoin, are you?"

He shook his head. "I am not."

"Billions of dollars in trades and transactions happen every day. Coins move across the internet at the speed of light. But the first wallet, the one with those 1.1 million coins? Not a single coin has moved in fifteen years. Fifty billion dollars of wealth. Just sitting there."

"And if they moved?"

"It would be read as a signal from Nakamoto himself for everyone else to do the same. It would set off a run on bitcoin."

He decided to play devil's advocate. "What if Satoshi Nakamoto doesn't have access to the private key that opens the wallet for those funds?"

"That's one theory in the bitcoin community. But those first coins have become important for another reason. Many people have claimed to be Satoshi Nakamoto, but nobody has managed to definitively prove that they hold the private keys to any of the addresses thought to be owned by Nakamoto. Possessing those would be conclusive evidence proving they are Satoshi Nakamoto. Of course, you and I know that Kelly Austin is Nakamoto. Up until yesterday the Bank of St. George controlled those one million bitcoin. Along with, at our best estimate, another three and a half million more."

Her intel was spot-on, matching exactly what Kelly had reported. But he wanted to know, "How do you think those gunmen back there knew where to find you?"

"I assume they were watching, waiting to see who would come."

"But they obviously have no idea about me," he said. "They didn't make a move when I arrived."

Which might offer him an open field to run in. And with Kelly under his exclusive control he might be able to dial things back a notch. His grandfather liked to say, *He'd waddled in the mud with pigs before, so why not now.* Good point. And allies were always a good thing. No matter how suspect they might be. Right now he could use the help. So he made a field decision, hoping Koger would later agree.

He said, "We need to go get Kelly."

CHAPTER 42

CASSIOPEIA SWAM DOWNWARD.

The murky water was cold, becoming colder, though the wet suit offered ample protection. Only bubbles marked her progress as they percolated away with each breath and started their journey back to the surface. She kicked steadily, letting the fins, not her arms, do the work. The depth gauge connected to her vest read fifteen meters.

She kept descending.

Pressure built in her ears and she pinched her nose through the mask, equalizing them. Interestingly, the deeper she went the clearer the water became. She switched on the underwater light, illuminating about ten meters ahead within the swath of its beam. Below she began to see a darker shadow in the inky water. Visibility was about twenty meters and she spotted the lake bottom.

Sandy. Barren as a desert.

Except for the hulk of a wreck.

KYRA HAD WATCHED AS A GUN BATTLE ERUPTED IN THE GROCERY STORE parking lot. Three men had arrived and started shooting at the

PSIA agent, then another man came out of the building and drove them away with more gunfire. Two of the original three were shot, one managing to help another away, leaving the third on the pavement.

Then the new man had left with Aiko Ejima.

She'd managed to snap several photographs, but none of what she witnessed concerned her any longer. Catherine Gledhill had been clear.

"I'm going to give you a location. Go there and retrieve Kelly Austin. She's expecting you."

That had been a surprise.

Austin was surrendering?

So much for the promised bonus.

She followed the navigation on her phone and located a *gasthaus* about ten kilometers away. Small. Quaint. Only a handful of rooms. A woman stood at the base of a set of steps. Slim, fit, attractive, with pale-reddish hair cut short. Kelly Austin. Looking anxious. Studying the road.

She parked and exited the vehicle. "I'm Kyra Lhota."

Gledhill had instructed her to use her name as a code phrase for a positive identification.

Austin headed for the car.

CASSIOPEIA KICKED TOWARD THE SUNKEN BARGE, WHICH HAD DEFInitely been down there awhile. Plants and algae populated its exterior. Fish darted in and out among openings in its hull. Some of the gashes were fairly good-sized. She settled on the bottom at thirty-two meters, resting on her knees, and appraised the situation.

Okay, there was a barge.

She'd not actually expected one to be here.

But she supposed that whatever game Citrone was playing had to include at least partial credibility. She scanned the water around her, looking for anything remotely associated with gold. Crates?

Debris? The bars themselves? But saw nothing. She estimated about ten minutes of bottom time so far. Five more to go. Ten at the most.

Fresh lights suddenly appeared.

A ghostly green incandescence. On the far side of the barge. Growing larger by the second as they approached.

Two divers. No bubbles.

Which meant they were wearing rebreathers.

Sophisticated equipment. But dangerous at depths like this. That meant they knew what they were doing.

And they were swimming straight for her.

Nothing about that was good.

COTTON HAD BOUGHT HIMSELF A TON OF GOODWILL BY SAVING AIKO Ejima's life. The question had become how to capitalize on that investment. This woman's, and her nation's, motivations were not the purest.

"When you had Kelly Austin," he said, "you told her you knew about the Atlas Maneuver and that you had a source within the bank. Why compromise that source?"

"It was important she understood the extent of our interest. She clearly has no love for her former employer. I thought her knowing we had eyes and ears inside would show her we are on the same side, and that we are informed."

"And when the CIA made a move on her, you thought she might need a friend."

"That had been our intention. Of course we never calculated you into that equation."

Or the fact that he and Suzy knew each other.

No one but he and Cassiopeia knew that.

Ejima drove as fast as the road and traffic allowed back to the *gasthaus*.

"Austin thought she was doing the right thing contacting the

CIA," Ejima said. "What she did not realize was the extent the CIA would go to suppress what she knew. They are not her friend. And now the bank has been made impotent. Once that is discovered the CIA will, without a doubt, try again to kill her. That way whatever she knows dies with her and the bank is rendered moot. We do not want her dead. I was trying to convey that fact to her."

"By strangling her?"

"We have found that an element of fear is good in those situations."

He didn't agree, but let it go. "Why not just come to Koger and tell him all that?"

"We thought it better to work unnoticed."

"How'd that work out?"

He saw that his sarcasm had registered. The Japanese were after something, and it did not involve helping America.

They were approaching the *gasthaus* and he motioned for her to park.

"Wait here," he said, as he opened the car door.

He hustled up the stairs into the building and found Kelly's room. He tapped on the door. No answer. Another knock. Nothing. This was not a high-tech locale. Locks with real keys only. He tried the knob.

Which turned.

Not good.

He opened the door and saw that the room was empty.

He rushed off to the front desk.

"The woman who came here with me," he asked the man behind the desk. "Do you know where she is?"

"I saw here leave. About half an hour ago."

"How did she leave?"

"A car came, with another woman driving."

A woman? "Did it look forced? Was she in trouble?"

"She opened the door herself and climbed in. That was after she used my phone."

Not good.

"I need to see your phone."

The man seemed to grasp the urgency and found his cell phone, tapping the screen, locating the last number called, which he showed. Cotton locked the numbers into his brain. He then told the guy where he'd left the car he'd borrowed and retreated to the car with Ejima. "She's gone. She made a call, then a woman came to get her. We need to know who she called."

He told her the phone number.

Ejima found her own phone and made a call. He was fluent in several languages, another benefit of his eidetic memory, but Japanese was not one of them. He listened as she spoke, waited, spoke some more, then ended the call.

"That number is a Luxembourg exchange belonging to Catherine Gledhill."

"Who is that?"

"The head of the Bank of St. George. Her former employer."

Really?

What the hell had happened?

CHAPTER 43

CASSIOPEIA DECIDED THAT THE LIGHTS HEADED HER WAY WERE NOT carried by pleasure divers. Especially considering the lack of other boats above when they'd arrived and the weather. Which meant these divers had been waiting and were coming for her. Which also meant that Rob Citrone was definitely a traitor.

She and Koger would deal with him.

But first things first.

The lights grew in intensity, then stopped, maybe twenty meters away, the sunken barge between her and them. The forms were more splotches than defined shapes in the water. But she caught the unmistakable outline of spearguns.

Aimed her way.

She doused her light and kicked hard, moving left, then upward in the darkness. She heard the swoosh as the spear propelled through the water and kept going past her previous position. The divers' lights were aimed in that same direction. It was too far and would take too long to make it to the surface. They could locate and take her out before she found air. And even more pressing was the time. She was dangerously close to her twenty-minute limit.

So she opted for the barge and the openings in its hull.

Perhaps she could hide there.

She kicked and swam straight for a yawning gash. Her bubbles would give her away until she was inside, then the hulk itself would capture them. She was not concerned about other residents of the enclosed space. Thankfully the lake contained no sharks or other predators.

Only men with spearguns.

She kept her light off and entered the barge. She could make out a few shapes and wondered if any of those were piles of gold bars, but she dared not risk a look. The barge, about ten meters long, lay at an angle with its port stern embedded into the bottom. Other gashes marred the hull and offered more ways inside. Beyond, back out in open water, she saw the jerky beams of the divers' lights. They'd most likely determined that she'd not surfaced, which left only one place she could be. She was unarmed and outnumbered, thirty-plus meters underwater, with her bottom time about to run out.

Not the best situation in the world.

But not hopeless either.

She decided to risk a look and switched on the flashlight, placing her left hand over the lens and diffusing much of the beam. A quick survey showed that the inside was littered with barrels, most open and empty. Nothing else of any interest or value caught her eye. Except some strips of metal, mostly intact, with sharp edges and little corrosion.

Which might work.

She grabbed one and extinguished her light.

KYRA WAS FOLLOWING THE ORDERS GIVEN BY CATHERINE GLEDHILL. Her usefulness in finding Kelly Austin had waned, but she still served a purpose by being Gledhill's eyes and ears on the ground. And at the moment, her employer needed that service.

Her instructions were to deliver Austin to the Basel airport where the bank's private jet would be waiting. No talking. No questioning. No discussion. Just deliver her, then both women were to climb aboard. The only exception to that was if Austin inquired about one particular subject.

"Do you know anything about my daughter?" Austin asked.

"I might."

For all her attempts at aloofness, she could see that Austin was bothered by the surprising turn of events. So, per Gledhill's instructions, she turned the knife. "She looks like you."

"You've seen her?"

She nodded. "She seems a lovely young woman. Happy. Full of life."

"Where is she?"

"That is not for me to say. Ms. Gledhill will speak to you about that."

"I'm not going anywhere unless you tell me what you know."

Gledhill had likewise predicted resistance.

"The only way," she said, "and I mean the only way you will learn anything about your daughter is for you to do exactly as I say. There is no other alternative. Ms. Gledhill told me that if that is not sufficient, you are free to leave and this will be handled in a different manner."

"I can find her on my own."

"No. You cannot. That trail has been wiped clean. There are no records to find. And I know this because I eliminated them."

Another lie that Gledhill had instructed her to use.

Silence reigned.

Perfect.

Cassiopeia readied herself.

The lights from beyond the hull openings indicated that the divers had split up, one on either side of the barge. They apparently intended on attacking on two fronts, trapping her inside and making their spearguns that much more lethal. She positioned herself to the side of one of the openings. The beam outside was progressively brightening.

A diver was coming in.

Her gaze alternated between the two openings. One to her immediate right, the other across the barge's interior on the other side, where that light's intensity was likewise increasing. She slipped her flashlight back into her vest pocket and readied the metal strip she held tight in her right hand. Careful with her air. The deeper you went the faster you breathed. Stay calm. She'd only have a moment to use the element of surprise.

Make it count.

The end of a speargun poked through the hull gash first, followed by the light gripped in a gloved hand. She sucked in a long slow breath, conscious of the fact that she could not hold it in her lungs for long at this depth.

She waited, keeping a watch on what was happening outside the other opening. The diver closer to her was now about a third of the way in, entering ever so slowly. She reached out, grabbed the speargun by the barrel, and yanked the diver inside. He reacted to the attack, but not fast enough. She zeroed in on the hoses leading from his mouth regulator back to his rebreather. She released her grip on the speargun and wrapped her left hand around one of the hoses. Then, using the sharp metal like a knife, she sliced the hose, releasing a burst of air bubbles.

No way the diver could make it back to the surface.

He was a dead man.

And knew it from the wild look in his eyes.

She released her grip on the piece of metal and wrenched the speargun away. While he died she took aim at the other opening. Surely that diver had seen the erratic light beam and had to be wondering.

Yet he kept coming.

The light growing brighter in the opening.

She waited.

Aimed.

Then fired.

CHAPTER 44

CATHERINE WATCHED AS THE GOSHAWK CONTINUED TO ENJOY ITS meal of fresh deer. What remained would be fed to the other birds. A car emerged from the trees on the road and motored up to the rookery. One of her employees climbed out, then assembled a wheelchair from the trunk. He then helped her mother from the rear seat and into the chair, which he wheeled onto the covered porch. Maddy rarely left her room, and almost never the house. But she'd insisted on being here. Her mother sat beyond the morning sun, in the shade, a wool blanket draped across her lap for the cool air. The birds had once been in her mother's care. Her father was never interested in them.

"She is a good hunter," her mother said, motioning out to the field. "Her father was good too. I trained him myself. It's still impressive. A bird that size able to take down a fawn ten times its weight."

That it was.

But her birds were all determined predators.

"This has to be done," her mother said.

"I only wish it was not necessary."

Another car appeared, then motored down the dirt lane that bisected the trees at the far end of the meadow. The hawk seemed

231

unfazed by its presence as it drove past. The vehicle rolled up to the rookery and stopped. Lana Greenwell climbed out from behind the wheel and closed the door, dressed in a stylish business suit with low heels.

"What is this about?" Lana asked, approaching. "Kelly? Has she been found?"

Catherine understood the confusion, as Lana had only visited the estate as part of some official dinner or event, never early on a Friday morning after a personal summons.

She motioned for Lana to come closer. "Does anyone know you are here?"

Lana shook her head. "I did as you asked. My office thinks I'm running a personal errand before coming to the bank."

"I appreciate that. It's important this be kept confidential."

"You know you can count on me."

Catherine motioned. "This is my mother, Madeleine. I don't think you've ever met her."

Lana nodded an acknowledgment of the introduction, which Maddy barely returned. Pleasantries were not her strong suit.

"I asked you here because we have another security leak," Catherine said. "A major one. Japanese intelligence is fully aware of the Atlas Maneuver."

Surprised filled Lana's face. "How is that possible?"

"I've been wondering the same thing," she said. "The number of people privy to that information is severely limited."

The bank maintained a top-notch intelligence capability, the need made more acute by volatile world conditions. Knowing what was happening had become a necessity. Investments required protection. Economic, political, and social trends had to be constantly studied. Political risk analyses were made hourly, which improved decision making. The board required constant advising on technological developments, sociopolitical issues, terrorist threats, anything and everything that could affect business. Part of this intelligence division was an extensive array of internal security for both its own and its customers' protection. The team consisted of sixteen employees who worked away from the main building on the outskirts of Luxembourg City, maintaining a level of anonymity and independence. Among them were IT specialists adept at covert record gathering. Once Kelly Austin had revealed what she knew about a Japanese spy, Catherine had asked that Lana be given a quick scrutiny.

"You made a call yesterday," she said to Lana. "Thirty minutes after you and I spoke in your office, after we discovered Kelly's breach."

Lana stood still and said nothing.

"The call was on your personal cell phone, not the one the bank provides," she added. "An account that is in the name of your nephew. We know this, as your nephew is a named beneficiary on your company retirement account. That was careless, Lana. You know our security people are thorough. But you were probably in a rush to report what you knew."

She'd chosen this spot to confront her traitor since it was isolated and away from anyone and anything. Nowhere for Lana to go. No one to help her. Lana started to shake. Like that fawn who realized far too late that the hawk had the upper hand.

"Kelly is a traitor," Catherine said. "That is clear. But so are you, Lana. What I wonder is, why?"

COTTON WAS STUNNED.

Kelly had made two calls to Catherine Gledhill, her former employer, then she'd left, on her own, with a woman.

"Wait here," Aiko said.

And she left the car, retreating toward the *gasthaus* to use her phone. Obviously, this was a conversation she wanted kept private. Though they were temporarily working together, it was a reminder that they were not on the same team. He watched as the PSIA operative listened for a few moments, then ended the call and returned to the car.

"I could not make contact with our source within the bank," she said. "I must say, I did not anticipate Austin communicating again with the bank. Everything we know indicated that was not a possibility."

He agreed. Something had changed. He played a hunch. "You have eyes at the Basel airport?"

She nodded.

He thought as much. Any local asset worth their salt cultivated sources at all points of ingress and egress. You never knew when those might come in handy. "Find out if anything from the bank is there, or on the way in."

She worked the phone and spoke in Japanese, then ended the call. "A private jet belonging to the Bank of St. George landed thirty minutes ago."

"How far out are we from the airport?"

"An hour."

"Let's go. Fast."

CASSIOPEIA HAD TAKEN OUT BOTH DIVERS. ONE WITH A CUT AIR HOSE, the other with a spear to the chest. Bubbles continued to spew from the one man's splayed hose, the other man drifting away, blood dyeing the water. Quickly, she took a look around inside the barge and determined there was nothing there. No surprise since this was a trap, not a treasure site. Her bottom time was at an end, so she fled the barge. But before surfacing, she found the second man's speargun, which he'd dropped after dying.

She began her ascent.

Slowly, keeping her breathing steady, allowing her lungs to equalize to the changing pressure.

A quick check of the timer on the regulator indicated that she was past the twenty minutes of down time, but not all that much. Certainly not enough to cause concern. She should be fine for a direct ascent without a decompression stop. She reached the fifteen-meter mark and noticed something odd on the surface.

Two boats.

Nestled close to each other.

That meant they had company, which explained who would have retrieved the divers.

Trouble. Absolutely.

With a capital *T.*

She realized her bubbles were giving her away. But whoever was here surely expected the two men to be the ones surfacing. Buying time and creating confusion seemed the smart play. So she removed her buoyancy vest, then unbuckled the tank, slipping it off her shoulders. She secured the vest to the tank, sucked one more breath, then let it go, watching it sink.

With the speargun in hand, she started swimming.

Up toward the boats.

CHAPTER 45

CATHERINE WAITED FOR AN ANSWER FROM LANA GREENWELL.

She hated everything about what was happening. Two people she thought close friends had betrayed her in a big way. Years of work and millions of euros had been spent on what was about to happen.

All now in dire jeopardy.

But for what?

"I could not bear the thought of Kelly succeeding. She's shown me nothing but disrespect for years. And you, Katie, allowed it to happen because you valued her over me."

Business jealousy? It couldn't be.

People being people, personalities clashed. Usually, though, the consequences from such pettiness were only a nuisance. Unlike here. Where they had become a catastrophe. Thankfully, the situation might have come under control with the deal she'd made with Kelly. By now Kyra should have her in custody and be on the plane headed for Morocco.

"I tried to warn you," Lana said. "I told you, repeatedly, that she could not be trusted. I despise her. Kelly is a reckless individual."

"So, because of your hatred," her mother said, "you sold yourself out to the Japanese? You are a liar. You may have started out doing what you did out of resentment, but you kept doing it for the money."

Catherine glanced out into the meadow. The hawk was still feeding. She had to be careful and not allow the bird to gorge itself. "We were able to locate an account this morning in Singapore, in the name of the same nephew who was tagged to the cell phone. The balance is far more than we've ever paid you."

"Which is another matter, all to itself," Lana said.

Now she was curious. "Your compensation is generous."

"It's a tenth of what you and the consuls make. And not even half what Kelly was paid."

Employee compensation was another closely guarded secret. The bank was known for higher-than-market salaries and annual bonuses, which attracted the best from around the world. To lessen animosity and jealousy salaries were known only to a few, all inside human resources. Lana was not one of those, but she'd obviously managed to breach that security.

"Kelly's contributions, and yours, are vastly different," Catherine made clear.

"How did the PSIA connect with you?" her mother asked.

"They didn't," Lana said, contempt in her voice. "I contacted them. I volunteered. At first they just wanted information on the gold—"

"But you increased your worth by telling them about Atlas," her mother said.

"They were willing to pay."

"You are a fool," her mother declared in a strong voice, the eyes fierce and intimidating. "That gold is gone to them, and they know it. They used you to troll for something of greater value, and you gave it to them."

Lana waved off the accusation. "I had no choice. They demanded more and more or they would have sold me out."

Which was the natural result of betrayal. The person being pressured always thought themselves in charge, that somehow the blackmailer would be satisfied with what was offered, never asking for more. Big mistake. It never ended. Her mother was right. Lana was a pathetic, idiotic fool.

Her mind was working. Thinking. Adapting.

True, Kelly had changed everything with her seizure of the bitcoin keys. And what was a single security leak had expanded into a full-fledged flood. Personnel within the bank were fully aware of the effort to steer countries toward more bitcoin use, but that was all part of the hype generated worldwide for cryptocurrency. The bank financed websites, newsletters, and other publications all designed to extol the virtues of bitcoin versus fiat money. A sales pitch designed to generate bitcoin usage. None of those people knew the true extent of what was about to happen.

Secrecy was vital to what they had in mind. Sure, the PSIA and the CIA were now involved. And the CIA, as they'd done in the past, might try a calculated PR campaign designed to discredit both bitcoin and the bank. But they could weather that storm. Bitcoin enthusiasts were accustomed to governmental degradation. No one listened to such noise. What would the PSIA do, though? That was a vexing inquiry. Clearly they'd known of the Atlas Maneuver for some time yet had kept that knowledge to themselves. So what was their endgame? Had what Kelly done changed things?

Surely.

So much was happening so fast, and her flight to Morocco was due to leave in two hours.

She found the lure and started to swirl it in the air.

The hawk knew what was expected of it and left the fawn, taking to the air, swinging up, then down onto her outstretched arm. She stroked the bird, its beak red with the deer's blood.

"Needless to say, Lana, your employment with the bank will be terminated. And that money you have on deposit will be forfeited too."

"Like hell," Lana spit out.

And she turned to leave.

Her mother reached beneath the blanket draped across her lap and removed a small pistol.

"No, you are not leaving."

CHAPTER 46

Cassiopeia kept swimming, careful to slowly exhale the air from her lungs as she rose. That last breath had come from the compressed air in her tank so it was important to rid her lungs of it as she kept ascending. Otherwise, she risked an embolism.

Her destination was the far side of Citrone's boat. She took a moment to assess her situation. Most spearguns were band-powered, working like a combination of crossbow and slingshot. A gun was loaded by stretching strong rubber bands from the end of the barrel to the back of the spear. When the trigger was pulled the rubber band snapped and propelled the spear forward. All that happened in the water. Not in the open air. But that didn't mean a speargun was impotent out of the water. She figured maybe four to five meters of defined flight was possible before the air began to affect the spear's trajectory.

Which should be enough.

She made it to the far side of the new boat and carefully poked her head from the choppy water. The rain had slackened to a fine mist that the wind blew onto her face mask in a layered gauze veiling her vision. No one was in sight. Hopefully, their attention was elsewhere. The weather was definitely a distraction. Lots of noise and movement. She needed to know what she was facing and there

239

seemed only one way to find out. So she grabbed another breath and submerged, swimming away about ten meters. The fins helped in the rough water. Once in position she carefully returned to the surface and snuck a peek, seeing one man with a gun and Citrone but no Koger. The two men stood on the rocking open deck, their backs to her. She debated whether what she planned could work. There'd only be one shot. At least from her standpoint. The guy with the gun would get more opportunities. What she hoped was that Citrone and the other guy were waiting for the two divers to surface, after dealing with her. So she had the element of surprise. Koger's absence, though, was worrisome.

In fact, this whole thing fell into that category.

Normally, it could be difficult to get Cotton to leave his bookshop in Copenhagen. He'd done his tour with the Magellan Billet, working twelve years as one of Stephanie Nelle's Justice Department agents. As he liked to say, *That was someone else's problem now.* More and more, though, it had become simply a matter of making money for him to freelance. *Everyone had to eat,* and his skill sets were definitely in demand. She, of course, went along because she loved him, wanted to be part of what he did, and, like him, loved the chase. This foray, though, started off as a favor but had morphed into something unexpected.

More personal.

A woman from his past.

She still wasn't sure how she felt about that.

She considered herself lucky to have found someone like Cotton. He was a few years older, tall, broad-shouldered, sandy-blond hair, blessed with a handsome face full of character. His green eyes seemed to always captivate her, as did his fight to keep the depth of his feelings to himself, which had clearly become harder and harder for them both to achieve. Once there'd been a time when she'd wanted no one to invade her world. When she became angry at her own weaknesses and her heart rebelled. They'd even broken up for a while. But she'd decided not to make the mistake again of thinking she could live without him. She could not. She loved him.

And he her.

He would not be happy with what she was about to do. But as he'd said on more than one occasion, *Sometimes you just gotta do what you gotta do.* At the moment dealing with the two men in the boat was the priority. Where things led from there was anybody's guess. But that was the great thing about an adventure. Whether it be in life or love.

You simply never knew how it would end.

Another deep breath and she submerged.

She wielded the speargun with her right hand. With her left she released the weight belt at her waist, which made her much more buoyant. She turned, facing the boat, which floated about ten meters away, and pointed the speargun. Fear played havoc with her mind, but she'd learned over the years how to control it. Using the fins she kicked hard and powered upward, breaking the surface, her upper body momentarily freeing the gun from the water.

"Hey," she yelled.

Both Citrone and the man with the gun turned.

She pulled the trigger and the spear zipped through the air and impaled the man with the gun. She tossed her weapon aside as she slipped back into the water and dove, swimming hard back under the two boats to the far side of the other one.

She heard shots.

Rounds ripped into the water behind her.

Damn. Citrone was firing at her.

He'd regret that.

She swam hard, fighting to keep panic down and maintain a smooth steady stroke. Her lungs burned and she barely felt the cold as she made her way back to the other boat, freed the fins from her feet, and surfaced where Citrone could not see her. The two boats blocked his field of vision. She carefully made her way to the stern and climbed aboard, slipping the mask from her face. Citrone was in his boat, his back to her, studying the water where she was last seen. This guy may know a lot about stolen gold and the Bank of St. George, but he was a lousy field operative.

She straightened her legs and felt the solid deck beneath her feet, making her way across the one rocking boat and onto Citrone's.

The big man was still oblivious to her presence. The wet suit minimized any dripping and the weather added additional coverage for sound. She came up behind him and tapped him on the shoulder.

He whirled around and she planted a fist into his face.

Citrone released his grip on the gun, which clattered to the deck, shrieking in pain as blood gushed from his nostrils.

She retrieved the weapon and asked, "Where's Koger?"

CHAPTER 47

KELLY STEPPED FROM THE CAR.

They'd driven straight to the EuroAirport, which lay north of Basel, across the Rhine River into France. The woman who'd retrieved her had said little after revealing a few tidbits about her daughter, surely more bait designed to keep her on the hook.

The whole thing about everything being her choice?

She could walk away?

Just more enticement.

She had to wonder if what she'd been told about her daughter's physical appearance was true or false. But she had no choice. That mistake, made so long ago, had to be rectified. She'd been told at the time that there were positive feelings that came from giving a child up for adoption—relief, gratitude, acceptance—but none of that held a candle to the grief.

There was a definite loss.

She read once that feelings of grief were activated in the same areas of the brain associated with pain. And that was right. For her the loss began with the unplanned pregnancy, which came out of nowhere. She'd thought an IUD enough protection, but she'd been wrong. She'd had such plans for her life, none of which involved a child. An abortion had been considered but by the time she'd learned of the baby many weeks had passed, making it no longer a viable option. So she rationalized things by convincing herself that an adoption would result in a better life for the baby. Unfortunately her parents were both dead and she had no siblings. She'd been alone with both the decision and its aftermath.

She recalled with sharp focus the birth and the actual surrendering, the next day, when she signed the papers. Never once had she seen the child, though she was told it was a girl. Nothing close to relief or resolution had ever arisen. Instead, there'd been feelings of numbness, shock, denial, along with deep painful grief. For an instant she'd considered not doing it, but then she'd succumbed to a selfishness that she'd always regretted. Even worse, nothing marked the loss. When a mother miscarried, or experienced a stillbirth, there were things that could be said in conciliation. Comfort that could be offered. But when someone came home from the hospital without their baby, because they chose to surrender him or her to adoption, no words existed.

Nothing at all.

She'd experienced all of the stages of grief. Denial, at first, served as a buffer to the loss. That had been followed by sorrow, then depression as the sense of regret resonated. Anger and guilt were next, directed at the absent father who, in her mind at the time, bore some responsibility for the surrender. Later she realized that had been ridiculous since the father knew nothing of the child. Finally came acceptance and resolution.

But not really.

Acceptance of the loss and working through the grief did not mean you forgot the child. It simply meant that, in some small way, you'd been able to integrate the loss into your life and move on. She probably should have sought some professional help, but with her accident, paralysis, and disfigurement, other more pressing matters had taken over. No one fantasized about having a baby, then giving him or her up.

She'd constantly wondered what that child might have become as hers. Those thoughts reemerged every June 8, her daughter's birthday. She'd learned that it was impossible to forget. She'd tried to adapt. Focusing on work and career, becoming really, really good at what she did for a living, moving up the ranks from the military, to the intelligence services, to finally the Bank of St. George. Ultimately, she'd invented something utterly incredible. Blockchain. Which led to something equally amazing. Bitcoin. She'd used those successes as a way to come to terms with regret, integrating the loss into her life and gaining some feeling of control.

A few years back she read an article on adoption. Its author wrote of entrustment ceremonies. Where birth parents engaged in a ritual, or ceremony, that took place when they entrusted their child to the adoptive parents. For newborns that usually happened at the hospital. A way for the birth parents to say goodbye, while maintaining a sense of purpose over the placement. The article suggested that even if such a ritual did not occur a birth parent should give themselves a ceremony, using it for reflection and healing. The idea seemed to be focusing not on the painful emotions felt at surrender, but on the optimism and encouragement that came with knowing the child would be raised in a good and loving family.

What bullshit.

For her nothing could right the wrong.

Reality was clear.

She'd made a mistake.

It had taken a lot of time and effort for her to realize the depth of that error. But an error it was, and no ceremony, ritual, or self-analysis was going to make her feel better about it. She'd wondered for years what happened to her daughter. Now Katie Gledhill said she knew.

Was that true?

She had to find out.

She stood in the midday sun outside a building that indicated it was for private charters into the Basel airport. Out on the runway she saw a small jet glide down for a landing, painted in a distinctive combination of blue and gold. On its tail fin, atop a royal-blue background, was the golden image of St. George atop his horse. She knew the plane. Owned by the bank. One of its latest purchases as the Bombardier came with the smoothest ride, largest cabin, most comfortable seats, cleanest air, and longest range of any private jet. It could literally take her anywhere in the world, most destinations on one tank of fuel.

The woman who brought her stayed close.

"Is your name really Kyra Lhota?" she asked her.

"It is."

"Where are we going?"

"We'll both find out when we get there."

"You're a terrible liar."

"I really don't know. That's what I was instructed to tell you."

"And you're a good little order-follower?"

"Something like that."

The plane taxied from its landing and came to a stop about a hundred feet away, engines in neutral. Its forward cabin door opened and landing stairs unfolded. Kyra Lhota motioned for them to head that way. They walked over and both climbed inside, settling into two white leather seats. She wondered if any of this made sense, but it was too late now to turn back. She hated running out on Cotton, but this wasn't his fight.

It was hers.

And always had been.

One of the pilots appeared and told them, "Our flight time will be about three and a half hours. There is food and drink in the galley. Help yourself."

"Where are we going?" Kelly asked.

"Ms. Gledhill instructed me to say, if you asked that question, that this is not a prison and no one is forcing you to go anywhere. If you want to leave the plane right now, you are free to do so. It's your choice whether you stay or not."

The moment of truth.

She looked at Kyra, who, along with the pilot, waited for her decision.

"I'll stay. Do I now get to know where we are going?"

"Not until we are close," the pilot said.

He then left them, retracted the stairs, and sealed the cabin door.

"Am I going to regret this?" she asked Kyra.

"I have no idea."

The only thing that brought her some measure of comfort was that she controlled those bitcoin private keys. Katie wanted them. The CIA wanted her dead. The Japanese? Who the hell knew. So it seemed she'd chosen the lesser of many evils.

But that realization brought little comfort.

CHAPTER 48

COTTON STEPPED FROM THE CAR AND ENTERED THE BUILDING LABELED TRAVEL SERVICE BASEL. The small terminal incorporated a passenger lounge and pilot's briefing room. Two hangars were attached and he noticed that all of the expected amenities were there. Limousine arrangements, catering, direct ramp access, and customs clearance. Everything and anything private charter services required.

Ejima's eyes and ears on the ground had described the jet, which clearly belonged to the Bank of St. George. Unfortunately, the plane had stayed for only a few minutes, taking on two female passengers before taking back off.

That was forty minutes ago.

He approached a service desk where a bright-eyed twenty-something in a smart uniform greeted him with a smile, asking in French if she could help him. He decided to stick to her language, which might garner him some brownie points.

"I seem to have missed my flight," he said. "I was supposed to be on the Bank of St. George charter."

"Oh, I am so sorry," she said. "That left nearly an hour ago."

Ejima stood behind him, near the doors, keeping watch.

For what, he wondered.

"I realize that," he said. "There are two scheduled to come this way. I need to find out which one it was."

He knew that, just like in the United States, for every flight in European skies, pilots must submit a flight plan before its initial departure. These were then distributed electronically across the European Union. But to make sure his request was not dismissed, he reached into his pocket, found a hundred-euro note, and handed it over, adding, "Of course, I don't expect to use your time for free."

Back in the States that type of incentive was nearly always seized upon with vigor. But in Europe he'd come to learn that the gesture did not always work. He supposed it was the difference between capitalism and the socialism that dominated across the European Union. Just not the same degree of hunger to get ahead. It was there, but not as strong as in the United States. This young lady, though, readily accepted the offer and turned her attention to the desktop computer, tapping the keyboard, studying the screen before saying, "It's headed to Marrakesh. Morocco. Three and a half hours flying time. Expected to arrive at 3:35 P.M. local time."

Morocco was an hour behind Swiss time.

He thanked the woman and walked over to Ejima, who'd heard everything.

"Catherine Gledhill owns an estate in the High Atlas mountain range, south of Marrakesh," she told him. "She retreats there often. But tonight, she is hosting a gathering of national representatives there to convince them on the wonders of bitcoin. It's been scheduled for some time."

"And you're just now mentioning this?"

"It was not relevant. Until now."

"You have operatives there?"

She nodded. "Several."

"Why are you being so cooperative?" He was having a hard time determining if this woman was on the good or bad side.

"Could we walk outside?" she asked. "Where we can speak more privately?"

They retreated into the midday sun, the air at a comfortable room temperature.

"Malone-san—"

"Call me Cotton. Please."

She smiled. "It is not our way to be so informal with people we have just met."

"Humor me."

"As you wish. It is true we have long sought the return of the war gold. But we abandoned that quest some time ago. What we did not give up on was the hypocrisy of the United States. That gold was used to covertly further American interests postwar and to do some highly despicable and illegal things. Unfortunately, history does not note those quite so clearly."

"And your point?"

"We want to rectify that situation. Expose to the world what really happened after World War II. The truth of the evil we did is there for all to see. But the truth of what the United States did is not. Not to mention that the CIA has lost all semblance of control. Compounding this is the Bank of St. George, which not only has taken command of the gold, but now secretly dominates the entire bitcoin market, which some nations are heavily dependent upon. We think they, and everyone else, deserve to know the truth."

"One-upping the United States?"

"Exposing your ineptness. And why not?"

Good question. Why not?

"What we never anticipated was Kelly Austin's betrayal of the bank. Having her in our custody assured that the bank remained impotent regarding the Atlas Maneuver. No manipulation would occur. Our hope was she would eventually see us as a friend and cooperate. She is the single most important live witness to it all. She is Satoshi Nakamoto. But now the bank has her back. You can take comfort in the fact that nothing will happen to her. They need her alive and well."

"Until they get those private keys."

"Something tells me that Kelly Austin can take care of herself in that regard."

He could only hope. But he still wondered why Kelly had gone voluntarily. Then there was, "Do you know a Robert Citrone?"

"I am familiar with him. He was the CIA's liaison to the Bank of St. George for a long time. An opportunist who personally benefited from his service. But he's no longer important. He retired a few years ago."

"He was attacked by two men and taken prisoner. Both Japanese."

"I assure you, those men did not come from me. We have no interest in Citrone."

His instincts had always been spot-on and served him well. And though he too had been retired for a few years they remained sharp. Every one of those told him this woman was being truthful.

So he decided to trust a little.

"I need you to check and verify that the PSIA doesn't have Citrone in their sights. Derrick Koger and a woman I care a great deal about are dealing with Citrone, and they need to know the facts."

She nodded. "Excuse me while I make that call."

She stepped away and used her phone.

He too needed to make some calls.

First, to his old boss Stephanie Nelle.

Next, to Geneva.

CHAPTER 49

CASSIOPEIA SETTLED ON THE ROCKING BOAT AND KEPT THE GUN SHE'D retrieved from the deck aimed at Citrone. Koger lay still under the covered portion, near the helm, not moving.

She spotted a bucket.

"Dip that over the side and fill it," she ordered.

Citrone hesitated, still nursing a bleeding nose. She cocked the hammer on the gun. "I won't kill you, but I sure will hurt you."

"You are a violent woman?"

"Coming from a man who shot at me in the water."

"It seemed necessary at the time. I assume the divers below are dead?"

"You're on your own."

"I underestimated you."

"Your mistake."

Citrone bent down and lifted the plastic bucket, which he dipped over the side and filled.

"Dump it on Koger," she said.

Citrone emptied the pail onto Koger's head. The big man sprawled on the deck roused from unconsciousness, shaking off the fog in his brain, blinking his eyes, and coming back to reality.

"What happened?" she asked.

"I got coldcocked," Koger said, rubbing the back of his neck. "Where's the other guy?"

"Somewhere over the side with a spear through him," Citrone said.

Koger faced her. "Your doing?"

She nodded.

Koger slowly rose from the deck and immediately advanced on Citrone, grabbing the man by his jacket. "What are you up to?"

"You rattled the wrong cage this time," Citrone said.

The wind and rain began to ease, but the deck continued to rock. Luckily, she'd always had a stout pair of sea legs.

Koger released his grip. "Explain that or you're going swimming."

"The Japanese have returned and want what they believe belongs to them. Since I have no intention of journeying to the Philippines, and America isn't interested in digging up any more gold, I thought I would sell them the map. They, of course, do not want your interference so they insisted you be handled. I had no choice but to comply."

She heard the buzz of a phone and saw Koger reach back with his free hand and retrieve his from a back pocket. Koger answered the call, listened for a few moments, then said, "Do what you have to. We got it on this end."

The call ended.

Koger grabbed back hold of Citrone again and yanked him to the stern diving platform. "I'm going to give you five seconds to tell me the truth about all of this, or over you go."

Citrone seemed not to believe the threat.

But she could see Koger was serious.

That call had been important.

Koger glanced back her way. Then, with a twinkle in his eye, he whirled around and shoved Citrone over the side. She knew firsthand how cold that water was, especially with no wet suit. She stepped over to see Citrone treading water, the chill surely enough to bring his senses to full alert.

"He can't stay there long," she said.

"I know. But that pain in the ass is going to tell me the truth."

"Who called?"

"Cotton. Kelly Austin is on the way to Morocco. The bank has her. But he's learned that the Japanese have no operation ongoing relative to Moby Dick out there in the lake. This is all his, and I suspect Langley's, doing. He's got to be working with Neverlight. That other boat appeared right after you went into the water. Citrone popped me on the neck from behind. But not before I saw the divers."

"I will tell you everything," Citrone called out.

"I'm listening," Koger said.

"Get me out first."

"No way in hell. Talk. Then you get out. I figure you have maybe ten minutes before hypothermia sets in."

Citrone kept treading water. "Operation Neverlight. They are serious about this. They want you to disappear."

"And your involvement?"

"I know the bank. Langley wants the bank neutralized. They decided the two of you were problems. They were going to take Ms. Vitt out, then you."

"And you went along with that?" Cassiopeia asked.

"I...had no...choice."

"Keep talking," Koger called out.

Citrone was drifting away from the boat in the rough water. "They were going to prosecute me, even though everything I ever did was with Langley's okay. The bastards were going to put me in jail. You need to get me out."

"I'm still listening," Koger said.

"Langley wants you dead, Koger. Her? She's just in the wrong place at the right time. My task was to make it easy for them to take you both out."

"What about yesterday?" Cassiopeia asked. "What was that about?"

"A staged event, for your benefit," Citrone called out. "We wanted you to think the Japanese were the culprits. So we tossed the house and made an escape, wanting you to follow. You did.

When you appeared with the map we gave you what you expected. The idea was to kill you then. Of course, Ms. Vitt appeared and was quite brutal."

"You really want to insult me?" she called out. "I just killed three people."

Citrone continued to tread water. He had to be getting tired.

"We need to bring him in," she said in a low voice.

"Another minute," Koger replied. "Rob, do you actually have the real map?"

"I do."

"Do you know where the bank's gold is?"

"I think I do."

"Are you going to share that information?"

"I will. I swear."

"Are we still in the crosshairs?"

"Absolutely."

"Can you get them off us?"

"I'm afraid not. But thanks to Ms. Vitt, I will now be joining you in those crosshairs."

Citrone had drifted about twenty meters from the boat in the choppy water.

"He's right about that," Koger said. "They'll take him out now. We're all he's got to stay alive. Work the helm and let's get him in the boat."

CHAPTER 50

AIKO STOOD OFF FROM THE PRIVATE AIR TERMINAL, ON THE FAR SIDE OF one of the hangars, where she could talk in private on the phone. She'd placed the call a few minutes ago and was told the emperor emeritus would be available shortly. Her phone was vibrating, indicating that the former emperor was ready to talk. She thought an update was definitely in order, along with obtaining some guidance. Things were changing. Fast. So she answered the call and recounted all that had happened since this morning, including the decisions she'd already made.

"Not exactly what we had in mind," the emperor emeritus said.

She was touched by the intimacy of the conversation—the use of *we*—and the sincerity of the old man's words.

"Can you proceed forward?" he asked her.

"I believe so. I may still be able to retrieve Austin."

"Or perhaps find something else of interest."

She agreed.

"Journey safe, Aiko-san. Heed the *honne* and *tatemae*."

Truth and lie. The way things were and the way we liked them to be. The real reason and the pretext. Westerners believed the Japanese stressed harmony.

Not true.

They merely pushed the *image* of harmony.

Big difference.

What lay beneath might be, and usually was, completely different.

Like here.

COTTON MADE A CALL TO STEPHANIE NELLE.

Time to bring in the cavalry.

He found her at Magellan Billet headquarters in Atlanta.

"You didn't get your fill of Koger in Germany?" she asked.

"I do seem to be a glutton for punishment. But this is more serious than I imagined."

And he told her all that had happened, including what Koger had just reported about Robert Citrone and the attempt on Cassiopeia's life.

Which he had not liked to hear.

"The CIA has gone off the deep end," he said. "Again."

"Give me a few minutes and I'll call you back."

Ten minutes later his phone buzzed.

"I still have friends inside Langley," she said. "Operation Neverlight is definitely happening. There was sharp disagreement inside management on whether to do it. But the radicals won out."

"Does the White House know anything?"

"My first thought too. I texted Trinity Dorner. She checked and says they are in the dark."

Trinity was the former deputy national security adviser, now director of the National Counterterrorism Center. A friend, whom he'd worked with recently in Germany. Her word was gold.

"President Fox needs to know," he said. "The more the merrier here."

"I agree. I'll get Trinity to do that. But that's not going to help your immediate problem."

"I need to get to Morocco," he said.

"And your newfound travel buddy?"

"I'm taking her with me."

"Keeping your enemies closer?"

"Something like that."

"You do realize there's nothing the Japanese are doing that is good for us."

"I get that. But she knows more than I do. And she has assets on the ground, in place. Besides, I've worked with trouble before."

"That you have. It's your call, Cotton. Make it work. I'll have a plane there shortly. Keep me informed."

He ended the call and found Aiko Ejima. "You and I need to have a talk."

She stared at him.

"There's a story. A little girl and her father were crossing a bridge. The father became concerned and instructed his daughter, *Sweetheart, please hold my hand so that you don't fall into the river.* The little girl said, *No, Dad, you hold my hand.* The father was puzzled and asked, *What's the difference?* The little girl answered him, *If I hold your hand and something happens to me, chances are that I may let your hand go. But if you hold my hand I know for sure that, no matter what happens, you will never let my hand go.*" He focused hard on her. "Are you going to hold my hand? No matter what?"

"I could ask you the same thing."

Yes, she could. "You've been on this longer than me. And the only thing keeping me here, talking to you, is the fact that you're smart enough to know that the gold is gone. Were you going to stop the bank? Take control of the Atlas Maneuver for the Japanese government? Or gain control to expose the CIA and embarrass the U.S.? I don't know. Nor do I care. But I'm still going to trust you. I hope it won't be a mistake. We need to work together. Now please tell me what's happening in Morocco."

"The bank has scheduled for some time a large gathering of representatives from countries considering a switch to bitcoin as either currency or their national reserve. That gathering is happening this evening in Morocco. Unfortunately, I have just learned that

Catherine Gledhill has rooted out the source we cultivated within the bank, a woman named Lana Greenwell, who is now traveling with Gledhill to Morocco."

"A one-way ticket?"

"I would assume. Kelly Austin is being escorted by a hired assassin named Kyra Lhota, who is working for the bank. My assets here secured photographs that confirm this."

So he got the picture. "We have everybody in one place, where they can be dealt with."

She nodded. "Precisely."

Including you, he thought.

He'd been to Morocco several times. The rules there were vague and loose, law enforcement dependent on who you knew. An ancient class society dependent on how much wealth you possessed. Not one of his favorite spots on the globe. But Suzy was in serious trouble, regardless of the fact that she'd gone voluntarily. And as Stephanie had said, he was working point on this one.

"This gathering," he said. "Any way to get an invite?"

She shook her head. "No way. But we have eyes and ears on the ground."

"Okay. We're going to Morocco."

CHAPTER 51

CASSIOPEIA WATCHED AS KOGER TOSSED A LIFE RING OUT, THEN HELPED Citrone from the water, the big man struggling to climb back onto the stern platform, shivering. They were practicing, as Cotton would say, *some tough love*. But that's what it took sometimes.

"You two are evil," Citrone said. "Pure evil. I'm freezing."

She harbored little sympathy for the lying bastard who'd just tried to have her killed, then shot at her himself. Citrone found a few towels in a cabinet near the helm and wrapped himself.

Koger adjusted the cabin heater and blower to provide more warm air. "Rob, neither one of us is in a good mood. I got banged on the head and Cassiopeia barely avoided being skewered."

"Or shot," she added.

"I'm going to give you one chance to tell me the truth," Koger said. "If anything even hints at a lie, back in the water you go and, this time, we leave. Understand?"

Citrone said nothing.

Koger moved toward him and grabbed the man's wet clothes, ready to drag him back to the gunwales.

"Okay. Okay," Citrone said. "I understand."

"Talk," Koger said.

Cassiopeia kept the boat in neutral. The rain had eased to a mist and the wind had died down. The day remained gloomy with no other boats nearby. The one that had brought all the trouble had been released and drifted a hundred meters away.

Citrone moved himself closer to the vent pouring warm air out. "You two are in an ocean of trouble. The agency wants you dead. That effort includes not only your demise, but Catherine Gledhill and Kelly Austin too. They then intend to attack the bank and stop what it is planning."

"Forcibly?" Koger asked.

Citrone nodded. "Whatever it takes."

"The Atlas Maneuver?" Koger asked.

Citrone nodded.

"And what about the treasure from Golden Lily?" she asked.

"It's real," Citrone said. "What you two now find yourselves in the middle of dates back to the early days of the CIA, right after it was formed."

"We know that," Koger said. "Golden Lily and the Black Eagle Trust."

Citrone shrugged. "You have no idea. What do you know about James Forrestal?"

She glanced over at Koger, who did not seem as clueless as she was.

"The first secretary of defense," Koger said, "after the job was created in 1947. He worked for Truman, but they never got along. Eventually, Truman forced him out."

"In 1949," Citrone noted. "Then something odd happened. Two months after resigning, Forrestal suddenly died."

"What does that have to do with anything?"

"That's always been your problem, Derrick. No appreciation of history. You are indeed the proverbial bull in the china shop."

"Insulting me is not the best strategy," Koger said.

"In 1949 there was a war brewing within the intelligence community," Citrone said. "Nothing new, huh? This one was between the military and the newly formed CIA. The military wanted no part of a civilian spy agency. But others had different ideas. One of those was Forrestal, along with Allen Dulles, who was emerging as a leader of the CIA. Dulles was part of a team that submitted a report to Truman. It recommended the CIA be the central organization of the national intelligence system. Run by civilians. All clandestine operations to be headed by the CIA. No FBI involvement. No military. And, most important, full secrecy of the CIA's budget to provide what they called *administrative flexibility and anonymity.*"

"The Dulles-Jackson-Correa Report," Koger said.

"Look at you," Citrone mocked. "And here I thought you never cared about history."

"The Cold War had begun," Koger said. "Nobody wanted another Pearl Harbor, and everybody hated the Soviets, so anything and everything was on the table."

"Including using stolen war loot to finance covert operations," Cassiopeia added.

Citrone wrapped the towels tighter around him. "Precisely. The Black Eagle Trust. But that's where Forrestal drew the line. He wanted a strong CIA, but not financed by what he called *blood loot* stolen during the war. He and Dulles broke ranks on that one. Luckily for Dulles, Forrestal had some serious mental health problems. He'd been suffering from depression for years and was hospitalized at the Naval Medical Center in Maryland right after his resignation."

They listened as Citrone explained that the navy surgeon general handpicked a psychiatrist to treat Forrestal, who was housed on the hospital's sixteenth floor, supposedly to afford him more privacy. No one wanted the media to discover that the former secretary of defense was in a psych ward. At the time secrets like that could actually be kept. Forrestal himself prized anonymity, calling obscurity his hobby. And his relationship with the press was not amicable. Columnists Drew Pearson and Walter Winchell particularly disliked him.

"Forrestal was getting better," Citrone said. "Gaining weight. Holding a better grip on reality. But the man knew way too much, and he was bitterly opposed to the Black Eagle Trust. Remember, Truman himself had okayed all that and Forrestal hated Truman for forcing him to resign."

"He was going to expose it all?" Koger asked.

Citrone nodded. "But who knows? In the early-morning hours of May 22, 1949, about six weeks after he'd been hospitalized, his body, clad only in the bottom half of his pajamas, was found on a third-floor roof below the sixteenth-floor kitchen. The official navy review board waited five months before saying it was a suicide jump, offering no explanations."

"Why could it not have been?" Cassiopeia asked.

"Beside his bed Forrestal left a written statement. The contemporary press and later biographers called it a suicide note. But it hardly fit the mold. It was part of a poem from a translation of Sophocles' tragedy *Ajax*. Seventeen lines."

She knew the poem, having read it as a teenager. Her father had been a student of the classics and wanted his only daughter to be the same. After the great warrior Achilles had been killed in battle, a debate arose over who should receive his armor. Ajax, as the greatest surviving Greek warrior, felt he should be given the armor. But Kings Agamemnon and Menelaus awarded it instead to Odysseus. Ajax was furious and decided to kill all three of them. But the goddess Athena deluded Ajax into killing an entire herd of animals, thinking them men. Once he realized the deception, and the extent of what he'd done, overcome by shame, Ajax killed himself.

She told Citrone what she knew.

"And who said the classics cannot be instructive," Citrone said. "The symbolism and connection to reality are clear, provided you know the facts. The CIA and the fools conducting the Forrestal investigation did not make the connection between the poem and reality. Of course, the investigators knew nothing about the Black Eagle Trust. That was a closely held secret. The CIA tried to suppress what Forrestal wrote, but too many people knew about it. So they let it remain, thinking everyone would believe it the ramblings of a crazed mind. Which is exactly what happened. But Forrestal was anything but crazy. He was sending a message. Subtle, but loud and clear."

"And the point of this history lesson?" Koger asked.

"James Forrestal was probably murdered to keep him silent. And if the people involved with the creation of the Black Eagle Trust were willing to do that, what do you think the people involved with ending it will do?" Citrone paused. "There's just the two of you, plus Cotton Malone. Yes. I know about him. Neverlight does too, and they have their sights set on him. Three people against the Central Intelligence Agency. Derrick, you were not sent here to protect Kelly Austin. You were sent here to set her up to die."

The boat continued its steady rock back and forth on the choppy water. Cassiopeia now realized that she'd just killed three CIA operatives. That would not go unanswered. But she was more concerned about Cotton.

"I assume," Koger said, "I've now become a problem for them too?"

Citrone nodded.

"All right, Rob. Time for you to choose sides. And I swear to all that's holy, if you double-cross me again, I will put a bullet in your head. You get my meaning?"

She could see that Koger was not bluffing.

"Derrick, I am now as expendable as you," Citrone said. "They will kill us all. So I have no choice but to align with you. The enemy of my enemy and all that bullshit. Thankfully, there might be a way to get ahead of them."

"I'm listening," Koger said.

"As I told you, I actually do have the map for the Philippine caches. The original is safely tucked away. I also know where the gold is being held here in Switzerland."

"We've heard this before," Cassiopeia added.

"Yes, you have. But as Derrick has so eloquently pointed out, the situation has changed and he will kill me if I lie to you again."

"Keep talking," Koger said.

"The one thing the agency fears most is public exposure. They don't want any of this to see the light of day. That could be our main weapon. All we need is physical proof of the gold. Some wonderful color images would do the trick."

Koger stayed silent a few moments, considering the suggestion. As was she. It made sense.

"Okay," Koger finally said to her. "Let's get out of here."

And she restarted the engines.

CHAPTER 52

Kelly's head swirled.

She seemed in a daze.

Similar to how she felt twenty years ago when faced with the most difficult decision of her life. She'd prepped herself for months during the pregnancy, waiting for the inevitable. For so long she'd tried to live with the decision. Not forget it.

That was impossible.

She'd always wanted to know what happened after that day in the hospital. Finally, six years ago she'd used some of the money made from the bank and hired a top-notch investigator from New York to look into the matter. But that woman had found little to nothing. The adoption had occurred in Texas, with everything under seal, no public access allowed. They'd tried bribing a local clerk, and that had led to the name of the petitioners and information that the adoption file itself was destroyed in a fire a decade earlier. No electronic versions existed, and finding the adoptive parents had led to several dead ends.

But not so for Katie Gledhill.

Or was she lying?

"I need to speak to Catherine," she said.

KYRA OPENED HER EYES.

Kelly Austin had spoken to her.

They were cruising at thirty thousand feet, headed south toward the African continent. She'd lied to Austin. She knew exactly where they were headed. She'd left the woman alone, just as Gledhill had instructed, waiting for her to make the first move.

I need to speak to Catherine.

"Tell me more about my daughter."

She heard the pain in the request but, in truth, she personally knew nothing. She'd not been involved with that matter, until today.

"Have you really seen her?"

She nodded. "I have."

Not a lie, as a photo had been included in the e-file.

"Does she know she's adopted?"

"I have no idea."

The file had made no mention if anyone had made contact with the daughter, who would be approaching twenty years old now. Surely Austin had often wondered about appearance, manners, personality.

And the ultimate question.

Had any of her been passed on to the child?

Then there was—

"What about the father?" Kyra asked.

KELLY HAD NOT CONSIDERED THAT QUESTION IN A LONG, LONG TIME. When it all happened, involving the father had never been an option. She'd wanted nothing to do with him. So she'd lied to the lawyer handling the adoption and said the father's identity was unknown, adding that there'd been several men in the picture at the time of conception, impossible to say which one was the father. She'd signed an affidavit swearing that his identity could not be *reasonably ascertained*. The lawyer had warned her that lying could prove disastrous. The father, if he later became aware, could challenge the adoption, no matter how much time had passed.

His rights last forever.

But the father had never known about the child and she planned to keep it that way.

"He does not exist," she said.

"The presence of your daughter says otherwise."

She hated the condescending tone. "Have you ever made a mistake?"

"Who has not?"

"I mean a truly epic mistake. One that alters the course of your life. One you can never, ever take back."

The plane buffeted from turbulence. Truth be known, she wasn't all that keen about flying. But answers to lifelong questions might exist at the end of the journey.

"You have an opportunity to reverse the mistake regarding your daughter," Lhota said.

"You don't understand."

"Enlighten me."

"The mistake came when I chose to exclude the father."

And she meant it.

It had been a selfish act by a rash young woman thinking of no one but herself. Would things have been different if she'd done otherwise?

Hard to say.

But she probably never would have found herself on that dark road when a deer decided to dart out in front her. And definitely not at the Bank of St. George when the CIA came looking for an alternative to a potential economic disaster. One a tragedy. The other an opportunity. She *was* Satoshi Nakamoto. Creator of blockchain and bitcoin. But she was also the woman who gave up her child.

"Perhaps you can rectify the mistake regarding the father too," Lhota said.

Doubtful.

But perhaps.

CHAPTER 53

CATHERINE STARED OUT THE WINDOW AS THE JET CROSSED OVER Marrakesh. She loved Morocco. Her parents had been the first to buy an estate there. The purchase made sense as the kingdom was big on investment and low on rules and taxes. The bank itself had maintained a long-standing relationship with the ruling Alawi dynasty, the current king a close friend.

Humans had occupied the land for nearly a hundred thousand years. The Carthaginians, Phoenicians, Romans, and Arabs had all invaded. The first Moroccan state was established in the 8th century. At one time its sultans controlled most of the Iberian Peninsula. Then colonization came and the Ottomans, Spanish, Portuguese, French, and British each occupied parts of it at times. Its strategic location near the mouth of the Mediterranean had always made it politically important, the region a volatile mixture of conquest and trade. It had been an independent nation, beholden to no one, since 1956.

Hundreds of kilometers of Atlantic Ocean coastline stretched along its western border, reaching eastward past the Strait of Gibraltar. The Rif Mountains rose in the northern regions. The Atlas Mountains ran down the backbone of the country, twenty-five hundred kilometers from northeast to southwest. Most of the southeast portion was Sahara Desert, sparsely populated and unproductive. The majority of the population lived toward the north, the mountains generally inhabited by Berbers. Especially in the High Atlas where they dominated. A simple people with a straightforward way of life, unaffected by luxuries the world offered. Many lived in houses made of clay with no electricity. Resources were few, but the Berbers had never been dependent on anyone. A healthy, self-sufficient people who appreciated the natural world surrounding them. They took care of themselves.

Her father had loved them.

The jet began its descent.

Lana Greenwell sat toward the rear of the cabin, alone, on one of the leather sofas. They'd said nothing to each other on the three-hour journey. Her mother had remained in Luxembourg. Lana had been terrified of the gun pointed at her, and eventually came along without resistance after Catherine offered assurances.

"You must understand the situation you have placed me in. I have to keep you close so as to avoid any further lapses in security. Surely you can see that."

"Your mother aimed a gun at me."

"I know. Please forgive her. But she is protective of me and the bank. I want us to work together tonight. I am counting on you."

"I want my job back and my money to remain untouched."

"I will agree, we can discuss that. After the gathering. Provided you work with me tonight."

All of which had calmed Lana down.

Kyra was on her way with Kelly. Eventually, the problem with Lana would be turned over to Kyra and she'd take care of the matter. There was no way she could ever trust Lana again, and no way could she turn a blind eye to what had happened.

"You have no choice," her mother had said. *"She can, and will, jeopardize everything."*

"You want her dead?"

"It is not what I want. It's what's necessary. That woman chose her own fate when she became a traitor."

True. Without a doubt.

But still regrettable.

She'd already read the news reports about how Samvel Yerevan had been found floating in Lake Baikal, the victim of an apparent drowning. Access to Yerevan's bitcoin had required that the Armenian be dead. It was the only way. The same was true for Lana.

Conscience had no role in her line of work.

The plane began to lose altitude.

Hopefully, Kyra had sufficiently prepared Kelly. Sadly, she too would have to be dealt with. But only after the keys were returned to the bank's control. Never would she see her daughter. But that realization would not become clear until it was far too late.

"I made a mistake, Katie," Lana said.

"To say the least. You sold me out for money."

She'd known from the start that what she and her mother had devised came with risks. The covert manipulation of varying national economies was something many had tried through the centuries. None had ever succeeded for long. But here they had devised something innovative, something utterly new that no one, outside of their inner circle, would know even existed. Something so clever that its use could not be anticipated.

Her mother had been right.

Brainwash your subject well enough and control is easy. Say the right words, paint the right picture, make their minds believe what they so desperately want to believe, and the response is guaranteed.

Thankfully all cryptocurrency carried an aura of mystique.

It was what made it special.

But in reality it was nothing more than another financial bubble.

And there were many in the world.

Real estate bubbles. Stock market bubbles. Dot-com bubbles.

In every one people paid exorbitant amounts for things that shouldn't have been worth anything near the going price.

An anomaly.

That traced its way back to tulips.

Something else her mother had taught.

People associated tulips with Holland, but the plants were not native there. They were introduced to the Dutch in 1593, brought in from Constantinople and planted to research their medicinal purposes. But people broke into that test garden and stole the beautiful plants, selling them for quick money and, in the process, starting the Dutch bulb trade.

Over the next several decades tulips became a fad among the rich of Holland, and prices rose to astronomical levels. At the height of the mania, in what seemed a complete loss of sanity, the bulbs were deemed too valuable to even risk planting. Wealthy purchasers began to display the ungrown bulbs on mantelpieces and sideboards. The height of the bubble came in March 1637. Tulip traders were making, and losing, fortunes regularly. A good trader could earn a year's salary in one month. Local governments could do nothing to stop the frenzy. Then, one day, a buyer failed to show up and pay for his bulb purchases. The ensuing panic spread across Holland and, within days, tulip bulbs were worth a hundredth of their former prices.

The bubble burst.

There were lessons to be learned there.

Buyers of bitcoin thrived on the hope that the blockchain network would continue to accrue in value and that they would find someone to pay more for their coins than they had. But people loved to gamble. They even sought out risk. And, she'd found, the less someone knew about a subject, the more they were excited. She likened it to Oscar Wilde's definition of fox hunting. *The pursuit of the uneatable by the unspeakable.*

It was truly all about the mystique.

She heard the landing gear deploy. They were on their final approach to the Marrakesh Menara Airport.

That mystique must continue.

Despite the two betrayals.

And the next few hours would be telling.

CHAPTER 54

COTTON HAD ALWAYS LIKED MARRAKESH. THE RED CITY. NAMED FOR its countless buildings of beaten clay. It sat in the Tensift valley, an oasis at the edge of the Sahara Desert, a river passing along its northern edges. A vibrant former caravan town and imperial capital full of Islamic architecture, steeped in ancient aristocracy, and littered with commerce. Nearly eight miles of powder-pink ramparts still encircled the old city. Once needed for protection, now they were just one more tourist stop in a place where over a million people lived.

They had flown from Basel straight to Morocco aboard a private United States Air Force jet. Stephanie had arranged for the quick transportation which had whisked them from Switzerland to Africa in just over three hours. Online flight tracking indicated that the jet with Suzy was ninety minutes ahead of them, which meant she was already on the ground. Thankfully, the PSIA had assets waiting and they'd already reported that Suzy and Kyra Lhota were driving south, toward the mountains, their destination most likely Catherine Gledhill's estate.

He and Aiko had remained in Marrakesh to touch base with other PSIA operatives and get a better idea as to the lay of the land. Knowledge was without question power, especially in this chaotic spot. A taxi had brought them from the airport to the central medina. He recalled the drivers who were notorious for saying the meter was broken and quoting rates ten times the standard. Aiko seemed to know them too.

"Here," she said, handing the man fifty euros.

The driver started to protest and she tossed him a glare that dared him to challenge her. The guy seemed to know when to hold and when to fold and pocketed the money before speeding off.

"I detest people without honor," she muttered.

The scene around him seemed to beat with a frenetic pulse and gave *bustle* a whole new meaning. The medina was the heart and soul of the city. It was easy to get lost among its countless narrow alleyways that all wreaked havoc with any sense of direction. A World Heritage Site. And his experience with those was anything but good. Bad things always seemed to happen when he visited one.

"Why are we here?" he asked her.

The sun had begun its retreat to the west, but a hazy warmth still cloaked the air.

"As opposed to heading for the Gledhill estate," he added.

"Follow me," she said.

They left the crowd for one of the looping *derbs,* narrow alleys lined with one storefront after another. Hawkers bid them welcome in a litany of languages. Smoke from restaurant grills plumed the air. Odd to be here. He should be in Copenhagen, closing up his bookshop for the day. They rarely stayed open past seven, after the busy summer months. But business had been especially good for the year. An upturn. And though he made some money from the buying and selling of used books and some new frontlist material, the big bucks came from the private collectors who were always on the lookout for the rare and unattainable. There, he'd excelled and gained a reputation as someone who could find what you wanted. He enjoyed book hunting. As much as the intelligence business? The jury was still out on that one.

Aiko marched at a steady pace, oblivious to the push and pull between old and new that surrounded her. They turned a corner and found a quiet, white-walled street lined with more houses squeezed tightly together. Closed doors lined both sides. Behind those he knew were *riads*, homes built around courtyards filled with palm trees and bougainvillea. She stopped at one painted an emerald green and turned the brass knob. Beyond was a passageway where a set of ladder-like steps led up to the next level. There another door waited, partially open.

She froze and he read her face.

"That's not good?" he asked.

"Not at all."

He reached back beneath his jacket and retrieved a Beretta. Two weapons with spare magazines had been waiting for them in the jet. Aiko had refused the one he'd offered her. Which he hadn't challenged. Carrying a gun was a personal choice every field officer had to make.

He eased open the door.

Beyond was a small apartment, the furniture a mismatched array. The air smelled heavily of tobacco. Nothing seemed out of place. But his senses were on high alert. He led the way inside with Aiko following, watching their backs. A small kitchen was visible past a counter. A second archway led to another room. He swiftly moved there and glanced past to see a bedroom with a man sprawled across the bare mattress, two bullet holes in his forehead, the skin drained white, death freezing the eyes and mouth open. Aiko came up behind him, stepped past, and approached the body.

"Your man?" he asked.

She nodded. "This is a problem."

"Who was he?"

"Head of the detail here. In charge of the contingent."

"How many?"

"Six."

"You need to see about them."

Not a hint of emotion filled her face, and he assumed that her docile and unassuming mask had seriously misled more than one enemy. He made a mental note never to play poker with this woman.

She found her phone and began tapping.

He took a moment to look around and see if there was anything there that might be useful. His soft-soled shoes moved noiselessly across the wood floor. But there was nothing. No phone. Computer. Laptop. Not even a piece of paper. Zippo.

"I can't contact any of them," Aiko said. "They made a report less than two hours ago. The CIA is clearly ahead of us."

And he knew for what.

Clearing the playing field.

Her phone began to vibrate.

She answered, listened a moment, spoke in Japanese, then ended the call.

"One of my assets," she said. "The one at the airport. They missed him. He was answering my call. We need to get to him."

CHAPTER 55

CASSIOPEIA CHANGED BACK INTO DRY CLOTHES. THEY'D FLED THE LAKE and headed straight to Citrone's villa. Koger was keeping an eye on Citrone, ever mindful of the fact that their newfound ally did not have a trustworthy bone in his body. After everything they'd learned, she was more concerned than ever about Cotton. He was flying blind into a hurricane. Problem was, Citrone had no idea what was happening in Morocco, only that the CIA was there. She found her phone and dialed Cotton's number.

He answered after the third ring.

"You okay?" she asked.

"Gettin' by. A lot happening."

"Same here."

And she told him about the day's events.

"You took a risk going into that water," he said.

"It was the only way to flush Citrone out. Of course, I had no idea he'd go to the lengths he did. But I was ready."

"I'm sure you were."

She loved the fact that he didn't criticize or lecture her. He knew she didn't need protecting, just supporting.

"Citrone says the CIA is there," she said.

"We've already determined that," he told her. "But it would be nice to know what they're planning."

"He swears he's in the dark, but we'll keep working on him. The problem is he's a pathological liar."

"Koger will shoot him. The guy's a loose cannon sometimes."

"As I'm learning. What are you going to do?" she asked.

"I'm not sure. We're making this up as we go. Keep me posted if there's anything else I need to know."

"Be careful." She had to say it.

"Same to you."

"I always am."

The call ended.

She did not like that he was in danger, but realized trust was a two-way street and she couldn't make things better for him, just as he couldn't for her.

They were both on their own.

She left the bedroom and walked to Citrone's room, where Koger was standing watch as their host showered and changed clothes in the bathroom with the door nearly closed.

"I have his phone," Koger said to her. "And I told him that I'll put that bullet in his head if he tries anything. You hear that, Rob? A friggin' bullet right between your eyes."

"I understand," Citrone replied from the other side of the door.

Citrone waddled out, dressed in black slacks and an expensive silk shirt, his thin hair dry and combed. He was back to his more polished self. Unlike flailing away in freezing lake water. She realized that Koger was making sure this man stayed just enough out of his element to keep him off guard. Though, if pushed enough, Koger might just shoot him.

Citrone allowed his girth to settle comfortably on the bed. The house staff had straightened the room. "Derrick, you have to believe me. Yamashita's gold exists. It was merged with the Nazi gold in 1949, but the Japanese gold was five times the size of Germany's. Historians love to talk about Nazi plunder. But the Japanese put the Germans to shame. It was an enormous cache, worth in the many billions. The Bank of St. George has that gold and has used it regularly as a source of unaccounted-for capital. They currently have one of the largest concentrations of gold on the planet."

"But it's unknown," Koger said. "Not counted in the world's inventory."

Citrone pointed a stubby forefinger. "Exactly. So the bank was always careful and trickled it in ever so slowly. They are masters of what they do. And controlling that much bullion is a challenge. Believe me. That is why there remains only a single repository for it all."

"And you know where that is?" she asked.

Citrone nodded. "I do. And you've already been there."

"That wine depository?" she said.

"Exactly. I wanted you to take a look at the one vault to see if, by chance, the gold had been returned there. But as you discovered, it was empty. There's another vault, though. The bank does not know I am aware of its existence. But I am."

She could see that Koger was suspicious.

As was she.

Like, who wouldn't be?

"Rob," Koger said, and he cocked and aimed the gun at Citrone. "I'm not screwin' around here. I'm going to get this done whether you're dead or alive or badly maimed."

Citrone showed not a hint of fear. "Langley didn't really want to partner with me in the first place, but I offered them a quick way to get to you. That failed. So I have no choice but to work with *you* now. It's my only shot of getting past this alive."

Koger kept the gun aimed. "Okay, partner. Talk."

"The gold is in the wine vault. In another location."

She stared at Koger and he seemed to sense her thoughts.

Do we believe him?

"I worked with the bank a long time," Citrone said in a bitter, almost defeated tone. "I made many friends there. Friends that keep me informed. For a price, of course. The gold is there. It was put there decades ago and left after the vault was converted to wine storage. That much bullion would be impossible to move out of that building without drawing a lot of unwanted attention."

Koger motioned with the gun. "That's the first thing you've said that makes sense. Can your friends get us in?"

"No. But I can."

Cassiopeia had been thinking about what Citrone said earlier.

"The one thing the agency fears the most is public exposure. They don't want any of this to see the light of day. All we need is physical proof. Some wonderful color images would do the trick."

"If the gold is there," she said, "only publicity will protect us."

Koger said, "I agree."

"Do you have the ability to make that happen?" she asked.

Koger smiled.

"I know just the person to call."

CHAPTER 56

KYRA ADMIRED THE UNCLUTTERED COUNTRYSIDE OUTSIDE THE CAR windows, the Moroccan landscape grand, rugged, unassailable, as if no one had ever walked there before. The distant Atlas Mountains seemed an impassable wall with no straight lines, the ragged, tranquil giants scored with snow, the tops capped even thicker. She'd always thought mountains revealed nature's essential character. Hard, cruel, totally uncaring about anything.

She and Kelly Austin were headed south, away from Marrakesh, on the RN7, a main highway that eventually led to Agadir on the coast. The car had been waiting when they deplaned. The pilot had informed them just before landing where they were setting down and Austin had not been surprised.

"I'm not an idiot. I know about the event in Morocco. It's a big deal. And I assumed Katie would move ahead, telling no one about what I did."

"And what was it you did?" Kyra had asked, trying to learn more. But Austin had only smiled. "I'll trade you."

Clever. But not possible.

So she'd let it go, though she wanted to know what was going on. Gledhill was usually the picture of cool. Nothing got to her. But the older woman had seemed agitated and anxious today.

Both surprising.

A lack of a passport for Austin had not been an issue as no one had met the plane, nor demanded to see any documents, at the airport. Kyra assumed that was more of Gledhill's influence.

Money truly did talk.

They were rising in altitude, the terrain stretching away in undulations of the sallow, sunburned grass that belonged to high-up places. She'd never visited Morocco before, though she'd heard tales and stories. Lots of men with money, but not the type who routinely used services like hers. And, if they did, they surely kept those in-house.

"There it is," Austin said.

Perched on a mount. High in the shelter of the mountains. A *kasbah*. A grand fortified house built by the rich, made of compacted red mud. Its castle-like shape came from four turrets, one at each corner, once used by other similar buildings to keep a lookout or to fire down at enemies or bandits. Its windows were intentionally small both to keep weather out and to make the target difficult to acquire. More buildings stretched out around it, but the kasbah remained the tallest. High walls washed in pink tones encircled the compound. Great old cypress and palm trees stood close to the outer walls softening the monolithic effect. The sun's last rays fought to stave off the coming evening chill that would accompany long shadows.

"Banking pays well," Austin said.

That it did.

"This land was once owned by the king," Austin said. "It was given to Katie's father long ago."

"No telling what favors were being repaid."

"Her father built the house, and she has maintained it."

"You've been here before?"

"Several times."

"You know a lot about her."

"More than anyone else, I imagine."

The car motored to a gate arm that blocked the road. Kyra did not at first see the guards until they stepped from the shadows. Two men. Both armed with assault rifles. They spoke to the driver in Arabic, which she did not understand. But they were quickly waved ahead, the barrier lifted, and the car headed farther up the mount toward the main gate in the high walls. Security was everywhere. Men with rifles outside the walls, more atop, all of them patrolling. She wondered what was happening here.

I know about the event in Morocco. That's what Austin had said.

"What's going on here tonight?" she asked.

"Changing the world."

Which told her nothing.

She wondered if the time would come when she'd have to kill Kelly Austin. Definitely, she'd do it. Only rarely had she ever regretted doing her job. But she might here. Austin seemed like a decent person. And the whole thing with her daughter, given up at birth. Tough break. But she still wanted to know what was happening.

She asked, "Does this involve bitcoin?"

The car stopped at two huge wooden gates. Both closed. Other men with rifles waited. More discussions with the driver. Then the gates slowly swung open.

"Do you own bitcoin?" Austin asked.

"Who doesn't?"

"Why did you buy it?"

She couldn't tell her the truth, so she said, "I considered it a good investment."

"Why? There's nothing of any tangible value there. Not a thing you can hold or touch. Just a blip on a computer screen."

"That people are willing to pay money for."

"What happens when they don't want to do that?" Austin asked.

"I guess I'm in big trouble. But could not the same thing be said for any money? It's all based on a belief that it's valuable."

"That's true, with one big difference."

The gates were now fully open and the car began to slowly creep inside the compound.

"With fiat money a government issues and regulates it. Yes, nearly all of them manipulate it, printing more and more, devaluing what already exists, and a person's wealth is totally dependent on that manipulation. But all of that happens in the open. There are many, many people involved. The media watches everything. There are countless eyes and ears on what is happening, so there are few surprises. If the people don't agree with the manipulation, they can change the government. But with bitcoin, everything, and I mean everything, is hidden away. Sure, every transaction is recorded on the internet. But you have no idea who is buying and selling, who is manipulating, and the entire system is designed to make sure you never do. That's good in one respect, but dangerous in another. Especially for a commodity that is nothing more than ones and zeros in a computer program."

She'd never really considered it all before this moment.

"And how is it you know all this?" Kyra asked.

"I created the whole damn thing."

The car eased its way into a large, paved courtyard that fronted the main house and the driver switched off the engine.

"When you check in, like good guard dogs do, I want you to deliver a message to Katie Gledhill," Austin said.

She was listening.

"Tell her, I created it all and I can end it all. So don't screw with me. I want the information on my daughter."

CHAPTER 57

CATHERINE STOOD AT HER OPEN BALCONY DOORS AND STARED OUT. The evening sun slanted at a low angle and its golden light made the contours of the distant Atlas Mountains seem deep, the colors rich, yellow-green on the western face, darker to the sides, snow atop, the vibrance of every ridge against the valley's shadow like an inner glow. The air was dry and pristine, which was one of the things she really loved about Morocco. No haze or heat gave any illusion of motion. No wind swayed a thing, no clouds drifted in the evening sky. Every peak, every rock lay still, like when a breath was held.

Her father had worked hard to create a working estate. Carrots, turnips, potatoes, and onions were still grown in irrigated fields, as well as wheat. Date palms and olive trees dotted the land, sheep and goats grazed on patches of grass alongside free-range chickens. In recent years she'd opened a carpet workshop that produced some impressive Berber rugs sold in the markets. Beyond the walls, toward the west, stables housed purebred Arabian horses, another of her father's passions that she'd continued, the animals compact, powerful, and highly intelligent.

She'd arrived in Marrakesh ahead of Kyra and Kelly, and had just been informed that the two women were now within the compound. Good. Everything was finally contained.

She loved the estate. Her father had seen to every detail in the construction. Architecture had been another of his many varied interests. He'd modeled it after other *kasbahs* in the region and she'd lovingly maintained his vision, new stone added to old and scraped to a corresponding gray-brown pallor. Gardens abounded everywhere, the largest now filled with a tent large enough to accommodate the eighty guests who were here for the evening. She was climbing to the pinnacle of her life, ready for her latest performance, eager to erase the failures of the past two days.

Prepared to change the world.

A soft knock came on the bedroom door.

She stepped across and opened it.

Kyra Lhota entered and she closed the door behind her.

"Your guest is safely in her bedroom," Kyra said.

"Did she offer anything meaningful?"

"One thing."

And she listened as Kyra told her what Kelly had said about being capable of ending it all.

That was not an idle threat.

Especially coming from Kelly.

Bitcoin ran through a collection of software programs that tens of thousands of computers around the world used, solving mathematical challenges and constantly adding to the universal blockchain. In the beginning Kelly had interacted with the bitcoin community through mailing lists, message boards, and emails using her Satoshi Nakamoto persona. She was the one who moved the Genesis block on January 3, 2009, which first started the chain. Catherine had been there, watching. Kelly personally maintained and developed the network for the next two years, all as Nakamoto. Then she backed off and encouraged other open-source developers to step in.

And they had. Many, in fact.

Which allowed bitcoin to take on a life of its own, now through its growing number of participants. To signal Nakamoto's withdrawal from the process Kelly had sent out a message on December

12, 2010. *I've moved on to other things. It's in good hands now.*
In the years since then, contributing developers had made the net-
work better, more secure, more functional, or at least that's what
Kelly had told her.

"*Satoshi Nakamoto doesn't matter anymore. It's all a collabo-
ration now. The network runs itself.*"

"*Is that not dangerous? Should we not have more control?*"

Kelly smiled. "Who says we don't."

Indeed. Who says?

"Did she mention anything else?" she asked Kyra.

"That's all, besides wanting to know more about her daughter."

"My plan is to get what I need from Kelly, provide her with
what I know on her daughter, then have you deal with her after
she leaves Morocco."

She saw that Kyra understood what that meant.

But what Kelly said could not be ignored.

I can end this.

She had to be careful with what she revealed since Kyra was
unaware of what was at stake. No need to involve her with such
sensitive information. But that didn't mean she did not need Kyra.

"This situation is fluid," she said. "For now we must keep Kelly
alive and well and cooperative. She'll stay here on the estate until
we come to an understanding. There's plenty of security. But I
have another problem that needs your immediate attention. Her
name is Lana Greenwell. She's here too."

"I assume you want that problem to disappear?"

"Permanently. But it needs to be explainable. She came here
for the event, with me, and plenty of people know she is here.
I thought perhaps she leaves for a walk in the countryside, or a
visit to a local village, and never returns. Her body is found. Say
at the bottom of a cliff. An accident, a tragedy. Like with Samvel
Yerevan."

"When would you like that situation to be resolved?"

"All of the bank's consuls are here for the event tonight. Lana
wants desperately to believe all is forgiven. So she'll cooperate.

288

Everyone will leave tomorrow. Lana and I will stay. Take care of it in a few days."

Kyra nodded.

She also realized that the task would be made much easier by the fact that no one, Lana included, would suspect the first consul of the Bank of St. George of being a murderess.

"There is an even more pressing matter, though," Catherine said. "One I need you to handle in the meantime." She stepped over to her leather satchel and removed a file folder, which she handed over. "That is a copy of all the information I have on Kelly Austin's daughter. I want you to find the daughter, then keep her in your sights. I suspect we are going to have to exert extreme pressure to get Kelly to cooperate, and I have found show-and-tell to always be quite effective. I will need you nearby, ready to provide photos or video at a moment's notice."

Kyra opened the file and pursued a few of the investigative reports, surely searching for her destination.

"The jet is at your disposal, waiting in Marrakesh. Contact me when you have the daughter in sight."

"And my fees for all these additional services?"

"Double the bitcoin you just made."

Which had been the fee for finding Kelly Austin. That had not worked out, but now the opportunity was resurrected and she saw that Kyra appreciated the generosity.

"I can live with that," Kyra said.

I bet you can, she thought.

And Kyra left the room.

Catherine took a moment and composed herself. She'd just orchestrated the deaths of two former friends. One quite close. And the daughter? Hopefully they would not need to involve her at all.

But as bait?

She was perfect.

She stepped back to the French doors overlooking the central garden. Below was a sea of wildflowers, cacti, palm trees, and fountains. At its center an ancient fig tree, tall and broad, thrust out its twisted arms. Beyond, toward the far end in a large open patch, a huge canvas event tent had been erected. Dinner tonight was for too many to host comfortably inside the house. But the evening's weather was perfect for an outdoor gathering, though the tent itself was air-conditioned.

The staff had been working all week to make things ready. Representatives from Panama, Paraguay, Venezuela, Nicaragua, Brazil, Argentina, and Malta were staying at the Four Seasons in Marrakesh. Cars had been sent and everyone should be arriving within the hour. Representatives from six other nations that had already made the switch to bitcoin would also be here. It helped to have people with firsthand experience present to answer questions and ease concerns. It also maintained the façade that the bank was neutral relative to bitcoin, acting merely as a conduit for the exploration of new alternatives, something financial institutions had been doing for centuries. Her message later to the gathering would be carefully chosen, never advocating, merely reporting facts and allowing the participants to make up their own minds.

Say the right words, paint the right picture, allow their minds to believe what they so desperately want to believe, and the response is guaranteed.

She checked her watch: 6:40 P.M.

Here she was plotting life and death. Her father would have never appreciated the gravity.

But her mother certainly did.

Which was all that mattered.

CHAPTER 58

CASSIOPEIA STARED UP AT THE LEADEN SKY THAT LAY LOW OVER Geneva, enveloping the city in a premature dusk. A biting wind howled off the lake, whipping the water into frothy waves, driving birds to seek cover beneath the bridges. Pedestrians hurried themselves along on the sidewalks, bending low in a quest for shelter from the unpleasant weather. The time was approaching 8:00 P.M. She, Koger, and Citrone had driven back to the city after Citrone had finally—supposedly—told them all he knew.

From 1949 until the 1980s the Black Eagle Trust gold was stored in a secure mountain bunker, one of many that dotted the Swiss Alps. When the underground vault in Geneva was created the gold was moved. That had been a huge undertaking, accomplished in pieces so as not to draw attention to the extraordinary quantity. The gold had been crated by CIA contract help, then transported by armored cars to its new home. That had all happened during the good times between the agency and the bank, and Citrone had been provided access to the entire operation. When the vault was converted into a wine repository, the gold was never moved. Instead, it had stayed and the remodel of the facility had taken place around it, unknown to the contractor. The vault Cassiopeia had entered apparently acted as a decoy. A place to show and say the gold was gone.

The information made sense, but it was dependent on whether Citrone could be believed.

And believing him was a big leap.

Koger had driven, parking right in front of the wine depository. This was going to be the direct approach, especially considering that Citrone knew the custodian, Wells Townley.

"Wells and I have done business together," Citrone told them. "Thankfully, he is a negotiable soul. He likes the good life. He just can't afford it. I make sure he can. And it's not easy. The bank operates at a security level comparable to Langley. They keep a close watch on their people."

"That's just a challenge for you," Koger said. "Not an obstacle."

Citrone smiled. "Exactly the way I view it too. Langley wanted me to cultivate the relationship. But be warned. Wells is loyal to the bank. He will not reveal its secrets easily."

She noticed the tone, not that of someone cornered or caught, more the natural exasperated voice of someone genuinely bemused.

Which made her wonder.

"Just so we're clear," Koger said. "I'm going to hurt you bad if this turns out to be a wild goose chase."

"It won't."

She was somewhat encouraged by Citrone's confidence but kept reminding herself that this man was a proficient liar.

And that was a problem.

The city was bustling for the evening, cars darting back and forth on the busy boulevard that stretched past the repository. Both she and Koger were armed. She was still worried about Cotton. They'd heard nothing more from him about what was happening on the ground in Morocco.

"You ready?" Koger asked her as they all walked toward the repository's front doors.

"I'm always ready."

"You sound just like him."

"And the problem?"

They stopped at the glass doors. Koger tested them. Locked.

More plate-glass panels formed walls to either side. Past the glass and into the foyer a reception counter waited. The elevators were around the corner, as was the conference room where she and Townley had met. No one was in sight.

"That's odd," Citrone said.

"How so?" Koger asked.

"Someone is always watching the front doors."

"Not this evening," Cassiopeia said.

A door opened behind the reception counter and Wells Townley appeared. The stolid, bland-faced little man wore a houndstooth jacket, maroon slacks, and a pale-blue shirt with a bow tie. Townley approached the doors but made no effort to unlock them. Koger motioned for that to happen. Townley shook his head no.

"Okay," Koger muttered. "Have it your way."

The big man raised an arm then twirled his pointed index finger round and round. Behind them, from down the street, three white vans motored up and hopped the curb, parking directly in front of the repository in the small cobbled square between the building and the street. Doors opened and a host of armed Swiss military poured out. Men and women. They assumed a position in front of the glass doors, weapons at the ready.

Back at Citrone's villa Koger had made one call.

To a woman named Trinity Dorner.

He'd explained the situation and asked that President Warner Fox be informed. Intentionally he'd bypassed the CIA, since there was no way to know how far knowledge of Operation Neverlight existed up the chain of command. Dorner, Koger had explained, had been with him and Cotton in Germany, proving invaluable. She was closely connected to the White House and the president in particular. The call had been short and to the point. Twenty minutes later a return call came into Koger's phone.

From the president of the United States.

They talked for a few moments.

We're ready, Koger had said at the end.

And apparently that was the case.

Another car hopped the curb and came up beside the vans. From the passenger side a woman emerged, dressed in a smart red business suit.

"Is that Dorner?" she asked.

Koger shook his head. "No. That's trouble. With a capital *T*. I asked Trinity for help and, of all the people in the world, this is who she sent."

The new woman stopped to talk to one of the uniformed men.

Koger explained that the Financial Market Supervisory Authority was the Swiss governmental body responsible for financial regulation. That included the supervision of banks, insurance companies, stock exchanges, and securities dealers, along with any other financial intermediaries and private vaults. It was an independent institution based in Bern, functionally and financially separate from the central federal administration and the Department of Finance, reporting directly to the Swiss parliament.

The authority granted operating licenses for companies and organizations subject to its supervision and made sure every one of them obeyed the law. It could investigate, issue warnings, cancel licenses, even liquidate a company if need be. One particularly testy subject was that of World War II plunder and wealth. Swiss banks had come under repeated fire for harboring Holocaust-obtained wealth. In the 1990s the banks finally agreed to a $1.25 billion settlement. New laws were passed to make it harder for Swiss banks to retain any ill-gotten plunder. The Nazis' and Yamashita's gold represented the Holy Grail of plunder and had effectively evaded detection since 1945. All thanks, of course, to the Central Intelligence Agency.

"I'm assuming," Koger said, "that when the authority was contacted and apprised of the situation its interest was immediately piqued."

He told her that the authority consisted of a board of directors and an executive board, all headed by a chairperson, the current one walking straight over to them and introducing herself as Kristin Jeanne. She was middle-aged, dark-haired, with a face and expression that seemed utterly comfortable with armed military personnel standing behind her.

"So good to see you," Jeanne said to Koger. "Again."

"Are we good?" he asked her.

"Let's see. We date for a month, then you haven't called me in, what, three months? What do you think? Are we good?"

"I get it. I'm sorry. I really am. Things have been a little hectic."

"Relax, Derrick. I just enjoy watching you sweat. We're good." She paused. "We're always good."

Cassiopeia was intrigued. "You two know each other?"

"That's one way of putting it," Jeanne said.

"You were briefed?" Koger asked her.

She nodded. "Oh, yes. We have had our eye on this place, and Sir Citrone there, for a long time. Trinity said you may have hit the jackpot."

Citrone stayed silent.

"You're about to get a look at what's behind the curtain," Koger said, stepping aside and gesturing for her to do the honors. "But we need your...gentle touch."

She stepped to the glass and said, "I am Kristin Jeanne, here on behalf of the Eidgenössische Finanzmarktaufsicht, the Financial Market Supervisory Authority. I have an order for an immediate inspection of the premises. Open the door."

Townley shook his head no.

Jeanne shrugged and stepped back.

"Blow it open," she ordered.

CHAPTER 59

COTTON FOLLOWED AIKO AS THEY NAVIGATED THE CROWDED STREETS of Marrakesh. The time was approaching 7:00 P.M. and the sun had begun its fall in the west. Operation Neverlight had made it to Morocco, apparently now focused on the PSIA. To take out assets from a friendly ally was a serious matter, tantamount to an act of war, one that usually came with long-term repercussions. Most likely the official assumption was that none of this was any of Japan's business. That issue had been settled long ago when the country lost the war along with the spoils, which the CIA had ultimately claimed and enjoyed for a long time.

Finders keepers and all that.

They passed a clutch of art galleries and stayed to the fringes of Djemaa El Fna, the nightly circus of commerce in full swing. A sea of *souqs*, the stalls laid out according to a labyrinthine medieval plan, spread out into an ancient shopping mall, all of them doing a brisk business in olives, spices, clothes, rugs, and pottery.

The heart and soul of the city.

He caught sight of the minaret for the Koutoubia Mosque that stabbed the ever-dimming sky. He knew the name meant "of the books," because of the many book stalls that once surrounded it. Which he liked, given he was a bookseller too. Aiko seemed to know where she was going as she never hesitated in her steady pace, taking each turn with confidence within the scrawls of the close-knit alleyways.

"Did you see it too?" she quietly asked.

Oh, yeah.

A man, sitting on a bench, feeding the birds from a bag of something. Everything was right except for the way he fed them, tossing a few morsels at a time away from the bench. But when the birds pranced close, he moved his foot, scattering them. Odd. Feeding something you didn't like.

"A lookout," she said.

He agreed. And not a good one.

She cut down a side street lined by more shops with residences above.

"I assume we're moving away from where you want to be," he said as they walked.

"Not at all. We're going straight in."

"And the reason?"

"*Koketsu ni irazunba koji o ezu.*"

He waited for her to translate.

"If you do not enter the tiger's cave, you will not catch its cub."

He smiled. "We say it another way. Out of the frying pan and into the fire."

She made a few more turns and they found a café that seemed shabby, but he wondered if that was part of its ambience. Aiko stopped a moment outside and looked around before entering, but it would be tough to know if they had company as the narrow street was crowded. At a table to the back sat an eagle-beaked man, brown and lean with vigilant eyes dressed in dirty clothes. Aiko went straight for him. Cotton knew what was expected of him.

Keep watch.

Be ready.

Something was going to happen.

He drew close, his back to them, eyes focused on the café's entrance, one hand ready to grip his weapon, tucked beneath his jacket.

"I need a report," she said to her operative in English. "And fast."

AIKO REMAINED ANXIOUS AND CAUTIOUS.

She'd had a team on hand, here for the past two months, ready to deal with the international gathering that was happening about a hundred kilometers to the south. Six days ago she'd received a report of unusual CIA activity within Marrakesh. She'd ordered further investigation. Then, with all that had happened in Switzerland over the past two days, what was happening here had become even more important.

Now it was vital.

"They came for us," her man said. "They were waiting. All five of the others are dead."

"Why are you alive?"

"I was at the airport to watch the incoming flights and managed to get away from the people sent after me."

"I need to know what you found out."

"The Americans are planning an attack. Tonight. At Gledhill's compound."

Malone's gaze kept scanning the small eatery and the front entrance, surely mindful that it was an open doorway with easy access.

He glanced back and she spotted the concern in his eyes.

"Tell me more," she said.

"We've been watching a location here in the city. There's been plenty of activity there over the past few days."

"Doing what?" she asked.

COTTON WAS BOTH LISTENING TO THE CONVERSATION BEHIND HIM and watching the room, which contained about twenty patrons at small tables. Aiko was right. In order to catch fish, you had to lay out some bait. But this might be a bit foolish, though his new Japanese friend did not seem reckless. Quite the contrary, in fact. Still, they were pushing their luck.

Two men appeared in the doorway.

Brown-skinned, stocky, ready for a fight, their gazes locked on him.

One of the men vanished back out into the street.

The other advanced.

Cotton had already spied, through the kitchen, a door half opened to the outside. A rear exit.

"Get him out of here," he said to Aiko, not turning around. "Past the kitchen. There's a way out."

His adversary produced a length of chain, brandishing it by his hip. Patrons reacted and leaped from the tables, fleeing toward the entrance. He debated whether to find his gun and end this Indiana Jones–style.

But somebody might get hurt.

The chain whistled close to him.

He threw himself back just in time, the links rattling so close he felt the rush of air across his face. Metal found stone. Chips flaked off the wall in a shower of blue sparks. Cotton scrambled to regain his footing. With a wild scream the man pounced, swinging the chain in a wide deadly arc. Cotton lurched back, barely evading a blow that would have broken ribs, but the end link nicked him.

Which hurt.

The man grew bolder, lunging and swinging.

Cotton fell back on one of the tables, dodging and feinting, but the lengths caught his thigh. He staggered as if hit by a hammer, his leg momentarily numbed. A quick follow-up strike could be a problem, but the blow did not come. Instead the guy hesitated, as if assured of success, and took a moment to grab a breath, chest heaving from swinging the heavy chain.

Big mistake.

One thing he'd learned long ago about a fight.

No retreat. Not ever. Hold your ground.

The man began to swing the chain in small circles, seemingly enjoying the anticipation of a final blow, stepping forward. Cotton waited to the last second as the man bounded in, cocking his arm. He lunged, not away, but toward the chain. For another millisecond the guy hesitated, then, instead of completing his swing, he protected it. Which left his body open and vulnerable. Cotton drove his foot into the exposed solar plexus. A whoosh of sour breath spewed out the man's mouth and he doubled over.

A kick to the face finished him off.

The other man reappeared from outside with a knife.

Long, wide, serrated, a dull silver.

Sweat stung Cotton's eyes.

He glided toward his attacker, pivoting on the balls of his feet, the knife swinging in a small circular motion of intense readiness. Cotton lunged, sliding to the right and resisting the impulse to move back. Instead, just as with Chain Man, he moved in, causing the slash attack to miss over his shoulder. He then caught the knife arm over his hip so that his body weight worked in his favor. Twisting, he flexed the guy and somersaulted him to the ground with a thud.

The knife spun free and he kicked it away.

He slammed his foot down on the man's chest. The body convulsed, jerked, then went still.

He glanced up.

Aiko and her associate were gone.

He headed after them.

CHAPTER 60

CATHERINE DESCENDED THE STAIRCASE THAT DOMINATED THE FOYER, gilt banisters gleaming under the illumination of an iron chandelier. She exited the house through a rear door into a tiled courtyard, where she walked through an archway and emerged in the garden, the grounds intersected by wide gravel paths that formed a series of rectangles. Within them other paths radiated outward like spokes in a wheel from both a fountain and an enormous fig tree. Replicas of old lamps cast dim but adequate amber light.

She headed straight for the tent.

It was shaped like a traditional *caïdal*, draped in burgundy and royal blue and gold silk taffeta with sweeping sculpted peaks. An upholstered banquette wrapped the sides and blocked all views of the inside. She wore heels and a starkly simple black dress with a striking Van Cleef & Arpels necklace.

A present to herself.

The evening's fading sunlight lay like gold leaf on the garden, the air pleasantly dry, the sky clear and without menace.

She stepped inside onto a wood floor that had been specially built in a series of alternating squares, or diamonds depending on the angle. Cloth-draped tables filled the space beneath the canopy, guests standing in clusters chatting. Sounds of conversation and laughter filled her ears. Servers circulated with trays of drinks and hors d'oeuvres. A three-piece combo played soft music in a far corner. From the tent's peaks hung three large, ornate chandeliers of black metalwork supporting electric Moroccan lanterns. Air-conditioning cooled the inside. She readied herself for the constant stream of introductions, as she was the star of the party.

Time to build a consensus.

She headed toward a podium that fronted a large LED screen and settled before a microphone.

The crowd quieted.

"Ladies and gentlemen, on behalf of the Bank of St. George, we welcome you to the first day of your new future. To set the tone, and start the night's discussion, we have a short video for you to watch. So enjoy."

The screen behind her came to life, the film narrated by her.

At the turn of the 2nd century the Roman Empire controlled all of Western Europe, parts of North Africa, and the Middle East. Between fifty and sixty-five million people lived under Roman rule, approximately twenty percent of the world population. Yet a mere 150 years later the empire was near collapse. Many factors caused the end, notably political disorder, corruption, slowing expansion, and constant war. But the worst malady was the debasement of the Roman currency, which led to overtaxation and inflation, which in turn caused a fatal financial crisis.

The physical composition of the Roman money itself is illustrative.

The silver denarius was minted for use during the first two centuries of the empire. A four-gram coin in 60 A.D. was composed of ninety-five percent silver. Within fifty years that dropped to eighty-five percent silver. Another sixty years passed and the denarius was only seventy-five percent silver, then sixty percent after another forty years elapsed. By the year 270 it had been reduced to a mere five percent silver. Not long after that Rome abandoned using silver in their coins altogether, switching to bronze. Toward the end of the 3rd century, prices of goods in

Rome were seventy times what they were two centuries prior, most of that increase coming in just over ten years. What began as a steady devaluation became a rapid destruction of the Roman currency.

It was actually easy to debase in the beginning. Shave a little silver here. Add a few more coins there. What's the big deal? The problem was that currency debasement is a lot like heroin. The first time you use it is the most potent. Afterward, you're constantly trying to take more and more just to find the same high. In the end you always overdose. The same is true for currency debasement. In the end the denarius simply collapsed.

What's shocking is the striking similarities between the Roman silver content decay and the balance sheet of any central bank in the world today. The rate of decay—or in today's language, the reduction in purchasing power—follows a similar path. The problem with currency debasement is that it is a hard habit to kick. Even worse, those engaging in it don't even realize that it's bad.

They just do it.

This held true in Rome, it held true in Germany during the 1920s, in Argentina in the 1970s, and it still holds true today.

Currency debasement is a one-way street.

Downhill.

Nations today simply cannot turn off the money printers. Just last year the United States Federal Reserve printed forty percent more new money, which instantly devalued the rest of the money already in existence. This move was done in lieu of other, more painful options. If they attempt to slow down inflation by raising interest rates, within months, if not weeks, bankruptcies rise, unemployment increases, and a recession takes hold. The government, and by extension the banks, find themselves backed into a corner, which was exactly what happened in Rome nearly two thousand years ago.

No one willingly chooses inflation.

But few take the steps necessary to protect themselves from it.

The video ended.

She stepped back to the microphone. "Tonight, we will discuss the steps that each and every one of you can take to protect your nations." She paused. "Without the problems that come from debasement."

The group applauded.

So many before her had attempted to impose their dominance across the globe. Governments, tyrants, conquerors, syndicates, religions, corporations. All tried, but none ever succeeded.

And for one reason.

They all openly tried to impose *their* will and desire on the unwilling. She would be doing the opposite. Providing the willing what they themselves desired.

Here that desire was simple.

They all wanted freedom from America, China, Russia, the European Union, the International Monetary Fund, and the World Bank. Which was understandable. Smaller nations were treated with utter disrespect. All of them were deeply in debt. So much so that they were forced to do business with people they despised. She'd heard the same complaint from one country after another. Thankfully, she harbored no politics, possessed no ties to any ideology, and cared for nothing but the pursuit of her own endeavors. Her task was ridiculously simple. Just provide information, all true, from which others could make an intelligent choice for change.

She focused on the faces staring back at her.

Eager men and women from around the world.

The applause subsided.

"Please," she said, "enjoy dinner and, afterward, we will discuss the future."

CHAPTER 61

A<small>IKO FOLLOWED</small> M<small>ALONE'S INSTRUCTION AND FLED THE CAFÉ</small> through the kitchen and out the back door. Her man came with her. He was not a PSIA-trained operative. Just local hired help. Which explained the panicked face.

"I was not paid enough for this," he said to her in English.

She could not care less. "Finish your report."

"I want my money."

"You'll get it. After you report."

"I don't want to die. Pay me now."

She stood her ground.

He shook his head and, sensing she was not going to budge, turned to walk away down the narrow alley, but she grabbed him by the shirt. "Leave now and you will have two people hunting you."

She saw he got her message.

"Like I said inside, we've been watching that location." And he told her where it was, talking fast. "There's a CIA team here in the city. All American or European people. They've been working out of that location for the past week. Coming and going with a lot of heavy supplies."

"Did you learn what they were doing?"

He shook his head. "But they have explosives."

That grabbed her attention.

"They have a van. It's stored inside, but I was not on the team watching that place. The others handled that, but they're dead. That's all I know. I want my money."

"Take me to that location and you will get it."

"I'm not going anywhere near that place. I tell you what, keep the money. I'm out of here."

And he ran off.

COTTON DARTED FOR THE KITCHEN. NO EMPLOYEES WERE IN SIGHT. They all must have fled. He left too out the rear door. Outside was an alley. Aiko stood a few feet away and rushed over. He saw her man running away.

"He's scared," she said.

"Aren't we all."

And he hustled after the guy, who turned a corner fifty yards ahead and vanished from sight. He kept running, rounding the same corner where the alley drained into a busy street. His target was preparing to cross to the other side where a short wall and iron fence separated the sidewalk from a treed park. A car's engine roared to life and leaped away from the curb, speeding right at the fleeing man, who tried to vault out of the way, but his foot slipped and the bumper caught him at the knees. The grimy front of the car smacked into the body, bowling it backward, the skull slamming the pavement with killing force. Two wheels ran over him then the car rushed on, skidding at high speed around a corner.

Aiko came up behind him. "We need to get out of here."

He agreed. "Where to?"

"The only place we have to go."

She turned and headed in the opposite direction.

Okay.

He followed.

Kelly sat at a cloth-draped table adorned with crystal glasses and beautiful porcelain plates bearing the image of St. George on a horse. It sat in a prominent place just before the podium and she listened as Katie addressed the gathering. The audience was a mixture of male and female, all dressed casually, enjoying a glorious evening in southern Morocco. Katie seemed right in her element, exuding her trademark poise and confidence, in total command of the room. The video they'd just watched had been slickly put together, making its points with facts that no reasonable person could counter, playing off already established fears, cleverly utilizing images that drove the minds of viewers to obvious conclusions. She'd heard people at the bank say it a million times. When it came to impressing a prospective client, *Be prepared, listen, focus on the need, know the customer's business, acknowledge the problems, tell a story, use the right jargon, keep it simple, and always be persistent.*

Katie left the podium and came to the table, sitting beside her, then leaning close. "I want you to enjoy your dinner. During the next few hours we need a truce. For both our sakes."

"I mean it, Katie," she whispered. "I can end all of this."

"And I believe you."

She agreed, though. This was neither the time nor place. But she wasn't bluffing. That was the thing about creating something. You knew every detail. All the minutiae, including the weaknesses. The Atlas Maneuver sprang as a natural extension from what she'd conceived with blockchain and bitcoin. It was clever, and smart, but not invincible.

She surveyed the room once again.

Ten tables were spread out beneath the huge tent, each holding eight guests. This event had to be costing hundreds of thousands of euros. And all to impress. But it was just a con. What was it she once read? *The greatest friend of a con artist is lack of knowledge.*

Ain't that the truth.

This was just another modern-day Ponzi scheme.

The pitch back then, in the early 20th century? Charles Ponzi claimed he could turn the average workingman into a multimillionaire overnight. But the scheme only worked to turn Ponzi into a multimillionaire.

Everyone else lost their money.

Ponzi exploited the system by buying massive quantities of postal coupons from countries with weak economies and redeeming them in countries with stronger financial systems. He operated the scheme under his invented Securities Exchange Company. He even trained sales agents to pitch potential investors, telling them that they would receive double their money, plus interest, back within forty-five days. The sales agents pulled in a healthy ten percent commission for every investor they managed to corral. Forty thousand investors eagerly dumped money into the scheme. And instead of using that money to buy and ship postal coupons Ponzi simply pocketed it all himself. Then he used portions of the money, along with the money paid by new people, to pay off previous investors, creating an infinite cycle of non-profitable investments.

And made millions for himself in less than six months.

In the end it all collapsed and Ponzi went to prison, eventually dying broke. What had he called the whole thing?

The best show ever staged.

Maybe so.

Until now.

CHAPTER 62

CASSIOPEIA STOOD BEHIND ONE OF THE VANS AS THREE OF THE uniformed soldiers attached explosive charges to the doors, then detonated them, shattering the thick glass to pieces. Townley had disappeared, but several of the armed personnel rushed inside and returned with him in custody.

"This is private property," he called out.

"Which is under the full jurisdiction of the supervisory authority," Jeanne made clear. "My order gives me the right to inspect these premises, in any matter necessary."

"I need to call Luxembourg," Townley demanded.

"You're not calling anybody," Koger said.

Jeanne stepped over to Townley. "This entire facility is owned by the Bank of St. George, which makes it subject to the authority's jurisdiction. Unfortunately for the bank this facility does not appear to have a license to operate as a bullion repository within the confederation. That makes this location illegal. You oversee this facility. Which places you in a great deal of trouble."

Townley seemed to finally grasp the seriousness. "What do you want?"

"Access to every square meter of this building," Jeanne said.

"You can have it," Townley said. "Go ahead and search."

Koger glared at Citrone, who nodded toward the reception desk and the closed door behind it.

"Bring him," Koger said to the soldiers.

"I thought I was in charge here," Jeanne said.

Koger shrugged. "Whatever floats your boat."

Cassiopeia followed them behind the counter and into a large office. Townley's quick concession to a full search bothered her. Obviously, if there was something here to find, Townley figured nobody would. One wall of the room was filled with LED screens that showed different views of the facility both inside and out. She saw the same corridor below that she'd visited yesterday.

Citrone approached a control board. "This opens and locks every vault in the building. Including the one you have already visited."

She studied the board. One bank of switches obviously controlled the refrigerated wine vault doors. Another seemed to be the entrance and exits to the building. More could override the elevator. Another switch sat apart from the others. A simple OPEN/CLOSE noted in English, a keyed lock beside it. She reached down and moved the switch from CLOSED to OPEN.

Nothing happened.

What interested Cassiopeia was the lock on the panel. Which probably activated the switch. "Where's the key?"

They all faced Townley, who said nothing.

"Cuff him," Jeanne ordered.

Two of the soldiers grabbed the irritating man by his arms and wrenched them back while another applied a plastic zip tie to the wrists. Koger stepped over and frisked Townley. Then he loosed the man's tie, unbuttoned the collar, and checked for anything around his neck. Cassiopeia spotted the chain just as Koger ripped it away. On its end was a small brass key.

"Herr Townley," Jeanne said. "You may consider yourself under arrest." She then spoke to the soldiers. "Take him outside and hold him until we are finished here. We will hand him over to the local *kantonspolizei*."

"This is outrageous," Townley yelled. "I am a Swiss citizen."

"Then act like one," Jeanne said, her voice rising. "You are operating an illegal vault, possibly harboring a massive amount of stolen war gold. Did we not learn our lesson about that a long time ago?"

Cassiopeia could see that Townley was unaffected by any appeal to nationalism. No surprise. This man, as Citrone had warned, was a loyal servant to the bank. She saw that when he delivered the message to her during the first visit. He took his job seriously. And obviously the bank thought him beyond reproach, empowering him with the management of the vault. Sure, he'd take Citrone's money for the small stuff. But not for full-scale treason.

Did he know the secrets? No doubt.

But what exactly were they?

Koger stepped to the control panel and inserted the key into the lock, which clicked into place.

Cassiopeia came over. "Let's leave it alone. We have no idea what that is and we're not going to be told if it's good or bad."

Koger nodded and withdrew the key without turning it.

But she wondered. Why had Townley kept it around his neck? Hidden. Only available to him. Koger had already told her that the Swiss were merciless on banking violations by foreign entities. The days of the country being a financial free-for-all, open for anything and everything, were over. The nation had taken a huge PR hit with how it handled stolen Holocaust wealth, learning the hard way that arrogance and stonewalling were no longer options.

"Herr Townley," Jeanne said, "the legend of a huge cache of World War II gold has long existed within Swiss banking. Now so much time has passed that few still believe it was real. But here we are and, lo and behold, it is real. And the Central Intelligence Agency being involved? Perhaps even the originator of it all? Between seventy and eighty-five million people died during World War II. Three percent of the world's population. The gold that may be below us was pillaged from its rightful owners through blood and death, then held by America for who-knows-what."

"Good luck with your search," Townley said, defiant.

Cassiopeia stared at Koger, who seemed as puzzled as she was on what to do next.

"Get him out of here," Jeanne ordered, and the soldiers removed Townley from the room. She then dismissed the other uniforms, leaving the four of them alone.

Koger faced Citrone. "Okay, pal. What now?"

"That gold is here. I came to that conclusion a long time ago. There was no practical way to move that much bullion away."

"I went to the lower floor," Cassiopeia said. "There was nothing below the wine vaults."

"So that means," Citrone said, "it has to be on the wine vault level, as is the empty vault you opened."

Koger seemed irritated. "Quit telling us the obvious. We need information."

"Lucky for us," Jeanne said. "I may have just that."

CHAPTER 63

COTTON FOLLOWED AIKO AS THEY HUSTLED THROUGH THE STREETS OF Marrakesh. She'd stopped and sought directions from a vendor, who even drew them a rough map. They knew precious little other than that the CIA was here, working Neverlight, cleaning up every last loose end. He was still greatly concerned that the woman spotted with Suzy, who deplaned and accompanied her south in a car, was, according to Aiko, a high-end, for-hire assassin whom the bank had obviously employed.

This situation was escalating.

Fast.

They kept following the narrow ocher-dusted lanes, finding an area of town where grease-streaked men in cubbyhole shops worked on motorbikes. Other businesses were closed for the day. A tailor shop. Laundry. Grocery. Aiko kept going past the closed doors and boarded windows, turning two more corners, until finally stopping.

"This it?" he asked.

She nodded. "If the map is to be believed."

They stood before another shop with dusky ivory walls, this one with a single wooden door for entry and no streetside windows. The route ahead led to another corner, which hooked left. Nobody was around. He tested the knob. Locked. He pounded on the wood.

No reply.

He tried again.

"Seems nobody's home," he said.

He had nothing to pick the dead bolt with and noticed that the door swung inward. So he gave the wood a frenzied heave.

But it held.

Another.

And the jamb gave way.

He reached for his weapon.

Beyond, the door opened into a compact warehouse-like space with lots of open containers in varying sizes and a stack of long aluminum poles. Workbenches fronted one wall. On the far side an overhead garage door was closed. Raised, it would expose a large rear exit. For loading? Aiko had said that her man mentioned a van had been inside.

But it wasn't here any longer.

He pushed the broken door closed. Aiko fanned out and began investigating. He did too.

"Take a look at this," she said.

He walked over to where she stood before one of the workbenches. Beside it was an open plastic bin that contained a quantity of olive-black Mylar film with adhesive tape on one side, the peelable covers still there. Also scattered among the waste were some oversized white plastic envelopes.

All of which he recognized. "Those are plastic explosive wrappers."

"M112 and M118 to be exact," she added. "Both C-4 composition."

She was correct. His eidetic mind recalled the details.

Gray, malleable, like modeling clay, able to be fashioned into any desired shape. Safe. Easy to transport. And exploded only by the shock wave from a detonator or blasting cap. Popular stuff. Used by the military and terrorist organizations worldwide.

A small wooden box sat beneath the workbench. He crouched down and retrieved it. Inside were wireless detonators, two remote controllers, and three blocks of C-4 still in their wrappers. Another box of detonators was empty. He bent over and sniffed the waste container, catching a faint, oily odor. Like tar. C-4 was odorless but, like natural gas, there were additives that generated a smell to aid in detection.

"Seems the information regarding explosives was accurate," Aiko said. "They were building a bomb."

"And a big one too."

Knives lay on the workbench, its wooden surface scarred by long lines. Plastic residue filled the marks. He sniffed them. Same odor. He pointed. "It has to be cut on a non-sparking surface."

"Cut for what, though," she asked.

Good question.

He looked around some more.

Two cardboard boxes lay open on the floor, which he walked over and inspected. Inside both was a layer, a few inches deep, of ball bearings, but both boxes were otherwise mostly empty. On the far side he found a spray gun, along with open cans of red paint, most of their contents gone. On the grimy concrete floor lay a stencil, stained red from use.

He held it up.

VOYAGEZ & AMUSEZ-VOUS. French. Travel and Have Fun.

"They had a van here," he said. "Looks like something was painted on it." He'd already noticed that the paint was for a metallic surface.

Aiko found her phone and tapped. "That's an event planning company here in Marrakesh. My guess? They are handling the event at Gledhill's compound."

His mind was adding, subtracting, fitting, piecing, trying to assemble the various elements into a coherent message. Then another of the boxes caught his eye, along with what looked like an invoice tapped to the outside. He stepped over, ripped it free, and read.

"This contained pure oxygen cylinders," he said. "Small, compact ones."

He walked back to the aluminum poles. Some eight to ten feet long, others longer. Stout. All of them around six inches wide and hollow.

"These are struts or supports," he said. "Does that event company have a website?"

She nodded.

He came close and studied her phone. The site was in English and advertised the company's expert services for high-impact corporate and private events all over Morocco. He noticed the images. Some of indoor and outdoor parties, an elegant meeting room, a banquet hall full of red-clothed tables, an outdoor wedding, and a large tent set up among palm and cypress trees.

He glanced over at the poles.

Then he stepped back to the workbench.

From the number of discarded wrappers a lot of C-4 had been used. He counted the discarded wrappers. Thirty-two for the M112. Along with a dozen plastic sleeves for the M118.

"M112 could turn a metal pole like those over there into flying shrapnel. The M118 can level a building. Together, that's one powerful bomb loaded with ball bearings."

"Something is wrong here," she said.

He agreed. "It's all so obvious. As if it was left to be found. No disposal of anything. No cleanup." He pointed at the waste bin. "They even left the wrappers for us to count. I suspect the CIA wants the world to think someone else is to blame for whatever they're doing. Do you have anyone at Gledhill's estate?"

She nodded. "One operative. Another inexperienced local. Not trained for anything other than watching and listening."

"You seem to have a lot of those."

"This was thought to only involve surveillance. Locals are the best to hire for that."

"This is way beyond a look-see. We need to get to Gledhill's place."

"You think that C-4 and those ball bearings were stuffed into those poles?" she asked.

His sixth sense tapped away at his brain and he nodded. "If there's an event tent there, it could now be one huge bomb."

"You in there," a voice yelled from outside.

Both he and Aiko reacted and turned for the door.

"Come out, with your hands in the air. This is the Moroccan security police. We have you surrounded. There is no escape."

CHAPTER 64

CASSIOPEIA STEPPED FROM THE ELEVATOR. SHE WAS BACK ON THE lower level, the same refrigerated wine vaults stretching out before her on either side of the wide corridor.

Koger, Citrone, and Kristin Jeanne followed her.

The corridor ended about twenty meters ahead at the familiar steel door with an electronic lock. She walked straight to it and entered the code from yesterday. The lock released and she pushed it open. Lights sprang to life and fluorescent ceiling fixtures brightly illuminated the space.

Still empty.

"Do you think the other vault is adjacent to this one?" she asked.

"It's doubtful," Citrone said. "Too obvious. But it is definitely on this level. Somewhere."

"I anticipated this problem," Jeanne said. "So I came prepared. We have the schematics for every vault in Switzerland in our files, including the floor plan when this was a bullion vault, along with the revised plans when it was converted to this refrigerated site. I compared them, and there is some missing space beyond that room there." She pointed at one of the refrigerated wine rooms to their right. "I'm assuming they believed no one would notice. After all, this was going to hold wine, not gold. And they were correct, no one did notice. Until now."

Koger headed for the door and entered the room.

Cassiopeia and the others followed.

The air inside was cold and dry, perfect conditions for wine storage. The rectangle had solid walls on the two short sides. One long wall was of plate glass, and the other held about a hundred numbered wooden cabinets, each with its own keyed lock. The doors were a latticework with screening. Beyond, the necks of bottle after bottle lay on their sides each in its own individual slot. Probably hundreds of thousands of dollars of wine, chilling away in comfort and safety.

"The unaccounted-for space is beyond that wall," Jeanne said, pointing at the wine.

"It could have simply been eliminated," Cassiopeia said.

"Maybe," Koger said. "But nothing about this place seems haphazard. Everything has a purpose. So my guess is there's something there."

Citrone stepped close to the wall of cabinets. "How do we access it?"

"We can tear it all down," Koger said.

Jeanne began her own inspection of the wall. "It might be easier than that. The authority has experience with the ingenuity of Swiss bankers and brokers. They can, at times, go to great lengths to conceal things. Unfortunately for us Swiss storage operations don't have the same strict reporting standards as the banks do. Old bunkers once used by our military have become the new locales for hiding bullion." The older woman continued her scrutiny. "I'd say we're looking at a hidden panel among these cabinets. Activated by a remote control. It would be a lot quicker to use that, as opposed to tearing this entire wall down."

"Townley has to have it," Cassiopeia noted. "But he would not be stupid enough to carry it on him."

She stared at Koger, who seemed to read her thoughts.

"I agree," he said. "Let's take a look."

They reentered the security office back at ground level and decided this was not the place.

"Does Townley have an office?" Koger asked.

Citrone nodded and led the way out of the room and down the hallway, past the reception counter, toward the elevators. Farther on was a single door that Citrone opened. Beyond was a corner office with windows dotting the two outer walls, the others filled with an array of modernistic art. A desk, credenza, a few chairs, and a leather sofa rounded out the décor. Everything was in perfect order, the desk devoid of paper. Not a surprise considering Townley's stiff personality.

"There's a safe here," she said, "somewhere, with a controller inside. If that other vault really exists, it's probably not a place visited all that often."

"That makes sense," Citrone added.

Koger checked the desk. All the drawers were unlocked. Which did not bode well for something to be concealed within. Cassiopeia studied the pictures and quickly checked them. None concealed a safe behind, like in the movies where the frame smoothly swung out on hinges. Jeanne was examining the credenza, and behind the left side door she found a small iron safe.

They all rushed over.

"Okay," Citrone said. "Now what?"

Jeanne reached for a mobile phone. "That's easy."

Cassiopeia watched as a two-man team used acetylene torches to burn through the safe's hinges.

"We many times have to forcibly enter vaults," Jeanne said. "I came prepared."

"She always does," Koger muttered.

"I don't recall you ever complaining."

"Do I ever get the last word with you?"

"Now, what fun would that be?"

The men finished their work and extinguished the torches. One of them then removed the metal door. Cassiopeia and the others crouched down and stared inside. There were some papers, two stacks of euros, and a remote control.

Jeanne reached in and retrieved it.

They headed back down to the wine vault and faced the wall of

CHAPTER 65

E*L* S*ALVADOR* BECAME THE FIRST COUNTRY IN THE HISTORY OF THE WORLD *to adopt bitcoin, the world's new currency. Remember those words, as they will be engraved in the history of money. But as of today, opinions differ. Was it a bold move, a smart move, a dumb move, or simply a gamble?*

Of course, it was none of the above.

It was the obvious move. The only logical one.

The real question is not if other countries are going to adopt bitcoin, but when. We are so early in this paradigm shift that any logical, commonsense move is controversial. It has many people cheering it on, but it also has many, many detractors. On this occasion I will not analyze the supporters, only the detractors, and they can be separated into three groups. The ones who genuinely think it's the wrong decision. The ones who think it's a good decision, but for the wrong reasons. And the ones who are afraid of our decision.

Now, the interesting part is that the first and second groups exist mostly because of the third. Why? Because the most vocal detractors, the ones who are afraid and pressuring us to reverse our decision, are the world's powerful elites. They are accustomed to owning everything, controlling everything, and in a way they still do. Who are they? The media, the banks, the NGOs, the international organizations, and almost all the governments and corporations in the world. And with that, of course, they also own the armies, the loans, the money supply, the credit ratings, the narrative, the propaganda, the factories, the food supply. They control international trade and international law.

But their most powerful weapon is the control of the truth.

And they are willing to fight, lie, smear, destroy, censor, confiscate, print, and whatever else it takes to maintain and increase their control over the truth.

Just think about the hundreds, if not thousands, of articles about how El Salvador's economy was supposedly destroyed because of its bitcoin gamble, about how we are inevitably heading to default, that our economy has collapsed, and that our government is bankrupt.

Most of you have surely seen this, right?

They're all over. Reported in every financial publication, every major news organization, every newspaper in the world. All of the international financial organizations are saying the same thing. You just need to read their articles and listen to their experts saying that all of this happened after El Salvador lost around $50 million because of bitcoin's recent plummeting price.

Since we are not selling any bitcoin, this statement is obviously false. But for the sake of making a more profound analysis, let's say it was all entirely true. A whole country's economy was destroyed by a $50 million loss? Yes, El Salvador is a relatively poor country, but in the last year alone, we produced $28 billion in products and services. Pushing the idea that a $50 million loss—less than 0.2 percent of our GDP—would destroy our country's economy, or even put it in trouble, is ridiculous.

According to the International Monetary Fund, our GDP rose 10.3 percent. Income from tourism rose fifty-two percent. Employment went up seven percent. New businesses up twelve percent. Exports up seventeen percent. Energy generation up nineteen percent. Energy exports went up 3.291 percent. Internal revenue went up thirty-seven percent. All without raising any taxes. And this year, the crime and murder rate has even gone down ninety-five percent.

These are real numbers, facts that cannot be distorted by any false narrative.

But with all that we still ranked as the country with the highest risk of default in the world.

To counter that narrative we did exactly the opposite of not paying our debts. We offered to pay in advance. And that is why, this month, we will be buying all of our future bonds that the holders want to sell, at market price.

You may have also read in the media of huge anti-bitcoin protests in El Salvador. But those have been anything but huge. Furthermore, my government has an eighty-five to ninety percent approval rating, according to every poll conducted in the last year—including several polls conducted by the opposition and several by independent international polling firms. How could this be, if we are handling things so badly?

Even better, come ask the people of El Salvador, see the transformations for yourself, walk in the streets, go to the beach or to our volcanoes, breathe the fresh air, feel what it really means to be free, see how one of the poorest nations in the continent, and the previous murder capital of the world, is changing to rapidly become the best place it can be. And then ask yourself, why are the world's most powerful forces against those exact transformations?

Why should they even care?

You see it now, right?

The reason for all of this is because we're not simply fighting a local opposition, or the usual roadblocks any small country may face. We are fighting the system itself, for the future of mankind. El Salvador is the epicenter of bitcoin adoption, and thus, economic freedom, financial sovereignty, censorship resistance, unconfiscable wealth, and the end of the kingmakers and their printing, devaluing, and reassigning the wealth of the majorities to interest groups, the elites, the oligarchs, and the ones in the shadows behind them, pulling their strings.

El Salvador has succeeded.

Will you play their game?

Or will you become aware of the truth?

Catherine was pleased.

The audience gave the speaker, the president of El Salvador, a standing ovation. She'd brought him here as a powerful show-and-tell, and the man had delivered. He was an excellent speaker. Of course, her people had drafted the speech and it had been perfected through a series of test audiences.

Dinner had been a Moroccan feast. Pre-dinner nibbles of olives and some crispbreads to dip in a homemade ghanoush. Main courses of lamb, chicken, beef, and a tasty vegetarian option of vegetables and chickpeas along with basmati rice. Dessert had included pomegranate seeds, some mint, natural yogurt, preserved lemons, and toasted almonds. She'd eaten little and had, instead, worked the tables, moving around, talking with her guests. The conversations leaned toward the light and amusing, but there was lots of shop talk about money, finance, and the future.

The consuls had been fanned out, one to a table, there to lobby the various national representatives. Lana had eagerly participated, believing that she could redeem herself. Kelly had also behaved, talking with the president of El Salvador, who'd dined at the head table. Catherine had made sure both Lana and Kelly were properly dressed, having clothes brought down from a Marrakesh boutique.

El Salvador was the showpiece. That small Central American nation had been the first in the world to adopt bitcoin as legal tender. The government spent about $375 million U.S. on the bitcoin rollout, including incentive programs to encourage citizens to start using it. Privately, the bank was not all that happy with the stats there, but given that El Salvador's economy was generally cash-based, with a population not all that schooled in high tech, the results were acceptable. The initial idea had been to help save hundreds of millions of dollars in remittance fees paid by migrants on money sent home from foreign jobs, which accounted for more than twenty percent of El Salvador's gross domestic product. Some households received over sixty percent of their income from that source alone. Banks and other service providers charged ten percent or more in fees for those international transfers, which could sometimes take days to arrive and require someone to go physically retrieve the money.

None of that would be required with bitcoin.

Every transfer could be made at the speed of light.

The fees nominal.

It helped that the president himself owned bitcoin, secretly bought by the bank, which had adequately persuaded him to become an outspoken advocate for change. He'd made speeches all over the world, including one at the United Nations. Catherine had asked him to come to Morocco and assist in their latest push. The more countries that came on board the better for everyone, and all of the nations here tonight were ready to make the move. Mexico's announcement, coming next week, would greatly aid in producing more converts.

Kyra was gone, headed back to the airport, then off to get close to Kelly's biological daughter. There, ready, just in case.

But things were going well.

Only one warning sign.

Kelly had not clapped at the end of the president's speech. Nor participated in the standing ovation.

She just sat in her chair and stared.

While everyone returned to their own conversations, she stepped close to Kelly and whispered, "You and I need to speak. In private. Now."

CHAPTER 66

AIKO WONDERED WHY THE LOCAL AUTHORITIES OUTSIDE HAD NOT JUST stormed inside, unannounced. Morocco maintained several military commando and intelligence units. Each highly trained and respected. The main agency was the Direction de la Surveillance du Territoire, which conducted most of Morocco's intelligence operations. The DST had made a name for itself working with other agencies on counter-terrorism. But its history was one of human rights violations that included the arrest, detainment and torture of Moroccan political dissidents. So everyone kept their distance unless absolutely necessary to engage.

"The CIA had to tip them off that we're here," Malone said. "Blame us for all this."

"More accurately, blame our corpses."

She knew killing a retired Justice Department operative was one thing. But a full-fledged investigator for the PSIA? That was another matter entirely. The CIA would have a hard time explaining that one to a close ally. So they'd done what any self-respecting intelligence agency would do. Let others handle it, along with any fallout that might happen.

"I wonder what they told them," Malone muttered. "To get them to act."

"Nothing good, I assure you."

The front door still hung partially open, a fact that the people outside, surely with guns, had observed too.

Gunfire erupted.

A burst of rounds chewed on the damaged door, which swung inward from the barrage that thudded into it from the outside.

Aiko dove to the floor.

COTTON LEAPED DOWNWARD.

On the way he grabbed one of the three remaining C-4 blocks.

The gunfire stopped.

"That was a warning," the voice outside yelled. "Last chance. Come out. With your hands in the air."

Where they'd both be shot where they stood.

"Stall them," he said to her.

She stepped closer to the front door but stayed off to the side, keeping the thick stone wall between her and the guns.

"We are coming out," she said in a loud tone.

"Weapons first," the male voice said.

"I understand. But I need assurances you will not open fire."

Like they were going to do that.

But Aiko was doing what he asked.

Stalling.

He knew C-4 could not be detonated with a gunshot, or by dropping it onto a hard surface, or even by setting it afire. An explosion could only be initiated by a shock wave from a detonator. Like the ones he was staring at in the box beneath the workbench. High tech too. No more hot wires to a power source to ignite the detonator. These were activated remotely from a controller. The detonator then exploded in a charge that produced just enough heat and pressure to ignite the C-4.

He fished three detonators from the box and inserted them through the Mylar covering, deep into one of the C-4 blocks, twisting the ends and activating them. He grabbed a controller from the box and switched it on. A green light indicated it was powered and ready. Thank goodness. Aiko stared straight at him, her face saying, *Really?*

He nodded. Really.

They needed to leave the city and head south, and they didn't have the time to try to convince the DST of the situation. Those folks had already chosen sides. No time either to involve Stephanie and jump through the diplomatic red tape. Operation Neverlight was in full swing and now it had its sights set on him and Aiko.

"We are coming out," Aiko called out, still staring at him. "Weapons first."

He crept close and handed her his gun, which she tossed out the open doorway.

That should make them happy.

This wouldn't.

He underhanded the C-4 out the door.

Both he and Aiko rushed to the other side of the room and dove to the floor. He pressed the button on the controller. The brick exploded, releasing hot gases that traveled outward at tens of thousands of feet per second. The initial blast would inflict most of the physical damage. But then the gases would rush back, creating a second inward energy wave. The building's thick stone walls provided them with a measure of protection, as one block of C-4 was not enough to take them down. But the blast wave rushed in through the open door in a burst of heat and debris.

They had to move fast.

He raised his head from the floor and blinked away the dust.

Aiko was doing the same.

"We need to go," he said.

They came to their feet and approached the doorway. He took a quick survey and saw through the haze two vehicles, one left, the other right, bodies lying on the ground. Six. The blast had taken them all down. They made their way through a choking cloud that was beginning to settle. A few of the men were coughing, reorienting themselves, struggling to stand. He headed for the car on the right but, before climbing inside, he retrieved one of the automatic rifles and fired a salvo into the front tires of the other car. He then climbed inside behind the wheel. Aiko did the same on the passenger side.

Keys were in the ignition.

The engine rumbled to life and he shifted to reverse.

More of the men with guns were starting to stand. He floored the accelerator and backed down the narrow lane that stretched between the buildings, using the mirrors to keep the car heading straight. He kept going until he reached the end of the street then shifted into drive, whipped the wheel to the right, and sped off.

CHAPTER 67

KELLY WALKED WITH KATIE AS THEY LEFT THE TENT AND HEADED OUT into the garden, finally stopping near the center beneath a huge fig tree. The air-conditioned tent's thick side panels provided them with privacy. Two security men guarded the tent's entrance. Katie told her that there was a break between speakers to allow dessert to be served. After, Katie was scheduled to address the gathering. The pitch from the president of El Salvador was powerful, especially coming from someone with firsthand experience with bitcoin as currency. It was a full-court press, but she would have expected nothing less.

"Those people back there have no idea what they're getting into," she said.

"We offer them freedom and independence with a currency that will hold its value."

"As long as you allow it."

She knew the entire scheme had been created right here among the Atlas Mountains over the course of several winter days three years ago. She'd been instrumental in formulating the plan since, after all, it depended on her creation. At that point the bank owned nearly three million bitcoin. The original million that Kelly had mined in the beginning, along with those acquired from covert mining she herself had organized over the years utilizing an array of high-speed computers. During the past three years the bank's inventory had grown to over 4.5 million bitcoin, which effectively vested it with total control over the entire system. No one should have that much power.

"Not a single person in that tent knows what you and I know," Kelly said. "They have no idea what they're buying into."

Katie shook her head. "What does it matter? It's for their own good. They will benefit. The bank will benefit. Our clients will benefit. How is this so wrong?"

"If it's so good, tell them the truth and let's see if they want in."

Katie did not reply.

"I didn't think that was an option," Kelly said. "What you're planning is not what I, or they, envisioned. Bitcoin was supposed to belong to the twenty-one million people who owned it. They set its price, among themselves, as the coins are bought and sold in an unregulated market. No government, no corporation, no bank would interfere. A true marketplace commodity. You've now weaponized it and turned the whole thing into something else entirely."

"Which was your idea."

She pointed a finger. "That's a lie. I suggested that it would work as currency, maybe even as a reserve currency, and it can. It's as good as U.S. dollars or euros. But I said nothing about covert manipulation of its price. That was all you."

"There is no point debating this, Kelly. The Atlas Maneuver is in play. Give me back our bitcoin, then go find your daughter and live your life. You're a wealthy woman."

"What's to stop me from exposing it all, after we trade the coins for my daughter? I could tell the world I am Satoshi Nakamoto."

"You and a hundred others. Your story will just be another of the countless ones that exist. Nobody will care, nor will they listen. Your precious bitcoin owners will just keep buying and selling and wondering."

Which was true.

So many had claimed the title as the founder of bitcoin that nobody would believe anyone any longer on the subject. Sure, she knew far more than most, but she lacked the ultimate proof. The most definitive? Access to those original million or so coins that everyone attributed to Nakamoto. Move those? Sell a few? That would be the proof. And, right now, she had access to them. But revealing herself as Nakamoto was not the point of all this. Stopping the bank and, now that she knew, finding her daughter were the priorities. Hopefully, that young woman would understand and forgive her. Maybe they could even become friends. Hard to say. But she wanted to try.

Though first—

"Let me make this clear," she told Katie. "To get your coins back there's a precise code that has to be entered. If done wrong more than twice, the server will wipe the wallets clean. Gone. Forever. Three tries. That's all you get."

"I do not plan to underestimate you," Katie said. "The woman who brought you here is currently on her way to your daughter. If we come to an agreement, she will be there to help you make contact."

"I won't need her help."

"That's your choice. But I sent her there so you would know that I am serious about making this agreement. You and I will stay here, in Morocco, until we come to an understanding. But just as I will not underestimate you, don't you underestimate me."

"What does that mean?"

"It means that you and I were once close friends. But you have placed me in a difficult situation. No. An impossible situation. So I am prepared to do whatever has to be done to regain those keys."

Which made her wonder. How far would this woman go? How far had she already gone? She decided to deliver a promise of her own. "Don't screw with me, Katie. I don't give a damn whether you get those keys back or not. Let's be clear. Your job is to make me care enough to want to do it."

"And your job is to not make me angry, or desperate enough, to do something you're not going to like."

CHAPTER 68

COTTON NAVIGATED THE CAR THROUGH THE MAZE OF MARRAKESH'S many streets, finally leaving the busy medina behind and heading south out of the city. The car they'd appropriated contained nothing to mark that it was an official vehicle besides a flashing red light that could be placed on the dashboard. No radio or other communication devices. He hoped no one was seriously injured with the explosion. He hadn't wanted to hurt people, but sometimes you had to do what you had to do. The DST had come for a fight. He just obliged them. There was a strong possibility that something really bad was happening at Gledhill's estate, something that might endanger Kelly. Ordinarily he would have involved the locals but, thanks to that block of C-4, that was no longer an option.

"They will put an alert out on this car," Aiko said.

"I know. But we'll be long gone out of town."

They were past the city lights, now on a darkened highway that bisected open terrain on either side. Marrakesh seemed to end quickly, bleeding off into the countryside. He increased their speed with Aiko navigating off her phone. They were on their own, which seemed the story of his life. He'd always been a lone ranger. But over the past few years he'd learned to be a team player too.

"How far?" he asked Aiko.

"It says about forty minutes. This route will take us straight there."

The time was approaching 8:00 P.M. and the road was nearly devoid of traffic. A full moon illuminated the stark landscape, a lonely vista of bare mountains and valleys. He wondered what was happening with Cassiopeia and hoped she was being careful. The thought of something happening to her seemed unbearable. Oddly, the thought of something happening to Suzy Baldwin, now known as Kelly Austin, seemed equally unbearable.

And not because he still carried feelings for her.

Those were long since purged.

But the woman had once meant something to him. What started as a stupid, reckless affair became something more. Not necessarily love. At least not on his part. But definitely an element of caring.

On both of their parts.

Which, more than anything else, explained her anger when he'd ended things. He'd been angry too. At himself. For allowing his life to get out of hand. He'd thought by ending it, and never doing it again, he could make amends to his wife. But Pam had other ideas. Ones that he would know nothing about until many years later. Was Suzy in trouble?

He had no idea.

But he needed to make sure she'd be okay.

He owed her that.

"We need to agree on what's going to happen, once we are there," Aiko said.

He knew what she meant. "I have no idea how this is going to play out. Last I knew Kelly Austin controlled everything. So it seems what happens is up to her."

"Neither one of us can allow the bank, or the CIA, to regain control of those coins."

"On that we agree. But I can't allow Japan to acquire them either."

"I understand. Perhaps a joint operation? With joint decision making? Neither one of us taking advantage of the other."

He liked the sound of that.

And hoped her desire for honor in others worked both ways.

Everything about this was risky.

And for what?

Unlike a stock, where there was a company behind it, one with people, places, and a history, with bitcoin there was not a single tangible thing of inherent value to represent an investment of tens of thousands of dollars for each coin. Just blind faith. From uncritical minds. No questioning, no suspecting. What had somebody once said?

Belief can be manipulated. Only knowledge is dangerous.

He kept speeding south.

Less than half an hour to go.

He'd lost his pistol but gained the automatic rifle retrieved back at the blast site. Surely the DST would be after them. He wondered if these cars were equipped with trackers. He hoped not. No matter. They were way ahead of any pursuers unless there were agents at or near the Gledhill property.

Which he doubted.

From everything he'd heard so far about Gledhill, and the people at the Bank of St. George, none seemed the type to involve the authorities. They were all working outside the lines, using subterfuge and secrecy to the max.

To cross paths with Suzy Baldwin after all these years seemed a sign. What did it mean? Hard to say.

What had Einstein said?

Coincidence is God's way of remaining anonymous.

Yep.

Suzy came along at a turning point in his life. He could have kept cheating on his wife, accomplishing little to nothing in a mediocre navy career as a JAG lawyer. Instead, he came to his senses, then Stephanie Nelle changed his life forever. She saw something in him that he'd never seen in himself, and for that he was eternally grateful. Now here he was in Morocco dealing with another matter of life and death, the stakes unusually high.

Miles passed without comment from either one of them.

Finally, Aiko said, "Our main problem is getting inside. They're not just going to allow us to enter."

He'd already been thinking the same thing.

"Don't be so sure about that."

CHAPTER 69

C<small>ASSIOPEIA HAD CALLED OUT ON INSTINCT.</small>

Something was wrong.

"This is too easy," she said.

Koger stopped and stared at her. "What are you thinking?"

"Billions in gold protected by these concealed panels? And Townley. The man's facing prison, yet refused to do a thing to help himself? He just wished us luck."

"You think this is a Trojan horse?" Citrone said.

Good question.

"There's one way to find out," Koger said.

And she agreed.

It took ten minutes for two soldiers to bring Wells Townley down to them, his hands still cuffed behind his back.

"We broke into your safe and found the controller," Jeanne said. "Now we're here. There's nothing left to hide. Please open the door."

Townley shook his head.

Koger grabbed the irritating little man and shoved him toward the door.

"No," Townley screamed, trying to regain his balance as he stumbled toward the stainless steel. "I will not help you. I demand to be taken into custody. Take me away from here. Now."

"That's a strange request," Jeanne said. "Rarely do we have offenders wanting to go to jail."

"You are going to take me there anyway. Right? I prefer to get it over with."

Jeanne paused for a moment, then said, "Maybe not. I can grant you full immunity."

Townley seemed to consider the proposal. "I'll need more than that. The bank has an enormous reach."

"So do I," Jeanne said.

"I would want full protection."

"We can provide that. But you will have to offer sworn testimony that incriminates the bank, its officers and directors."

The stout little man went silent for a moment. Then finally nodded. "All right. I can do that. I have the code that will open the door."

Citrone moved forward. "Allow me."

The big man stepped into the concealed passage and approached the keypad. The rest of them waited in the refrigerated room. Townley rattled off a series of numbers, which Citrone entered.

The panel beeped, then the red light changed to green.

An excitement tingled through her.

"It seems we have permission to enter," Citrone said.

That it did.

Citrone reached for the door handle with his right hand, gripping it, ready to twist. Suddenly, his body went into violent convulsions, shaking uncontrollably. Spittle and a moan seeped from Citrone's mouth, but the big man did not let go of the metal latch.

He just kept shaking as if in a seizure.

Cassiopeia reacted and lunged forward.

Koger stopped her with a grab from his hand.

They watched as Citrone's legs gave way and his bulky frame collapsed to the floor, finally letting go of the door, his body shaking for a moment before going still.

Koger crouched down and checked for a pulse. "He's dead."

Cassiopeia realized what had happened. "Electrocuted."

They all glared back at Townley, who stood in the refrigerated room, beside the two soldiers, with a sly smile on his face.

"You didn't think it would be that easy," Townley said. "We are not something to be trifled with. I have no need for immunity."

Bitterness and confidence laced the voice.

As if they truly were untouchable.

Koger stood. "You son of a bitch."

"That gold is not America's," Townley said.

Koger reached for his gun.

She moved to stop him but was too late.

Koger brought the weapon up and planted a round right into Townley's forehead. The bang rattled off the walls. The impact threw Townley back, off his feet, his cuffed hands unable to maintain any balance, the back of his head thumping the stone floor hard. The two guards reacted by reaching for their own weapons.

"No," Jeanne ordered. "Stand down."

"You feel better?" Cassiopeia asked Koger.

"Much. I hate smug pieces of—"

"I get it," she said.

Jeanne walked over to Townley's body. "This might be hard to explain. Especially with all these witnesses."

"No explanation needed. I work for the CIA. We kill people. It's part of the job."

"You don't actually believe that, do you?" Jeanne said.

"It doesn't matter what I believe. Rob is dead. That prick is dead. And I want to see what's behind that damn door. You like to tell me all the time how good you are. Then show me and make that happen."

Cassiopeia was ahead of Koger. She'd already moved closer to the steel door and noticed that the red light had returned to the control panel.

"He just let Citrone walk right up and die," Cassiopeia said.

"Another reason I shot him," Koger muttered. "My bullshit tolerance level is right at zero."

"You know who you sound like," she said.

"I know," Koger said. "I wonder how Captain America is doing too?" He faced Jeanne. "Any bright ideas?"

"The key you found might turn off the electricity to the door. Then again, there could be more traps. But I have a thought that should guard against that."

CHAPTER 70

KELLY HAD EATEN LITTLE DURING DINNER AND PASSED ON THE CRUSTY almond treats for dessert, but she was nursing a cup of sweet mint tea and considering her options. Katie had told her that Kyra Lhota would be near her daughter by tomorrow. Ready. No matter what was said to the contrary, she assumed having Kyra there was supposed to convey some sort of threat. But she was not intimidated. Far from it. She held all the cards and no amount of bravado would change that superior position. Without the bitcoin the bank could do nothing. The Atlas Maneuver would be totally impotent. But she reminded herself that desperate people did desperate things.

She glanced around at the dinner guests.

All were busy chatting and eating.

Katie had excused herself and left the tent again. Kelly assumed the big push would come shortly after everyone's belly was full and enough wine and liquor had been consumed. The bank spared no expense with events like this. They usually hired the best event planners and caterers available, and this night seemed no exception. Waiters were busy serving the tables, more hired help cleaning away the dishes and refilling glasses. Odd that Lana Greenwell was here, but Lana was probably thinking the same thing about her. Neither of them in the past had been included in any outside activities. Both she and Lana were behind-the-scenes participants, two of only a few within the bank who knew what was truly happening. She had an urge to flee, but knew there was nowhere to go. She was a prisoner, albeit one with bargaining power, but a prisoner nonetheless. If this worked out, what would she say to her daughter? How would she explain why she gave her up? She'd fantasizeed about that conversation for a long time, and soon that dream might become a reality. But she was playing a dangerous game. One that could place not only her own life, but now also her daughter's in jeopardy. She'd never figured someone else into the mix. The risks had been designed to be hers alone. But there was no turning back now.

Everything was in motion.

This had to play itself out.

To the end.

Cotton sped up the car, the flashing red light now on the dashboard announcing their presence. They were approaching the Gledhill compound, which sat on a mount that overlooked a black valley. Lights illuminated the outer walls and the main gate. Armed men waited in the wash of brightness. More men were atop the walls. The gates leading inside were closed. Everything seemed sealed tight. Which made sense. Considering there was some high-profile event occurring within.

He rolled up, came to a stop, and opened his door.

As did Aiko. They both stepped out.

Two of the armed men approached.

Cotton had learned long ago if you spoke fast, straight, and clear without a speck of hesitation and acted like you knew what you were doing, your listener would come to the same conclusion.

"Do you speak English?" Cotton asked.

The man shook his head. He'd also learned that a smile was the best substitute for not knowing a language. So he offered one and asked, *"Parlez-vous français?"*

The guard nodded.

He'd always been able to depend on his memory, especially when it came to languages. He could speak and understand quite a few.

"We're here from the DST," he said in French. "You have a situation brewing inside."

A puzzled look came to the leathery face. "What situation?"

"Is there a van and personnel in there from Voyagez & Amusez-vous?"

The guards traded stares, and the one nodded.

"We have reason to believe they could be impostors. Something may be happening behind those walls. We need to get in there."

The guards seemed hesitant.

"Do I look like a problem?" Cotton said, voice rising. "We didn't drive here from Marrakesh for no reason. Open the damn gates."

And he slipped back into the car, as did Aiko.

The guards still hesitated, so he laid on the horn.

"Now," he yelled.

CATHERINE HEADED BACK TO THE EVENT TENT AFTER TALKING PRIvately with a few of the consuls, listening to their reports and perceptions. Those observations would be important during her upcoming remarks.

Know your audience.

Good advice.

She was to address the gathering in a few minutes with a last attempt to sway the representatives into recommending to their respective governments that bitcoin become an integral part of their economies. Nothing would be decided here tonight. The idea was for these representatives to return home and become champions for the cause. Of course, a fair number of them had been bought and paid for with bitcoin of their own, now safely secure in e-wallets to which only they had access.

But not everyone was bribed.

Sometimes just the idea itself was enough to inspire passion, but when needed money was always a convincing incentive.

Everything seemed to be going great. They'd planned this night for a long time, taken special care to make sure that the food, the atmosphere, and the message were all in sync. Too hard a sell would drive them away. Too soft would never reel them in. A balance had to be achieved, and she'd become quite adept at finding that equilibrium.

She stopped outside the tent for a moment at one of her favorite spots, a cluster of low shrubs beside a solitary palm that had been planted by her father. She crouched and removed a few dead fauns from the flower bed. One thing she'd learned from her father had served her well. *Anything you could not be absolutely sure about, take no chances with.*

But this she was sure of.

She reentered the air-conditioning and checked to make sure Lana and Kelly were still in their seats. Both were. She'd assigned one of the hired security guards to keep a watch on them both in her absence. That man stood to the rear of the tent, just inside one of the entrances, his attention on the crowd. She passed him and walked toward the main table, retaking her seat beside the president of El Salvador on one side and Kelly on the other.

Give it a minute or two, she told herself.

Then head for the podium.

COTTON DROVE INSIDE THE COMPOUND AND PARKED. HE QUICKLY assessed the lay of the land and noted a variety of multistory buildings with lots of windows. Beyond the tall one ahead he spotted a glow of light above its roofline. More armed guards appeared, surely alerted by the gate sentries.

"Is the event there?" he said, pointing and sticking to French.

One of them nodded, saying it was inside the main garden.

"Where did the tent company park their van? We need to see it."

Thankfully no one had, as yet, questioned why an American man and a Japanese woman were working with the DST. But apparently, the car and its light, his attitude, and the automatic rifle he produced from the back seat were enough to convince them.

They followed the guards around the buildings to a small courtyard that seemed to be acting as a parking lot for the night. A façade of four floors with deep-set widows rose to one side, the outer wall on the other. Several cars were there along with a white van with Voyagez & Amusez-vous stenciled on the side in red. They approached with caution, he to one side, Aiko to the other, the remaining two guards standing back, weapons ready.

Cotton banged on the rear doors.

No reply.

He grabbed the latch and opened one door.

Aiko freed the other.

Empty.

Just some tools.

No weapons. Nothing that pointed to a bomb.

"Where are the people who came in this van?" he asked the guards.

"Most likely at the tent."

"How many came?"

"Four."

"Take us to them," he ordered.

CHAPTER 71

CASSIOPEIA STOOD BACK AND ALLOWED KRISTIN JEANNE'S TEAM TO DO their work. They'd cut all power to the building, including a backup generator, and discovered that the door to the vault was wired to electrocute anyone who touched it. The voltage and amps were obviously more than sufficient to kill. Surely there was a way to disarm the trap, and it most likely had something to do with the key Townley had concealed, but they did not have the time to learn more. Jeanne's team was specially trained in gaining access to vaults and, during their examination, discovered that the door itself was made of copper, plated with stainless steel. Both excellent conductors of electricity. With all power off to the building the idea was that any other traps would be rendered useless.

Except, of course, if they ran off batteries.

To be sure, the key they'd discovered was inserted back into the lock at ground level and turned to the off position. The bodies of Townley and Citrone had been removed and stored in one of the other refrigerated rooms. Those would be dealt with later. The main mission at the moment was discovering what was inside the vault.

Battery-powered lights were brought down and illuminated the door. Torches were being used on the keypad. Once the steel

346

covering was breached her people could then see about bypassing the keypad entirely and releasing the lock.

"We're going to take the Bank of St. George down," Koger said to her. "All of them are going to jail."

"Your superiors might have a different opinion," Cassiopeia pointed out.

"One thing years of bucking authority has taught me is that you don't stop bucking. I want them in jail too."

"Was it necessary to kill Townley?"

"He killed Rob. Eye for an eye."

"The Swiss might look at this another way."

"Kristin could not care less that that fool is dead. She's a tough cookie. And I really don't give a crap what the Swiss think. Their damn banking secrecy laws are what fueled all this. They're only here now, Johnny-on-the-spot, because the White House has intervened and they don't want a PR nightmare."

The men with torches finished their work and removed the keypad from the wall. They then began working on the wiring beneath. Jeanne watched it all from a few meters away, just outside the wash of the portable lights. They'd brought down a small temporary power source to operate the door's locking mechanism. Once opened they would disconnect the power, hopefully leaving the metal harmless.

Jeanne's radio crackled.

Neither Cassiopeia nor Koger could hear what was being reported as she wore an earpiece. All they heard was *thank you* and *maintain position*.

"A contingent of CIA officials are outside," she said to them. "They are demanding to be allowed inside, claiming any gold found here is theirs."

"Pretty damn bold," Koger said, "considering they've been hiding their ownership for eighty years. Not to mention that it's all stolen war loot."

"Which could work to our advantage," Cassiopeia said. "Frau Jeanne, do you have media contacts?"

"Many."

"Perhaps it's time to alert them to what's happening here."

Cassiopeia caught the glint in Koger's eyes.

He pointed toward her. "I like the way you think."

"We're ready to open the door," one of the men called out.

Jeanne signaled that they should proceed.

One of the men did something that caused a click. A slight hiss of air and the thump of pneumatic bolts signaled a release. The men disconnected the battery, then checked the door with voltage meters, signaling all was safe. One of them swung the metal panel open and motioned for the others to hold for a moment as they cautiously entered the room with flashlights.

"There's a cutoff switch," one of the men called out. "It disarms the voltage. I have activated it, just in case."

Jeanne used a portable radio and contacted more of her team, instructing them to switch the power back on. Lights sprang to life. Fluorescent ceiling fixtures illuminated the vault. The two men again tested the door and the jamb with voltage meters and indicated that all was clear.

Cassiopeia followed Koger and Jeanne inside.

The room beyond was maybe twenty meters square, the walls more stainless steel, the floor concrete. Which brought a measure of comfort since concrete was not an electrical conductor. Wooden crates in rows were stacked five-high. Several hundred, at least. Koger stepped over to one stack and tested the weight of the upper container.

"Super heavy," he said.

Jeanne motioned and her two men brought the crate to the floor, then pried off the lid, which had been nailed down. Before removing it she dismissed them both and they left the vault.

Cassiopeia understood. The fewer eyes the better.

Koger crouched down and removed the lid, revealing stacks of shiny gold bars. Each stamped with a number. He lifted one out and gave a low whistle that said what they were all thinking. *It really does exist.* "I was told they smelted down all the Nazi and

Japanese stolen gold and made new bars. Each with its own number for inventory. Amazing how careful they were with other people's wealth."

Cassiopeia heard the disgust in his voice. "It's got to be one of the largest caches of gold on the planet."

"By far," Jeanne added. "This is a quantity of gold that nations maintain, and only precious few can even do that."

"Like you pointed out, this gold came from millions of people dying," Koger said. "It's blood money. Used by so many, for so long, for God knows what. That's now over."

"I will issue a confiscation order," Jeanne said. "We will take charge of this entire vault. The claims of ownership for all this will be countless."

That was true. But Cassiopeia said, "How would anyone be able to establish a claim? The gold has been re-smelted. There are no records of anything. Nobody could ever prove a thing. And eighty years have passed."

"Unfortunately," Jeanne said, "that will not stop them from trying. This much wealth will attract an unprecedented storm of attention. Perhaps enough that the gold will never leave this vault." She faced Koger. "We still have a problem outside with your employer."

Koger smiled. "I know exactly how to deal with them."

But something else was on Cassiopeia's mind.

Cotton.

And what was happening in Morocco.

CHAPTER 72

COTTON FOLLOWED THE GUARDS AS THEY ALL APPROACHED THE EVENT tent. Walls on all sides shielded what was happening inside, but there was an entrance straight ahead, past a huge fig tree ripe with fruit, manned by two guards. The murmur of many conversations could be heard. The travel and constant alertness had left him weary, but his mind and body remained sharp.

"That whole tent could be a bomb," he whispered to Aiko.

"How do we convey that fact to these people, without sounding insane?"

"I don't know. But you were right. We have to be sure before acting. We could be wrong. What we found could have been planted. Why? I have no idea, but this whole thing fits into the category of extraordinary. Let's find Kelly and the people who came in that van."

He turned to one of the guards and explained that he was looking for an American woman, offering a description. The guard told him that one had arrived earlier and was taken inside the main house.

"Lead the way there," he ordered, then he turned to Aiko. "I'll check that out. Can you see about the tent and the people who brought it?"

She nodded and walked off with one of the guards.

He followed the other man to a side door that led inside the main house. The interior was a mix of Moroccan latticework, tadelakt polished walls, exquisite mosaic-tiled columns, and marble floors dotted by Berber rugs. Muted palettes of cream, rose, pale green, chalk blue, yellow, and white cast an Old World charm. A woman in a black burka appeared and said she was the night maid. The guard explained who they were looking for and she led them upstairs to a closed bedroom door. Cotton entered to find the room empty, but the clothes Kelly had been wearing back at the inn were littered across the bed. She'd obviously changed. But at least he knew she was here.

In the tent?

God, he hoped not.

He stepped to the window and gazed down to the garden. The two guards remained at their post outside the tent entrance. The conversations from earlier had died down. Someone was speaking inside the tent, the voice amplified. A woman. But he could not make out the words. Applause came from inside. Two men appeared and approached the guards from either side of the large tent. They drew weapons and fired a single shot into the head of each. No retort. Sound-suppressed.

They then zipped the tent panels shut and fled, heading his way.

Aiko was impressed with Malone.

She'd always liked American vitality. It was what set them apart. As a nation they were headstrong, proud, and ideologically confused. But no one could match their spirit, their eagerness to tackle a problem, and their refusal to fail. Like a wolf, cunning and hungry, always on the prowl.

Malone seemed the perfect example.

He'd pushed their way right into the compound.

She'd carefully explored the outside of the tent. Now on its far side away from the entrance. She'd sent the guard off in another direction. Her nerves pulsed each time the wind rustled. She kept moving, feeling the tension settle over her muscles like a cold, sodden blanket.

Could the tent explode at any moment?

CATHERINE STOOD AT THE PODIUM AND ADDRESSED HER GUESTS. SHE was a confident performer, the text she was reading the product of inspired minds, carefully drafted, redrafted, and splattered with common sense. But she told herself not to project the air of a conquering general surveying territory claimed in battle. This war was not over, its outcome remained in doubt. Her job? To bring home victory.

"You may be wondering why the Bank of St. George cares so much about your financial independence. Why the bank thinks bitcoin is a smart move. Why it matters even to consider such a thing."

She paused.

"It's quite simple. The time has come to dissolve the bond between currency and state control. For centuries we have been betrayed, lied to, stolen from, extorted from, taxed, monopolized, spied on, inspected, assessed, authorized, registered, deceived, and reformed. We have been economically disarmed, disabled, held hostage, impoverished, enervated, exhausted, and enslaved by debt."

Another pause.

"Then came bitcoin."

Heads were nodding in agreement.

"Governments and many financial institutions will tell you that bitcoin is volatile in value. A risky investment. But these are the words of those who don't understand it, from those who fear it. The crusade to absorb bitcoin into the cracks of the existing financial systems around the world has begun. The goal of many seems to be to swallow bitcoin, process it, integrate it, devolve it, and keep it stagnant in the gears of a failed financial operating system. The Bank of St. George rejects that. Why? Because bitcoin is inherently anti-establishment, anti-system, and anti-state. It undermines governments and disrupts institutions because bitcoin is fundamentally humanitarian. Something the existing financial systems are not in any way whatsoever. But that philosophy does not scare us."

She'd delivered similar speeches before, but tonight's felt especially poignant. And her audience seemed receptive.

"Bitcoin is not supposed to work within our current financial mechanisms. It needs no entities of authority to acknowledge it, incorporate it, regulate it, or tax it. Bitcoin does not pander to power structures. Quite the contrary. It disarms them."

Heads were bobbing.

They were listening.

"Bitcoin exists in anonymity. Satoshi Nakamoto's facelessness is symbolic of this characteristic. Privacy is the whole point. Bitcoin means to channel economic power directly through the individual. It was never intended to be integrated. It is not just a currency, a commodity, or a convenience. Just like the internet gave information back to all of us, bitcoin will give financial freedom back to the people. Bitcoin will allow you to shape your world without having to ask permission."

Time to bring the message home.

Gunfire erupted.

CHAPTER 73

Cotton unlatched the window and swung the double panes outward. The two men were fleeing right toward him through the garden twenty feet down. They'd yet to notice him so he grabbed their attention with a burst from the automatic rifle that peppered the ground right in front of their path. Both men stopped, looked upward, and sent silenced rounds his way. They both scrambled for cover behind two tall palm trees with thick trunks. Cotton dropped back from the window, his rifle remaining at ready.

"Two men below," he said to the guard with him in the room. "They just killed your guards at the tent. Get down there and cut them off."

The man nodded and rushed from the room.

He turned his attention back to the window. The two below seemed to be waiting for him to reappear, ready to fire. But they were using small-caliber pistols with sound suppressors. Not all that accurate at this distance. He had a short-barreled automatic rifle and, more important, knew how to use it.

He planted rounds into both trees.

That should get their attention.

AIKO ADVANCED TOWARD THE GUNFIRE, ROUNDING THE TENT AND spotting two bodies on the ground. She then saw two more men huddled behind trees, their attention on a second-story window where a rifle was firing. That had to be Malone. She was unarmed but saw that the two dead guards had carried weapons. So she eased herself close and relieved one of the corpses of a pistol. Then she quickly assumed a position behind another mature palm and readied herself. It had been a while since she'd fired a weapon.

But she was an excellent shot.

The garden before her was illuminated from both ground lighting and floods atop the surrounding buildings. More than enough for her to see. The two armed men were unaware that they'd been flanked, so she decided to alert them by firing into one of the tree trunks.

Both men whirled to face her.

COTTON HEARD THE SINGLE SHOT THAT CAME FROM THE DIRECTION OF the tent and spotted Aiko huddled in a defensive position. The two men had turned her way so he used the distraction to lay down another salvo of bullets that stirred the dry ground into a dust storm.

"Lose the weapons," he called out. "You're surrounded. And I won't say it again."

Aiko came to her feet and fled the tree, her weapon aimed ahead, advancing straight for the two threats, her focus down the gunsights on the targets. Damn. He liked her courage. No hesitation. Just jump right in.

The two men dropped their guns.

"Hands up where I can see them," Aiko yelled, still moving.

Both raised their arms to the night sky but Cotton noticed something in one of the hands, the fingers cuffed around a small object.

Not a weapon.

He focused hard in the dim light and aimed the rifle. "Drop whatever that is you're holding."

The man did not comply.

AIKO HEARD MALONE'S COMMAND AND ALSO SPOTTED SOMETHING IN the one man's upheld hand.

"He's got a controller for a C-4 detonator," Malone called out from above.

And she knew what that meant.

"You need to drop that," she told the man, keeping the gun trained straight on him.

Suddenly one of the doors from the main house burst open and a guard, armed with a rifle, emerged. He seemed frantic and anxious.

Malone screamed in French, "Don't shoot."

The man planted his feet and pointed the weapon.

She had no choice.

She aimed her gun at the guard and fired.

CATHERINE TRIED TO CALM HER GUESTS WITH A REASSURING VOICE. "Please, remain in your seats. We have an extensive security detail and I am sure they are dealing with the problem. It's important for us to stay out of the way and allow them to handle things. I will check to see what's happening and report back in a moment."

Several had risen from their chairs and started for the exit.

"Again, please, just relax and let me see what the problem is. You're safest inside here."

She'd heard a variety of gunfire. One report was a single round. Others were staccatos of rapid fire. None of which could be good. But the bank had employed a huge array of local private security and she'd been assured that the compound was safe. She caught sight of Kelly, who remained in her chair, surprisingly calm, just watching everyone around her, perhaps thinking the gunfire was a supposed rescuer. Hardly. How could anyone even know she was here?

Another shot rang out.

The side walls of the tent prevented any line of sight. She should exit and see about things. Where were the guards? She heard raised voices from outside but could not make out what was said. The purr of the air conditioners blocked all but the loudest of noises.

More gunfire.

Like a machine gun.

She moved toward the exit and noticed that the flaps had been zipped shut in the middle. She reached up to grab the zipper, then something strange washed over her and a rush of air filled her ears. Intense heat and pressure swept across her face.

Which burned.

A sick feeling of dread filled the pit of her stomach as a concussion of pressure threw her off her feet.

And the world dissolved.

CHAPTER 74

CASSIOPEIA STOOD IN THE REPOSITORY'S MAIN FOYER AND STARED OUT the plate-glass windows. The small cobbled square that separated the building from the street was filled with armed, uniformed Swiss military who stood before the entrance and a contingent of plainclothes individuals closer to the street. Four men, two women.

"The tall guy," Koger said, "is my boss. A deputy director from Langley. I'm assuming he's in Europe overseeing Neverlight. A butt kisser to the highest degree. But one thing is sure, he only does what he's told. Not a bone of self-initiative in that man's body."

"It's a stand-off out there," she said.

Koger glared out the glass. "That it is. But I think we may be able to break that stalemate."

He headed for the opening blown in the glass and stepped outside. Cassiopeia followed. Jeanne was still below, in the vault, dealing with the gold. Koger had recorded a video of the entire room and forwarded it somewhere on his phone. Where? He'd not shared that info. And she knew better than to ask. They marched past the Swiss officers and approached the Americans.

"Surprised to see me?" Koger asked.

The other man said nothing.

"Cassiopeia," Koger said, "this is my boss, deputy director of something or another, I'm not really sure. I don't even like to use his name. I call him PIMA. Pain in my ass. He got stuck with me and made it clear from day one that he was no friend of mine. I suspect he's been waiting for a report that I was dead. Along with you too, I might add."

"I told the director that promoting you was a horrible idea. You're nothing but trouble."

Koger pointed. "That's right. Trouble that has you now in its sights. You lose this one."

"Don't be so sure," his nemesis said.

Beyond where they stood, at the street, another car approached and stopped. The rear door opened and a woman emerged. Striking, with steel-blue eyes and thick dark hair. She marched straight toward them sporting a long wool coat, hands in the pockets. Expensive. Chanel, if Cassiopeia wasn't mistaken.

"I'll be," Koger muttered. "TOO herself."

She recognized the moniker. Cotton had told her about this woman. Trinity Dorner. Little sense of humor, with a penchant for avoiding small talk. An accomplished listener, thinker, and watcher, an expert at political weather forecasting, practical and pragmatic, attuned to the slightest change in breeze. Supposedly, her stoicism was legendary. During briefings she'd always sat in the back of the room, out of the way, so nondescript that people who didn't know her would ask afterward, *Who was that other one in the back?* So many asked the same question that the tag stuck. *The other one.* TOO.

Dorner marched straight over to where they all stood. "Mr. Deputy Director, I'm here on behalf of the president of the United States. You are ordered to stand down. Operation Neverlight is ended. Is that clear?"

Cassiopeia could see that PIMA seemed unsure how to take the rebuke.

TOO was unfazed. "I also was told to convey to you that your services are no longer required. You're fired. The director is also being fired by the president himself, as we speak. Operation Neverlight is over."

PIMA said nothing.

"All of this is now classified," Dorner said. "And be grateful that you're not being arrested and charged for a variety of crimes, including murder."

"That gold is going to be a huge problem," PIMA said. "More than you or the president realize. A big problem."

"I think we are more than capable of dealing with the situation," Dorner made clear. "You may go. And take these others with you."

TOO stood tall, hands still in her coat pockets, waiting for her commands to be obeyed. The deputy director turned to leave and motioned for the others to join him.

"And you," Dormer said to Koger. "You're also lucky not to be charged with murder."

"The little prick had it comin'."

"That's what I was told. And losing Rob Citrone is not the end of the world either. He pushed everyone to their limits."

"Obviously, Kristin called you," Koger said.

"For some incredible reason she actually likes you."

"And you just happened to be in the neighborhood?"

"Something like that." Dorner faced Cassiopeia and introduced herself. "We appreciate all of your assistance here. Needless to say, it has to remain confidential."

"Not my first rodeo."

Dorner smiled. "I know where you learned that phrase."

"What now?" Cassiopeia asked.

"Derrick sent me a video. But I'd like to see, firsthand, what you found."

They reentered the subterranean vault, this time with Dorner in tow. Kristin Jeanne was there speaking to one of the uniforms. The two women spotted each other and smiled, then hugged.

Dorner surveyed the crates, circling their outer perimeter. "This is amazing. Only the CIA could have pulled this off for so long."

"You know about the Black Eagle Trust?" Cassiopeia asked.

"I do now. Something the agency created, just like bitcoin."

"Somebody's been doing their homework," Koger said.

"And that surprises you?" Dorner asked.

Koger shook his head. "What's the game plan here?"

"It's real simple," Dorner said. "This gold is going to disappear. The world will never know it exists. It cannot ever know."

"Why not?" Cassiopeia asked.

But it was Jeanne, not Dorner, who answered. "Nothing is to be gained by any great revelations. This has to be handled in secret."

"President Fox has spoken directly to the Swiss government," Dorner said. "They are in agreement. The gold will be divided fifty-fifty between the two governments and absorbed into each nation's national reserves. That way it goes unnoticed and will have no effect on the world economy."

She could understand the logic associated with that decision but still had to say, "It's war plunder. People died for its acquisition. It came from the horror of the Axis armies. It doesn't belong to either one for your countries."

Dorner nodded. "You're absolutely correct. But it's the only viable solution. The Bank of St. George cannot be allowed to keep it, and we definitely are not going to alert the world to its presence."

"But that's just it," Cassiopeia said. "The bank knows it's here. You can't keep this secret."

"But we can," Jeanne said. "A threat of prosecution should be enough to ensure everyone's silence. Our guess is that only a few within the bank know about this. So we should be able to contain it. My officers are sworn to secrecy on threat of jail. They are accustomed to classified missions. None will talk. And besides, once it's gone, there's no way to prove anything."

A few minutes later they all emerged back out into the cool evening air.

A soft hum interrupted the silence.

Trinity Dorner removed a phone from her coat pocket and tapped the screen. Not a call. An email or text.

Which seemed to be important.

"You need to see this," Dorner said, and she displayed her phone.

They all came close and Cassiopeia saw what appeared to be a high-altitude image.

"Cotton Malone is in Morocco," Dorner said. "I assume you're both aware of that. There's a gathering there within Catherine Gledhill's estate. Malone and a PSIA agent are on the scene. We have a drone in the air monitoring, and this just happened."

Dorner tapped the screen and the video sprang to life.

Cassiopeia saw the roofs of buildings within a large walled compound. There were several gardens, one filled with what appeared to be a large tent.

Which exploded.

CHAPTER 75

KELLY STRUGGLED TO BREATHE.

A blinding flash had come first, then a bang and she was pitched backward by a blast of displaced air, her vision gone, ears ringing, face hit by a wave of intense heat. Then everything had gone black, a total cloaking darkness, as if she'd been struck blind. The air around her had turned hot, clammy, and close, pressing onto her skin, hard to breathe in, burning her throat. Panic clamped her lungs. A foul odor swelled in her nostrils. Flesh burning? A weight seemed heavy on her chest, pinning her down, and she was shaking bad, her body cold. In the turmoil that assaulted her stunned mind the only impulse was to flee. But none of her muscles responded.

She opened an eye.

The tent was gone.

The night sky now above her clouded by smoke.

Intense pain radiated from her midsection, through her back, and into her brain. Her left arm would not move but, with the right one, she carefully examined her abdomen. Blood coated her hand. Red, warm, fresh. She was bleeding. Bad. Slowly, she turned her head and saw more bodies, many covered in smoking vinyl. The scene around her winked in and out and she fought to stay conscious. Her strength was waning and nothing she did rallied her stamina. She stiffened and struggled to bring herself under control.

Was she dying?

Bleeding to death?

God. No.

AIKO RESTED IN THE DEPTHS OF BLACKNESS, A WHIRLPOOL OF LIGHTS swirling ever larger, ignoring her subconscious pleas to go away. A voice could be heard, soft at first, in sync with the light, growing in volume as things grew brighter. A familiar voice, that never grew older, never lost its strength.

Her father.

Urging her to wake up.

COTTON ROSE FROM THE FLOOR.

Pain and apprehension were compounded by shock and confusion. He'd dived down once he realized that the guard below was not going to heed his warning and intended on firing at the man with the controller. Aiko had shot the guard, but not before the man sprayed the two attackers with automatic weapons fire and the one with the controller flicked the switch.

He stepped to the window and saw Aiko slowly coming to her feet, shaking off the cobwebs caused by the blast. Her legs ebbed and she stumbled forward, seemingly trying to regain her senses. He recalled the moment of the explosion. The tent rearing up like a balloon expanding upward atop an orange cloud. At the peak of its ascent it began to separate, the vinyl surely flame-retardant but not immune to the effects of searing heat, pieces shearing off and melting in a cloud of hot gas. Fragments from the aluminum supports flew in all directions, most likely accompanied by ball bearings that had become lethal projectiles. Another explosion blotted everything from view before the tent reemerged from the fireball, dropping back to the ground wrapped in flames. Shrapnel had burst outward, most heading downward within the tent but some had made its way beyond thudding into the stone walls. Many of the glass windows near the tent were gone. The one here in this room had survived but only because it had been swung inward.

He'd hit the floor, his head covered with his hands and arms.

Always get low.

That's what he'd been taught.

He now saw that the aluminum support poles were nearly all gone. But the vinyl fabric of the tent itself had settled back down like a searing blanket of melted material coating the charred tables, chairs, and bodies. The two men who'd brought the terror and the guard lay dead on the ground. More sounds cut through the haze that clouded his brain. Screams. Yells. The crackling of fire. And an unmistakable odor. One he'd smelled before.

Flesh burning.

"You okay?" he called down to Aiko.

She nodded, seemingly back in control of her balance. He had to get down there, so he fled the bedroom and headed outside. More of the security detail had arrived and were headed for the blast site.

He and Aiko stared at the devastation.

Was Suzy in that tent?

He had to find out.

AIKO HAD NEVER EXPERIENCED ANYTHING LIKE THIS BEFORE. SHE'D dealt with cars driven into pedestrians, a bus and plane hijacked, and the deadly sarin attacks conducted by Aum Shinrikyo.

But nothing even close to this magnitude.

She followed Malone into the devastation. A few of the people who'd been inside were moving on the ground, moaning in agony, one screaming with pain.

Malone began searching.

She knew for who.

Kelly Austin.

COTTON SCANNED THE CARNAGE LOOKING FOR SUZY AND HE SPOTTED her among half a dozen other bodies. He rushed over and knelt down. Her skin had been pierced with multiple wounds from the steel balls, leaking blood at an alarming rate. Her hair was singed and awful burns were on her arms and legs, her face charred black from the heat, one eye sealed shut. Blood gushed from a deep cut to her forehead, trickling down over her left eye. He held her limp, torn body in his arms, anguish in his eyes.

"It's Cotton, Suzy. Can you hear me?" he asked her, voice low and soft.

She did not rouse.

He gently nudged her and she came alert.

"Suzy, you need stay with me. Can you do that?"

She blinked her one eye, trying to focus on him.

"That's good," he said. "Try to stay awake. I'm going to get you help."

But he realized that would be too little too late. She was bleeding badly, no way to stop the flow. He quickly glanced around and saw that most of those who'd been inside the tent were dead.

"Cotton."

He turned back to her. She'd breathed his name. "I'm here."

"Listen...to me...please."

"Save your strength. There'll be time to talk later."

Aiko was moving among the carnage, but had stopped at one body where she bent down.

"Cotton," Suzy breathed out. "Listen."

He turned back to her. "Okay, what is it?"

"Remember my...favorite...book?"

He did. They'd often talked about books. It had been a subject they'd shared. Unlike Pam. His wife had harbored no interest in reading. Suzy's likes had varied from biographies, to history, to science fiction. She especially loved history books. One of which ranked as her all-time favorite.

"*A Distant Mirror.*"

She gave a slight nod. "Remember that."

"I never forget anything."

He was trying to make a little light of things. Take the edge off.

"No...you....don't. I still...have my copy."

He'd given it to her.

A present to someone special.

He wondered about the choice of subjects, but indulged her. Anything to keep her awake, talking, engaged—until help arrived. Problem was, the compound was a long way from the nearest hospital and Suzy didn't have enough blood to wait.

"Fix it...please...you have...to fix it."

He was puzzled. "Fix what?"

"Atlas Man—

She started to gasp, struggling to breathe. Blood seeped from her lips. He wanted to do something, but there was nothing he could do. She'd been shredded by shrapnel and singed by the heat of the explosion. His initial assessment now seemed correct. C-4 had been packed into the tent's support structure along with the steel balls. Once exploded the aluminum and the balls shredded outward with the force of bullets, doing immeasurable damage.

"What do you want me to fix?" he asked her.

"All of it...everything. Use the...code. It will make it all... right...again."

Death seemed impatient. The words edged falteringly past her blue lips flecked with red. Her left hand reached for his and he gently grabbed hold. She was staring at him with her one eye, watery, oily, the life fading from it. It broke his heart to watch this happening. Others were being administered to, but they were all surely in the same bad place.

Aiko walked over. "Catherine Gledhill is dead. She's over there.

My source within the bank, Lana Greenwell, was here too. Also dead."

He was still holding Suzy's hand.

Aiko stared at the wounds and nodded her understanding. Nobody was going to survive this.

"Cotton," Suzy suddenly said, with surprising firmness.

He faced her.

"You have to make it...the way I wanted."

Desperation filled her eyes.

"Okay," he said. "I'll fix it."

"I need to tell you—"

Her words trailed off in an indistinct jumble. She sputtered, coughed, and gasped. Her breathing went ragged. She struggled for air. Then her eye went wide, her mouth opened, and she stopped breathing.

Damn. Damn. Damn.

He waited to see if she might rebound.

But nothing.

He closed his eyes. He had not felt the pain of loss in a long time. Not since Antarctica. Then again in Paris. He'd thought those had been the worst.

But he was wrong.

This hurt worse.

He checked for a pulse.

None.

CHAPTER 76

KYRA HAD FLOWN DURING THE NIGHT AND ARRIVED AT THE DESIGNATED location by midmorning. Catherine Gledhill had been emphatic. Get there but make no contact. Gledhill had also provided adequate background information on how to locate Kelly Austin's daughter.

She remained apprehensive about this whole endeavor. Running errands for her clients was not part of her services-rendered portfolio. Still, this whole job had turned into the unusual. Considering the compensation she'd made an exception. This was turning into the largest payday she'd ever experienced. So if the Bank of St. George required a babysitter for a few days, then that was what it was going to get.

What was next?

She'd already received two inquiries through her usual channels. Never did potential clients contact her directly. Instead, she employed a variety of brokers who acted as a filter. She paid them generously for both the service and the risk. Their contact with her was always by text using coded messages with alert words that would signal danger without any outsiders being the wiser. Both of the current inquiries had come through with no alerts, which meant she now needed more details to determine which job would be next.

Or maybe she'd just handle both.

Her best asset was that she never appeared deadly. Quite the contrary. She made every effort to blend in. Be part of the surroundings. Do nothing that drew unwanted attention. She could always tell when a pair of insistent male eyes focused on her, flashing the unspoken message of desire. Which she rarely returned. Attachments were risky, and even the most casual of acquaintances came with dangers. It helped that she was no stranger to fear, but the downside to that was she never really felt secure, always possessing a contingency plan. A way out. Hard to keep count of the number of people who'd not shared her good fortune and died by her hand. She was getting older, and with age came contemplation. Was it time to stop?

Not yet.

She was enjoying a delicious breakfast. She'd called ahead and reserved a room at the best hotel in town, thinking she might be here for a few days. Gledhill had told her that she would be negotiating with Kelly Austin. Some pictures and videos of the daughter might prove helpful in bringing those discussions to a close.

So be ready.

That was the last instruction she'd been given.

She'd flown most of the night, arriving right after dawn local time. A shower, along with washing her hair, and a change of clothes had been welcomed. Now she was enjoying some fresh croissants, sweet blueberry jam, and hot coffee. She sat on a spacious stone terrace, enjoying a rare moment of personal satisfaction. Someone once told her, *Be led first by your wisdom and second by your passion.* Good advice.

Which she'd followed for years.

The plan for the day was to make indirect contact and ensure that Austin's birth daughter was actually nearby. Gledhill had instructed that she would call when necessary. Otherwise, there was to be no communication. Fine by her. She was ready for this whole job to end. Her bitcoin was secure inside her personal wallet, protected by a confidential key, backed up by an envelope in a Swiss safe-deposit box. Thankfully, she had millions of euros in a variety of banks spread across the globe. More than enough money for her to live comfortably for the rest of her life. But she was still young and there was so much more to do. Her services would always be needed.

For a price.

She indulged in another of the fresh pastries. She ate little when working. The rush of adrenaline that kept her senses sharp also dulled her appetite. But this job was essentially over. No more risks. Just a little recon.

She signed the bill for her breakfast and headed out the hotel's main entrance. The concierge had arranged for her to use a hotel car for the day. She thought it the most innocuous of vehicles, one that should allow her to move around unnoticed. She left the grounds and headed out, driving along on a two-lane highway. Her destination lay about ten kilometers away. Traffic was light for the morning, only a couple of cars and a bus had passed in the opposite lane. The weather was perfect, bright and sunny and warm.

Something banged.

Loud.

A tire blown?

The steering wheel lurched to the right. One of the front tires must have punctured. She fought to slow down and regain control.

Then another bang.

Two tires?

The rear end of the vehicle swung left. She tried to counter by steering in the opposite direction, but the timing of the blowouts, as she was making a sharp right turn, compounded her inability to tame the car. The passenger side slammed hard into the guardrail. Momentum kept the vehicle going, up and over the top of the rail, then down, somersaulting, turning over and over, crashing against the rock face, twisting, screeching as the metal pounded against the stone, bouncing off a ledge, finishing in a crumpled heap.

Amazingly, right-side up.

The seat belt and shoulder harness had kept her in place and the air bag had deployed.

She'd never experienced anything like that before.

A damn car accident?

After all she'd been through?

She tested her arms and legs. Everything moved. Nothing seemed broken. She tried the door, which partially opened. It took effort but she forced it to move enough outward so that she could roll out onto the ground.

Her head spun to the point of nausea.

Her stomach erupted and she vomited her breakfast, retching until her gut hurt. A concussion? Probably. She stared upward, trying to clear her head. That was a lot of tumbles down fifty meters of rocky bank. She needed to find her cell phone and call for help. It had been resting in the center console, surely tossed about during the crash.

She heard footsteps. Approaching. She rolled her body over and saw a man walking her way. Slow, steady, deliberate.

Thank God.

"I need help," she said.

The man did not reply.

He just kept walking, then stopped before her.

"I had a wreck," she said.

He was middle-aged with short-cropped black hair and continued to make no effort to render any assistance.

Which concerned her.

More vertigo swept through her brain and she retched again.

"Not so tough now, are you?" he said.

She stared up from the ground.

He held a gun.

But she wanted to know, "Who are you? Why are you here?"

He did not answer.

Her body started to jerk, blood and froth foaming from her mouth. The man bent down and grabbed her hair.

"Closing loose ends," he said.

Then he shoved the muzzle of the gun into her belly and fired.

She felt the bullet enter.

Then nothing after that.

CHAPTER 77

COTTON STOOD BEFORE THE APARTMENT DOOR.

He'd stayed at the compound in Morocco until the wee hours of the morning. The death toll had been extensive. All eighty-four people inside the tent died. Most during the explosion, the rest in the hour or so after. No one made it to a hospital. Among the dead was the entire governing board of the Bank of St. George, including Catherine Gledhill. In addition to Suzy, as Aiko had told him there, another bank employee, Lana Greenwell, had also perished. Then there'd been the envoys from all of the nations and the president of El Salvador.

Gone.

The Moroccan government had been informed of the attack and the DST had come to the scene. It had taken direct White House intervention to smooth over the C-4 incident in Marrakesh. Luckily, none of their people had been seriously hurt and, as Stephanie Nelle told him, *They're big boys and will get over it.*

They'd managed to keep the media at bay. The isolation of the compound helped. The story would finally be released in about another hour. Terrorism would be floated, but far more questions than answers would be presented. And he assumed that's the way it would remain.

Particularly considering the truth.

He'd contacted Cassiopeia and learned what happened in Geneva and the discovery of a massive cache of World War II gold, all of it part of the Black Eagle Trust. A TOP SECRET label had been slapped on the gold by both the American and Swiss governments. Derrick Koger had assured him that not a bar would ever see the light of day. And now, with the decimation of the entire leadership of the Bank of St. George, keeping that secret had become a thousand percent easier.

Which also helped with Aiko Ejima. She knew nothing about the gold being found and seemed satisfied that the Atlas Maneuver was effectively rendered moot with all of the deaths in Morocco. So they'd said their goodbyes and she flew back to Switzerland.

"It was a pleasure working with you," she said to him.

"I know things did not work out as you planned."

"They seemed to have worked out for the best. Perhaps it was time for all this to be put to rest."

And he agreed.

The culprits who'd triggered the explosion, along with the dead men found in Marrakesh, were second-rate mercenaries who'd obviously been well financed and supported. All that C-4 had to have come from somewhere. And the bomb itself had been supercharged by the addition of pure oxygen being fed though the tent's air-conditioning system, amplifying the effects a hundredfold.

That took expertise to both know and make happen.

The real van from Voyagez & Amusez-vous, along with four bodies, was found abandoned outside of Marrakesh. He doubted anything would ever be traced back to the CIA. Too many layers. Too many middlemen. That trail would stop long short of Langley. But there was no question it had all been part of Neverlight. What started at the end of World War II had ended in the Atlas Mountains of Morocco.

There'd been nothing left for him to do so he'd left, taking an early flight out to Rome, then on to Luxembourg. Why had he come? Hard to say. But every instinct he possessed told him that he had to see this through. Suzy had been trying to tell him something, but she died before completing the message.

Fix it, please, you have to fix it.

She'd started to say *Atlas Maneuver*, but could not finish, so he'd asked, What do you want me to fix?

All of it, everything.

And there'd been something else.

Right before she died.

I need to tell you—

But she never finished.

So he'd come to Luxembourg to find answers. Stephanie had obtained an address for Suzy's apartment, which was located in the Cloître de Saint-François, a former convent that had been converted into luxury housing in the heart of the old city. Records indicated that Suzy owned the space outright, its current valuation, according to tax records, at a little more than six million euros. Apparently she'd been extremely well paid.

But for the inventor of bitcoin he would have expected no less.

The Police Grand-Ducale, part of Luxembourg's Ministère de la Sécurité Intérieure, had been briefed and called in to assist. They had met him at the airport and driven him straight here, arranging for access to the apartment. He'd asked to inspect it alone but they had not agreed, so three of the national police now stood with him. Considering the owner was deceased there was no need for subtlety, so one of them used a battering ram and crashed the door open.

He stepped inside.

Impressive.

Especially the view of Luxembourg City, bathed in sunlight through plate-glass doors past a terrace. He walked around and noted the exposed beams, fireplaces, gold leaf, beautiful herringbone floors, intricate moldings, and some top-of-the-line appliances. In a walk-in closet off the master bedroom he noted her wardrobe, an assortment of high-end designer clothes, shoes, and handbags.

The three national policemen had fanned out and were looking around too. He wondered what for since their briefing had been extremely limited, only that the apartment's owner had worked at the Bank of St. George. Other officers, along with Europol, had already appeared at the bank's headquarters and taken control, effectively shutting the bank down. Both Bern and Washington had requested this through the European Union.

Remember my favorite book?

A Distant Mirror.

By Barbara Tuchman.

A self-trained historian and double Pulitzer Prize winner. The book detailed the tumultuous 14th century and postulated that the death and suffering then reflected that of the time in and around World War I. An excellent narrative history. He loved the book too. He and Suzy had discussed it during their time together, and he distinctly recalled that she ranked it as her favorite.

I still have my copy.

That's what she'd told him.

So he continued his survey, moving slowly and casually, eventually making his way into the den and the bookshelves to the left of the flat-screen television. His expert bibliophile eye perused the shelves. Biographies, some novels, but mainly histories. No surprise. Her favorite. From different times and periods. None overrepresented. Not a lot of books. Nothing that ranked collectable or valuable, except to their owner.

Then he spotted it.

The distinctive beige cover with block lettering.

He glanced around. The three officers were off in other rooms. He slid the book free and admired the front jacket and the painting depicted. From a famous 15th-century book of hours. Showing the fourth horseman of the apocalypse. He noticed that the cover was wrapped in clear plastic, like books were in libraries for protection. Others on the shelves were likewise sheathed.

Book lovers did that.

He cradled the hardcover in his left palm. Maybe nine hundred pages. Gently, he opened the front cover to the end papers that showed a map of Europe during the 14th century. He turned the page carefully, respecting the fact that the book had been printed nearly fifty years ago. The next page was blank save for the distinctive feminine signature of Barbara W. Tuchman in soft blue ink.

A signed copy.

He'd found it in a Jacksonville, Florida, used-book shop and bought it just for Suzy. A first edition. This volume carried some worth as Tuchman had been dead for a long time. But the epigraph page had been defaced with writing. In pencil. No self-respecting bibliophile would permanently damage a precious book. Sure, Suzy had written in this one but only in the faintest of lead, easily erased without a trace remaining.

A series of letters and numbers.

He counted. Twenty-eight different characters.

Hos730#DF$2936GRVOZX37/?fy%&

Which she'd recorded beneath the book's epigraph. A quote from John Dryden, who penned a work titled "On the Characters in the Canterbury Tales."

> *For mankind is ever the same*
> *and nothing is lost out of nature,*
> *though everything is altered.*

Suzy had deliberately left a message and, with her dying breaths, directing him straight to it. But when this message had been left she'd had no way of knowing that he would appear in Basel.

Yet she'd still made this choice of book. Why?

The twenty-eight characters were now engrained in his mind.

But he could not leave this for someone else to discover, and there was no way those police were going to allow him to leave with the book.

So he did the unthinkable—

And tore the page free.

CHAPTER 78

Cassiopeia entered the Bank of St. George.

She, Koger, Trinity Dorner, and Kristen Jeanne had traveled the 250 kilometers north by car. She and Koger had spent the night in a Geneva hotel, then reteamed with Trinity and Kristin for breakfast. She'd spoken to Cotton and he'd told her about the massacre in Morocco. Koger and Trinity had made inquiries and learned that the entire governing body of the bank had been killed, including Catherine Gledhill. Most disturbing, Kelly Austin was among the casualties, along with all of the national envoys.

A team of international investigators had been called in to examine and analyze anything that could be uncovered at the bank. They were already on the scene, in the building, interviewing employees who'd been ordered in to work on a Saturday. She was excited to finally see Cotton, who'd told her on a call earlier that he would be there, and she found him in Catherine Gledhill's office.

She gave him a long hug, which he returned. "Good to see you in one piece."

He smiled. "Same to you."

"I'm sorry about Kelly Austin."

"It was a terrible way to die. She didn't deserve that."

Koger entered the office.

"I'm sorry about what happened," the big man said.

She noticed no arrogance, nicknames, or grandstanding. Instead, his tone sounded sincere.

"And thank you," Koger said. "I appreciate all that you did."

"It wasn't enough. We lost them all."

Trinity Dorner entered the office. "I told you in Munich we'd see each other again."

He said, "That you did."

"I've spoken with the president," Trinity said. "The CIA director has been fired, as have six deputy directors. All were implicated with Operation Neverlight. Everything about that really stupid idea has now been stamped CLASSIFIED. Nobody is going to speak of it to anyone, unless they want to go to prison."

"And the fact that the CIA engaged in mass murder?" Cotton asked.

"You know the answer to that," Dorner said. "We can't afford that heat. We'll deal with this internally. I promise you, there will be retribution."

"Citrone had the original map that details where the Japanese hid all the gold across the Philippines," Koger said.

"Good to know," Trinity said. "We'll make a search. But we can only hope that the map's location died with Citrone. That's another door from long ago we don't want to open."

"We still have a big problem," Koger said. "This bank controlled a huge amount of bitcoin, which Austin hijacked. We need to retrieve those coins."

"Why?" Cotton asked. "Let them vanish into the wind."

"That is an option," Trinity said. "But we can't risk someone else gaining control of them. As we have discovered, the damage that could be done from that is immeasurable."

"Contrary to what the idiots at Langley thought," Koger said, "bitcoin isn't going away. You can't stop it."

"It can only stop itself," Cassiopeia had to say.

"Which is why," Trinity said, "we can't risk someone acquiring over four and a half million of them."

"And what would happen if we could reacquire them?" Cotton asked.

"The United States government will keep them," Trinity said.

COTTON DID NOT LIKE WHAT HE'D JUST HEARD.

That would be the last thing Suzy would have wanted. *The whole idea was total and complete independence.* That's what she'd told him two days ago. Now for the government to take control of a quarter of all the bitcoin known to still exist?

That seemed unconscionable.

Bitcoin was Suzy's legacy. Sadly, he knew little to nothing about her family. That had not been a subject they'd ever explored. He did know she was an only child. He had no idea if her parents were still alive. Her life had to have meaning. She was the creator of blockchain. A brilliant mind. An innovator. Someone who literally changed the world.

And she was blown up.

For what?

Fix it. You have to make it the way I wanted.

"I think I have an answer," he said.

Cotton followed everyone off the elevator. They'd descended below the ground level into the most secure area of the bank. Where the servers were located, especially an air-gap version that kept the private keys for the online wallets. He'd been introduced to a woman named Kristin Jeanne from the Eidgenössische Finanzmarktaufsicht, the Swiss Financial Market Supervisory Authority. Like the Securities Exchange Commission, federal bank regulators, and FBI all in one.

"I need you to explain to me how this system works," he said.

"I can't do that," Jeanne said, "but we found one of the IT personnel from the bank who can. She explained the situation to me."

"Okay," he said. "I'm all ears."

"And who exactly are you?" Jeanne asked.

"I'm the guy that can solve this problem."

He caught the glances among Koger, Trinity, and Jeanne, ones that said *He's okay, you can trust him.*

Jeanne shrugged. "Okay, that server over there is not connected to the internet. It sits alone. On it are the keys to the bank's 4,556,298.6752 bitcoin. They exist inside 4,312 separate electronic wallets, each protected by an access code. Kelly Austin froze that server with a virus. Once that virus is released then the keys to those wallets will be available once again. They can then be transferred through this desktop here to the internet and the wallets themselves."

"How do you move them over?"

"With a flash drive," Jeanne said.

"Can you access the air-gap server?" he asked.

Jeanne stepped back to the door, opened it, and motioned. A younger woman entered and was directed to the chair before the keyboard. "She can."

The woman started typing and a prompt screen appeared on the monitor asking for the user name and password. The latter he was certain about. The former? Not so much. But Suzy had written the password right under the epigraph. So he went for the obvious. The man who penned the epigraph for *A Distant Mirror.* John Dryden. And he spelled out the last name.

Which was entered.

"Password?" Jeanne said.

And he repeated what Suzy had written.

Hos730#DF$2936GRVOZX37/?fy%&

Twenty-eight letters, numbers, and symbols.

When everything was entered he double-checked the screen.

"There could be a fail-safe here," Jeanne said. "We've seen them before. Use the wrong name or password too many times, or even one time, and everything is erased."

"I'm not wrong," he made clear.

And he tapped the ENTER key.

The screen went blank for an instant, then came back to life producing a list of numbered lines with identification numbers, each followed by a set of letters, numbers, and symbols. Cotton scrolled down. The last line was numbered 4,312.

"How about that," Koger said. "Those are the private keys for the bank's wallets. Unlocked."

"Move them to a flash drive," Jeanne ordered.

And the woman before the terminal did that, removing the drive from the terminal and handing it over to Jeanne.

"We need to see if they work," Trinity said.

He agreed and motioned.

Jeanne inserted the drive in the second terminal, which was connected to the bank's internal system and the internet. The woman tapped the keyboard, then looked at them.

"It requires another password."

He thought on that for a moment, then decided on the obvious.

For mankind is ever the same and nothing is lost out of nature, though everything is altered.

The epigraph itself.

He repeated it out loud and the woman typed, omitting the spaces between the words and running them all together. The screen went momentarily blank, then reappeared with typed text.

They all read.

CONGRATULATIONS, KATIE, YOU HAVE REACQUIRED THE KEYS TO OPEN THE BANK'S WALLETS. HOW? THAT'S HARD TO SAY SINCE I'M WRITING THIS BEFORE IT HAPPENED, BUT YOU HAVE APPARENTLY SUCCEEDED. THERE WERE ALWAYS TWO OUTCOMES HERE. ONE WHERE YOU REGAINED CONTROL OF THE KEYS AND THE WALLETS AND CONTINUED ON WITH YOUR ATLAS MANEUVER. THE OTHER WHERE SOMETHING ELSE ALTOGETHER HAPPENS. SINCE YOU ARE READING THIS MESSAGE THE LATTER HAS OCCURRED. IN THIS SCENARIO IT WAS IMPORTANT THAT YOU SOMEHOW FORCED THE ISSUE, GAINED THE UPPER HAND, WON THE BATTLE. BUT SADLY, YOU LOST THE WAR. ONCE YOU MOVED THE UNENCRYPTED KEYS FROM THE AIR-GAP SERVER TO THE MAIN SYSTEM

AND SENT THEM OUT OVER THE INTERNET TO CONNECT WITH THE BANK'S WALLETS, SOMETHING ELSE TOOK PLACE. THE KEYS WERE AN ILLUSION, THERE TO SATISFY YOUR INSATIABLE NEED TO WIN. HOW DID IT FEEL? SATISFYING? INSIDE THAT ILLUSION I CREATED A PROGRAM WHERE THE KEYS ACTUALLY DID OPEN EVERY ONE OF THE BANK'S WALLETS, THEN REMOVED THE BITCOIN THAT WERE THERE AND CONCENTRATED THEM INTO A SINGLE NEW WALLET OF MY CREATION. FROM THAT NEW WALLET THE PROGRAM ASCERTAINED THE TOTAL NUMBER OF ACTIVE WALLETS THAT CURRENTLY EXIST FOR BITCOIN, DIVIDED THAT NUMBER INTO THE TOTAL NUMBER OF COINS THE BANK OWNS, AND THEN DISTRIBUTED THOSE EVENLY TO EVERY ACTIVE WALLET IN THE WORLD. GRANTED, GIVEN THE SHEER NUMBER OF ONLINE WALLETS THE AMOUNT OF BITCOIN SENT TO EACH IS MINUSCULE. BY MY CALCULATIONS CURRENTLY THAT'S ABOUT A ONE HUNDRED AND FIFTIETH OF A BITCOIN TO EVERY WALLET. SMALL, BUT THE POINT IS MADE. THOSE COINS WHICH YOU PLANNED TO USE TO MANIPULATE ARE NOW WHERE THEY SHOULD BE, AMONG THE OWNERS. NOT YOU, NOT THE GOVERNMENT, NOT THE CIA, NOT ANY SINGLE PERSON OR ENTITY WILL HAVE THEM. WHAT I CREATED CAN NOW WORK AS INTENDED. THIS IS MY OWN ATLAS MANEUVER. AND NORMALLY THIS WOULD TAKE MONTHS TO ACCOMPLISH, BUT THE PROGRAM YOU HAVE UNLEASHED IS SOMETHING NEW, SOMETHING BETTER THAT I CREATED. A LIGHTNING NETWORK THAT PROCESSES TRANSACTIONS AT A MUCH FASTER RATE. ANOTHER GIFT TO THE WORLD FROM SATOSHI NAKAMOTO. NONE OF WHICH WAS DESIGNED FOR GREED OR PROFIT OR POWER. INSTEAD, THIS IS A GREAT EQUALIZER THAT RETURNS TO THE GOOD PEOPLE WHO WILL OWN BITCOIN THE FREEDOM THEY WERE PROMISED. I OWE THEM THAT. I OWE MYSELF THAT. ALL IS NOW RIGHT. YOU FAILED, KATIE.

"Can you verify what happened?" Jeanne asked.

The woman who sat before the keyboard tapped away, studying the screen, then tapped more.

CHAPTER 79

Cotton removed the books from the top shelf and carefully stacked them on the floor. He'd been meaning to reorganize the history section for a couple of weeks now and decided today was the day. Running a used-book shop meant that the inventory changed daily. People would bring in their old books by the boxful for either sale or trade. He took great pride in recycling them from one owner to the next. Along the way he made a living—that's what booksellers did—but he was careful not to price his wares too high. The idea was for every book to find a new home.

"Books are amazing," Suzy said. "Words on a page that transport us. We can switch off from everything, never notice the time passing, and experience smells, sounds, sights, and emotions from all over time and place. It's like chewing gum for the eyes."

He'd always liked that phrase.

She was always clever with words. Yet for all that cleverness she'd also had an insatiable yearning for adventure.

Just like him.

"Bitcoin is like a religious experience," Suzy said to him. "Like Christ himself."

He smiled. "A bit blasphemous, but I'll bite. How?"

"Both had a humble beginning. Christ in a manger, bitcoin

appearing on the internet, each a gift to the world, both loved by everyone. Bitcoin, like Christ, plays no favorites and lives forever. The establishment hated Christ and today it also hates bitcoin since it, like Christ, flips the money changers' tables. They are also both a central source of truth, selflessness, and morality, and they encourage the world to stay peaceful."

"How do you figure that?"

"It takes money to fight a war. Money nations borrow. To borrow they just create more of their own money, devaluing their own currency. You can't do that with bitcoin. It's finite. So if everyone used bitcoin there'd be a limited amount of money to wage war. Countries literally could not afford to fight. And finally, both bitcoin and Christ work as a savior, starting revolutions."

She'd been so excited to explain what she created. So proud. And deservingly so. He'd known from the beginning she was smart. A love of books had drawn them together. They'd first met in a Pensacola bookstore, she there buying a gift for a friend, he just browsing, avoiding having to go home to his wife. Her favorite stories had been ones about humanity coming through adversity and finding hope. How fitting that her own life became just such a story.

"You can't change the world, Harold. But you can do the right thing. We all behave according to the world, as we live it."

He stared down at the piles on the floor.

Yes. Books were important.

Suzy Baldwin / Kelly Austin had also been important.

More than the world would ever know.

He'd left Luxembourg yesterday and flown back to Denmark. Cassiopeia had headed for France, but she was due back here in a couple of days. She'd sensed that he needed some time alone and he appreciated the space. Suzy had come along at a crossroads in his life when two paths had opened. Over the years he'd come to realize that she'd indirectly pointed him toward the right road to take. But that choice had involved hurting her deeply. He'd seen it in her eyes that last day when he told her it was over.

Her pain changed him.

No question.

He'd noticed in her apartment little in the way of personalization. No family pictures. No travel experiences. No special person. Nothing at all. As if the past never existed. And perhaps it didn't for Kelly Austin. Suzy Baldwin? That was someone altogether different. But the books. Those were there. Which seemed to explain her life. Besides *A Distant Mirror*, one in particular on her shelves had caught his eye. A familiar colorful cover of a magician playing cards with the devil. The latter displaying four kings, the former proudly showing off four aces. At the time it was a relatively new book. Written by a man named Glen David Gold. His first novel. *Carter Beats the Devil.* He'd bought her that copy too, the inside inscribed FOR YOU, FROM ME.

Which she'd also curiously kept.

He'd loved the story.

It remained one of his personal favorites. It took place in the 1920s, the golden age for stage magic, and Charles Carter was a magician at the height of his fame. At the climax of his latest stage show Carter invited President Warren G. Harding on stage to take part in his act. In front of an amazed audience Carter chopped the president into pieces, cut off his head, and fed him to a lion before restoring him to perfect health. The show was a great success, but two hours later Harding was dead and Carter found himself at the center of some unwelcome attention from the Secret Service.

Apparently, President Harding passed a great secret on to Carter.

A young inventor named Philo Farnsworth had created a new device called television. And not everybody was happy about that. Both the radio industry and the military wanted it to go away, and they came after Carter to get it. The great magician had to draw on all his skills to escape kidnapping and death as he sought out the elusive inventor. Along the way Carter met a young blind woman with a mysterious past and encountered a deadly rival. At the end, in a magic show to end all magic shows, Carter had to beat the devil to save both Farnsworth and his magical new invention.

A gloriously fun tale.

Its major theme?

Making seemingly impossible escapes in order to change the world.

But the book also highlighted the way new and different things inspired fear, mistrust, and wonder. And how great things could be accomplished in secret. In the end Carter's greatest trick was performed with the knowledge of only a few close people.

Just like with Suzy.

No one would ever know what she accomplished.

The sequence of events from the past few days had reordered itself into a clear, horrible memory. One he'd never forget. So many memories had lain dormant for so long. All troublesome. So much that he'd chosen not to recall. But now only ugly lewd images reared up, and the pain of his thoughts was not easily brushed aside. True, he'd accomplished her goal and made things right, but he felt no triumph. Only uncertainty and a brooding unease.

He turned back to the shelves and brought more books to the floor. The shelves all required a periodic cleansing, with him removing duplicates and reorganizing what was left into some semblance of order. Customers liked order.

He liked order.

The bell on the front door tinkled. It had been doing that quite a bit all day. Business had been brisk. Out the plate-glass windows he'd noticed that Højbro Plads was busy with people enjoying a glorious late-summer day in Denmark. He went back to work and heard some conversation occurring at the main desk. Then footsteps across the hardwood floor and Trinity Dorner appeared at the end of the aisle.

Nothing about this could be good.

"What brings you by?" he asked.

"I was on the way back to Washington."

"This is not on the way from Luxembourg to DC."

She shrugged. "I'm flying private, so I can go wherever I want."

He wasn't fooled. This woman didn't do a thing without a reason. So what was her angle here?

"I'm sorry about Kelly Austin," she said. "Though you knew her a long time ago as Suzy Baldwin."

He went back to sorting the books on the floor for reshelving.

"Koger told me all about it," she said. "He learned it all from Cassiopeia. And she's a keeper, by the way."

"I agree."

"You and Suzy Baldwin were close?"

"I knew her when I was young and stupid."

"We've all been there."

"As much as I would want to explore that subject, I'm a little busy."

"President Fox stopped Neverlight. But not before they killed a woman name Kyra Lhota."

He knew that name. From the airport in Basel. She'd taken Suzy to Morocco. "She's a paid assassin."

Trinity nodded. "And was quite good. Or so I hear."

"Apparently not good enough. Why did they feel the need to take her out?"

"That was a question that bothered me too. So I ordered a deep dive."

He looked up from the books. "And?"

"All we found was an encrypted file that had been sent from Catherine Gledhill, the head of the bank, to Lhota. Our people broke the encryption and decoded the file. It was background information on a young woman, who seems to have no connection here whatsoever. But the file was sent just a few hours before Lhota arrived."

"Who is this woman?"

"That's a good question."

"Since you're here, telling me this, I assume this somehow involves me."

His voice was unusually deep from fatigue, and he had to concentrate to keep his thoughts together. Some sleep would be good.

But he was too wound up.

She reached into her shoulder bag and withdrew a large manila envelope, which she tossed to him. "From President Fox. With his thanks."

The tone—cold, unmoved, unquestionable—carried a sense of finality.

She turned and left.

He heard the front door open, then close.

The envelope lay atop some of the books.

He stared at it like it was cursed. He wanted to vent his anger and frustration by tearing it to shreds but his curiosity was too much, which Trinity Dorner had apparently known.

He opened it and shuffled through the papers. A lot there. Mainly field reports from an investigative agency, which apparently had located this woman a few years back. He skimmed through some of it. There were three color images showing a lean figure in a simple red dress, her face sharp-featured and attractive. At the bottom of the papers he found an order of adoption, issued by a Texas court. The petitioner was Susan Baldwin, noted as the natural mother. The adoptive parents' names were also there, with the court divesting Suzy of all her parental rights. He knew what that meant. Even the birth certificate would be changed so that Suzy's name would not appear. The order also provided that the petitioner had sworn, under oath, that she did not know the identity of the natural father.

He knew what that meant too.

The notice of the adoption would have been run in a local Texas newspaper for four weeks announcing to the world that the petition had been filed. If anyone had a claim, including the unknown natural father, there was a mechanism provided where they could assert it. Not the best way to let people know, but it was the only way available. Service by publication, it was called. A copy of the new birth certificate was there showing the adoptive parents now as mother and father, vested with the same rights as if they'd produced the child themselves.

But the last sheet grabbed his attention.

The original Texas birth certificate. Listing Suzy as the mother and the father as unknown. And the date of birth?

He did the math.

Seven months after Suzy left Pensacola.

A tingle of apprehension ran down his spine as an uncomfortable question forced its way into his thoughts.

Could it be?

WRITER'S NOTE

As to the settings for this story, Elizabeth and I visited Morocco and ventured into the Atlas Mountains. Separately, she and I have traveled to Switzerland. We were not able to make it to Luxembourg, but we will definitely be correcting that omission in the future.

Time now to separate fact from fiction.

The various locales are all faithfully represented. These include Basel, Lake Baikal, Luxembourg, Geneva with its lake, Morocco, the Atlas Mountains, and Marrakesh. Katie Gledhill's compound is fictional though it is based on others that exist in the region. Her Luxembourg estate is likewise my creation, but the village of Esch-sur-Sûre (chapter 28) is real. Wine vaults (chapter 4) do exist throughout the world, especially in Switzerland, but mine is fictional.

Falconry (chapter 40) is fascinating and I've been wanting to include it in a novel for a long time. And a hawk can indeed take down a fawn.

As to the various security agencies mentioned, the PSIA is Japan's intelligence service (chapter 19) and the DST performs a similar function for Morocco (chapter 66).

There are many references to Japanese philosophy. Darumas (chapter 39) exist, the concept of *Giri* noted in chapter 33 is alive and well, and the beliefs in *honne* and *tatemae* (chapter 50) have not been forgotten. In addition Japan has seen an emperor resign—Akihito did so in 2019. I seized on that historical event for this story (chapter 20), but my emperor bears no resemblance to the real one. Japan has always revered its emperor but, after its defeat in World War II, General MacArthur did in fact force Hirohito to renounce his claim as a deity (chapter 20). It is also surprisingly true that the World War II peace treaty between Japan and the Allies was not signed until 1951. That document also contained the incredible waiver of all liability for war reparations quoted in chapter 12.

A curious clause indeed.

Aum Shinrikyo was a Japanese terrorist organization that committed many violent acts (chapter 30). Its founder, Shoko Asahara, was eventually caught, tried, and executed. Japanese soldiers did secrete themselves in the highlands of the Philippines after World War II and continued to fight for decades (chapter 33). The last of them finally surrendered in the 1970s.

There was a Bank of St. George, founded in 1407 in Genoa, Italy. It was abolished by Napoleon in 1805. I just resurrected it and changed locations. Bank secrecy has a long tradition in Switzerland (chapter 38), dating back centuries. Only in the past two decades, though, have laws been passed that finally chip away at that sacred concept.

The fate of James Forrestal, as detailed in chapter 51, is accurate. He did suffer from mental illness, died under mysterious circumstances, and left a strange message behind tied to Sophocles' tragedy *Ajax*. His connection to Golden Lily and the Black Eagle Trust, though, was all my imagination.

Ponzi schemes began in the early part of the 20th century as described in chapter 61. The Bretton Woods Agreement, adopted in 1944 by delegates from forty-four nations, formally adopted the U.S. dollar as the official reserve currency and set a framework that governed the world's economic systems from 1945 to 1971 (chapter 28). The two books mentioned at the end of the novel, *A Distant Mirror* and *Carter Beats the Devil* (chapters 75 and 79), are among my favorites.

This novel deals with something that can't adequately be described as fact, but it also cannot be dismissed as fantasy.

Kin no yuri.

Golden Lily.

Named after a poem that Emperor Hirohito wrote.

It was a covert plan, hatched by the imperial family, designed to acquire and move plundered war loot to Japan. When transport of the massive amounts of gold, silver, platinum, diamonds, and other precious stones became impossible (thanks to an Allied blockade), the stolen loot was secreted away underground in the Philippines for later retrieval.

The internal CIA memorandum contained in chapter 12 is fake, but the information it contains is all part of the story behind Golden Lily. There is no doubt that General Tomoyuki Yamashita oversaw a huge Philippine engineering project in the waning days of World War II. One hundred and seventy-five underground vaults were constructed by soldiers and prisoners. Loot was stored inside them. We know this because gold and plunder have been periodically found in the Philippines, some even by its former president Ferdinand Marcos. But were the engineers treated to a celebratory dinner and then sealed underground to die as depicted in the prologue? Was Prince Chichibu, the emperor's brother, there? Nobody knows for sure. But supposed witnesses after the war testified to that occurrence.

History also notes that General Yamashita was captured, quickly tried, found guilty of war crimes, and sentenced to death. He appealed to General MacArthur, who upheld the verdict. He then appealed to the Supreme Court of the Philippines and the Supreme Court of the United States, both of which declined to review the case. In dissent from the U.S. Supreme Court's majority, Justices W. B. Rutledge and Frank Murphy questioned the legitimacy of the hasty trial, including various procedural issues, the inclusion of suspect hearsay evidence, and the general lack of professional conduct by the prosecuting officers. They called the trial a miscarriage of justice, an exercise in vengeance, and a denial of human rights. Strong words from two American judges regarding a suspected war criminal. After President Truman denied Yamashita's petition for clemency, Yamashita was hanged on February 23, 1946.

One historical note.

Evidence that Yamashita did not have ultimate command responsibility over all military units in the Philippines (some of which actually committed the atrocities) was never admitted in court. Nonetheless he was held accountable for their actions. Yamashita's case created the legal precedent labeled command responsibility, which holds that a leader can be, and should be, held accountable for the crimes committed by their troops, even if they did not order them, didn't allow them, did not know about them, or did not have the means to stop them. Doesn't matter. The person at the top is responsible. Eventually, this doctrine of command accountability found its way into the Geneva Conventions and has been applied to dozens of subsequent war crimes trials.

Why was it necessary to so quickly end Yamashita's life?

Historians have wrestled with the inquiry. Many have argued that the information contained within chapter 12 might be the answer. Yamashita knew about the gold and, true to his oath to the emperor, refused to cooperate in its extraction. Once the gold was found Yamashita could become a liability for those secretly holding on to the wealth. So the decision was made to eliminate him and see if his personal driver would be more forthcoming. Apparently that man was much more cooperative (chapter 12), and some of the largest caches were supposedly recovered. That wealth was then secretly transported and deposited in a variety of repositories (chapter 12) across the globe. My consolidation of those caches to a single institution (the Bank of St. George) is imaginary.

There is supposedly a map that details the locations of all 175 underground vaults. Images of it abound on the internet. But no one, to date, has been able to effectively decipher it. Clues as to where the vaults are located are scattered all across the Philippine highlands and jungle. They exist in the trees and rocks, left there by the Japanese in 1945. But just as with the map, no one has ever successfully deciphered them. A recent television series on the History Channel, *Lost Gold of World War II*, attempted to find those caches with no success. An excellent source on this whole subject is *Gold Warriors: America's Secret Recovery of Yamashita's Gold* by Sterling and Peggy Seagrave.

The Central Intelligence Agency was formed in 1947. It grew out of the Office of Strategic Services, which operated as America's primary intelligence agency during World War II. The CIA had a confused beginning (chapter 12). No one was quite sure what it should do. Eventually, the Dulles-Jackson-Correa Report laid out the agency's primary mission statement (chapter 51), making it solely responsible for the gathering of American intelligence worldwide. But thanks to Allen Dulles (chapter 25) the CIA also assumed an offensive role, trying to influence and change political situations around the world (chapter 17). Nothing was out of bounds, including murder. Having a huge cache of undocumented wealth at its disposal would have been a tremendous CIA asset. Some say the Black Eagle Trust existed (chapter 29) and was extensively utilized. Others disagree. We will never know for sure as everyone involved is dead and many of the records remain classified. Even when some of those decades-old documents were finally released to the public in the late 1990s, President Bill Clinton allowed them to be severely redacted.

This novel centers on bitcoin, a subject that has long fascinated me. The whitepaper mentioned in chapter 16, which first described blockchain on October 21, 2008, is real. Some have described it as one of the most revolutionary scientific papers ever published. Blockchain is indeed a marvel (chapter 13), and the concept has changed the world. Eventually, every time you pay a bill online, or buy something, it will be blockchain that makes it possible. Cryptocurrency directly sprang from it, the largest of which is bitcoin.

Legend says that both blockchain and bitcoin were created by Satoshi Nakamoto, who has never been seen or identified. In fact not a single communication has come from this person since December 12, 2010. It is also said that Nakamoto himself mined the first million or so bitcoin on the internet (chapter 41). Those coins remain inviolate, still there in e-storage since 2009. The source code for bitcoin was released to the world on January 3, 2009 (chapter 15). And so began bitcoin mining on the internet, which is not all that dissimilar to the quest for gold from the ground (chapter 15). As you might imagine, with all this uncertainty, it was easy to turn Satoshi Nakamoto into Kelly Austin.

The halvings of bitcoin occur on a regular basis (about every four years). The next one will happen in the spring of 2024. Miners are hard at work every day trying to solve the mathematical challenges. It's a bit like trying to guess the number of a lottery ticket. The first computer to move through the billions of possibilities and find the correct combination of letters, numbers, and characters broadcasts the result to the world signaling success. A new block is then appended to the blockchain. The difficulty is adjusted by the source code to make sure that one bitcoin block is created on average every ten minutes. If the number of miners or computational power in the network increases, the difficulty in calculating increases to keep the coin distribution and the block production predictable.

It's amazingly ingenious.

Currently, the first person to solve the challenge posed by the bitcoin program receives 3.125 coins. The total number of bitcoin that will ever exist is twenty-one million, no more, so it is a finite asset. The total number of halvings will be thirty-two. This specificity sets bitcoin apart from other cryptocurrencies and makes each coin more valuable (since there are only so many). It would be as if if there were a finite number of U.S. dollars. Each one would take on a greater value simply because of that scarcity (unfortunately, though, there seems to be an infinite number of dollars, which continually lowers their value).

As depicted in chapters 8 and 14 bitcoin are secured in online wallets, and accounts are protected by an access code called a private key, somewhere between twenty-four and thirty-two characters. These keys are personal to each owner, selected by them, and safeguarded by their own ingenuity. The device that Samvel Yerevan utilized is but one of countless methods bitcoin owners have created (chapter 8).

The first actual financial transaction involving bitcoin was the purchase of the two large Papa John's pizzas (as detailed in chapter 15). That day, May 22, 2010, is remembered within the bitcoin community as Pizza Day. That initial financial transaction played itself out exactly how the creators of bitcoin imagined. A peer-to-peer trade of coins for goods and services, one that did not involve any government or third party.

Millions more transactions, just like that, have happened since.

Billions of dollars in bitcoin are traded across the world every day.

There is a persistent story that blockchain and bitcoin were a creation of the Central Intelligence Agency (chapter 15), as was Satoshi Nakamoto. Supposedly, this was done as a precaution, in the event that the world's financial systems collapsed, which was a real possibility in 2008. The CIA wanted a simple means of exchange ready where people could buy and sell among themselves and keep the world afloat. Thankfully there was no global monetary collapse and, once the crisis was averted, supposedly the CIA wanted bitcoin to disappear. But by then, it had been released to the world and taken on a life of its own. No one knows if this story is true, but it was too good not to use in this novel.

It is true, though, that the CIA, the United States government, and law enforcement in general have expended a lot of effort in labeling bitcoin notorious (chapter 39). Most of those arguments are weak and baseless, unsupportable with the facts (as related in chapter 39). But those pundits nonetheless continue with their negative marketing campaigns.

Which again begs the question, Why bother?

How is bitcoin so threatening?

Russia is particularly interesting. Openly it discourages bitcoin use within its borders (still regarding it as property, not currency), but privately the Federal Security Service (FSB) has long been accumulating large quantities. The FSB was connected to the bitcoin that disappeared from Mt. Gox (chapter 11).

Money is a subject that has long vexed economists and historians. Its history, as related in chapter 32, is accurate. The fate of the Roman Empire ultimately turned on the value of its money, which steadily deteriorated to nothing (chapter 60). Modern fiat currency has similar problems (chapter 56), which is definitely disturbing. Through the centuries many varied things have acted as a means of exchange—salt, tobacco, dried fish, rice, cloth, almonds, corn, barley, coconuts, tea, butter, reindeer, sheep, oxen, cacao seeds, animal skins, whale's teeth, copper rings, flattened iron, brass rods, precious metals. Bitcoin can now be added to that list.

Enthusiasts have long advocated that countries should change the way they view bitcoin from mere property to a unit of currency (chapters 18 and 28), taking the concept to another level. In the novel several have made that choice, most of those even taking the next step and adopting it as their reserve currency (chapter 40). In reality, only one nation has thus far gone there.

El Salvador.

The speech given by my fictional president of El Salvador (chapter 65) is taken nearly verbatim from a written message the current president of El Salvador released in 2022. Catherine Gledhill's speech on bitcoin (chapter 72) is a merger of the many pro-bitcoin statements made by people around the world. The use of a lightning network (for even faster transactions) in chapter 78 is something currently evolving within the bitcoin world.

It will eventually become a reality.

This novel explores a flaw in the entire bitcoin scenario, one that enthusiasts do not like to discuss. With there only being twenty-one million coins in existence, and with some ten to fifteen percent of those no longer accessible to their owners (through lost private keys), that means only around fifteen to sixteen million coins will be available and active. Control enough of those and you would effectively control the market. Bitcoin's price is a factor of its buying and selling. There is nothing intrinsically valuable about a bitcoin. Its worth comes mainly from what another buyer is willing to pay for it. So I asked myself, What if someone gained control of a large quantity of coins, then just bought and sold to themselves, moving money and coins from one account to another, setting their own price in buying and selling? With enough transactions that person or persons could drastically affect bitcoin's value, essentially costing themselves nothing. And if that same person or persons had access to billions of dollars in unaccounted-for gold? Then so much the better.

Hence the Atlas Maneuver was born.

But then it was pointed out to me that the whole thing could be reversed and those same coins could be put to a different use. A different kind of Atlas Maneuver. Which is what Cotton ultimately accomplished in chapter 78, fulfilling Kelly Austin's last wish.

Of course, all of this is fiction. Not real. Made up.

Could it ever happen?

That's hard to say, but perhaps we should take heed of Proverbs 28:20.

A faithful man will abound with blessings,
but he who makes haste to be rich will not go unpunished.

ABOUT THE AUTHOR

Steve Berry is the *New York Times* and #1 internationally best-selling author of eighteen Cotton Malone novels, five stand-alone thrillers, two Luke Daniels adventures, and several works of short fiction. He has over twenty-six million books in print, translated into forty-one languages. With his wife, Elizabeth, he is the founder of History Matters, an organization dedicated to historical preservation. He serves as an emeritus member of the Smithsonian Libraries Advisory Board and was a founding member of International Thriller Writers, formerly serving as its co-president.